PRAISE FOR

THE

LINE

BETWEEN

"VERDICT: Lee's perfectly crafted dystopian thriller will keep readers up all night and have them begging for a sequel."

—*Library Journal* (starred review)

"A tight, fast-paced thriller, with a winding, twisty plot and an intrepid protagonist.

—*Booklist*

"A fast-paced and deeply human story. Tosca Lee has put together a terrifying apocalyptic scenario, made all the more real through the eyes of a protagonist who comes to life on the page."

—Patrick Lee, *New York Times* bestselling author of *Runner*

"*The Line Between* blurs the line between science fiction and terrifying real science. Tosca Lee gives us a cautionary tale that is beautifully written and deeply unnerving!"

—Jonathan Maberry, *New York Times* bestselling author of *V-Wars*

"The perfect blend of spellbinding and heart stopping, *The Line Between* is an absolute must-read. Tosca whips up a thriller that is emotionally wrenching yet utterly believable, the kind of story that is sure to leave readers breathless and begging for more. This well-written, carefully plotted tale is apocalyptic fiction at its finest!"

—Nicole Baart, *New York Times* bestselling author of
You Were Always Mine

"Everything you want in a thriller: suspense, intrigue, and, best of all, a truly captivating protagonist to cheer on. Throw in a white-knuckled race from Chicago to Colorado over back roads that this author obviously and respectfully knows well. This one's a slam-dunk that'll keep you reading, non-stop until the very last sentence."

—Alex Kava, *New York Times* and *USA Today* bestselling author of *Breaking Creed*

"[A] moving dystopian thriller . . . Lee gets readers to invest in the characters, particularly her well-defined and sympathetic lead."

—*Publishers Weekly*

"Relevant and frighteningly real, *The Line Between* is an infectiously good read. Be prepared to lose sleep."

—Brenda Novak, *New York Times* bestselling author of *Face Off*

"Tosca Lee nailed the twists and turns in this masterfully crafted thriller."

—Steena Holmes, *New York Times* and *USA Today* bestselling author of *The Forgotten Ones*

"Tosca Lee's *The Line Between* is terrifyingly close to a future reality. An utterly immersive tale of apocalyptic cult manipulation and all-too-possible infectious epidemics, this story will have readers holding their breath on every page and dearly wishing for their own basement survivalist shelter. Perfect, chilling entertainment."

—Lydia Kang, bestselling author of *A Beautiful Poison*

"An edge-of-your-seat, nonstop, apocalyptic rollercoaster of a thriller! As only she can, Tosca Lee pulls the reader in and refuses to let go until the final heart-pounding page!"

—J.D. Barker, international bestselling author of *The Fourth Monkey*

"Wynter's daring escape draws the reader into a maze of intrigue and false realities, as a bona fide apocalypse grips humanity. This frighteningly topical page-turner from Tosca Lee is a wild ride that will leave you breathless."

—Maria Frisk, producer, Radar Pictures

"A tremendous thrill-ride that is sure to linger long after you turn the last page. With compelling and memorable characters, this is a true run-for-your-life, end-of-the-world, amazingly realistic tale full of twists and turns that will have your heart pounding."

—E. C. Diskin, bestselling author of *Broken Grace*

"Shades of *The Handmaid's Tale* and *The Walking Dead* blend together in an epic novel of depth and power. Tosca Lee's *The Line Between* is a breathtaking story of a woman who rises above her own dark past to stop civilization from descending into madness. Brilliant."

—K.J. Howe, international bestselling author of *Skyjack*

"Smartly written, tautly paced, with an utterly irresistible protagonist, *The Line Between* is pure exhilaration on a page."

—Emily Carpenter, bestselling author of *Burying the Honeysuckle Girls*

"*The Line Between* is a nail-biter . . . one horrific thriller fans will want to read. The conflicting urges rampant in the story resonate with our world today, making this both a great read as well as a cautionary tale."

—Nancy Kilpatrick, award-winning author of the Thrones of Blood series

"*The Line Between* by Tosca Lee had me captivated from page one! I give this book five stars and plan to keep it in my bug-out bag, along with my MREs, first aid kit and Swiss Army knife."

—Merrie Destefano, author of *Valiant*

"A true wordsmith, Tosca has crafted another page-turner, a nonstop thrill ride that will leave you breathless."

—Steven James, bestselling author of *Every Wicked Man*

ALSO BY TOSCA LEE

Firstborn

The Progeny

The Legend of Sheba

Iscariot

Demon

Havah

THE
LINE
BETWEEN

TOSCA LEE

HOWARD BOOKS

NEW YORK   LONDON   TORONTO   SYDNEY   NEW DELHI

HOWARD BOOKS

Howard Books
An Imprint of Simon & Schuster, Inc.
1230 Avenue of the Americas
New York, NY 10020

First Howard Books hardcover edition January 2019

HOWARD and colophon are trademarks of Simon & Schuster, Inc.

For information about special discounts for bulk purchases, please contact Simon & Schuster Special Sales at 1-866-506-1949 or business@simonandschuster.com.

The Simon & Schuster Speakers Bureau can bring authors to your live event. For more information or to book an event, contact the Simon & Schuster Speakers Bureau at 1-866-248-3049 or visit our website at www.simonspeakers.com.

Interior design by Jaime Putorti

Manufactured in the United States of America

10 9 8 7 6 5 4 3 2 1

Library of Congress Cataloging-in-Publication Data has been applied for.

ISBN 978-1-4767-9862-2
ISBN 978-1-4767-9863-9 (ebook)

For Jimmy and Julie.
I waited half a lifetime for the chance to say I love you.

I've got a lot of tattling, breaking your stuff, and embarrassing
you in front of your friends to catch up on.

prion

noun pri·on \' prī -, än\

An infectious agent that causes proteins to misfold, causing progressive deterioration of the brain and nervous system in mammals, including humans. It is always fatal.

ALASKAN INTERIOR, JUNE

The farmer moved into the woods looking for his pigs.

"Jilly! Jilly!" he called. He'd named the sow after his first wife, who'd grown about as fat as the woolly Hungarian blonde, if not quite as hairy. But unlike his ex-wife, Jilly usually came when called, which meant it must be time. The sow was expecting her third litter, and for some reason beyond his understanding, every pig in the sounder had to traipse off into the forest with her to make the farrowing a community event.

He stepped over fallen tree trunks and bent to duck several others. There wasn't a single tree in this patch that was plumb. "Drunken forest," the climate change people called it—a more subtle sign of melting permafrost than the sinkholes in town. Aside from the new buckles in his road, he didn't mind much; warm weather meant more growing days for his new garden. Soon as the pigs got done rooting up this patch, he planned to clear the fallen trees and plant some vegetables. Just enough to beat back the high cost of fresh produce a little, maybe even sell some at the Tanana Valley farmers' market. Who knew—maybe in a year or two he'd look into growing some midnight sun cannabis.

"Jilly girl!" he called, nearly tripping over what he thought was a root until he recognized it for what it was: a bone. He squatted down, tugged, and came away with half a shoulder blade. Caribou, by the size of it. Thing still had gristle on it, leathery and black except where a hunk had been freshly torn away. God only knew how long that thing had been buried in the mud.

He stood up and kicked around, unearthing what was left of the carcass, which wasn't much. One thing he'd learned, the Mafia legend held true: a dead body wouldn't stand a chance against pigs. Nor did living chickens that wandered too close to the pen. He'd learned that the hard way.

He wandered deeper, hacking at the fallen trees with the shoulder blade until he finally found Jilly—and Romeo and Petunia and Walter—nestled in the pine needles with a fresh litter of blond-haired piglets. Ten in all. Well above the European average and two more than her last litter.

He patted Walter when he pushed his snout into the farmer's hand and let him have the shoulder blade, already doing the math in his head.

It was going to be a good year.

TWO DAYS LATER, the farmer found Petunia milling around the yard with a bloody stump for a tail. She ran when he tried to inspect the wound, and only Romeo came when called. The farmer's first

thought was that someone—or something—had terrorized the animals. A wolf, maybe, or even a bear.

After retrieving his shotgun from inside the house, he struck out
for the wood.

He found Walter sprawled near the base of a leaning tree, snout
bloody, corpse bloated. Just beyond him lay his prized sow Jilly, belly
torn open, her piglets savaged around her.

NORTH WOODS FARMS QUALITY ALL-NATURAL PORK

A farmer-owned network offering restaurants the best pork available—in partnership with Midnight Sun Farms, purveyor of 100% Alaskan-raised Mangalitsa pigs. The healthy pork.™

Pigs raised the way nature intended: free ranging, without hormones or antibiotics. Old-world pork for today's farm-to-table connoisseurs.

SUSTAINABLE PRACTICES FOR DISCERNING PALATES

Our focus on environmental responsibility and humane farming produces a naturally marbled, far more flavorful meat. The bacon and pork chops your grandmother remembers—voted Best Bacon and People's Choice at the Bellevue, WA, annual Baconfest.

Our farmers are committed to the practice of raising happy, limited-stress pigs who spend their days digging, rooting, and exploring within stable community groups—resulting in a more tender cut with a pH superior to that of commodity pork.

ALL NATURAL!

- Free range, never corn fed
- Gluten free
- No growth hormones
- Uncured—no nitrites or nitrates
- No antibiotics or steroids, ever!

CHAPTER ONE

Conventional wisdom dictates that there's an insurmountable divide—an entire dimension of eternity and space—between Heaven and Hell. Lucifer managed to make the trip in nine days, at least according to *Paradise Lost*. That equates to a distance of about 25,920 miles, assuming standard rules of velocity.

But I can tell you it's closer to a foot and a half. The distance of a step.

Give or take an inch.

Magnus stands near the gatehouse, shirtsleeves rolled up, collar unbuttoned beneath his brown vest. He nods to the Guardian in the booth and the industrial gate begins its mechanical slide. There's a small door to the side of it just large enough to admit a single person, but I won't be leaving by the Narrow Gate. My departure must be a spectacle, a warning to those assembled behind me.

I can feel their eyes against my back like hot iron. The glares mottled by anger and fear. Sadness, maybe, but above all gratitude that they are not me.

Two Guardians stand at my sides ready to forcibly walk me out in case I balk or my twenty-two-year-old legs give out beneath me. I glance at the one to my right and swear he looks impatient. Hungry, maybe; it's just before lunchtime. I'm crossing into eternal damnation, and all he's thinking about is an egg salad sandwich—and not even a good one. It's Wednesday, Sabbath by the solar calendar. Rosella is managing the kitchen, and that pious sandwich is full of chickpeas without a single real egg in it.

The gate comes to a stop with an ominous clang. The road beyond is paved with gravel, a gray part in a sea of native grass strewn with gold and purple flowers in stark contrast to the carefully and beautifully manicured grounds behind me. A meadowlark sings somewhere nearby as a combine rumbles in the distance.

I grip the plastic bag of my sparse belongings: a change of underwear, my baby book stripped of its photos, a stone the color of sea glass. Sweat drips down the inside of my blouse as I stare out at that feral scape. At that barren drive through untouched prairie that leads to the road half a mile away.

A car idles at the corner, waiting for me.

Don't look. Don't glance back. That's Pride talking, a voice so faint this last decade I wasn't aware it was still in there. Still, I turn. Not because I need a parting glance at the compound I called home for the last fifteen years or even Jaclyn, my sister. But because I need to see *her*.

My niece, Truly.

I scan the nearly five hundred Select assembled across the broad drive until I find her small form near the front, her hand in Jaclyn's, curls wafting around her head in the breeze.

I'd planned to mouth the words *I love you*. To tug my right ear-lobe in our secret sign so she'll remember me long after she's told she can never speak my name again. To fight back tears at the sight of hers, to combat her confusion with love.

Instead, my heart stops.

She's glaring at me, her face pink, growing redder by the instant. I open my mouth—to say what, I don't know—but before I can, she tears her hand from my sister's and runs away, disappearing into the assembly.

"Truly!" I gasp, and stagger a step after her. The Guardians grab my arms.

"No. Wait—Truly!" I twist against them, plastic bag swinging against my thigh. I can't leave her like this. Not like this. It wasn't supposed to happen this way.

None of it was.

I shift my gaze to my sister, where she stands beside the six Elders. Her cheeks are hollow, features chiseled far beyond her twenty-seven years.

"What did you say to her?" I shout as I'm jerked back around and hauled toward Magnus, who stands before the open gate, this side of that invisible line.

"Wynter Roth," Magnus says, loudly enough for those behind us to hear. Which means he's basically shouting right at me. Gone, the brown-and-gray scruff that was on his chin yesterday. I can smell his aftershave from here.

"Please," I whisper in the space between us, trying to snag his gaze. But he stares past me as though I were a stranger.

"Because of your deliberate, prolonged disobedience . . ." His words carry to those behind me even as the breeze whisks mine away.

"Just let me say good-bye!"

". . . including the sins of idolatry, thievery, and the willful desire to harm the eternal future of those most vulnerable among us . . . because you will not hear the pleas of the brethren and refuse repentance, you are hereby delivered to Satan for the destruction of your flesh."

I hear the words as though from a distance. I've seen and heard them spoken before—I just never thought they'd be aimed at me. So this is it. There will be no good-byes. And I realize I hate him.

Magnus lifts up his hands. "And so we renounce your fellowship and cast you out of our holy number even as we pray for the restoration of your salvation, which you forfeit this day. Now, as it is bound on Earth, so let it be bound in Heaven." He lowers his arms as the assembly echoes his words and says, more quietly as he meets my eyes at last, "You have broken our hearts, Wynter."

He moves away before I can respond and the Guardians walk me to the line as I glance back one last time.

But Truly is gone.

I face the gravel drive before me.

One step. That's all it takes to span the distance of eternity.

Welcome to Hell.

CHAPTER TWO

An eye in the corner blinked from above Jaclyn's bed.

"Are people spying on us? Are they gonna watch us in our underwear?" Jaclyn asked, squinting at it skeptically. She was twelve—five years older than me—and worried about these things.

Now that she mentioned it, so was I.

"No, of course not," Mom said as she got down in front of us to take both our hands. "That camera is here for our protection, just like the big walls all around this place. Which is why you never need to be afraid of monsters ever again. Got it?"

Jaclyn looked unconvinced but kept her mouth shut as she reached out to tuck a strand of hair behind Mom's ear.

"Now, isn't this place cute?" Mom said, getting up. We followed her out of the bedroom and down the stairs past a picture of Jesus and some other guy as she admired the carved wooden railing, the doily on an end table in the living room below. "See? There's another camera." She pointed at the blinking light in the corner and waved at it. I did, too.

"This feels like a grandma house," Jaclyn said, hugging herself.

"It's part of the charm," Mom said. "Look at these braided rugs. I bet someone here made these just for us. Did you know this is a working seed farm?"

Jaclyn plopped down in a wooden chair. "There's no TV. And the toilets are weird."

"I like it," I said. Because it was bigger than our apartment. And I had my own bed.

"I do, too," Mom said as I followed her into the tiny kitchen where she opened the only cupboard. "And look—homemade jelly!" She took out the jar and showed me the handwritten label. "Wild plum!"

I'd never seen her like this, so excited about jelly or the cloth bundle that turned out to be a loaf of bread. I didn't like the look of it; it wasn't sliced or even in a bag. But as she searched through the drawers for a knife, she was smiling. I couldn't remember the last time she hadn't looked sad.

That afternoon two girls Jaclyn's age came over to hang out with her. They brought a girl my age named Ara, who was nicer that day than my best friend in Chicago had been my entire life.

That night when Mom made us kneel by our beds, I prayed we could stay forever.

NEXT MORNING, MOM put on her going-out clothes.

"Why are you dressed up?" Jaclyn asked, arms crossed.

"I've got a meeting with the Elders," Mom said, tugging her denim skirt down until the hem covered her knees.

Ara, who had shown up with a little basket of brown eggs for our breakfast, stood silently by, a doll made out of a handkerchief in her hands. It bothered me a little, that it had no face.

"Better?" Mom asked, glancing at her.

Ara nodded.

"That looks dorky," Jaclyn said.

Mom untucked her blouse, hiding the waistband hugging her hips. "There. Now, listen to your new friends while I'm gone. This place has rules and we don't want to do anything wrong. You won't let Wynter get into trouble, will you, Ara?"

Ara shook her head.

Mom kissed us both and left as Jaclyn's new friends arrived.

The minute she did, Ara sat down on my bed near the nightstand I had set up to display my most treasured possessions: my *Fancy Nancy* and *Amelia Bedelia* books propped up by my pink piggy bank and a soup bowl from the kitchen containing my barrettes and hair ties in a happy riot of color. Leaning over the bowl, Ara reached in and started examining them, one at a time.

"You want me to put one in your hair?" I offered. Hers was braided the same way it had been yesterday, tied by a rubber band too tough for the fine strands falling down around her face like a halo. I plucked the pink butterfly from her palm. "How 'bout this?"

Ara shook her head.

"This one?" I asked, choosing another.

She shook her head again.

I went through them all. She refused each one.

"Okay . . ." I said, feeling slightly rebuffed at my offer of friend-ship. "Wanna read a book?"

She peered curiously at my piggy bank. But when I picked it up and suggested we dump it out and count the coins in it, she pulled away.

"Let's go to the Banquet Table," she said, reaching for my hand. "Haven made ice cream."

I didn't know what the Banquet Table was but thought ice cream sounded good. I followed her downstairs, where one of the older girls was showing Jaclyn how to hold a guitar.

"Stay out of trouble," my sister mumbled, barely looking at me.

Outside, we skipped all the way up the garden path toward the chapel. I'd already decided that this place was a cross between a farm and what I imagined church camp to be like, with long houses Ara called "barrows" and a church in the middle. I pointed to a large metal building in the distance.

"What's that?" I asked.

"Where they package the seed orders," Ara said. "Children aren't allowed. Come on."

The Banquet Table turned out to be a big building filled with long tables and a giant stone fireplace. Ara took me straight into the kitchen where a lady with an accent smiled and wiped her hands on her apron before introducing herself like I was someone important.

"You two take a seat," she said, glancing around as though it were a secret. We went out and sat across from each other, Ara's faceless doll staring up at the ceiling as Haven brought out two little dishes of tan-colored ice cream and spoons.

I picked up the spoon and hesitated. I'd never seen ice cream that color.

"It's pumpkin," Haven said, beaming. "Well, go on."

I thought it tasted weird—Jaclyn definitely wouldn't like it—but decided it was delicious because I was eating it with my new best friend.

"There's kittens in the barn," Ara said when I finally finished. "Want to see them?"

I did, very much, having never had a pet in my life.

On the way there we passed yet another long barrow where a mom was singing with a group of little kids on the front porch. As I watched, she looked up and put her hands together like she was praying. I glanced at Ara for an explanation and noticed her doing it, too. But she was facing the other way.

Then I noticed the man walking past us. He was tall, with curly dark hair. His long shirtsleeves were rolled to the elbow and he carried a laptop under one arm. When he saw me he stopped, and the corners of his eyes crinkled as he smiled.

"Well, you must be Wynter," he said, leaning down. I nodded. "Did you have some ice cream?"

I nodded again.

He glanced around as though to make sure no one was listening. "Say, did you leave any for me?"

I grinned and shook my head.

He chuckled and patted me on the shoulder. "Smart girl." He gestured me closer. When I leaned in, he cupped his hand to my ear. "Be sure Ara shows you the rope swing, okay?"

I grinned and nodded.

He straightened, and Ara put her hands together again. And because Ara did it, I did it, too.

"Who's that?" I asked when he was gone.

"That's Magnus," she whispered.

OUR THIRD MORNING at the Enclave we went to church even though it wasn't Sunday, which Jaclyn said was weird. But she liked her new friends, all of whom were homeschooled, and she had already learned to play a few chords on the guitar—a thing for which she was treated like some kind of genius, though I didn't think it looked so hard.

That day was the second time I saw Magnus, who I now understood was the preacher, except they didn't call him that. He read from the Bible about the Garden of Eden and talked about how special everyone here was, how bad the world was, and some other things I didn't understand.

What I did understand was that he looked strong. Like a baseball player, I thought. Like someone who knew how to fold perfect paper airplanes and have a job. Who smiled and talked to me like he was glad I was here. Like a man who wouldn't make Mom cry.

When he was finished he said our names and we stood up and everyone nearby hugged us.

We started going to morning service, which was led by a different man each day except on Sabbath Wednesday. None of them had eyes that sparkled like Magnus's—but by then Jaclyn had a crush on one of the boys and he attended service, so she wasn't any help convincing Mom to let us stay home. Jaclyn had become instantly popular, which she had never been back in Chicago. So had I. In fact, I had so many friends who came to our house after children's session to play or take turns braiding my hair like theirs that we could barely all sit on my bed at once.

We spent the last days of summer playing with the kittens, eating raw rhubarb straight from the garden and peaches right off the trees. I forgot about the cartoons I loved so much as I learned prayers and the songs that everyone clapped to at service, and never once missed the noise of the train that clacked by our apartment. Though I did miss pepperoni pizza—a confession that caused Ara to wrinkle her nose and, I suspect, prompted the lesson in children's session the next morning about why we should never allow death to enter our bodies or eat the grains of the fallen world. How the eggs and wheat allowed to guests were forbidden to God's Select.

My cheeks burned as the teacher read a volume of the Testament written by Magnus himself about eating the flesh of animals. Humiliated tears welled in my eyes until Ara and the teacher both hugged me and said how very good it was that I was learning to live the way God intended.

And I did want it, more than anything. Because there had been no safe walls in Chicago except those that kept the monsters inside.

A month after our arrival at the Enclave, Mom cleaned and tidied the house all morning, saying we were going to have a visitor. And I thought it must be someone really special since everyone else just showed up whenever they wanted.

I hoped it was Magnus and said so.

"It's his wife, Kestral," Mom said, fussing with the braid she, too, had begun to wear. But I was strangely disappointed to learn Magnus was married.

When Kestral showed up, I was surprised to recognize her as the woman I had seen singing in service onstage. Every time I thought she looked like an angel. From her white skirt and blouse to her blond hair, I thought she was magical. She moved like a princess, as though she had never worried about anything in her life—a look I had never seen in my mom until recently.

"Sylvia," Kestral said, kissing Mom on the cheek. "Girls." She smiled, her blue eyes shining. "I have something very exciting to talk to you about."

She slipped out of her shoes and came to sit down on the sofa, holding Mom's hand.

"I'm so happy. Do you know why?" she asked, looking from Jaclyn to me. "Because here at New Earth we are a very special family. And we want *you* to be part of our family. We want you to stay!"

Jaclyn sat up straight and looked at Mom, who held a finger to her lips so Kestral could finish.

"This is a very special decision. Because if you say yes, the girls you play with will be your sisters. Would you like that?"

"And you'd be like our mom, too?" Jaclyn asked.

Kestral laughed. "Something like that. Or a big sister."

But all I heard was that if Kestral would be like another mom to us, then Magnus would be like our dad.

"And one day"—Kestral gave that beatific smile of hers—"if we are obedient to the Testament of our Interpreter, Magnus, we will all be together forever."

"In Heaven?" I asked.

"In the new Earth, which is what Heaven will be."

"But aren't we already in New Earth?" Jaclyn said, looking confused. I was, too. Because I'd seen the sign outside the gate when we got here.

"That's a very good question! And the answer is that we call our home New Earth because we know that it is coming. Girls, this sick and ruined world is ending very soon and only a select number of people will get to live in the new one. Do you understand?"

No. I didn't. But as I watched Kestral's fingers tighten around Mom's and the hope brimming in Mom's eyes, I understood enough.

"I want to stay," Jaclyn said. "Mom, can we?"

Kestral raised a finger. "One thing you need to know about our family," she said soberly, "is that we choose to lay down things of the old world that might keep us from entering that new place. We don't do it because of rules—I don't like rules, do you?"

We shook our heads.

"We do it because we want to be ready. Because on the day that this world ends, it will be too late. So you see why this is such an important decision. The most important one you'll ever make in your life."

"I want to stay, too," I whispered.

"All right," Kestral said as Mom wiped her eyes with a smile on her face. "I need you to show me you no longer want to be a part of the dying world."

"How?" Jaclyn said.

"Let's go upstairs," Kestral said, reaching out to take me by the hand.

We all went up together to the bedroom with the blinking eye where Kestral walked to the closet and lifted one of Jaclyn's Star Wars T-shirts from the shelf.

"Jaclyn, we don't wear clothes that glorify worldly entertainment," Kestral said. "Nor do we wear clothing that is immodest or tempts our brothers. Nor do we dress like a man. We're honored to be women and for our brothers to treat us with respect. See how pretty your mother looks?"

That's when I realized Mom had quit wearing her denim skirt that she had to tug down to her hips to cover her knees. Or her jeans. I didn't know where she got the skirt she was wearing now, but I thought she looked a little like Kestral in it.

"If you want to be part of our family," Kestral said, "you can take all these things out to the salvage pile yourself . . . or you can give them to your mother to take there for you."

Jaclyn lowered her head and walked into the closet and slowly started pulling things from the shelves.

I couldn't believe it. Jackie loved Star Wars—had been obsessed with it as long as I could remember. But a moment later she somberly handed over an armful of clothes that amounted to nearly everything she had brought in her duffle.

Kestral leaned over and kissed Jaclyn on the forehead. "Bless you for choosing the way of life," she said.

They went through all of Jaclyn's belongings. Her sixth-grade yearbook, which she no longer needed because she had new friends who were real family now. A girl wouldn't keep a picture of an old boyfriend around once she got married, would she? It had to go. Her headphones and iPod, because we were called to make holy music. Her tennis shoes, because they weren't feminine.

"For all of these things, you'll receive so much more," Kestral said as Mom got out a trash bin and helped pile the things in.

When it was my turn, Kestral looked at my nightstand. "Wynter, how does *Fancy Nancy* fit into our heavenly family?"

"It doesn't?" I guessed.

No, Kestral said, because dresses and jewelry did not make us beautiful. And wasn't that a nice thought?

I wasn't so sure, but I handed over the book and *Amelia Bedelia* as well, because I figured there was something wrong with it, too.

"And this," Kestral said, pointing to my piggy bank. "Do you know what this is?"

I frowned. "My piggy bank."

"That's what the world wants you to think. But the world is an evil place that lies to children."

"My mom gave it to me."

"And to moms," Kestral said with a glance at Mom.

"If it isn't a piggy bank, what is it?" Jaclyn said.

"Magnus has taught us that this is an altar. But not to God. To Mammon, the false god of greed."

My books, clothes, hair things, and shoes had filled a second trash bin by the time I carried my piggy bank outside to smash it with a hammer Kestral gave me from the kitchen.

Now I understood why Ara had never wanted to wear my barrettes or play with my things. And even though I knew it was a small price to pay to see Mom happy, I couldn't stop my lower lip from trembling as I turned over the coins to Kestral to be given to the Important Work.

Afterward, Kestral knelt down and took our hands. "It's never easy to cut worldly ties in our journey to be worthy," she said, brushing the tears off my cheeks. "But the *good* news is that it will never be this hard again. Your new sisters will bring you fresh clothes and new toys. Because we share everything we have, you never have to feel jealous of anyone ever again—especially those living in destruction. But more than that, and above everything else . . . it means you're *home*."

At that, Jaclyn started crying uncontrollably. I was embarrassed for her and then for myself. But even then I sensed Jaclyn was coming from a place I was not old enough to understand.

Kestral got up and clasped Jaclyn tight, her cheek against my sister's hair. "Everything is going to be perfect. And one day, so will you. Thank you," she said, though I didn't know what she was thanking us for.

Kestral let me keep the tissues, saying that when they were gone I'd have a nice clean handkerchief to keep in my pocket. Which meant I'd be carrying my boogers in there as well, though I didn't say so. If it kept us safe and Jaclyn from crying those horrible, broken tears, I could do that, too.

That night we said our prayers on the upstairs landing beneath the picture of Jesus and the man I now knew to be Magnus.

Three weeks later, we moved into the barrows. The guest cottage was needed to house a new family. When they showed up—a mom and dad and three boys—the ice cream, which had gone away after our decision, resurfaced again for a few days. But only for the kids who went to play with them, which is why I welcomed the youngest boy with open arms.

That fall, Jaclyn was relocated to the young women's dormitory and I to the girls'. Mom moved to a barrow for single women that everyone called the Factory. We weren't allowed to visit.

Which is why I didn't know when Mom got sick.

CHAPTER THREE

The meadowlark is still singing as my soles crunch against the gravel. The wildflowers look the same as they did ten minutes ago or on any of my rare excursions into Ames while I was still protected by the invisible bubble of my salvation. The sun is shining, promising temperatures in the seventies. By all accounts, it's a beautiful day.

Of course it is. The world is filled with deceptive beauty.

Magnus's words.

But the only beautiful thing I know is trapped behind those walls.

I stop and turn as the gate begins to grind shut. Watch as that nondescript wall cuts off my view of the parking lot and the admin building behind it, traveling across the assembled brethren like an iron curtain. Until there's just Magnus, his back to me as he walks up the drive to put an arm around Jaclyn, my sister.

His wife.

Others come to embrace them both and someone starts up a hymn as they head up the hill to lunch.

The gate rumbles shut with the finality of a vault. I stare at it for a long minute. Wait for the earth to swallow me. Lightning to fry me from the inside.

My stomach grumbles. The meadowlark sings.

I start down the drive toward the road where a woman is getting out of that car. As I get closer, I falter and then break into a run, the plastic bag crinkling with every beat against my thigh.

Mom's former best friend, Julie, grabs me into a hug. "Got you," she says. "I got you."

I shudder a sob I didn't know I had in me. It sounds like a strangling person trying to breathe.

". . . told your mom she was making a huge mistake," she whispers fiercely against my hair. "Argued with her the whole time she was driving to that crazy place . . ." She holds me away from her and looks me up and down. "Never mind. You're safe now. God, you look so much like her. Are you all right?"

I nod numbly.

"Let's get out of here," she says, hustling me toward the car with a glance over her shoulder. "I don't trust those people not to change their minds. Can't believe your sister—no, sit up front. Are you hungry? You look hungry."

I get in and realize there's a teenage girl slouched behind the driver's seat in a tank top and shorts, tapping at her phone. She's wearing a big pair of headphones over a sloppy grass-green ponytail. When she glances up, she tugs them down to her neck.

"Hey," she says.

I glance back at that wall as the car pulls away. Some invisible cord between Truly and me is pulling tight, tighter, until I think I might scream.

"Wynter, this is Lauren, the boys' half sister. She's sixteen."

The boys. Half sister. I parse her words as though through a fog until I realize she's talking about *her* boys, with whom Jackie and I used to play on weekends—or any other time Mom could shuttle us out of the apartment to Julie's house, which had everything we did not. Video games. The Cartoon Network. Popsicles and smoke bombs on the Fourth of July—a holiday I haven't celebrated since the summer they moved away and my world went dark a year before we arrived at the Enclave.

"Lauren was born in Atlanta, where we moved with Ken, her dad, after my divorce. You remember Ken? We've been married for fifteen years."

I can't help it. I keep hearing what Magnus would say about Lauren's shorts, the tank top, the hair. About Julie's divorce and remarriage, Lauren's birth before that marriage. The charm bracelet dangling from Julie's wrist as she drives. About the charms themselves.

Tinny music drifts from Lauren's headphones. I strain to listen, if only to shut Magnus up.

Or is this what it means to be in Hell—having to hear and see Magnus in everything?

"So what's it like?" Lauren says.

"What's what like?" I ask.

"Being in a cult."

"Lauren!" Julie says, glancing in the rearview mirror.

"What? That's what you called it," Lauren says.

Julie holds up her hand. "Lauren Zandt. Not another word."

Cult.

I know the word. Had been warned one of the few times I helped out at the farmers' market I might hear this worldly lie. That I ought to count the derision of anyone not one of us as a badge of honor. It hadn't kept my cheeks from burning when I saw the way other teenagers looked at us—as Lauren is now.

I turn in the seat, but when I look back, the walls are gone, swallowed by the horizon.

Several miles later Julie pulls into a diner. There's a TV on in the corner and the red booths remind me of the times we went to Denny's when I was little. How we'd stopped there on the drive to Iowa for a "nice" dinner, Mom saying, "Better have a cheeseburger. Who knows when we'll get one again." Which I did.

The thought nauseates me now. The smell of the kitchen—all greasy meat and frying potatoes—does, too.

I stare at the laminated menu on the table, but all I see is the last look on Truly's face.

"Wynter, hon?" Julie says. "What would you like?"

I realize the waitress is there, that everyone's waiting on me.

"Do you have anything without grain or dairy?" I ask the waitress, noting her pierced nose, the tattoo on her inner wrist. Her pink lipstick.

She squints up at the ceiling. "Pot roast, roasted chicken . . ."

"Or meat?"

"Salad?" She shrugs.

"Salad, please."

"Hold on. Give us a minute, will you?" Julie says to the waitress. When she's gone, Julie leans across the table and says, quietly, "Sweetie, you have to eat more than that. You're skin and bones the way it is."

"Are you like vegan or something?" Lauren asks.

"Look!" Julie points at the menu. "Soup. How 'bout soup? Right here: black bean and rice."

But something else has caught my eye. "Can I have some ice cream?" I ask.

"Yes!" Julie says and slaps the menu. "Thank God. All right, we're ready." She waves the waitress over. I watch her as she orders; she's changed. She's prettier than I remember, the hollows around her eyes gone despite the fact that she used to be heavier. Her hair's lighter, practically blond. Sunglasses perch on the top of her head and I think, for a minute, that she looks like some kind of movie star.

A *beautiful deception* . . .

Shut up.

I excuse myself to wash my hands. Inside the bathroom, I hesitate before drying them on a paper towel. And then, when I do, I take a second and then a third. Stuff a fourth in my pocket, just because I can.

I cover my fingers with my sleeve before opening the door.

Over a lunch of chocolate ice cream—I try not to stare at Julie's grilled cheese—I ask how they got here so fast from Atlanta.

"Oh, we moved back five years ago," Julie says. "We're in Naperville now, just a half hour from Chicago."

"It sucks," Lauren says.

Julie levels a look at her before turning to me. "So. Tell me about your mom."

I poke at the ice cream, which is a lot sweeter than I remember. I keep looking around, I don't know what for. Black-clad Guardians come to drag me back, maybe. Given how sideways this whole thing went, I'm not sure I wouldn't let them take me.

"She got sick," I say.

"When was this?"

"I was twelve. So ten years ago, I guess."

Julie pushes her fries toward me. I take one, nibble the end of it, and then drag it through my melted ice cream like I used to do when

I was a kid. And for a minute, I swear I can smell cherry Popsicles and bean burritos.

"What did she have? Did they tell you?"

"They said her spirit was sick from the time she'd spent in the world before we got there."

Julie puts down her fork with a loud clang and a call on Jesus Christ that is not a prayer.

"Wynter, listen to me. People get sick. Period. It just happens. It's germs, not the Devil. Or stress. God only knows how much of that she's endured in her life. Did they even take her to a doctor?"

"I don't know."

I remember the morning Mom was missing from service. I asked my dorm warden and then Jaclyn where she was. No one would tell me. I finally went to the administrative office looking for answers—only to be hauled out by a Guardian and marched to Percepta Hall, where I spent the rest of the night in Penitence.

Three days later one of the girls whispered that Mom was back. But I wasn't allowed to see her.

"Did they treat her with anything at all? Did they even give her the choice?" Julie asks angrily.

You shall not take the sick to the sick to be healed, but they will live among the well and be restored.

Suddenly I'm no longer hungry. "They said I had to pray that she'd confess whatever was keeping her from getting better and search my own heart for sin. That if I did that, I could save her."

Lauren gapes and Julie closes her eyes for a brief moment before saying, "Honey, you know that's not possible. Right?"

I nod. I don't say that I turned myself over to Penitence and fasted there for a week in solitude, combing through each detail of my life until I had written down every possible thing I had ever done wrong—from the time I drew a face on Ara's doll to the time I rigged it with a bunch of thread I filched from one of the older girls' tatting baskets and casually told her it looked possessed. After which I'd disappeared around the corner from where it was perched on Ara's bed to pull the little threads like a demonic puppet master. Ara's scream had brought both of the girls' wardens running for the dorm at full speed—until one of them tripped and went sprawling across the floor and cut her chin. The whole thing landed me my first night in Penitence, during which I screamed and kicked the door and had not prayed once, which I also duly noted.

I had confessed that I missed cake with icing, hated learning to can tomatoes, and daydreamed during service about kissing boys, whom I listed in order.

I confessed that I had taught one of the other girls a Bon Jovi song and reenacted scenes from *Pinky and the Brain* when we were supposed to be cleaning and had covertly farted on Ara's pillow—numerous times—for making it her mission in life to report any infraction of mine she could ever since the Satanic doll incident.

I don't say that I declared it all before the six Elders upon my reemergence: twenty-three pages of sins—in deed, thought, or imagined—read with shaking hands and shameful tears. And though I knew it would lose me the friendship of those implicated in the process, I did it, convinced I had completed the work that would save my mother's life.

I don't say that the moment I finished, I knew my mother would be healed. That I felt reborn by the experience and fasted an extra day, I was so light and full of gratitude afterward.

I couldn't wait to see my mother, tell her that she was going to be fine. Which is why I waited so patiently when they told me she was resting. I believed she was recovering her strength.

"So what happened?" Julie asks.

"She died." Short, insufficient words.

Julie looks away, her chin quivering as Lauren's eyes dart between us. A few seconds later Julie dabs at her lashes with the crease of her napkin, and then reaches across the table to take my hands.

She hasn't washed hers in all this time. Not even once.

"Now, you listen to me," she says. "It isn't your fault. None of it. If it's anyone's fault, it's your mom's for taking you all to that place—no. Forget I said that. That's not fair, no matter how much I disagreed with her decision. She didn't want to go to a shelter and wouldn't come to Atlanta. She said it was the first place Nate would look, which was probably true. But I kick myself all the time for not just driving up to get you girls and telling her to get her ass in the car."

Nate.

It's the first time I've heard my father's name in fifteen years.

"Which reminds me," Julie says, squeezing my fingers, "I need to tell you something. Your father passed away a couple years ago."

"How?" I hear myself ask.

"Shot himself in the head."

Suicide. A damning offense. As though Nate hadn't committed enough already.

"I wish I could say I'm sorry, but I'm not," Julie says, her lips set in a tight line. "The minute one of your old neighbors emailed me I tried to get a message to your mom. I was hoping once she knew she'd have the courage to start over on her own. You can imagine my shock when they said she had passed away."

She lets me go to swipe at an eye, smudging her mascara. "And no one would let me talk to either one of you girls. Said you didn't want any contact with anyone from your past." She lets out an angry, ragged breath. "Which I knew wasn't true!"

But she's wrong. Two years ago, I wouldn't have taken that call. Because even though I missed Julie, I still believed. Could still chalk up the inconsistencies around me to my own lack of understanding or misguided nature. Because it was far easier to rationalize what didn't make sense than accept the truth glaring me in the eye.

And because Jaclyn—and Truly—were all I had left.

"I even consulted an attorney who specializes in this kind of thing," Julie says. "But of course neither one of you was a minor anymore."

My head snaps up. "Jackie has a daughter."

Julie blinks. "She does? How old?"

"Four. Can the lawyer get her out?"

Julie sighs. "Honey, no one's going to take her from her parents without some proof of endangerment or abuse. Has anyone hurt her? Has she been molested? You know—touched inappropriately?"

But no one would dare harm the daughter of Magnus. I shake my head.

"What'd you do, anyway?" Lauren asks.

"About what?"

"To get kicked out."

I feel their gazes—Lauren's, watching me as though I might sprout a second head, Julie's sharp curiosity primed for outrage.

But I can't talk about the last four weeks. "I quit believing."

"Well, thank God you've always been able to think for yourself. We'll just have to pray Jackie comes to her senses. Meanwhile, you're lucky you got out."

Lucky. It's a forbidden word. Am I lucky?

No. I'm free, with no sense of up or down. With no money to my name and everything I own in a plastic bag on the front seat of Julie's car. Without family, a home, or any idea how to function in the outside world.

Not so lucky then.

The waitress pauses at the booth across from ours, coffeepot forgotten in her hand as she stares at the TV. I follow her gaze to live footage of three people standing on top of a parking garage.

"Turn that up?" she calls to another waitress.

A younger woman in an identical black apron grabs the remote from the counter and punches up the volume until the announcer's voice reaches our booth.

"... in downtown Chicago where a couple and their unidentified nanny have told authorities they're teaching their children to fly," the announcer says, clearly baffled. "A truly bizarre and horrifying scene . . ."

"What is *wrong* with people?" Julie says, shaking her head.

"Probably drugs," Lauren mutters.

I cannot make sense of anything I'm seeing, even as a family photo flashes across the screen—of the couple on the garage, I assume. They're smiling and wearing matching white, from the blond mom and darker-skinned, laughing dad to the adolescent girl and younger boy—who's got his arm around a German shepherd.

All of a sudden, the announcer's voice raises in pitch. The picture disappears and returns to live feed—just in time to show one of the figures soaring out from the ledge of the garage in a swan dive. Julie gasps and the waitress screams, coffee splashing in the pot as the feed cuts back to the anchor.

"Oh, my God!" Lauren says, yanking her headphones off.

"Excuse me, miss?" Julie says, trying to get the attention of the waitress as a few patrons come over to get a better view of the TV. "Can you turn the channel? My girls don't need to see this."

The waitress turns. "Is that what they said? They're trying to teach their children to fly?"

Behind her, the TV abruptly goes dark—along with all the lights in the restaurant. The waitress glances up, curses, and strides off toward the kitchen.

"What happened?" Lauren says, looking around.

"Who knows," Julie murmurs, pulling her wallet from her purse. "But we're leaving." She plops down some bills on the table.

I slide from the booth, palms sweaty, my fingers cold.

"Does—does stuff like that happen often?" I ask when we're back inside the car. I can't not see the image of that swan dive, playing over and over again in my mind.

What kind of world have I returned to?

"The power?" Julie asks, glancing at the screen on her dash as we back out.

"No," I say. I've been accustomed to power outages at the Enclave during storms, though right now the sun is streaming through the window. "The people on the news."

"More and more, it seems. If it's not some crazy idiot, it's a nut job with a gun."

"Or terrorists," Lauren volunteers from the back seat.

"Like I said," Julie says. "Nut job with a gun."

"Or someone trying to dance in traffic," Lauren adds.

"What?" I say.

Julie chuffs and rolls her eyes. "Some lunatic decided to moonwalk down highway 59 and got run over. Not by me—thank God— but it happened while I was out buying things for the guesthouse.

Shut traffic down for an hour, and of course the car was on empty because someone didn't fill it up when she used it to drive to a concert"—she glances in the rearview mirror—"and I ran out of gas and had to call AAA . . ."

"I said I'm sorry!" Lauren says.

"And I said you're not borrowing the car for a week."

I glance between them. Someone got killed on the highway and, according to all I've been taught, is writhing in Hell this very moment . . . and they're bickering about how inconvenient it was?

But that was horror on their faces back at the diner. Which means this kind of thing can't be normal.

"Wait," I say slowly. "How did you make it to Iowa by noon?"

"That was yesterday, or we wouldn't have," Julie says.

"But I only called this morning." It was the first time I'd dialed a phone in fifteen years, and I hadn't even known who'd be on the other end of the number written in my file.

Julie glances at me and then back at the road, brows drawn together. "Hon, I got a voicemail three days ago that you were going to need a place to stay for a while."

"What?" Three days ago I hadn't even been turned in yet. "From who?"

"Your sister, Jaclyn."

CHAPTER FOUR

The new girl was about my age: fifteen, give or take a year. Her bored look and sullen scowl reminded me of Jaclyn when we first arrived.

No, it was worse.

But unlike Jaclyn, who still took in the world from the corners of her eyes, this girl had the distinct air of someone who didn't care about the judgment of others—whose half-shaved head and heavy makeup seemed to invite it, even, in a way that instantly drew me toward her.

"Want to get some ice cream?" I asked in the living room of the guesthouse, trying not to sound too eager to get out. This was our house, once. Or at least I thought it was going to be. Now I couldn't look at the braided rugs and doilies without remembering how Mom admired them.

Without feeling the ache of her absence.

The girl turned to look at me with an expression that clearly said, *Seriously?*

"There's a new pond in the garden," I offered. "Sometimes we put our feet in it, in the summer . . ."

It was the middle of January.

"Got any smokes?" she asked. And even though I was the only other one here—Elder Omni had personally taken her dad for a tour of the compound—I wished she hadn't said it so loudly as I glanced fearfully toward the eye in the corner.

"No, sorry." Guests were given pretty much free run of the Enclave, not subject to the same rules as the Select. Still, the thought of this girl in the torn black T-shirt sauntering around the Enclave with a cigarette hanging between her lips made me bite back a laugh as I wondered what Ara and her band of disciples would say about that.

"Weed?" she asked.

"What?"

"Got any?"

"It's winter," I said, confused.

She rolled her eyes and turned away. The side of her head was shaved into a grid of lines, and the rest of her chin-length hair flopped the other way. I thought she would have looked like a really pretty boy without her black eyeliner. Or the five studs in each ear. Which I didn't think made her any prettier as a girl, either.

But I liked her. She was feral and dangerous, and I imagined she even *smelled* like the outside world—a thought that should have repulsed me. Instead, I craved her friendship. Especially now that Jaclyn had been reassigned from the warehouse to the clothing and counseling outreach in downtown Ames two days a week. Though we'd never spent much time together, it stung each time she left the Enclave.

"Um, hey. Come look at this," I said, getting up and waving for her to follow me.

She sighed and, after a beat, trailed me into the kitchen where

I pulled the ever-present fresh jar of jam from the cupboard. Strawberry this time.

"There's a camera in there," I whispered.

Her brows raised. I had her interest at last.

"This is homemade here on the grounds," I said, loudly enough for anyone listening to hear. "Want some?"

I gestured for her to answer.

"Uh. Sure," she said. "Looks . . . scrumptious."

"What's your name?" I asked softly.

"Shae. *What kind of crazy-ass place is this?*" she hissed. "Don't tell me there's a camera in the bathroom, too? I just peed in there before you got here. Sickos."

"Where're you from?" I asked, clattering a knife from the drawer and locating the loaf of bread.

"San Diego," she murmured, leaning back against the edge of the counter, arms crossed.

I had never met anyone from California—at least as far as I knew. No one here ever talked about where they lived before.

"Have you seen the beach?" I asked.

"Every day. We live on the beach."

My brain partially exploded. "What's it like?"

"Frickin' awesome." She pulled her phone from her pocket and began to scroll through a bunch of photos. My heart thumped in my chest as I leaned close enough to see her with her friends, obviously partying. Making stupid faces. Playing Frisbee with a dog, lying out in skimpy bikinis. I was shocked by them in a way I never would have been as a child, envious and in awe all at once. At the laughter on their faces, the color of the water.

It's what I've always thought Heaven should look like—not gold but blue.

"Here," she said, handing me the phone and reaching for the piece of bread.

I knew not to touch it.

I took it anyway.

I swiped slowly through picture after picture of blue water and frothy white surf. Past surfers, palm trees, and pristine skies, purple and orange sunsets and kids my own age sitting around firepits. I took in their clothes, peace signs, and makeup. The plastic cups in their hands, the sucker in one woman's cheek, the sunglasses and tans.

When the beach pictures ran out, I kept going. Past images of some cute guy with a pierced eyebrow cuddling Shae and the two of them kissing. I wondered what it was like to kiss a guy like that—so openly and unafraid that you take pictures of yourself doing it.

I blinked when I realized he—not she—was wearing the black nail polish.

"That's my boyfriend. Part of the reason my dad brought me here." She rolled her eyes as she took back the phone.

"Why's he wearing nail polish?" I asked, wondering what she possibly saw in him.

"Why not?"

It wasn't my place to school a guest. Besides, I desperately wanted to see more.

"Do you have any music on there?" I whispered.

"Sure. Lots."

"Got headphones?"

We grabbed our coats and slipped out the back of the kitchen, hands in our pockets as we crossed first to the Banquet Table for the requisite ice cream.

"Gross," Shae muttered, sliding her bowl away. "What's in that?"

"Molasses," I said, helping myself to hers. After so many years, I no longer knew the difference.

Afterward, I made a show of taking her through the greenhouse before leading her to the barn with the rope swing, where we hid on the stairs to the loft, listening to music for a full twenty minutes with one earbud each, my heart hammering the entire time.

I wasn't to be touched by her influences. I was to make her feel embraced and loved unconditionally, while condemning with silent judgment every unholy thing about her. But that day as I served her jam and the promise of acceptance, I felt like she fed something starving inside me. I was elated, alive in a way I hadn't been in five years, since Mom's death.

Every day for three weeks we sneaked off between morning service and my chores to listen to music and look at the pictures and videos on her phone. I made Shae recount the storylines of her favorite movies and TV shows, tell me all about California and her friends, who called her "Coco." ("For Chanel," Shae said. "My fave perfume.") She talked about high school ("sooo much *drama*"), parties, and the boys she dated before her nail-polished boyfriend as we laughed at her friends' goofy expressions and stole minutes with Paramore, Radiohead, and The Killers.

I replayed the songs in my head as I worked, emoted their lyrics in the shower, fell asleep to them at night, toying with guilt but unable to find the Devil in this music, which felt more alive than the songs we sang in service. What was wrong with me that I swore I heard God in those electric guitars and pining voices?

Shae had been taken in by other new friends as well, including the ever-pious Ara, and it became harder to find time with Shae alone as she and Ara went off to play with the little kids together or climb to the top of Percepta Hall. I was jealous and glad. Jealous at the way she brightened at their fake overtures of friendship and because I desperately needed to know what happened to Elena in *The Vampire Diaries*. Glad because the more she felt loved, the more she might want to stay.

When Shae and her father committed to the Select, I was ecstatic. Because in her, I'd found a way to live a life more vibrant than my own from the safety of the Enclave. In—but not of—the world. Even without her phone, which I knew she wouldn't be allowed to keep, Shae had enough stories, songs, and memories to sustain me until the coming apocalypse.

I even imagined that a part of her fearlessness had transferred onto me.

I watched the bins of their things get carried off to the storehouse to be sold for the benefit of the Enclave or given away at the New Earth shelter in town. But I didn't see Shae again for weeks. When I asked, I was told she'd gone into intense study and contemplation to purify herself from the life she had now forsaken.

The next time I saw her, the rows of her earrings—like the eyeliner I once watched her draw on with rapt fascination—were gone, the gridlines in her hair grown out and covered by a straight middle part.

And I could already tell that a part of her had gone with them.

Two days later, I ended up in Penitence for all the filth I had eagerly ingested during my time with Shae, who had reported me in her initial reckoning.

I emerged to new strictures put in place for my benefit—including only supervised access to guests. No more temptations from the tainted world . . . no more ice cream or last summer's jam from our holy garden.

Shae and I rarely spoke after that.

THE DAY BEFORE my seventeenth birthday, I watched Shae cross the parking lot toward the van, a flat of seedlings for the farmers' market in her arms. Jealousy spiked in my gut. Ever since I'd finished high school curriculum the year before, I'd done everything I could to prove myself worthy of working the market or clothing outreach with Jaclyn, who ran it now.

But I had been deemed "too vulnerable" for placement in the outside world even as Shae—not even here two years—had been allowed to leave every Saturday now for a month.

That afternoon, Shae disappeared into the sweaty Ames crowd with a hundred dollars from the money box.

Now I understood why she had been so perfect since her conversion. She'd never meant to stay but had waited all these months for an opportunity to escape.

Which was also why she'd never been able to associate with me, the troublemaker she had implicated in the process.

I thought I hated her. At the very least, I was disappointed. But at night, as I lay in bed, I wondered if she was back in San Diego in the arms of her nail-polished boyfriend. Or, barring that, in her bikini.

CHAPTER FIVE

So this is "Hell": an entire apartment over Julie's second garage. A bigger bed than I've ever seen in my life with a thick white comforter and three fluffy pillows. A dresser with more drawers than I have clothes for and a bookcase filled with novels. A bathroom with a real toilet, a mirror that spans the entire wall over the sink, and a soft loopy rug in front of a bathtub shower. A TV the size of a window sits across the living room from the couch, and the little kitchen has its own set of plates, glasses, and silverware—as well as a small refrigerator that Julie's busy stocking with plastic bottles of water.

"Lucky," Lauren scowled when we arrived.

There was that word again. But this time, I agreed. I was overwhelmed by the sheer size of the main house, which they showed me first. I thought Julie's old house in Chicago was nice, but her house here is bigger than the barrow I shared with nineteen other girls. It also has two more garages attached to it in addition to the one beneath my apartment, where an RV and boat are parked.

"There's soap and shampoo and a toothbrush and all that in the bathroom. I'll pick up some juice and snacks for you tomorrow," Julie says, straightening.

"Mom, why can't I have the carriage house?" Lauren says. "Wynter can have my room."

"Because she's older than you and needs her privacy."

"I need privacy," Lauren mutters.

"Where are the boys?" I ask, not having seen a trace of them since we arrived.

Julie sighs. "Caden lives with his fiancée in New Mexico. Stefan's at college in Columbus, and Brendan chose to stay with his dad," she says with a sad smile.

I join them in the house for Chinese food Lauren's dad picked up on the way home from work—my second restaurant meal of the day. There's fried meat for everyone, vegetables for me. And fortune cookies.

Ken, Lauren, and Julie laugh as they scramble them on the table.

I like Ken. He kissed Julie first thing when he walked inside and there are laugh lines around his eyes. He doesn't seem concerned about the fact that he married a divorced woman or that he's a doctor tampering with divine will.

Most important, he wears his shirtsleeves all the way down, buttoned around his wrists.

"Wynter picks first," Ken says.

I hesitate.

"Um," Julie says, studying me. "Maybe we should save these for later." She starts to gather them up, but I reach for the closest one.

"I want this one," I say.

"All right! No whammies!" Ken snatches the farthest one from him as Lauren and Julie dive for the last two. They crack them down on the table, shattering the cookie, and then open the plastic, laughing.

"'You are stronger than you know,'" Lauren reads. "Whatevs."

"'Laughter is the best medicine,'" Ken reads. "That is true."

I peel open the plastic, break open the cookie, and search for the little piece of paper. But there isn't one. I glance up, puzzled.

"Looks like you get to create your own destiny," Ken says, getting up to clear the dishes. I've never seen a man do this. He waves us off.

"You girls go fire up a movie," he says. "Unless Wynter's tired."

I beg off and thank them for dinner. For everything.

Back in the carriage house, I wander through the apartment. Study the mismatched soaps and little bottles of shampoo, conditioner, and other toiletries in the drawer. Read their tiny directions.

Out in the kitchenette, I touch the dishes on the open shelves. Eight plates. Six glasses. Four mugs. I straighten the side table so it's even with the counter and then kneel down in front of the bookshelf to peruse the shelves.

Big Little Lies. Hex. The Ghost Mine. 16th Seduction. The Lost City of the Monkey God. They're the kind of stories that would never have been permitted in the Enclave, where we were only allowed a handful of inspired classics and then only to satisfy the state requirement. I study the worn spines, settle on *The Art of Racing in the Rain.*

I climb into bed with the book and, seeing the remote on the nightstand, finally locate the button that turns on the TV.

I click past alien movies, crime dramas, and some show about arguing wives. I'm appalled, fascinated, transfixed. I'm trying to find

more on the family that fell from the parking garage until a commercial with a girl Truly's age hits me with a jolt and sends Magnus's
voice booming through my head. Blasting me for abandoning her,
eating the unnatural food of the world, and practicing divination by
opening a stale packaged cookie.

Shut up. I clench my fists over my eyes. *Shut up. Shut up!*

I click until I find the Disney Channel, which I used to love. Fall
asleep to *Finding Nemo*.

CHAPTER SIX

The Sabbath after Shae disappeared, service began with a silent parade of headlines from around the world on the screen above the apse.

INFECTIOUS DISEASE

ON THE RISE . . .

GUNMAN KILLS 13 . . . GUNMAN KILLS 27 . . . KILLS 56 . . .

KILLS HUNDREDS . . .

AVALANCHES, HURRICANES, EARTHQUAKES,

LANDSLIDES . . . THOUSANDS DEAD . . .

FLOODING KILLS HUNDREDS . . .

DROUGHT KILLS THOUSANDS . . .

ETHNIC CLEANSING, STARVING REFUGEES . . .

CHILD PORNOGRAPHY RINGS, HUNDREDS OF CHILDREN
MISSING . . .

THREAT OF NUCLEAR WAR . . .

The Select watched with escalating gasps and cries.

When Magnus took the pulpit, he stared out at us in silence.

"Have I not told you what is to come?" he said quietly at last.

Murmurs of agreement hummed around me.

"Did I not say: not in *an* age, but in *this* age? I tell you today: it is here. *This*"—he pointed to the screen—"is the beginning of the end. It is happening even now. Even as I speak, the Deceiver lays waste to a humanity *drunk* on its own cesspool of immorality! The police cannot stop it. World leaders cannot stop it. And God *will not* stop it!"

Shouts of "Amen!" issued from the pews behind me.

"And yet! And yet . . . *some* of you wonder. Why do we not aid the sick and dying? Why not comfort those about to perish as the Samaritan comforted the man beaten by thieves? *Why?*" He gestured to the screen behind him. "Because this world cannot be saved. Because God *hates* this world and therefore *this world must perish*. Do *I* say this? No. *I* do not say this. *God* says this! Anyone who asks, 'What are we to do for the world?' questions the Almighty One, who says, 'I *will* lay waste on that coming day because I *am* righteous!' So it was spoken to me."

Shouts and clapping. Behind me, someone launched into a prayer so rapid it sounded like one long stutter.

He spread his hands and the chapel fell silent once more. "Brethren. Beloved. Even so, God is merciful. He has revealed He will call more to us. And we will welcome them. Their souls will be crowns on our heads. We do not know how many will arrive, but I tell you in that last day they will come as rats fleeing a flood! And I tell you something else." He dropped his head, blew out a long breath. "Not everyone here will see that glorious day. Because the Lord has revealed deception among you."

Somewhere behind me a woman cried out.

His shoulders sagged. "It's true. I've seen it. Now, you might be saying, 'But I've been accepted! I'm part of the family!' My friends, it's one thing to be accepted by this body, which is human and can be deceived. It's another to make yourself acceptable to the One who will broker no lies. What you have hidden in the darkness of your heart—you think no one knows? The Lord knows! And because *He* knows . . . I know. He has *already spoken the names*."

A pall fell over the sanctuary as he stalked toward the pews and up the center aisle. I felt, more than saw, those around me shrink back as he passed . . .

Until his eyes fastened on me.

I dropped my gaze, heat springing to my face as a chill poured down my spine. Because even though I had been outwardly perfect, I also knew I had become two people: the penitent shunned for her failure with Shae and vindicated by her escape. Who clung to stories about TV vampires and sang rock songs in secret. A member of the Select longing for the world. A believer subsisting on her sin.

Kestral and a man with a guitar ascended the dais and started to sing. Only when those around me finally joined in did I dare look up, heart thudding in my chest so loud I was afraid the girl sitting next to me could hear it.

EVERY MORNING FOR the next week, I woke up wondering if I would be summoned before the Elders and told I was no longer worthy. Worse, I knew they would be right. I repented a hundred times in those seven days, terrified of being cast out to my own destruction, eternally separated from God and the only family I had left.

The following Sabbath, when the Select were summoned to the yard after morning service, I could barely breathe. I'd never seen a casting out. How would it happen? Would Magnus call out my name? Would the Guardians drag me from the assembly?

My knees turned to water at the sight of a figure being escorted from Percepta Hall: Thomas, one of the boys from the first family I had welcomed to the guesthouse, now in his twenties. The Elders—including Shae's father, who had joined their ranks last winter—stood near the front as Magnus read the words accusing Thomas of disobedience and theft.

I watched, as terrified for him as though I stood there myself.

His mother howled and fell to her knees as a single step stripped him of eternity. The gate ground on its tracks, locking into place before he was even halfway down the drive.

And just like that, he was gone.

I felt somehow that I had been spared—a thing I didn't dare take to Penitence. Which only made me feel that much more fraudulent as I made my confession to God alone, praying it was enough.

The following week we assembled again, my head so light I thought I would faint until a young woman was dragged before the gate. Her hair was so disheveled, her face so splotchy and tear-stained that I didn't recognize her at first. The minute I did, ice pricked my back in the late-summer heat. *Lyssa?* We'd done our schoolwork together and slept three beds away from each other until she moved to the Factory last spring. She'd always been quiet, saying only what was necessary in a voice too small for a grown woman's frame, as though she were not a person but a wisp of one, invisible in the right light.

She collapsed at Magnus's feet, arms flailing in the space between them as her begging devolved into terrible sobs.

Magnus read the words. But when he accused her of promiscuity and fornication, I thought I must have heard wrong. I glanced at the chiseled expressions around me, the narrowed gazes taking in the girl they'd only ever half noticed before. But the Lyssa I knew bore no resemblance to the figure on the ground—and even less to the woman of the accusation.

Someone wailed as the gate opened. But when the Archguardian hauled her to her feet, Lyssa clung to his arm until he had no choice but to summon another Guardian and march her down the road as the gate slid shut behind them.

I alone stayed to watch the two Guardians return by the Narrow Gate, after which they headed up to lunch—the thought of which made me bend over and retch right there onto the gravel.

Worst of all, we were never to speak their names, which of course, only made them louder in the silence until I wanted to scream them.

A FEW DAYS later during the laundry shift, a girl with catty eyes named Candace whispered that Lyssa and Thomas had been caught together in the storehouse.

"That doesn't even make sense," I snapped. "Why was she the only one accused of it?"

"She tempted him. She was a whore," Candace said. "We're lucky he's the only boy she took with her. Maybe," she said, her eyes glinting a little too much, "they're out there, right now. *Fornicating.*"

Fixing her with a stare, I threw the linens I'd been folding into a bin and marched straight to Penitence to file my first report in years. I couldn't defend Lyssa, who effectively no longer existed. But I could inform on another for delighting in evil.

Candace wasn't seen for three days.

THAT FALL, KESTRAL died in the middle of the night.

A massive aneurysm, Magnus informed the morning service, had delivered her instantly to the throne room of God where she would wait to rejoin us in her heavenly body when the world was made anew. Which was why we weren't to mourn.

But I did anyway.

Magnus told stories of her piety, which was all we had to remember her by; her body had been removed before dawn, turned over to local authorities.

The same as my mother's had been.

Three weeks later, two marriages were announced at the first fall service: Jaclyn's, to Magnus.

And mine.

Dr. Angie Bohlman was a harassment suit waiting to happen. With those curves, that long red hair, and those evergreen eyes, she was the kind of woman who looked like she had paid for medical school by modeling bikinis. The kind of looker Frank Kerns had gravitated to when he was a resident and had even married once, three wives ago. Now at the tender age of sixty-eight, he found it hard to reconcile that a Jon Stolk Award recipient could have gams like that.

Oh, brave new world.

Today, as she made room for him to join her at the table in the doctors' lounge, the best he could hope for with a woman like her was to not spill his flimsy bowl of clam chowder all over himself or pass gas as he sat.

That, and to glean a little insight like detritus from the whirlwind of her already illustrious career.

"Dr. Kerns." She smiled, stabbing tiredly at her salad.

"How're things on the neurology service?" he asked, unscrewing the pepper shaker to dump a half teaspoon of the stuff on his bowl, making a mental note to buy this place a real pepper grinder.

She shook her head. "Crazy with this outbreak of encephalitis. I've got seven patients on the floor now, all under fifty, who've been here for days. One of them for weeks. All exhibiting symptoms of early-onset dementia but none of them with brain swelling."

"Any improvement?" he asked.

"None. We've worked them up for toxins, environmental exposures, heavy metals, drugs, and had immunology consulting . . . I've had enough patients complain of flulike symptoms at the onset that I was beginning to think it might be virally mediated, but then I saw yesterday's Department of Public Health email. Did you read that?"

Frank had quit reading those things ages ago. "Jog my memory."

"Thirteen patients with the exact same symptoms have just been linked to Overlake Medical Center in Bellevue, Washington. They all had surgery there within a month of one another."

He stirred the pepper into his soup. "Could be some tick-borne disease—have you tested for Powassan? There was memory loss and neurological symptoms in those patients, too."

"But why would all those surgical patients at Overlake get it in a cluster like that?"

"Hard to say." Frank had long ago accepted the fact that in medicine, much as in religion, you could go crazy plumbing for absolute answers. That one had to expect, and leave room for, a little ongoing mystery. He, too, had been zealous once, in his mission to save the world. Now he just thought what a shame it was to see the lines etched beneath her eyes. She'd lose her looks early to this career.

"At this point, I'm wondering if I should have the infectious disease chair from the med school take a look."

"Oh!" Frank said, with no small amount of pride. "Dr. Chen is the chair of ID. She's one of my former residents. I can ask her to come over if you like."

"If you wouldn't mind, that'd be great," Angie said, closing the plastic box on the remainder of her lunch.

"Happy to do it."

Alone in the lounge ten minutes later, Frank took his phone from his pocket and frowned. He had meant to call someone but now couldn't remember whom. He scrolled through his contacts, staring at the names, waiting for one of them to jump out at him. When none did, he opened his reminders, where he discovered a month-old note about a pepper grinder.

That must have been it, he thought, opening the Amazon app and searching for a good old-fashioned steak-house model.

CHAPTER SEVEN

The next morning Julie brings up some clothes. "You might feel more comfortable in these," she says, holding out a pair of jeans, a T-shirt, jacket, and a pair of sneakers—all obviously Lauren's.

When I ask her about Jackie's message, she dials the house phone from her cell and plays it for me on speaker:

Julie? This is Jaclyn Roth. Sylvia's daughter. It's . . . I know it's been a long time. Wynter's leaving. She needs a place to stay for a while. Our mom died a few years ago and you know I can't call Dad. It's this Wednesday at noon. I hope you get this. Please don't call this number back—it isn't mine—or call the New Earth office looking for me. It'll ruin everything.

The sound of her voice nearly breaks me. I wonder where she was, how she got a phone. She sounds nervous. There are voices, traffic in the background. She had to have been in Ames.

"Can you save this?" I ask after listening to it a third time.

"Of course," Julie says gently. "For as long as you like. Or until she's here with us." She gives a small smile, one I can't mirror.

"She won't leave Truly," I whisper.

Julie takes my hand. "Wynter, one day Truly will be old enough to make her own decisions."

But I know Magnus will never let her go.

WHILE LAUREN'S AT school, Julie takes me to a department store to buy clothes, a coat, a pair of winter boots. And though I recognize the virtue of clean underwear, I feel guilty about the amount of money she's spending on me and have already started a mental running tally of the amount I promise myself I will one day pay back.

She takes me to the grocery store to buy snacks for the carriage house, and I am overwhelmed by the volume of stuff for sale, the number of brands and varieties of each. Canned tomatoes. Diced tomatoes. Diced tomatoes with onions and peppers. Stewed tomatoes. Italian stewed tomatoes. Tomatoes and chili peppers. Farther down the aisle, I pick up a can of store-brand peas. I've spent days every year for the last decade of my life laboriously picking, shelling, washing, and canning peas . . . to the point where I couldn't stand to eat them—and here they are, on sale for eighty-seven cents.

I'm just putting the can back when I realize someone is staring at me—a woman with white hair and skin so thin as to be nearly translucent. She's easily the oldest person I've ever seen and gives a little cry as I take in her wrinkled mouth, the shadows beneath her eyes like bruises.

"Rose?" she says, coming closer, her purse dangling from her bony wrist. "Are you my Rosie?"

"Sorry, no," I say, confused. "My name's Wynter."

She gasps and her arms go wide. "My Rosie!"

I glance around, wondering where Julie went, not sure what to do. "I think you've mistaken me for someone else."

She stops as though struck. She looks angry. "Why would you say that? Rosie, come to Mother!"

She lunges for me and grabs me by the arm. Her eyes are clouded, a sheen of sweat on her forehead. I jerk away and hurry down the aisle.

"Rosie!" she calls, over and over, barking the name behind me.

By the time I find Julie, I can still hear the old woman shouting.

Julie looks up at the sound of the commotion. "What in the—"

I tell her what happened, but by the time she marches the cart toward the customer service counter, someone there is already on the phone describing the woman as two employees in matching shirts hurry toward the canned vegetable aisle. A moment later the woman is screaming.

We pay for our groceries, glancing back as shoppers skirt past the aisle, one of them furtively grabbing a box of saltines from the display on the end.

"If I ever get that bad when I'm old, just put me in a home," Julie says.

We're halfway to the house when we pass a bank with a long line outside of it. The parking lot is full, as are the drive-through lanes, a service truck blocking the ATM lane as someone works on the machine.

"What's going on?" I ask.

"No idea," she whispers.

THAT NIGHT, JULIE gives me an old iPhone, saying we'll get it activated tomorrow.

"Just in case you need to get hold of us," she says, programming in her number, Ken's, Lauren's, and the police.

Lauren spends the rest of the evening showing me how to send messages, search the Internet, and take pouty selfies, despite the fact that there's nothing fascinating to me about my own image and even less about making my lips look huge.

"Everyone takes selfies," Lauren says before making me watch some reality show about a girl who takes them all the time and is in love with her own butt.

Yeah. No danger of that slippery slope for me.

A few days later, Lauren shows me how to pull up entire series of TV shows on the carriage house TV, which I keep on even when I'm sleeping, if only to stave off the quiet and the voice that comes with it. Having worked every day at the Enclave, I don't know what to do with myself now that I have no responsibilities. And try as I might, I can't seem to sleep in past five.

I think of Shae. Wonder how it was for her, leaving the Enclave. If the first thing she did was eat a giant burger, smoke a cigarette, or find some of the weed she used to talk about.

On a whim, I grab my phone and pull up Safari. Type in "Shae Decaro" and "San Diego." Nothing. I delete "Shae" and type in "Coco."

Three listings come to the top. I click through and back and finally land on a social media site Lauren spends half her day on. I stare hard at the picture.

She's changed her hair. But it's her.

I wonder if she can tell I'm looking at her picture. That I searched for her name. I ask Lauren at breakfast, and when she says no, carry my bagel back to the carriage house and reopen the browser. And then I'm struck by a whim.

Opening a fresh search page, I type in "Magnus Theisen."

The screen fills with results, including a website for New Earth I never knew even existed, "CultWatch," "Former Hybrid CEO Renounces GMOs," and "Theisen's Ancient Vision for the Future." But it's the pictures of Magnus that stop me cold, his eyes glittering from the screen, staring at me even here, out in the world.

I shut down the page, heart thudding. Search for Paramore on YouTube. Crank up "Turn It Off." Play it over and over.

It takes me twenty minutes to figure out how to set up an account so I can send Shae a message.

Shae,
   This is Wynter Roth from the Enclave (well, not anymore). I hope you're okay. Hope to hear from you.
   W.

I check back the next morning, and the next.
The third day, her account is gone.

MY PLAN TO help out by keeping house for Julie falls apart when I learn she has a cleaning lady who comes every Friday.

"But I'll do it for free!" I say.

"Hon, give yourself some time to adjust," she says. "And to think about what you'd like to do with your life. You might've finished school early in the cu—the Enclave—but you've still got some catching up to do."

What I'd like to do with my life. It's a thing no one's ever asked me. Lauren seems concerned with nothing more than her friends and her phone. Julie's life is all about taking care of Lauren, Ken, and herself. Ken—I'm not even sure what Ken does for work except that he owns some kind of company that studies new medicines. Everything they do is about living for this life, today—a thing I no longer know how to do.

I read a lot. Meanwhile, the novelty of not having a regular schedule has started to make me edgy. Julie finally assigns me responsibility for cleaning my own apartment and doing the laundry. I offer to weed the yard and help cook as well. But all the while, unnamed anxiety has begun to gnaw at the back of my brain—especially when I inevitably turn to the channels I cannot resist.

The news.

There have been five new shootings in the last week alone, and there's more on the threat of cyberattacks by Iraq and Russia. But it's the rash of crazy people who eclipse political talk shows—including a man who tried to amputate his own leg because he thought it was infested with bugs and a lawyer who shot up his house after aliens moved into it. Also a pro football player who got let go from the Seahawks for tackling demons only he could see during scrimmage.

I ask questions during dinner: Where did ISIS come from? What's the difference between terrorism and hate crime, or between either of those and just being crazy?

"That's a good question," Ken says one night over veggie burgers. The fact that I've volunteered to cook has altered the way the family eats—at least a few nights a week. "One might even make the argument that extreme hatred *is* a form of craziness."

Three nights later, I'm pulling open a bag of microwave popcorn in the carriage house when a breaking news update on TV stops me cold.

A mudslide in China, nearly a thousand people dead.

Popcorn tumbles to the floor as the headlines from Magnus's sermons flash like lightning in the back of my mind.

Hurricanes, earthquakes, landslides . . . thousands dead . . .

Sweat breaks out across the back of my neck. I stumble barefoot out the door, hurry down the stairs and across the cold driveway to the main house.

Inside, the kitchen is empty, the low lights beneath the cabinets illuminating the countertops in a soft orange glow. Deceptively calm. I hurry toward the sound of the TV in the den where I find Ken working and Julie scrolling through a magazine on her tablet.

"There's been a mudslide in China," I say, out of breath.

Ken looks up from his laptop and Julie blinks at me. A glass of wine sits on the small table beside her as the TV drones on in the background about the uptick in dementia cases across the nation.

"It's wiped out an entire town," I say. "At least a thousand people are dead."

"I did see something about that. Tragic," Ken says, shaking his head.

I nod, not understanding their lack of concern. My heart is racing, panic biting away at my brain.

"Hon?" Julie sets down her tablet and then pauses the TV. The anchor freezes, midword. "Things like this happen. They're terrible every time. But tsunamis, hurricanes, tornados—they're natural. Well, most of them."

"Could be erosion or the aftermath of an earthquake," Ken says.

But all I can think is that it's happening. The terrible things that are supposed to herald the end of the world. And I realize a part of me was watching, checking for the signs ever since I got here, if only to prove Magnus was wrong and that I'm okay.

Now the full implications hit me like a hammer, knocking the wind from my lungs. Because if Magnus is right . . .

I can't breathe. My heart is pounding way too fast.

"Honey? Wynter." Julie says, getting up. "Ken."

Ken sets his laptop aside, comes over to feel my cheek and head. I want to scream at him that it isn't a problem with my body. It's my soul that's damned—and theirs are, too.

". . . bottle in my medicine cabinet . . ." Julie is saying as she leads me to the sofa. A minute later, Ken returns with a white pill.

"Wynter? Take this. Go ahead and chew it. It won't taste good, but it'll help."

A few minutes later, my heart begins to slow. I feel a little better. But I'm not. I know I'm not.

"Honey," Julie says, taking my hand. "Listen. Natural disasters happen. They're a fact of life."

I let out a broken sound with my breath. Feel like I might vomit. "Magnus said—"

She shakes her head. "I don't give a flying crap what Magnus said. Look. There was a tsunami in 2004 that killed maybe a quarter-million people. Hurricane Katrina killed at least a thousand."

"Mmm, closer to two thousand," Ken says, nodding. "I seem to remember a Chinese flood in the thirties that killed millions." He reaches for his laptop. A minute later he says, "Here it is. Yes. Nearly four million people."

"All tragedies," Julie says. "But the world didn't end. A landslide isn't the apocalypse. I promise."

I nod, the motion slow.

I get that they're not worried. But they're of the world. Deaf to the Testament. They don't know better.

But I did.

Which means if the world ends now I'm not only going to burn for eternity but will never see Jaclyn or Truly again.

Julie makes me a bed on the living room sofa where I fall into a thick and merciful sleep. The next day, she takes me to see a doctor—one of Ken's friends—who gives me a prescription.

I don't like how it makes me feel. But it dulls Magnus's voice and the war of logic raging like a torrent in my head. Because by all appearances, the end Magnus prophesied is coming. Is here. But neither can I reconcile his Testament with what I know.

A few days later, Julie takes me to talk to another doctor. Dr. Reiker doesn't wear a white coat. She doesn't have a stethoscope. She talks about PTSD and obsessive-compulsive disorder and gives me a prescription, which we pick up on the way home after my first flu shot ever.

THE MEDICINE SLOWS me down and makes me tired. I take it if only to get through each day. Because it's hard to function when you're facing eternal fire.

I sleep a lot. Julie says she expected this—that there had to be some kind of ramifications for being in "that place." That we'll get through it.

I don't know how to tell her that there's no way to get through an irrevocable decision. Or wishing every single minute you could go back in time . . . knowing you'd only make the same decision all over again.

That this must be what it is to be damned.

The new clothes Julie gave me hang off my hips and shoulders. Nothing tastes good. Julie fixes me soup and when I can't eat it, makes me a sundae. Says once I'm off my prescription—the sleepy one—we'll practice backing the car out of the driveway.

But I am, by now, so fixated I can think of little else. What good is ice cream? We're all going to Hell. What good is learning to drive when it won't save your soul?

At the end of my second appointment, Dr. Reiker suggests Julie remove the TV from the carriage house.

I stare at the churches we pass on the way home. "Purveyors of lies" Magnus called them. False prophets selling cheap imitations of a truth revealed only to us.

That night, Ken carries the television to the main house. But they don't take away my phone.

I track the news with panicked obsession. The death count in China has topped ten thousand. Two hurricanes are bearing down on Florida and another has just hit the Virgin Islands. But it's the contagious strain of early-onset dementia that dominates headlines as people wander into traffic and burn down their homes.

It is everything Magnus predicted.

And here I am, on the outside. The wrong side.

Sleep is my only relief.

The next day Julie and Lauren take me on a forced walk. I squint beneath the sun as Lauren asks whether she has to stay in school. Julie says they'll talk about it later, though what she means is not in front of me.

That night over dinner, Ken gently informs me that they're taking my phone—just for now.

"None of us has gone through this before, Wynter," he says, brows drawn together over the rim of his glasses. "So we're learning along with you. The fact is, I don't think we understood how overwhelming access to so much information was going to be for you. That's our fault, not yours. Just know that we're committed to getting you the help and resources you need. You're part of our family now. You don't have to go through this alone. Okay?"

But that's just it. They can't give me the help I need. No one out here can.

I take my medicine that night, sleep as late as I can the next day and the next. When I finally wake, I feel a little better. Lighter, maybe, the noise in my mind—once a roaring cyclone—having calmed to an eddy.

I eat a spinach, avocado, and provolone sandwich. Potato chips. Toaster Strudel and tea. The leaves are falling even as temperatures return to the seventies. By the end of the week, Ken and Julie announce that we're going to Indiana Dunes for a few days to unplug—for all of our benefit.

I am stunned by the sandy beach, the teal-green waters of Lake Michigan stretching to the Chicago skyline where a flock of birds swarms into the warm autumn air.

The next morning I learn that those weren't birds at all but a billow of smoke from a high-rise on fire.

NEW EARTH PURE LIFE™ ANCIENT SEEDS

- Heirloom seeds 100+ years old, including Hutterite Soup Bush Beans, Sikkim Cucumbers, and Old Greek Melons
- Unique seeds from more than 300 countries
- Ancient seeds, including the 1,000+ year Crapaudine beet, crookneck watermelon, "Methuselah" Judean date palm, and over 300 native American varieties of squash
- Seedlings (at select local farmers' markets)

Our Founder

After selling his GMO-based seed company to a top biotech company in 1994 for $53 million, young entrepreneur Magnus Theisen quickly realized that wealth, like fast life and fast food, failed to fulfill him. He spent the next four years on a personal quest to discover man's true meaning and value that ended with a spiritual revelation about the state of our environment, our world, and the human heart.

The result: the New Earth community and not-for-profit outreach ministry located north of Ames, Iowa, and the New Earth Pure Life™ Seed Bank and Company. Today, we are three things:

1. A community of like-minded souls intent on worshipping the Creator in all that we do—including what we put into our bodies and by sustainable living practices.
2. A clothing and counseling ministry to those in need of basic essentials—including compassion and guidance.
3. A private organic seed bank and small company offering some of the rarest seeds in the world, committed to the discovery of ancient varieties for the benefit of mankind.

READ MAGNUS'S PERSONAL STORY <u>HERE</u>

(Please direct all media requests to the link above.)

<u>LEARN MORE ABOUT NEW EARTH'S PHILOSOPHY</u> I <u>SCHEDULE A VISIT</u> I <u>DONATE</u>

<u>I'd like to know more about New Earth</u>

CHAPTER EIGHT

Jaclyn would marry Magnus in twelve days.

Two weeks after which, I was to marry Elder Decaro. Shae's dad.

The news—delivered to me and the entire assembly at morning service—left me numb. I barely heard the congratulations of the women around me as I endured their hugs.

He was forty-nine. I had just turned eighteen—the same age as Shae. Not that she would probably ever know she had a stepmom. Since her disappearance, Elder Decaro technically no longer had any children.

I moved as though through a fog as he came to take my elbow after service and led me outside to a bench, saying he'd like to get to know me. I listened as he told me that he had been born in Nevada, gone to college in California. That he had owned a financial company in San Diego before coming to the Enclave after his divorce—which wouldn't impede our marriage as it had happened outside the Testament. Erased, as though it never existed.

Just like Shae.

"I wanted to explain why I'm not coming to you chaste," he said. "And . . . you?" he asked, openly studying me.

I looked up, cheeks threatening to burst into flame. Affronted by the question. To be having this discussion at all. For Shae, wherever she was.

"No, I've never been married or fathered children," I said, before making some excuse about being needed in the Banquet Table and striding away.

I shut myself in the kitchen's equipment room and slid down against the shelves, heels of my hands pressed to my eyes. How had this happened? Whose idea had this been? Had he *asked* for me?

I couldn't do it. Could I? Was it possible I could ever look at him *that* way?

No. Not possible. Elder Omni's son, handsome and twenty-six, yes. Always. Though I'd repented of those ruminations years ago, or so I thought.

I'd been rude to Shae's dad—though I reasoned he'd been rude to me, too. We'd barely exchanged a dozen words in the last three years and *that* was the first thing he asked me?

I stumbled through my lunch shift, keeping well to the back of the kitchen, away from the serving line. Spent the rest of the day enduring the envious glances of the other girls in my barrow, feeling all the while tilted off axis, reeling out of orbit.

That night I prayed for a way out of my engagement. To be released from the honor.

And then I prayed to be forgiven for even asking . . . and asked again.

By morning, preparations for Jaclyn's wedding were already in full swing. Flowers. Food. Music. The two-hour service that would mark the union of human and divine when Magnus, the Mouth-piece of God, would deign to become one with his Select once more.

At least the focus was off me for now.

Were I not coming to terms with my own marriage, I might have been happier for Jaclyn. She'd be the Kestral of our age. Except that in every way Kestral had been angelic, Jaclyn was dour. Where Kestral had been gentle, Jaclyn was severe.

When the day came, she looked happy—radiant, even—as Elder Canon served her and Magnus communion and Elder Omni prayed for the blessing of children.

I wondered if Jaclyn was nervous—if not for tonight then at the prospect of childbirth. I'd heard another girl's screams from the next barrow over as she gave birth to a ten-pound baby girl just after her nineteenth birthday.

The next morning, I rode to Ames with two other girls and set up the New Earth booth at the farmers' market I had finally been allowed to work since the start of summer. The first week I had stared around us in wonder and shock. Fumbled over my words with strangers. Tried not to stare at the girls in their shorts, covet their painted nails and lip gloss, or envy their tank tops in the summer heat.

But today I was jealous. Of the girls laughing and flirting with boys their age. The young couples strolling with entwined fingers.

It was wrong. One day they—and the rest of the world that allowed them such freedom—would wish they were me as they burned in Hell. But for the space of those few hours, I wondered what it'd be like to be them. With no knowledge of the Testament or New Earth or the Enclave. To kiss so casually in public. Go on dates and to the movies. Cook dinner together, alone.

Today was both hotter and busier than any week I had worked so far. So when I made change for a customer and caught sight of something cylindrical and red against the side of the money box closest to me, I hesitated.

I knew what it was. Knew where it had come from—could recall the girl my age who had stopped to buy several packets of seeds for her mother, unloading the contents of her wristlet to dig for exact change in the process. I remember wishing I could look at all her things, smell her tiny bottle of perfume. Unfurl that lipstick.

That had been over an hour ago; the girl was long gone. I glanced at the two other women behind the table, both of whom were too busy to see me cover the shiny tube with my hand and deftly slip it into my pocket.

What was I doing?

I couldn't possibly keep it, let alone use it. Why, then, did I want it so much?

I was so distracted that I realized I had given a man a ten in lieu of a twenty only after he'd left our table. This, after being warned how important it was to represent New Earth perfectly—especially as we added free pamphlets and sermon CDs to bags.

Grabbing ten dollars, I dashed down the row of vendors in the direction most of the foot traffic was flowing, trying to remember if he'd had a hat on, the color of his shirt. But I'd barely been paying attention and had been so well trained to avoid the appearance of flirting that I hardly looked at most men directly to begin with.

I was just on the verge of giving up when the Guardian who had driven us here—clad in khaki instead of the usual black—grabbed me by the arm.

He didn't say a word. He didn't need to for me to realize what he

thought I was doing. His very presence at the booth was a result of
the day Shae disappeared into the crowd with a fistful of cash from
the money box.

And here I was with a ten-dollar bill in my hand.

"I miscounted someone's change," I said, showing him, his fingers bruising my arm through my sleeve.

"Everything okay here?" a male voice asked behind us. I twisted
around in time to see a guy in an Iowa State T-shirt step out of line
at a nearby taco stand.

He was suntanned and muscular, with a baseball cap backward
on his head. And I was mortified. At the heat in my cheeks. For what
this looked like—to the Guardian and to the guy. For drawing attention to myself at all.

"Fine, yes. Thank you," I said with a flustered smile before I
turned on my heel and marched back to the table.

By the time I got there, the others had already begun to pack up.

We left early. No one spoke to me in the van on the way back,
their gazes fixed in the other direction—which allowed me to slip
the lipstick from my pocket and hide it under the edge of my seat,
knowing I'd be searched in Penitence.

For the next hour, as I waited on the Admitter to take my statement, I thought about the guy who had asked if I was all right. No
man had ever done anything like that for me before.

Of course that wasn't true. Magnus and Jesus had saved me from
eternal fire. Still, I wondered what his name was. If he played bas-
ketball or football or worked somewhere.

If he had a girlfriend.

I confessed all of these thoughts as the Admitter repeated
the same questions over and over and shouted scripture at me for

an hour until my ears rang: THOU SHALL NOT LIE! THOU SHALL NOT STEAL! The works of the flesh are ADULTERY! FORNICATION! UNCLEANNESS!

In the end, the money box corroborated my story. Still, I'd cheated a man of ten dollars and tainted New Earth's reputation, for which I would no longer be allowed to work the market.

I never mentioned the lipstick, admitting instead to envying the trappings of the world and looking with desire on another man—a confession that landed on every Elder's desk the next morning in the Admitter's log.

My engagement to Shae's dad was abruptly annulled; I was deemed an unsuitable helpmate for a man of his station.

Three weeks later, he married Ara instead.

To show my relief would have been considered unrepentant. But I was relieved. I even imagined I was happy for Ara, who had gained the status I knew she craved and had no compunction about marrying the father of a girl she had once called friend or pretending that girl no longer existed.

In that way they were perfect for each other.

A few days after the wedding, I was assigned to clean the van. Crouched down between the seats with a cordless vacuum, I felt carefully beneath the seat I had been sitting in and then ducked down to stare beneath it.

The lipstick was gone.

THREE MONTHS AFTER Jaclyn's marriage, she announced she was pregnant.

It was received as a miracle—especially once our midwife calculated it back to Jaclyn's wedding night.

Magnus beamed as he read poetry from the Song of Songs with a tenderness I'd never known his voice capable of. And he sighed as he preached on the beauty of the coming kingdom from the fourth volume of his Testament.

I forgot my frustration. I spent every moment I could with Jaclyn and we grew close again for the first time in years.

The night Truly was born—three weeks early—my questions no longer mattered. They all had just one answer: her.

CHAPTER NINE

By mid-November, the panic attacks have nearly subsided.

I make homemade tiramisù (Lauren's favorite) for her birthday. Drive with Julie as far as the bookstore where, at Dr. Reiker's suggestion, I buy a journal in which I will record all I want to achieve in my new life.

I also agree to get my hair, which has not seen scissors in years, cut and layered at Julie's salon where the magazines are covered with bright headlines about losing weight and "beauty secrets after 30." I pick one up while I'm waiting, thumb past articles on the Mediterranean diet and how to talk to your doctor about your sex life. Nothing about the dead in China or the demented hacking off their own limbs. For a minute I wonder who's crazier—the man tackling demons only he can see or a world pretending such people don't exist?

A few weeks later, I'm given my phone back—with controls that keep me from streaming shows or searching the Internet. Soon after,

Dr. Reiker okays television on the condition that I log what I watch and how it makes me feel. The controls on the phone come off.

The news has taken a dramatic turn and now I realize how much Julie and Ken have kept from me over the last few weeks. Gone, the celebrity gossip, the sports and political updates. The headlines are devoted to the sharp uptick of early-onset dementia spreading along the West Coast and the "Bellevue 13"—a group of patients with the disease who had procedures at the same hospital. They're all under the age of fifty-five, and the second of them has just died.

Reporters interview coworkers, neighbors, and family of the sick in treatment. They're baffled, clearly afraid, hoping for a cure. Meanwhile, ginkgo biloba and herbal brain enhancers have sold out of stores nationwide as fresh cell phone footage of bizarre behavior is uploaded to video sites by the hour.

When I show a few of them to Julie, she snorts.

"There's a difference between having dementia and just being an idiot," she says.

But I notice she's begun setting the house alarm, even when we're home.

A FEW DAYS later at my weekly appointment, Dr. Reiker asks if it's ever occurred to me to do an Internet search on New Earth International.

I think back to the day I tapped out Magnus's name. The pictures of him filling the corner of the screen, staring back at me.

"Yes." Even as I say it, I feel the shadow of that former panic brush against the back of my neck.

"And did you?"

"I stopped."

"Probably a wise choice at the time," she says, crossing her legs. "But I think you're doing well enough now that you might find that it helps put some more things into perspective."

"Have you?" I ask. "Looked them up, I mean."

"As a matter of fact, I did after our first appointment," she says.

"What'd you find?" I ask, not sure I really want to know.

"Why don't you take a look when you're ready—maybe even invite Julie to search with you."

Alone in the carriage house that night, I type "New Earth" into the search bar of my phone. I haven't mentioned it to Julie, and my heart is pounding against my ribs.

I hesitate and then hit the "search" button.

The screen goes momentarily blank. And then it fills . . . and fills.

"New Earth Settles Lawsuit with Former Member." "Little Cult on the Prairie." "I Left a Cult—An Interview with an Ex-NEI Member." "New Earth International Investigated for False Imprisonment." "Sexual Harassment Suit Filed Against Elder 'Omni West' of Secretive Religious Sect." "Woman Files Lawsuit After Being Abused as Part of Iowa Cult."

Magnus's voice returns with a vengeance.

Persecution and lies! Our ways are not the ways of the world. The Deceiver is a roaring lion.

I click the first link about a lawsuit filed by a couple (listed as Jane and John Doe) against a college teacher, claiming the teacher brainwashed their son (name withheld) into joining New Earth and in turn recruited his sister and brother, alienating them from the family. Which, I suppose, is how it would appear to anyone on the outside.

I click on the Wikipedia page next.

New Earth International (NEI) is an apocalyptic religious group located north of Ames, Iowa. Founded in 1992 by Magnus Theisen, New Earth's theology centers around the End Times and teaches that only its members will advance to the new Heaven on Earth once the current Earth has been destroyed.

Theisen (formerly businessman and entrepreneur Jeff Gregory) changed his name in 1990 after selling his company, TG+ Hybrids, and claiming God had commanded him, as the New Adam, to prepare others to enter New Earth by strict adherence to spiritual standards and the ancient diet by which men were intended to live and eat.

"Jeff?" I say aloud.

There's a section below about Magnus's upbringing, how he dropped out of high school as a junior. A paragraph outlining his nine Testaments. Another about complaints brought against Magnus, Elder Omni, and New Earth as a whole.

I scroll down to the articles in the reference section at the end, click through to an article about a suit against New Earth for loans to the organization Magnus Theisen claims were "donations." I've been aware for years that new members sign over cars, property, houses—entire bank accounts—to the communal cause. Though I've never heard of anyone wanting anything back.

I return to the search page and hover over the sexual harassment link but can't bring myself to read it. Click instead on "I Left a Cult—An Interview with an Ex-NEI Member" on a site called Truth Watch. Scroll down to the account of "Ann" (not her real name), who joined as a teenager.

Because I can only think of one person this could be.

Shae.

But when I get to her photo, I freeze.

Because the eyes staring out at me aren't Shae's.

They're Kestral's.

But *Kestral's dead*!

I scroll back up. The article is dated last year.

We were married for fifteen years when Magnus told me he had had a vision that he was to take a second, younger wife. That God had told him he needed children—something I could never give him as a result of two abortions I'd had in my past. Except I had never had an abortion. I was seventeen when I met him soon after he received his first revelation and was a virgin when we married. Magnus knew this but claimed God revealed to him that I had aborted two children in my heart and would therefore not be given more.

I searched through my past, combing back for any possible negative thought I'd ever had toward children—mine or anyone else's—until I thought I'd go crazy. Until I no longer trusted my own mind or memory. Because I knew for a fact I had always wanted children—something that never seemed important to Magnus before. Once, when I thought I might be pregnant, I actually worried how he would react. Magnus requires a lot of attention, absolute devotion. It's the one thing he demands from every member of the Enclave. There were plenty of families at the Enclave, but the implicit understanding was that Magnus, as the Interpreter, always came first—before spouses, before children, before even the Bible itself . . .

When I balked at the idea of Magnus taking another wife, I was told I was in rebellion against God Himself. When two weeks in Penitence failed to change my conviction that I was not meant to share my husband [author's note: Penitence is a white, windowless room with only a cot and an altar, designed for the Penitent's undisturbed contemplation and prayer, where members are forced into solitary confinement and often not fed or given water for days], I was "sequestered" in a nearby garage and forced to sleep on concrete. When I still refused, I was given an ultimatum: go along with it or be cast out.

I was terrified. To be cast out [author's note: sent to live out the remainder of one's earthly life in the outside world before spending eternity in Hell] meant the loss of not only my salvation, but the only home or family I had. How could God demand this kind of choice from me— through the man who was His mouthpiece? Who had preached all my life about purity?

I began to wonder if Magnus was right and I was crazy. If Magnus was revealing something to me I myself hadn't realized. Because what you need to understand is that in the Enclave, you learn not to trust your instincts. They're base and fallible. You go by what the Elders and Magnus tell you instead.

Finally, I confessed that I had aborted two children in my heart. But I was too late. Magnus, I'm guessing, had probably realized the friction taking a second wife might cause inside the Enclave (if not the outside world, as we were never legally married—I couldn't even prove common-law marriage, as we never presented publicly outside the Enclave as a couple). All I know for sure is that he didn't want me to be his wife anymore, and for that to happen, according to our tenets, I had to "die."

Three days later, I was taken out in the middle of the night and driven a hundred miles west where I was let out at a truck stop with only the clothes I was wearing.

I sit back, reeling. But my first thought isn't of Kestral. It's Jackie. If this could happen to Kestral, what could happen to her? Jackie has no idea Kestral's alive.

All these years we thought she was dead . . .

I start.

Mom.

With shaking fingers I open a new tab and type in "Sylvia Roth Iowa."

The page fills with addresses, white pages, social media pages, a couple professional sites for an orthopedic practice . . .

And then I see it. The obituary. I click through, heart pounding in my ears. The picture is her. The date is the same.

Sylvia Roth, 39, of Ames, Iowa, formerly of Chicago, Illinois, died at home after a short and sudden battle with cancer. She is survived by her daughters, Jaclyn and Wynter.

Memorials may be made to the New Earth Clothing and Counseling Center.

I know what that last line means. I heard Julie talk about it just last week in relation to a friend who passed away in another state. I wonder if anyone sent money.

If New Earth profited off her death.

Now my hands are shaking for an altogether different reason. A new one: anger. At Magnus. For my mother. Jackie. Kestral. And at myself. For every minute I spent in Penitence. That I was cast out in a spectacle meant to keep the others in line, though I guess I should be glad I wasn't driven far away and released like some wild animal.

Most of all, I'm afraid. For Truly—always. But especially for Jaclyn.

There's an email address for Suzanne Ruckman, the writer of the article. I click on it and tap out a short message with my new email account I created to set up the social media one:

Dear Suzanne,

I am writing to you in confidence. Would you please forward
this note to "Ann," whom I knew at the Enclave? Please do not
share this note with anyone but her. Thank you.

K,

It's Sylvia's daughter. I'm so sorry this happened to you. I didn't
know. We didn't know. I'm out. Please write me back.

W.

I leave out my name; I have no desire for it to be associated
online with New Earth if the author doesn't honor my request for
anonymity or makes me an addendum to her interview.

I read until the early hours of the morning: personal accounts of
life at the compound by visitors who opted not to stay, unwilling to
sign over their assets; profiles about the secretive community behind
the charismatic leader of New Earth Pure Life Seed Co.; the sexual
assault story about Elder Omni as told by "Tamara," who is too afraid
to use her real name as she still has family living in the Enclave.

I wonder if "Tamara" is Lyssa or even Shae. But there is no picture for that one.

Finally, as the path lights in the yard below come on signaling
the hour before dawn, I type "Magnus Theisen" in the search bar.
There's far more on him, dating back to the 1990s, from more visible
outlets: ag industry reports, financial news sites, business profiles,
Entrepreneur Magazine, *People*. All about how he started TG+
Hybrids and later sold it for $53 million. The years he spent travel-
ing, partying, and getting asked for donations to causes that, in his
opinion, would never change the world. The cancer scare and conversion experience during which he claimed to hear the voice of God

telling him to prepare for the new Earth by returning to the "ways of Eden." His about-face on GMOs and obsession with acquiring rare, ancient seeds from around the world, including the "Methuselah" date palm in Israel—a tree germinated from a two-thousand-year-old seed—and, most recently, a four-thousand-year-old lentil purchased for $25,000. His rumored illegal purchases of seeds discovered at ancient archaeological sites in North America and the Middle East. The financial ruin of his former business partner, Blaine Owen.

I stare at that name a moment and then type in "Blaine Owen TG+ Hybrids."

His picture comes up with the dates of his birth . . . and his death.

Just four weeks ago.

I search through several articles until I find an obituary in the *Kansas City Star* stating that he lost his long struggle with addiction.

I go back, scroll down the results until I land on an old article about TG+ Hybrids' accounting violations. Hundreds of thousands in fines. Charges against Chief Financial Officer Blaine Owen, who spent five months in jail.

There's more, on Owen's allegations that Magnus forced him to take the fall, for which Magnus sued him.

Apparently no one believed Blaine.

I spend the rest of the night reading everything I can find on New Earth, Magnus, Blaine, cults, and their leaders.

By morning, I am numb.

I had a purpose once. Believed the lie that I was special if only because I had managed to claim a slot in Heaven. A reservation that was by no means guaranteed but had to be reclaimed daily by faith and toil if only to keep it from the hands of another. Faith had never been about being perfect—good thing for me—but about being more perfect than a world on the cusp of being devoured. The spiritual equivalent of outrunning the person behind you when getting chased by a bear.

But I am no longer one of the Select. I am one in 7.5 billion trying to figure out what's real. And right now all I know for sure is that I'm a jobless twenty-two-year-old vegetarian with exactly three friends and no job skills I can put on paper.

That afternoon, after finally getting a few hours' sleep, I open my journal to begin the list Dr. Reiker suggested of what I mean to accomplish in my new life.

But there's only one thing on it:

Get Jackie and Truly out.

That night, an alert flashes across my phone's screen.
An email.

SCHOOL OF VETERINARY MEDICINE, DEPARTMENT OF ANATOMIC PATHOLOGY UC DAVIS, BUILDING 3A

Grad Student Shon Goken stared at the obituary on the *Fairbanks Daily News-Miner* online, feeling vaguely ill. Just last summer the farmer had posted on a Mangalitsa breeders' board about the violent death of his sow by his boar. It had been a stroke of bad luck for the farmer but a boon to Shon's summer fellowship project on the normally disease-resistant heritage breed. Especially once the farmer had agreed to exhume the carcasses and send him several tissue samples of muscle, bone, and brain.

Shon had put them into storage and promptly forgot about them since his proposal wasn't due until February. Today, as he'd begun work on it, he'd realized he needed some more information. But now the farmer was dead, having been found in the woods last August after apparently wandering for days according to the farmers' sister, who had answered his house phone. She'd talked readily, like someone hungry for conversation no matter who was on the other end, and he'd offered her his condolences, trying to figure out how to tactfully ask if she had access to the purchase information on his boar.

She had sighed. "I can look if you want to leave me your number. But he burned a bunch of files before he . . . you know."

"Burned?"

"Yeah. You should see this place. It's . . . I never thought John was one to do drugs, but that's the only explanation anyone can come up with. Especially after two of his buddies he used to hang out with died a few weeks after he did. They weren't right in their minds, either."

"What do you mean 'not right'?" Shon asked.

"One of them, Cash Devries, who worked at the slaughterhouse, took the top half of his head off with a band saw."

Shon grimaced against his cell phone. "Oh . . . wow."

"The other one drove his truck into a building. Died a few days later in the hospital."

"Any idea what happened to the surviving pigs?"

"There was only two left," the sister said. "He slaughtered them. Had to. Said he was done, was talking about going into cannabis. Which is why I mention the drugs."

Now Shon toggled back to Cash Devries's obituary and that of the other man he believed to be the friend, if only because he had worked at the same slaughterhouse.

Something wasn't right. Pigs gone crazy. The farmer and two of his friends—who had possibly come into contact with the remaining pig—also gone crazy . . .

He called the sister a second time.

"Any chance your brother ingested any brain or spinal material of one of his own hogs?" Shon asked.

"He liked to fry the brains with eggs for him and his friends when he slaughtered. Only part he ever kept back for himself."

It *sounded* like a prion, but even a porcine variant of the spongiform encephalopathy responsible for mad cow disease in cattle or the human variant, Creutzfeldt-Jakob disease, would never present so quickly in humans. Assuming the farmer or his friends ingested the brain of a prion-infected animal, it would take years, maybe even decades, for symptoms to appear. And without studying a sample of the dead men's brains, there was no way to know.

Shon prepared several slides from the pigs' brain samples. And then, as an afterthought, took a sample of the dirt from the specimen bag as well.

Forty minutes later, he knew he had something far bigger than a summer fellowship project.

He grabbed his phone and placed a call.

"I found something," he said.

TWO DAYS LATER, Shon's summer fellowship project—and its $6,000 stipend—went up in smoke when his samples and their data went missing.

CHAPTER TEN

My hands shook as I crossed the yard. What could the office want with me? I'd striven to be silent, invisible, since Truly's birth, lest anything interfere with my ability to spend time with her. Because each time that sweet four-year-old girl ran into my arms, I knew God was good and everything in life made sense.

I knocked on the office door, hesitated, and at the sound of a voice, let myself inside. I remembered nothing of this place from my single visit here the day I barged in demanding answers about my mother. This time, I took in the cream-colored curtains and stuffed chairs just inside the door. The filing cabinets and bookshelves. The entire far wall lined with what looked like magazine covers featuring Magnus—*Entrepreneur Magazine*, *Organic Farmer*, *Forbes*, *Archaeology Today*. Magnolia, rising from her desk. Her shoulders had begun to hunch some time in the last decade, her chestnut hair grayer in the fluorescent light than I remembered, her jowls more pronounced. How that could happen on Rosella's cooking I had no idea.

"Wynter," she said, sounding relieved. She took me over to a smaller desk across from hers set up with a computer and piled high with papers.

"These are from last week's inventory," she said, pointing to one stack. "And these are last quarter's seed yields." She reached across me to grab the computer mouse. The monitor flashed to life.

"I don't understand," I said, wondering why she was telling me this as I stared at the grid on the screen. I hadn't seen a computer in nearly fifteen years; they weren't used in our warehouse or school where I taught math, as there would be no power on the Final Day or need for it in the New Earth to come. So I was more than a little shocked—even scandalized—to see not one but two of them here.

"You're assigned here in the afternoons from now on," she said, handing me a copy of *Excel for Dummies*.

The rules were simple: I was to work only on what I was assigned. I was not to touch the files. I was not to answer the phone. I was not to talk about what I did here with anyone or share any information that crossed my desk.

It took me three days to get my bearings with the computer spreadsheet—all while trying to work the mouse without the cursor jumping spastically across the screen. Elders Omni and Canon welcomed me with passing nods, Shae's dad not at all. Magnus's door was always closed, though I could hear his muffled answer any time one of the Elders knocked on it. The only time I ever saw him was the day he abruptly strode from his office right past me, phone held to his ear. He was out the door before I could drop the papers in my hand to press my palms together in greeting.

I loved the work, and the three hours I was there each afternoon flew by too quickly before I had to report for dinner prep. My fourth day there, Magnolia informed me I'd been relieved of second kitchen shift so I could work later in the office—a thing I did gladly. So gladly, in fact, that I stayed past the start of dinner.

Meanwhile, a strange shift had happened in the dynamics of those around me in just the last two days. My dormitory warden, Iris, who had treated me with a certain level of contempt since my broken engagement, became nervous and strangely agreeable when I returned to the barrow at night. The fresh clothing I regularly dug out from the bottom of the fresh laundry bin—rumpled after everyone else had helped themselves—began to appear neatly folded on my bed. And Arabella, the children's warden, who had mostly tolerated my regular visits to Truly if only because I helped with the other children as well, extended an invitation to come say prayers with the children that night.

Although working in such proximity to the Elders and Magnus himself had always afforded Magnolia a level of deference inside the Enclave, I was stupefied to find that it now extended to me—the same girl who had lived the last five years with sidelong glances after her questionable conduct at the farmers' market.

Which is why I suspected Rosella wouldn't mind my coming to the kitchen for a snack if I missed the meal tonight.

Just after six thirty, as I finished entering the latest yields, Magnus's door started to open. I got quickly to my feet, but before I could press my palms together, his phone sounded.

I heard him murmur to himself as it rang again and then again. His voice, by the time he finally answered, sounded tired.

"Yes?"

A floorboard in his office creaked over the background noise of the phone's speaker.

"Hello?" he said again.

A jostle on the other end, and then "Hey, man, long time!"

"Who's this?" Magnus said, sounding irritated.

"Whoa, it hasn't been that long, has it?"

A brief silence. And then:

"Blaine." Magnus gave a short, strained laugh. "Sorry, friend. It's been a long day. How are you?"

"Oh, you know. Good as ever. How's the religion business?"

"How many times do I have to tell you—"

"I know, I know. It's not a business. Okay, whatever. Hey, listen. I have something." Blaine, whoever he was, sounded distracted. Nervous.

Meanwhile, I was nervous, too. Did Magnus know I was still here? Everyone else had left for the day. No, he couldn't know, or surely he wouldn't have answered on speakerphone. I glanced around, not sure what to do.

"I'm really—thank you for thinking of me. But I'm not interested."

"No, seriously, you are. You will be. Trust me."

Magnus blew out a sigh. "You doing all right? I heard you did another stint in rehab a few years back."

"That's old news. I'm doing great." But his laugh was shallow.

"You still working in Kansas City?"

"Still in KC, but I'm in between. Guess our partnership was a hard act to follow. I was actually thinking of coming up to Iowa. Hell, maybe I'll join your cult."

When Magnus didn't respond, raspy laughter sounded on the other end. "I'm just kidding! Hey, listen. Any chance we could meet?" His words muffled as though he were rubbing his face.

"I don't think—"

"Listen, I'm telling you, this is worth something. As in, offer it to the Russians or Chinese for a hundred—a thousand—times more than what I'm asking for it. I'd offer it to them myself, if my name still meant anything. But as you know, it doesn't."

"Look, if you need money . . ."

"I'm telling you this is worth something! A lot to the right person," Blaine said. When Magnus didn't respond, he said, "Still there? Still with m—"

"Yeah. Yeah, I'm here," he said, and I realized he must have picked up the phone. "So what is it?"

I eyed the front door in the ensuing silence, but there was no way I could open it without it creaking on its hinges.

"Where?" Magnus said. And then: "What am I supposed to do with that? And no, it's not good—it's all derelicts and outcasts. We haven't had anyone with real assets in years and my last investor fell through. So I don't know what you think I have to offer. We're not exactly flush right now. No . . . that was a rumor. Of course not. That'd be illegal. Well, times have changed."

He sighed. "Look. I've got to go. I'll call you back tomorrow. But, Blaine? One word of this call to anyone, and I'll do more than deny it. I'll tell them you're a sad cautionary tale hitting up anyone you know for cash. I'm sure your parole officer would be really interested in our last conversation. Good. We understand each other then."

Now I was certain I wasn't supposed to have heard what I had. Sliding from my desk chair, I crawled into the leg well of my desk beneath my keyboard tray. Floorboards creaked as Magnus crossed to the door.

And then I realized that unlike Magnolia's screen, mine was still on, shining like a beacon above me. I darted forward, lunging for the power strip near the wall, fumbled for the switch at the end, and pressed it.

I recoiled beneath the desk as his door swung open. Held my breath as he strode out to the main office. Closed my eyes as he passed by my desk, catching a waft of his cologne. He was the only one at the Enclave who wore it.

A second later he turned off the light, opened the front door Magnolia had set to lock earlier, and left.

Sliding out from beneath my desk, I crawled to the window to peer over the sill, gaze following his figure toward the Banquet Table. The minute he disappeared behind Percepta Hall, I flipped the switch on the power strip back on. With a last glance out the window, I hurried to the door and slipped out.

I didn't dare show up in the kitchen after him now and so headed directly for the Factory, skipping dinner altogether.

That night after returning from the girls' barrow, I lay in bed wondering who Blaine was.

Derelicts and outcasts, he had called us. How could he say that about the chosen Select?

And what could someone—a drug addict, no less—have to offer the Interpreter of God?

I dreaded returning to the office the next day. I slipped into my desk chair without a word, relieved that Magnolia was too engrossed in whatever she was doing to even say hello.

I glanced back just once at Magnus's door, but the office beyond it was silent.

A short time later, Magnolia exclaimed, "How am I supposed to know what kind of nails we need when nobody specifies?"

I glanced up as she held up a request form where someone had written only "Nails."

I offered to take it to the farm, see if I could get an answer.

"No. I need to have a talk with them anyway," she said, getting up and marching out the door, slamming it shut behind her.

She was gone only two or three minutes before the phone on her desk began to ring. I ignored it until Elder Decaro poked his head out of his office.

"Is someone going to answer that?" he snapped.

I hesitated and then moved over to Magnolia's desk. After all, she couldn't gainsay an Elder. His door slammed behind me as I picked up the receiver.

"New Earth International," I said, as I'd heard Magnolia answer dozens of times this past week.

"Hi," a male voice said on the other end. "I'm calling from the *Ames Tribune*. Is Magnus Theisen available?"

"No. I'm sorry. Can I, uh, have someone call you back?"

I looked around for a scrap of paper to write down his name as he said something about wanting to do an interview. Told him I wasn't sure when he asked if we had a press release. That's when I noticed the open projects at the bottom of Magnolia's screen:

INBOX. ACCOUNTS PAYABLE. SERMON ORDERS. PRESS RELEASE.

I jotted down the man's number with a promise someone would call him back and carefully returned the phone to its cradle. Glancing back at the closed office doors behind me, I grabbed her mouse, hovered the cursor over "Press Release." Clicked it.

It was some kind of announcement about a seed New Earth had acquired. Some ancient lentil over four thousand years old purchased for $100,000.

One hundred thousand dollars. How was that possible? I had a fairly good idea by then what we sold in orders each month, and it wasn't nearly enough to cover that kind of a price.

Was that what "Blaine" had called Magnus about?

But no, it couldn't be. It was dated a week ago.

My eye ran down the page, scanning quickly.

". . . legume to be offered by New Earth International as early as next year, ancient Seed Hunter and religious leader Magnus Theisen claims . . ."

I ran the cursor over several other documents, accidentally clicking one. A news article sprang to life beneath my mouse: "Saving the World One Seed at a Time." There was a picture of Magnus holding a tray of seeds in what I assumed to be the vault.

The front door opened and I let go of the mouse and grabbed the slip of paper, ready to explain what I was doing sitting at her desk.

But it wasn't Magnolia.

It was Magnus.

I rose out of my chair, the phone message trapped in my fingers as I belatedly lifted my hands before my mouth.

"Why, Magnolia, have you done something different with your hair?" Magnus said with a chuckle.

I gave a small, nervous laugh. "I had to take a message. Someone called. They wanted to talk to you—" I stopped. I didn't know if I was supposed to know about the interviews. The news articles.

Including the one open on the screen in front of me.

He came over to the desk, gently took the slip of paper from me. His shirtsleeves, as ever, were rolled to the elbow, as though he were ready to weed in the garden or lug a crate of seeds. "Thank you," he said, not even glancing at it.

I was just grateful I wouldn't have to explain the call to Magnolia.

"Did you just start here?" he asked, leaning against the desk as though having forgotten whatever it was he had come here to do. As though there were something that fascinated him behind my eyes, though I had no idea what that might be.

Then I remembered his phone call last night.

"Just a few hours here and there," I said, stepping away, hoping to distract him from the open article.

But his eyes had already gone to the screen.

"Did you read that?" he asked, nodding toward it.

I bit my lips together for a second. But I didn't dare lie to his face. "Yes."

To my surprise, he smiled. "I'm flattered."

"I wasn't planning on it. It was just—"

"You look so much like your mother," he said, shaking his head faintly. "She was beautiful, too."

And then he walked to his office and shut the door.

I swiftly closed the article before Magnolia could return.

CHAPTER ELEVEN

I'm nervous as I open the email, though I'm not sure why. But the moment I begin to read, her sweet voice returns, the angelic smile of memory.

> Wynter!
>
> I'm so relieved you're out. How did you leave? Is your sister with you?
>
> Obviously, I'm not dead. I assume you know enough now to realize Magnus deceived you about so many things. Which means I hope you're not questioning yourself, wondering if you're crazy. I thought I was for a long time. Hang in there.
>
> Let me know how you are.
>
> Kestral

My gaze floats back up to that first paragraph. *Is your sister with you?*

She doesn't know. But of course not—how can she?
I slowly tap out a response.

Kestral,

I was cast out. I'm living with friends in Illinois. I'm doing better,
though went through a hard time.

W.

Her response arrives an hour later.

Wynter,

I'm so very sorry. What you need to know is that whatever
your so-called (or real) infraction, you are not damned. Do you
hear me? I'm shouting it all the way from Nebraska. Can you
hear me?

I hope one day you will be able to forgive me for my part in this.
I sold you a false bill of goods. I'm so sorry. I adored you all from
the minute you arrived and thought I was sharing something right
and good.

For now, you need to know there is life and love in the world.
I've seen it. God is far bigger than the Enclave.

Is Jaclyn still inside? I worry for her.

K.

Kestral,

I don't know how to tell you this . . . Jaclyn married Magnus.
She didn't know. None of us did. They have a daughter. I'm afraid
for them both.

W.

The next morning I still haven't heard back and wonder if I ever will. Maybe I shouldn't have told her, but I felt like a liar keeping it from her.

THE DINNER TALK that night is all about Ken leaving with an emergency team for Washington State and Lauren failing precalculus now that the friend she used to cheat off of has been kept home in the face of the "catching crazy." It doesn't help that her favorite teacher has been put on leave after someone noticed his Oregon vacation pictures from fall break online.

"I could tutor her," I offer.

"How do you know precalc? I thought you were homeschooled," Lauren says.

"I was." I don't say that growing up in the Enclave, school was the most fun part of my day.

"Ken, don't go," Julie says. "You started Zandt Research to get out of the field. Just because you miss the excitement is no reason to put yourself in danger."

"Bishop specifically requested me. How am I supposed to say no? I'll be fine," Ken says.

"Is it Bishop you don't want to say no to or the CDC?" Julie asks, giving him a level look.

"I'll be fine."

"'Fine'? Five cities in Washington and Oregon just declared states of emergency! London and Tokyo aren't even accepting flights from Seattle and Portland. There's nothing fine about that!"

"We're taking a charter plane," Ken says calmly.

"Someone shot up a grocery store just yesterday in Seattle,"

Lauren says. Julie gestures toward her as though she's just proven her point.

Ken quirks a smile. "Lucky for me, we're not going grocery shopping. I'll be safe and sound at a hospital across the lake in Bellevue."

"Because ground zero is so much better," Julie says.

"I saw Canada's refusing entry to US motorists traveling north to Vancouver," I say with an apologetic look. I don't want him to go, either.

"Why can't you video conference in?" Julie says.

"Because I can't run tests through a video feed." Ken sets down his fork with a sigh. "Guys, this could be really helpful to a lot of people."

"Just promise not to need an emergency appendectomy while you're there," Julie says.

"I promise," Ken says. "That doesn't appear to be how the majority of cases are being spread, anyway. Patients describe getting sick one to two weeks before their first episodes of confusion and erratic behavior. The main pattern of spread looks viral."

"You be extra careful," Julie says. "Wear your mask the entire time. Better yet, a whole hazmat suit!"

"Hey. Who's the doctor here? Hello, anyone remember those big framed paper things on my wall—the ones that say 'MD' and 'PhD'?" Ken asks. No one looks impressed.

"Can I be homeschooled?" Lauren asks.

"We'll talk about it," Julie says.

"Can I get my nose pierced?"

"No," Ken and Julie say in unison.

LATE THAT NIGHT, my phone chimes with a new email.

Wynter,

   Jaclyn's daughter, I'm sure, is safe for now. But I'm afraid for
Jaclyn.

   K.

K,

   Me, too.

   W.

KEN LEAVES THE next morning. Thirty minutes after Ken's plane
takes off, Lauren's school shuts down after a boy slashes one of Lauren's friends, claiming she's the Antichrist. We drive together to the
school where Lauren's waiting in the office.

Her shirt is covered in blood.

"Oh, my God!" Julie cries.

"It isn't mine," Lauren says, going into Julie's arms with a sob.
We drive home so she can change before going to the hospital and
donning masks from the dispenser inside the door to hold vigil with
her schoolmates while the girl's in surgery.

Her friend comes through, by which time the talk is all about
who else the boy had been around, and whether they're acting
weird, too.

Julie cranes her head as we drive past Walmart on the way home.
The parking lot is packed with people wheeling full carts to their
cars. A few minutes later, she turns in to Standard Market.

"Stay with Lauren and lock the doors," she says, grabbing her
purse. She returns twenty minutes later with a cart full of shopping
bags and several cases of bottled water. She drives to the gas station
after that, where we wait fifteen minutes for a pump.

Lauren spends the rest of the day huddled beneath a blanket on the living room sofa watching school closings scroll across the TV. The boys call off and on throughout the afternoon to video chat and ask how she's doing.

We eat in front of the news. Canada is refusing entry to motorists traveling Interstate 5 to Vancouver and several other highways that cross the border. A CDC briefing interrupts yet another panel of experts arguing about the difference between precaution and panic to report cases of rapid early-onset dementia in thirty-two states and more than two hundred confirmed cases and many more unconfirmed in Canada and overseas.

There is no treatment protocol.

"Ken," Julie says, video chatting with him when he calls to check in on Lauren. "Come home. Just rent a car and drive. I don't want you there anymore. That whole area's going crazy."

Ken, ever the prevailing voice of calm, says he'll be home in a few days.

"Just so you know," he says before they hang up, "I sent a company-wide email asking everyone in the office who can to work from home. No alarm, just a precaution. There's a box of surgical masks and latex gloves in my office. If you have to leave the house for any reason, use them."

It doesn't help.

The local news is all about the school incident. The kid with the knife has been hauled off to a psych ward, but he's not the only one; three more students from Benedictine and North Central were forcibly admitted.

"Are they all violent?" Julie demands, throwing her arms into the air. "Can't anyone go quietly crazy on their own without ruining people's lives?"

I don't say that the ones with shiny Hello Kitty obsessions probably don't make the news.

The next morning is filled with live coverage of office, mall, and traffic attacks throughout the nation, including a woman who mowed down three people in a Los Angeles parking lot claiming that the people she hit weren't real. Four more people have tried to soar off of buildings.

A guy in North Dakota only shot up the weight equipment in his local gym, saying they were Decepticons from Cybertron trying to kill the human race.

Luckily no human fatalities in that one.

Wynter,

Does Jaclyn still work the counseling center? Maybe when all these scary headlines die down you can get to her there. I won't lie, it's going to be very hard for her to get away with Magnus's child. If either of you needs a safe place, you're always welcome here in Sidney. Just ask for the Peterson farm. I'd love to hug your neck again.

It may not look like it right now, Wynter, but God is out here in the world. I've seen it.

K.

KEN CALLS THE next morning to say he won't be coming home as planned. That he's traveling by car to a field office in Boise.

"Listen," he says on speakerphone. "I'm not supposed to be sharing this—we're waiting for confirmation. But it looks like the disease is transmitted through a strain of influenza."

"Then it's good we all got our shots," Julie says.

I can practically hear Ken shaking his head as he blows out a sigh.

"It's an unusual strain not in this year's vaccine. The shot might offer partial immunity, but right now there's no effective vaccine."

Julie pales. "Flu season's barely started . . ."

"Just—stay in the house. Don't go anywhere you don't have to. Don't have anyone over. Wash your hands. Call the boys and tell them, too."

Lauren gives me a stark look as Julie carries her phone into the den and closes the French doors, but I can still hear them.

Probably because I'm eavesdropping right outside.

"I'm scared, Ken." She's crying. I've never heard Julie cry. "I want you to come home!"

"I can't. We have to go now, before they shut down the roads."

I step back. Shut down the roads? Has this ever happened before? For the first time in two months, the old fear spikes inside me. Is this how the world ends?

But Magnus lied. About Kestral and who knows what else. It's the truth I cling to, the missing strut in his house of cards.

Julie spends the rest of the afternoon on the phone with the boys, her mother, and Ken's parents.

That night, the CDC quarantines Bellevue, Washington, and several surrounding communities, and more in the Portland, Oregon, area. Restaurants and other businesses in quarantined cities have already shut their doors to paramedics, doctors, police, schoolteachers—and anyone else the proprietors deem unsafe. Others have closed completely.

Stefan calls back from Columbus to say Ohio State has suspended classes. Julie spends an hour redrilling him about not invit-

ing guests ("That means no girlfriends or parties!") to the house he
rents off campus with three other guys.

The next morning, federal police shut down Interstates 90 and
84 to the Pacific Northwest and 80 into Sacramento.

As national news covers alarm throughout the West Coast and
airport closings by the hour, local stations call them "precaution-
ary measures," citing panic as the most immediate threat to public
health—even as the public announcements across the bottom of the
screen flash their words in red:

Stay safe. Stay home.

HEALTH ADVISORY

Illinois Department of Public Health
Regarding: Rapid Early-Onset Dementia

The Illinois Department of Public Health is investigating multiple cases of Rapid Early-Onset Dementia (REOD) throughout the state of Illinois. Due to the volatile nature of the disease, the public is advised to study and know the symptoms:

- Increased confusion
- Memory loss, repetition of actions (due to not remembering)
- Sudden difficulty with balance or mobility
- Reckless or dangerous behavior toward self or others
- Hallucinations

Take precautions:

- Wash your hands with soap and water regularly.
- Be aware of your surroundings and those of any children with you at all times.
- Report any suspicious behavior.
- Avoid travel.
- Stay home.

Report symptoms of REOD to local authorities. Do *not* try to intervene in any situation, as such actions may prove dangerous.

CLICK HERE TO SIGN UP FOR HEALTH TEXT ALERTS

(STANDARD RATES MAY APPLY)

CHAPTER TWELVE

The next day as I worked across from Magnolia, Magnus emerged from his office. His shoes were freshly shined. He was wearing dark gray slacks. They were too nice to have been made in the Factory, and I knew for a fact Jaclyn couldn't sew more than buttons.

"Sister-in-law," he said, cheerfully, "I've got some business in town. Why don't you come with me?"

I blinked, not sure I had heard right. And then I was worried. Did he know I had overheard his conversation with Blaine? But when I looked up, his eyes seemed to laugh, crinkling at the edges just as they had the first time I met him.

"Well, what do you say?" He smiled.

"Of course." I stood uncertainly as Magnolia lifted her hands before her, knowing she wouldn't be pleased. But she wasn't about to object.

He held the door for me as we stepped outside, where a short man named Enzo waited by the Prius Magnus took into town for meetings. After gesturing me into the back, Magnus let himself in the other side as Enzo shut my door.

No one had ever done that for me before.

His was easily the nicest car I'd ever been in. Which wasn't saying much; the only vehicle I'd been inside the last fifteen years was an old van.

I kept my hands folded in my lap as the walls of the broad gate slowly pulled open. I hadn't been outside these walls in nearly five years, since that day at the farmers' market—a goal that had taken me years to achieve. And now here I was, leaving out of the blue.

I hazarded a glance through the window just in time to see Ara coming toward the office from the children's school, a box of something in her arms. But I didn't miss the way she stared. Or the others with her.

Was that alarm or envy?

I glanced over at Magnus, who sat comfortably, his legs crossed. His hair had grayed in tendrils near his temples, though it was still dark where it curled against his collar. I'd watched the transformation so slowly every morning for the last several years that I'd hardly noticed until seeing it just now, up close.

"So . . . where are we going?" I asked.

"Just into Garden City," he said. He looked relaxed, pleased even, that I was with him. "I thought it might be nice to get out and reacquainted."

Reacquainted. I'd exchanged more words with him in the last twenty-four hours than I had in the last fifteen years.

I clasped my sweaty hands together and hoped I didn't smell like the onions I'd chopped for lunch.

"Tell me," he said, after a few minutes. "Do you think Jaclyn is happy?"

"Of course," I said, puzzled by the question. But the truth was, I didn't know. The closeness between us during her pregnancy had waned in the years since Truly's birth. I saw her sometimes in the children's barrow, but we were rarely ever alone. And she was never *not* the wife of Magnus. Which meant she checked in on her daughter as she did any child. Because children weren't the property of their parents here, as they were in the world. They were members of the Select tended—and corrected—by the Enclave as a whole.

"Does she not . . . seem happy?" I asked, wondering what I'd missed.

He said it as though choosing his words carefully. "She hasn't seemed quite herself. I was wondering if you'd noticed any cause for concern."

"Not that I know of," I said. But I was no longer sure.

He shifted in the seat. "You know, I never told you that I knew the whole event several years ago was . . . difficult for you."

I glanced at him.

"You should know Elder Decaro was the one who requested you. I had my misgivings about the way he mistook personal desire for revelation but thought it best he be allowed to discover the mistake on his own."

I wondered what Elder Decaro would think, hearing Magnus say that, and took a little satisfaction in the thought. Especially since I'd been the one punished for it.

"The way you've learned to hear and submit to the word of our Divine Father is nothing short of impressive," Magnus said, openly studying me.

"Thank you," I said awkwardly, not exactly sure what he meant. I hesitated and then ventured, "I do miss working the market."

"You're doing more important work now." He leaned forward. "Enzo—the café."

Smiling at me, he asked, "Hungry?"

GARDEN CITY WAS a tiny hamlet with a convenience store, farm co-op, and a family-owned café. It was the closest settlement to the Enclave, with a population less than one hundred, but more people than the three closest hamlets combined.

Inside Gigi's café Magnus escorted me to a booth along the wall as Enzo took a seat at the counter and I quickly realized sitting across from Magnus was more awkward than sitting beside him. I didn't know where to look and so studied the silverware wrapped in a paper napkin in front of me until the waitress in the pink uniform came by with menus. I guessed her to be just a few years older than me. She was pretty, with red hair in a high ponytail.

"Afternoon, Magnus," she said, her gaze flicking to me as she delivered glasses of water. I was surprised that she knew him by name.

Magnus leaned across the table toward me as she left. "Your sister and I used to come here on occasion for lunch," he said with a wink.

"Oh," I managed even as I wondered how that could be for a dozen reasons. Chief among them that the Select didn't meet outside the Enclave or eat the food of the world. Let alone order it in a restaurant.

"You seem surprised," he said, watching me.

"Confused, I guess."

"Why?"

"Because . . ." Because everything. But I settled for, "The Testament."

He tilted his head, picked up the menu, and frowned at it. "Wynter, those strong enough in their faith have eyes to see. They don't look at this place and think, 'What a nice little business' or even 'Look at all the wonderful food on this menu,'" he said, gesturing vaguely around us.

"They take the protection of their salvation and the surety of their place among the Select with them. They come with a greater purpose than the rest who walk through that door. Because the Divine Father has guided their steps."

I nodded, but I didn't understand. Especially when the waitress came and he ordered two of today's specials—grilled cheese and tomato soup—for the both of us.

"Sound good to you?" he asked.

Was this a test? Gluten was off limits and I hadn't had real dairy in fifteen years. But this was Magnus. So I just nodded. And it did sound good.

He asked me about the office—if I liked the work. He asked about Truly. Wasn't she a smart and beautiful girl? I told him about how much she loved drawing pictures of the barn cats, whom she had named Shadrach, Meshach, Abednego, and Bob, at which he chuckled.

"I've heard of this mysterious Bob," he said, smiling. But a moment later, he grew serious. "I'm curious," he said, carefully unwrapping his napkin. "What are your thoughts about the future of the Enclave?"

I glanced around the table, searching for an answer. The right one. "I hope it'll expand. That we can bring in more people until the last appointed one." It had been the mission of New Earth drummed into me since I was seven: to welcome the remaining Select with the hope that each one would be the last one God had appointed to be saved. At which point the world would fall to ruin, the earth would be made new, and those who were "sleeping" like Mom and Kestral would return.

It was a thing I'd desperately looked forward to once I'd come to terms with the fact that Mom really was gone. That I had failed to keep her from death. A day when the pall of guilt would be lifted. Because she'd be alive and we'd be together again. She'd get to meet Truly and all would be forgiven.

To my mortification, thinking of that now made my lower lip tremble, unwanted tears to well in my eyes. Reaching blindly for my silverware, I unwound the paper napkin and lifted a corner to my lashes.

Magnus said nothing, quietly folding his hands as I tried to collect myself.

Which only made it worse.

Mercifully, the waitress appeared with our food a few minutes later—including a greasy pile of potato chips.

I'd eaten in Magnus's proximity before—if you call three tables away from the Elders' table in the Banquet Table "proximity." But it felt strange to bite into that first gloriously salty potato chip in front of him until he picked up his sandwich and took a big bite, studying me with an unreadable expression as he chewed.

"Why do you suppose I give this to you?" he said, gesturing at the plates in front of us.

"I don't know," I said honestly.

"I give it because it isn't what we eat that makes us unclean—the Divine Father tells us that. But we are called to serve our weakest members. To not become stumbling blocks to them. You wouldn't feed a baby adult food, would you? No. When you walk with a child, you don't walk as quickly as you do when you're with another adult, do you? No, you walk at their pace. It's all they're capable of. I feel you're mature enough to understand that we begin our lives with rules. The rules are our morality. But as we mature, we move beyond those rules. Because we understand that our journey is not the rules themselves."

I nodded slightly.

"In the same way, looking at a man or woman with appreciation is not a sin. The sin is in acting on that impulse outside the proper relationship. For instance, I can look at you, Wynter, and say you are a beautiful woman. There is no sin in that."

I felt heat rise in my cheeks. He'd said the same thing yesterday.

"But because we cater to our weaker sisters and brothers, we teach them to avert their eyes. To cover their bodies," he said, drawing on an imaginary cloak.

"The truth is," he said, his gaze intent, "we were made to be free. It was like that once. One day soon, it will be again. We will all be far freer than we are today, in that new place. But what so few people understand is that New Earth—Heaven—is already here, now, among and in us."

But it couldn't be here, now, or the world would be dead. And the precepts of the Testament were laws for the life to come. Hadn't he taught that? I glanced at Enzo as he chatted with the waitress, who had leaned so far onto her elbows in front of him I could see her cleavage from here. But her eyes were on Magnus.

Magnus followed my gaze and she smiled as he gestured with two fingers, at which she straightened and went to the pie case.

A moment later she set two slices of chocolate pie in front of us.

"You see," Magnus said, picking up his fork, "I knew that if we came here and I opened my heart to you, you would understand that rules are given for those without the discernment to exercise freedom. I sense you understand why we must act one way in the presence of others but can be *ourselves* around others who understand us. Which is why I feel I can talk to you. Why I can open my heart to you this way. And so we can sit here and eat this meal that will probably give us both a stomachache later"—he chuckled—"because we comprehend what others do not. And so we can *do* things other people cannot."

I nodded. But I suddenly wished he'd never asked me to come.

"I want us to talk freely, Wynter. I know you go to the Admitter and say the things you're supposed to say." He made a dismissive gesture. "But with me, I want you to say the things you would never dare tell him. And I will do the same. Because I feel like I can share things with you I can't share with anyone else."

"You have Jaclyn," I said quietly.

"Yes. I do. And she's a lovely girl. I'm so lucky. You know, we used to talk about things that would shock you." He smiled slightly. "But Jaclyn is extremely busy with the outreach. With important work that supports the Enclave—including you. It isn't fair to put any more needs on her. Mine or yours. Don't you agree?"

"Yes," I said. Because I had no choice to tell the man with absolute power over my eternal salvation anything otherwise.

He smiled then, the expression boyish. At grotesque odds with his fifty-something-year-old features, the gray in his hair. Hair that belonged to my sister's fingers to comb through. A face that should be looking on her with eyes ready to spill secrets only her ears should hear. Secrets, I somehow sensed, that she, too, might not want to hear, better confessed to God alone.

I choked down the pie, sickened by its sweetness.

On the way back to the Enclave, Magnus's eyes were twin smolders in the shadows of the back seat. When he looked down at my hand in my lap, I thought for a minute he might take it. Instead, he slid a finger thoughtfully across the top of my knuckles, the tip of his tongue pressed against his upper teeth.

"Isn't Wynter beautiful, Enzo?" he asked, not having taken his eyes off of me.

I willed myself not to hear Enzo's answer. Fled the car as they stopped to let me out at the parking lot before driving toward the warehouse.

THE NEXT MORNING at service, Magnus preached on the impending cataclysm. The coming of thousands. Why we must be ready.

"We will mortify our flesh in preparation as the cost of saving one more soul. And we will welcome them with open arms!" he said. "Because we know that the time is near when we will finally go home!"

Someone in the back shouted "Amen!" as an electric current ran through the hall. Magnus had that effect. I had felt it many times.

But that morning, I couldn't reconcile the Interpreter of the pulpit with the man who said he wanted to confide in me. Who had fed me forbidden food claiming the principles—that he had written in his own Testament—need not apply to us.

Who else did they not apply to here? The Elders, free to mistake desire for the will of God?

But those rules had been the pillars on which I'd built my life. Nothing was plumb without them.

I tried to catch Jaclyn's attention after service. But she was quick to extricate herself and by the time I reached the back of the narthex, she was gone.

THE ONE UPSIDE to all of the strange new deference paid me was that I finally had the leeway to visit Truly for longer than a few minutes at a time. The next day I took her to the barn to play with the kittens. Watched her chase after them and comforted her when they scratched her with their tiny needle claws. I took her to the kitchen where Rosella spared me one of the season's first tart apples to cut up into pieces that we shared before I returned her to the children's barrow, tugging on my earlobe in our secret sign that I'd be back soon.

Meanwhile, I was troubled. Should I go to the Elders? Even as I considered it, I knew I'd be the one condemned.

I met with the Admitter, and for once the urge to hold back was replaced with a longing to spill a truth I didn't dare voice. It welled up inside me like panic, filled my eyes with tears until I said something or other about missing my mother. I welcomed the rebuke not to grieve. The harsh reminder of the stark canon I had been taught to call the truth. But all the while, something was crumbling inside me.

My faith.

CHAPTER THIRTEEN

On December 4, the temperature dips below freezing for the first time this fall. National news covers airports turned into ghost towns. Even the commuter rail suspended service two days ago. News anchors and radio hosts report sleeping at the station as they replay viral footage of a talk show host having some kind of psychotic break on air.

I think of Truly, glad for the first time since I've left that she's safe behind the Enclave's walls. Jaclyn, too.

We turn on the fireplace, play virtual games of Scrabble with Caden and Brendan as I make stuffed mushrooms and butternut squash pot pies through the afternoon.

"Mom!" Lauren shouts a little while later. "They're talking about the CDC team on TV!"

We rush into the living room in time to see a photo of the hospital where one more member of the Bellevue 13 has died. Lauren turns up the volume as a picture of Ken's friend Bishop Williams appears in the corner of the screen.

A few minutes later, Caden texts that the power's gone out in Albuquerque.

The multistate blackout takes over the news. It's all up and down the West Coast to the panhandle of Nebraska. Being compared to something that happened in Ukraine.

"What about Dad?" Lauren asks, her expression stark.

"The field offices have generators. He'll be fine," Julie says. But she's chewing her lower lip.

Within an hour new panels of experts fill every major network to discuss cyberattacks, the failure of early-warning programs, "black energy," and point fingers at Russia, China, and North Korea in turn.

Just before 10 p.m., Texas loses power. Five minutes later, the lights in the house flicker.

"Girls," Julie says. "Go fill the bathtubs. And make sure you charge your phones."

KEN CALLS THE house from Boise that night.

"Hey, we saw you on TV!" Julie says and switches the speaker on. "Well, not you, but Bishop."

"Alas, he's far more photogenic," Ken says. "What's the power situation there?"

"Still on. We filled up the tubs just in case," Julie says. "Lantern, flashlights, and batteries are on the counter. Everything's charged. Don't worry about us. Are you keeping warm?"

"Warm enough."

Julie updates him on the boys and local news, which is all about crowded conditions in local clinics and the hospital where staff has been stretched thin for days—especially after a rumor that they were able to test for the new dementia, which turned out not to be true.

"There is no test," Ken says, sounding irritated. "There won't be for a long time. And by then, anyone sick now will already be dead!"

Julie blinks, startled to silence by the edge in Ken's voice. He curses softly—a thing I've never heard him do—and takes a deep breath.

"Sorry," he says. He sighs. "We've been trying to reconstruct where the first patient of the Bellevue 13 might have acquired the disease. Do you know how many places a person goes in the space of a month? Work, the gym, friends' houses, grocery stores, church, movie theaters, restaurants, the mall . . ." He drifts off.

"You sound like you need sleep, Dad," Lauren says.

"I will, promise. But now, Julie? Girls, there's something I need you to do."

"What's that?" Julie says, sounding worried.

"I want you to load the RV with all the food and water you can. Food, water, sleeping bags, cash, jewelry, anything else we could trade if needed . . ."

"What? What *for*?"

"You need to get away from Chicago."

"Ken, you're scaring me," she says.

"Load up the RV. Leave before dawn. Promise me."

"And go where?" Julie demands, her voice slightly shrill.

"Just—get out of the city. Head south."

"That's the other direction from where you are!"

"I'll catch up."

"All the public announcements are saying to stay home. You just told all your employees to stay home!"

"For once would you just do what I say?!" he shouts.

I cut her an alarmed glance. I've never heard Ken like this before. By the startled look on her face, neither has she.

"I'm sorry," Ken says as the house lights flicker.

A second later, they go out.

"Julie?" Ken says. "You there?"

"I'm here. We just lost power."

The house seems strangely larger than even a minute ago, the air eerily silent.

"Listen to me," Ken says. "Load up the RV with all the food, as much water as you can—everything you'll need. Tomorrow morning, when people wake up without electricity, there's going to be a run on gas. People are already lining up for it here. A bunch of them are going to leave the city—or try to. I need you to get out now. Okay? Go south. Get somewhere warmer. Try not to run the generator more than you have to—"

"Why can't we just go to my mom's?"

"Because we don't know if she's sick or not."

Julie barks a laugh. "My mom hardly leaves the house and has been crazy for years. I'll take my chances with her over strangers in the wilderness any day. Or am I missing something here?"

He sighs. "You're right. I don't know why I didn't think of that."

"It doesn't get much smaller than Jeffersonville, Illinois," she says with a slight laugh.

"But I mean it, Julie. If your mother is so much as flushed or even looks like she could have a fever—"

"Why can't we just stay here and lock the doors?" Lauren says. And I know she's thinking of her boyfriend, whom she's texted incessantly since the school incident.

"No. You need to get away from the city."

"What about you?" Julie asks.

"They're transferring us to the CDC. I'll join you as soon as I can. But for now, leave early. I'll be in touch. And don't stop for anyone by the side of the road."

We're quiet as the call clicks off. Julie's still for a moment, then she gets up, follows the glow of her phone screen to the counter, and turns on the camp lantern. It illuminates the entire kitchen. Grabbing a flashlight, she walks through the kitchen toward the garage.

Lauren's gaze follows her mom to the mudroom. The minute the back door closes, Lauren springs to her feet. "I've got to say good-bye to Riley. Can I come over, say I'm helping you pack?"

"No!" The last time she "crashed out" at my place and walked the half mile to his house, she came back drunk.

"I have to say good-bye to him," she says, practically in tears. "I haven't seen him for eight days!"

"And you won't tonight," I say. "It isn't safe."

"Everyone's fine at his house!"

"No."

She stares at me a moment longer, then slides her phone out and marches to her room. A few seconds later I hear her in tearful conversation.

I leave her alone to say good-bye. Not that she won't be talking to him every hour we're on the road.

Inside the separate garage, the RV door is open, the overhead light on. Julie sits in the driver's seat, staring out the wrap-around windshield.

I pause outside, flashlight trained on the steps between us. "Julie?"

"It's funny," she says softly. "I've never heard Ken raise his voice."

"He seemed pretty worried."

She looks down and nods. With a sigh she gets to her feet.

"The food's fine in the house for a few more hours. Let's get some sleep, load up in the morning. If we get up at three, we can be out of here by five."

UPSTAIRS IN THE carriage house, I pack clothes, shoes, my prescription, and toiletries in a duffle bag from Julie's basement, lay out my boots and coat. Gather up the cereal, crackers, and peanut butter from the counter, decide the things in the fridge will keep until morning. I don't like the idea of leaving, either, but hey, I'll get to meet Julie's crazy mom.

I've just chosen three novels from the bookcase to take along when a rapid knock sounds at the door. I sigh, irritated. Have no idea what Lauren sees in Riley and the wispy mustache he refuses to shave.

I consider not answering, but the last thing I need is something happening to her on my conscience.

I drop the books on the chair and yank open the door, shine my flashlight right in her face.

But the figure standing there in the surgical mask isn't Lauren or her mother.

It's Jaclyn.

CHAPTER FOURTEEN

Jackie," I call, hurrying to catch up to her on the path outside the children's barrow, where she had shown up, taken one look at me, turned on her heel, and left. "I need to talk to you."

"I don't want to talk."

I grabbed her by the arm. "We have to!"

She whirled around so fast I thought she might slap me. "There's nothing to talk about!" she said, eyes wild.

"Please," I whispered, trying desperately not to cause a scene.

She hesitated, and then snatched me by the wrist and dragged me off behind the vacant guesthouse.

"What do you want from me?" she hissed, pacing in the shadows. We didn't dare go inside or raise our voices. We both remembered the eyes.

"I didn't do this."

I didn't have to say what *this* was. The entire Enclave knew Magnus had taken me to Garden City. What they didn't know was that just yesterday he stopped by my desk while Magnolia was on the phone to lean over me and whisper, "You don't know how happy you've made me."

"Oh, stop," she snapped. "You've always wanted attention."

"What?" I said, incredulous. How could she say that when the whole time Jaclyn had been avoiding me, *I'd* been avoiding everyone else—not to mention fending off curious looks and silent questions from the other women in the Factory?

She reached back to rub her neck as though it hurt.

"Jackie, I didn't want to go."

That wasn't entirely true. I'd been flattered by the attention. To be noticed by Magnus was to matter. To know that God saw you.

And then there'd been that moment when he had looked at me as though fascinated. What did it mean that the divine could not only notice but seem delighted in me?

But that was gone, replaced by something else now, including a rising tide of doubt that threatened to drown me.

"Listen to me. The things Magnus says when no one else is around . . ." My voice dropped to a whisper. "When he doesn't know anyone is listening . . . and the people he does business with. Something's not right." I could hear the crack in my voice. But it was a fissure that went much deeper, into a foundation no longer whole.

"He's Magnus," she said dully. "You can't expect—"

"Did you go to a café together in Garden City?"

She looked irritated. "What?"

"He said you did. Together."

"I don't know! Maybe once, just so he could give his lawyer a check."

Why would he meet someone just to pay them? I saw checks go out from the office every day.

"He said you used to go for lunch."

"Maybe it was lunchtime. I don't remember! What's that got to do with anything?"

"The things he says—"

"Magnus doesn't have to explain himself to you," she snapped. "There are a lot of things you don't know about other people. Just because it doesn't make sense doesn't mean it's wrong. If anything, it means it's none of your business."

"It doesn't line up!"

She shook her head, a bitter smile twisting her mouth. "Don't you understand?"

"No. I don't."

"Magnus has revelations."

"So?" I stared at her blankly. Magnus had nine volumes' worth of revelations on the shelf of every building in the Enclave.

"It just had to be you, didn't it?" she said softly, tucking a strand of hair behind my ear.

I waited for some explanation. Instead, she left me standing in the shadow of the cottage where I had once felt safe.

CHAPTER FIFTEEN

I lower the flashlight. For a minute, we just stare at each other. She's thinner than I remember, green eyes large, surrounded by shadows. Even with the mask on, I'd know her anywhere.

She's alone, a metal carrier in one hand.

"How'd you get here?" I ask. And then: "Where's Truly?"

She glances over her shoulder. I follow her gaze. But the street, like the driveway, is empty.

"Please let me in. I don't have much time."

I reach for her but she steps back before I can touch her, a hand raised between us.

"Don't," she says. "Move away. I'll come in."

Only then do I realize she's wearing latex gloves.

Does she think I'll make her sick?

I back up and she steps inside, swiftly shutting the door behind her.

"I saw you come out here as I came through the yard," she says.

"Jackie, where's Truly?"

"She's safe. For now."

"Where?"

"At the Enclave."

"You *left without her*? *Why*?" Why would she do that? How will we get her out now?

"Because I had to bring this," she says, setting the carrier down on the table. Only then do I recognize it as one of the handled bins from the New Earth warehouse.

I glance at it, uncomprehending.

"You have to give this to Ken," she says, laying her hands on it. "He's a doctor, right? I remember that he was. That he studied some kind of—"

"Jackie, you're not making sense! Why didn't you bring Truly with you?"

"Because I'm sick!" she cries.

I stare at her. Only then do I note the slump of her thin shoulders, the faint sheen across her forehead.

No.

"I—I'll get you something," I hear myself say. "There's a bin of medicine in the house . . ."

"Wynter," she says gently, "it's not going to help. I know the symptoms. What's happening. I saw it at the center before we shut down last week."

And Truly?

"Is anyone else—"

"No. I don't think so. I spent the last four days in Penitence just to be certain I didn't infect anyone," she murmurs, her gaze roaming the small apartment in the glow of my flashlight. I reach for the nearest chair but she wards me off, pulls it out herself, and sinks into it.

"Do you have a mask?" she says.

I nod, numbly.

"You should put it on."

I move to the bed where I've laid out my coat, fumble in the pocket for the mask and gloves I wore last time I left the house, over a week ago. Loop the mask over my ears. Struggle with the gloves. My hands are shaking.

Jackie's saying something about Magnus and Des Moines. But I don't care about Des Moines, and the last person I want to hear about is Magnus. My sister is sick.

Julie and Lauren will have to go without us. I'll take care of Jackie here.

And Truly . . .

Jackie's right. She's safe, for now.

"Wynter!"

I glance up.

"Listen to me!" she says sharply. Her hands fly to her head as though it hurts. "There are things I have to tell you. Things it's hard enough already for me to keep straight. Things I worry I'm imagining . . . or that I wish I was."

I move to the table, set the flashlight down on it, the beam pointed toward the ceiling. "Okay," I say softly, sliding into the seat across from hers. "I'm listening."

And I will, for the rest of her life.

She takes a slow breath and begins again. "Two months ago Magnus took me with him to Des Moines . . . remember?"

"I remember." How could I not?

"Magnus was meeting with someone. I thought it was just another seed acquisition—some ancient kumquat or something . . ." She gestures vaguely. "He'd been short-fused, so tense the months before that. I attributed it to his lack of investors. He didn't talk to me about the company often, but when he did, he was angry and vindictive, saying that he looked forward to the day that everyone who had shunned him would be wasting in Hell.

"A few weeks before we left, he abruptly changed. He seemed lighter. Excited. I'd seen him that way before, when he'd come and go a lot from town. I used to think he might be seeing someone there, though the one time I dared ask him about it, he called me crazy and asked how I could question him, the Mouthpiece of God, and whether I really believed. I wondered how I could, too. And if I was—crazy."

"You weren't," I say, my gaze falling on the metal carrier in front of her. "He did the same thing to Kestral."

She looks at me strangely but goes on. "Which is why, when you came to me, told me what was happening . . . I couldn't accept it. It would have meant all of it was a lie—everything we believed. It was easier to think I was crazy and that you were, too . . . I'm so sorry, Wynter."

"Jackie, don't," I say softly. "Don't apologize. I know."

"And when I think of Mom . . ." She lifts her hand to her mask.

I close my eyes. The thought of Mom dying the way she did, believing she was doing the right thing, has haunted me since my first crisis of faith—along with the question of whether she'd still be alive if we'd been anywhere else.

"Des Moines," Jackie says, straightening.

I nod.

"When Magnus showed up at the counseling center to surprise me with the trip to Des Moines, I just knew it was about you. Some way to sweeten me up and bring me around. But then he didn't even bring you up until the trip home. All he could talk about was some new acquisition. Not another seed, like I'd assumed, but some strain of three-million-year-old bacteria and how he'd soon be able to do a deal to get it."

"*Bacteria?*" New Earth didn't deal in bacteria. Or believe the earth was even that old.

"Some lunatic Russian scientist found it frozen in Siberia and injected himself with it. Claims he hasn't had the flu since. I'd heard Magnus mention reading an article about it months before—about how it's melting into the water from the permafrost and the people nearby supposedly live longer. Now it was all he could talk about."

She coughs, and an instant later, she's doubled over, racked by a fit. I get up but she wards me off with an outstretched hand, so I go to the kitchenette and grab a bottle of water from the darkened fridge, unscrew the top, and hold it toward her. She takes it and lifts the mask just enough to sip off the top.

Her voice rasps as she continues, "He left me alone for a while that first night, and I thought he was meeting with his broker or whoever it was. When he came back, he smelled like perfume."

I exhale a harsh breath. "What'd you say?"

"What could I? I asked how his meeting went, and he told me that the next night he'd be busy up until time to go and that he needed me to pick a friend of his up at the bus station. But that night, I finally opened my eyes and began to *see*. And I began to see everything in a whole new light. Including all the things that didn't add up about him."

The expression on her face is weathered. But there's steel in her voice.

"The next night—the night we came back so late—Magnus loaded our bags and I left at nine o'clock and drove to the bus station. After about twenty minutes, a man came out to the car, told me to pop the trunk, and put his bag in. And then he got in and made me drive to a nearby hotel. It was terrible, being in the car with that man. He reeked of smoke and kept licking his lips. He was jittery and nervous. I didn't know what would happen when we got there, if he'd try to get me to go inside or what Magnus had said about me."

Something she's just said . . .

"Jittery how? Like a drug addict?"

She cocks her head. "A little like that, yes. He reminded me of some of the people who come to the center."

"Jackie," I say quietly. "Was his name Blaine?"

Blaine, whom I had overheard on the phone with Magnus, his former business partner. He'd wanted to sell him something.

She shakes her head. "I never knew his name."

"Where did he come from? Where had the bus come in from?"

She frowns. "Kansas City, I think."

It had to be him.

"What happened?"

"The minute we got there, he jumped out of the car, got his bag from the trunk, and left. That was it. I drove back to the restaurant where Magnus had his last meeting and we came home. Except one of the bags we returned with was different. Also, the bag I left with had been filled with money. I know, because I was nervous about picking up a strange man and pulled over on the way to get the pepper spray I take with me to the center out of my backpack. Which I thought was packed in that bag."

"Why didn't he send Enzo?" I say angrily. For Magnus to have used Jaclyn for his shady deals . . . *Why?* But I knew why. She was one of the few Select who knew how to drive. And whereas Enzo was publicly associated with Magnus, Jackie was unknown to anyone but those who visited the counseling center.

"He doesn't trust him. Not like me," she says bitterly. "I've turned against my own family for him. I'm sorry, Wynter! I did the only thing I could for you!"

Something within me shatters at the sound of her voice. My arms ache to hold her. My fingers to close around hers.

But right now new alarm is sending frost down my spine.

"Jackie, how did you get here?" I say slowly, glancing at the carrier on the table.

"I drove," she says, seeming baffled by the question. "I wasn't sure if I was followed, so I parked a block away."

"No," I say more gently. "I mean how did you get out?"

She shakes her head as though to clear it. "Sorry. This afternoon I was working in the office when Magnus got a call. He got up and left right away. I didn't think much of it until he came back a little while later and told me he needed me to drive some supplies to the center and stay there until someone came to get them. That if I ran or the supplies disappeared—if I failed him in any way . . . he'd kill me."

"He *said* that?"

"I passed two black cars I've never seen before on my way to the highway. I don't know if they were police, but they were headed toward the Enclave. Where my daughter is. A daughter I will never see again in this life." A tear slips down her cheek.

"Something in me snapped. I pulled over on the outskirts of Ames, opened the back of the van. It was filled full of boxes of sermons and two bins of clothing. That"—she glances at the carrier—"was inside one of them, buried beneath some coats. In the same bag as before."

"This is what you picked up in Des Moines."

"Yes. And what he planned to trade for the crazy Russian bacteria."

What could possibly be valuable enough to buy Magnus a fountain of youth?

I stand up, slide the carrier toward me, stare at it for a long instant.

And then abruptly pull it open.

Grabbing the flashlight, I shine it down into the refrigerated case on a set of plastic containers with screw-on lids. A case of glass microscope slides. A plastic bag of what looks like a chunk of dirt. All labeled *Porcine* and *muscle, bone,* or *brain.* All marked *Fairbanks, Alaska,* and dated last June with an abbreviation I don't recognize.

"What is all this?" I murmur.

"Tissue samples. Taken from pigs."

"Okay, but why?" I don't know what I expected, but it wasn't this.

She shakes her head. "I don't know but I'm sure of two things: they're valuable, and they're stolen."

A large envelope, folded in half, has been shoved in along the side. I fish it out, pinch the clasp together at the top, and pull it open. After peering inside, I upend it. A dual-end flash drive drops into my gloved palm.

"What's that?" Jackie says.

"Thumb drive," I murmur. Lauren has one like it that she downloads pirated *Game of Thrones* episodes onto for a friend who isn't allowed to watch it. I search for my phone, find it on the counter, and connect the drive.

It's full of files: A blank application form for a summer fellowship. A document with a few dates from June and the names "Walter," "Petunia," "Jilly (sow—10)," "Romeo." A contact for someone in Alaska. Several saved web pages. One of them is an obituary—for the same name as the contact. There's two more, for two other men. The home page of some gourmet pork supplier. A roster of vendors offering samples at an annual Baconfest somewhere in Washington.

The last item is a news story about the Bellevue 13.

The hair rises on my nape.

I scroll back and through them once more in chronological order, beginning in June with the pigs. Ending with the Bellevue 13.

"You're right," I say. "We need Ken."

I toggle to my contacts. Scroll to Ken's phone number. He's sleeping, I'm sure; it's after midnight in Idaho. I dial anyway.

It rings and rings, and it occurs to me that maybe the call won't go through. I don't know if the towers work without power.

He picks up on the fifth ring, voice groggy. "Wynter?" I hear him shift in his bed. "Is everything okay?"

"Yeah. Julie and Lauren are sleeping—"

"What?" he says, far more alert. "Why aren't you on the road? I told you to leave!"

"We will. Soon."

"No. You have to go now!"

"Ken, Jaclyn's here."

"Who?"

"Jackie. My sister."

For a minute I think the call's cut out. And then: "Ah, yes. You really need to go."

"We will. But Jackie brought something to give you that I think may be important."

"That's sweet of her—"

"No, not *for* you. Magnus acquired some tissue samples that I think you need to take with you to the CDC."

"Samples? What do you mean?"

"Ken . . . is it possible the first Bellevue patient could have gotten the disease from eating *bacon*?"

He gives a slight laugh. "Wynter . . . no. Are you all right?"

"So the catching crazy couldn't have come from eating pork."

"No. That'd be a prion disease. Like mad cow. This rapid-onset dementia is far too fast. Though—" He paused, then said again, "No."

"Though what?"

"Well, prions can't be destroyed by normal sterilization techniques. I guess, in theory, if one of the Bellevue 13 had a prion . . . All thirteen had medical procedures. It's already been established that they shared the same OR." I can practically hear him frowning. "There's samples, you said? Are they labeled?"

"Yes." I move to the carrier with the flashlight.

"Read them to me."

I do, lifting the containers and slides out one at a time, the baggie with the chunk of dirty flesh last of all.

"Porcine (boar #2) tissue and soil, Fairbanks, AK, PrP." I turn the baggie in the beam of light. "This one looks like it was dug up or something."

He's silent for a moment.

"It says 'PrP.' You're sure."

"I'm looking at it right now."

"Where'd you say these came from?"

"Magnus got them from some under-the-table deal but there's an application form on a flash drive that says 'UC Davis,' if that means anything to you." I glance at Jackie, but she's staring off toward the window.

"Magnus . . . ?"

I close my eyes, squeeze them shut. Say, very calmly, "The leader of New Earth. The . . . cult I came from. He's been acquiring ancient seeds for years. But I don't know why he'd have this."

When I open my eyes I'm startled to find Jaclyn's staring right at me, her expression stark.

What? I mouth. She doesn't respond. Doesn't seem to really see me at all.

I can practically hear Ken rubbing his forehead. "Yeah. No. They ruled out prion disease weeks ago."

"With tests?"

"The only reliable way to test for it is to study the brain after death."

I grab one of the slides labeled *Porcine (sow) brain, Fairbanks, AK, PrP.*

"Ken, I think you need to see this."

"Even then, it'd have to be a prion we've never seen before to misfold that rapidly—"

"There's notes," I say swiftly. "There's one about a Romeo—I assume that's a pig—digging up a caribou carcass from the permafrost. What if it *is* something no one's seen because it's been *frozen*?"

He gives a tired sigh. "I mean, sure. Anything's possible in theory. But it still wouldn't explain how it's spreading—especially among populations that don't eat pork. I know for a fact there are Orthodox Jews, Muslims, and vegetarians with the disease. Which means you and Jackie are equally susceptible. Which is why you need to do what I said and leave town tonight!"

"Ken, Magnus paid a lot of money for these. He planned to trade them to some Russians for some three-million-year-old bacteria—"

I stop. Because now I am starting to sound crazy. I might as well be talking about magic beans.

The silence fills with soft sibilance. It comes from across the room where Jackie's gazing out the window. Her lips move in the darkness. She's talking to herself.

"When are you leaving for Atlanta?" I say. "I'll meet you."

"No," Ken says. "That won't work."

"I'll make it work! I'll leave now. You can—"

"Wynter—absolutely not. Where's Julie? Get her on the phone."

I turn away from the table. "Ken, I'll slash the RV's tires, I swear to God I will. None of us is going anywhere until you promise to meet me!"

"I can't meet you!"

"Why?" I demand.

"Because the team's already back in Atlanta!"

I blink in the darkness. "But . . . you said you're still in Idaho."

"They left yesterday morning. They're already there. I . . . I had to stay behind." He's quiet a minute. "Do me a favor—don't tell Julie. Not yet."

I grab a fistful of my hair, squeeze shut my eyes.

I've already lost my mother. I can't lose my sister, too. I need her. And the world needs Ken. If there's even a remote chance the contents of this case can help them . . .

Magnus's voice returns to me with a vengeance.

The world cannot be saved!

I hear myself say, "Then I'll go to Atlanta."

"Wynter. The place is on lockdown. Surrounded by National Guard. After the attack on the—the . . ." He falters, searching for a word, "the lights . . . no one's getting in or out without high-level clearance."

"But if you call them—"

"Unless you're with the military or World Health Organization it won't matter! Especially with stolen samples. You'll be taken into custody as a suspected bioterrorist before you get through to anyone who'll hear you. And that's if you even make it through the city alive. They're already looting here—and this is *Boise*."

"What am I supposed to do?" I cry.

Ken sighs. "I can try to call UNMC in Omaha, though I won't be able to get through to anyone until morning. For now, you and Jozlyn go with Julie like I said. Okay? I'll be in touch when I can."

I don't bother to correct him about Jaclyn's name. Wonder if he'll remember that I mentioned her at all in a day or two.

He clicks off.

I lower my head, trying to think.

For all I know, Blaine put together a few pieces of bad meat and sold it for whatever Magnus would give him.

But while Magnus may be many things, stupid isn't one of them. He built and sold a hybrid seed company. The man knows something about science—or knows plenty of people who do.

"Ashley!" Jackie says. And I'm not convinced she isn't babbling to herself again. Or worse yet, that she's forgotten my name.

"What?"

"It's an animal disease. You need a veterinarian."

I feel my expression twist. I can't see her like this. Can't watch the way she stares at her gloved hands, hear the soft wonder in her voice. But neither can I turn away.

"You need to see Ashley," she says, glancing up. Her eyes are clear. "At the Veterinary College in Fort Collins, Colorado. He knows who Magnus is. And he'll believe you because of me."

"Jackie, who's Ashley?" I say, confused.

She gives a quiet smile.

"Truly's father."

CHAPTER SIXTEEN

"Come, Wynter," Magnus said, not even waiting for me to answer as he strode out the office door.

Enzo drove us to Story City, a town large enough to boast a McDonald's and an outlet mall—even a park with an old-fashioned carousel in the middle. I had only heard about it from Ara, who had been there several times for sewing supplies.

The entire way I felt the weight of Magnus's gaze heavy upon me, as though our first outing had been the prelude to some new level of intimacy between us.

"I've thought a lot about our last conversation," he said, turning toward me in the back seat.

So have I.

"You've brought something out in me that has been buried beneath this burden of leadership. That I thought had gone dry. You don't know how grateful I am to you, Wynter. You're a gift to me, and I have so much I want to tell you."

But I didn't want to hear it. He was *supposed* to bear that burden with only God to confess to.

He leaned forward to say something to Enzo, directing him to the far side of town.

"You should unbraid your hair," he said to me. "This town doesn't understand us and what we're about. There's people here who distrust the Enclave and some, even, who wish we'd go away."

Two thoughts assaulted me at once. First, it had never occurred to me that there were people who didn't want us. The second was: *Then why are you bringing me here?*

I reached back reluctantly, started to unpin my braids as Magnus openly watched me, hand over his chest, stroking the skin in the open V of his shirt.

"I'm supposed to be in the kitchen by three," I said. "Rosella asked if I'd be able to help with dinner."

It wasn't entirely a lie. I had volunteered just an hour ago to show up then. It wasn't my normal time.

"You're with me."

"But I promised—"

"Who cares? *Rosella*," his lips flattened as he said her name, "will never understand people like us."

"Rosella is a true believer," I said, aghast, having never thought I'd find myself in a position of wanting to defend her. She was a praise-hungry tyrant. But she was earnest.

"Are you chiding me?" he said sharply.

"No. No, of course not," I said quietly, looking down between us.

He tilted his head, seemed to appraise me. "You have such beautiful hair, did you know that? Now, if we wanted to make today extra special . . ." He paused, reached into his pocket, and pulled an object from it.

When he opened his fingers, my heart stopped at the thing nestled in his palm.

A lipstick.

"Go on," he said.

I took it slowly. The metal case was warm.

Did he know about that day?

But how could he?

I swallowed, throat dry, not daring to open it.

"I forget that you were too young to wear makeup when you came to us, weren't you?" he said softly, taking it from my hand. He pulled off the lid and twisted the tube until a bright red column emerged from its shadows.

Red.

The tip was uneven, concave in the middle where it had been pressed to another woman's lips before. I wondered whose it was. The waitress's at the café?

I didn't move as he lifted my chin and opened his mouth, indicating for me to do the same. He slid the color across my lower lip.

It's forbidden.

You didn't care that it was forbidden when you pocketed one at the farmers' market . . .

Hadn't I wanted to do this? Hadn't I planned to, in secret, while everyone was asleep?

He smiled as he finished. Twisting the lipstick closed, he returned it to his pocket, from which he produced a cell phone. Swiping his thumb across the surface, he held it up. A light flashed in my eyes, startling me.

"So beautiful," he said. "Now I can see you like this any time I want."

But photos, like cosmetics, were forbidden. What would happen to me if that picture ever came to light—of me, obviously outside the enclave inside a car, my hair down, wearing that forbidden lipstick?

My palms began to sweat as we pulled up in front of a row of buildings. And then he got out, reaching a hand toward me.

I forced myself to take it, to slide across the seat toward him and step out. His arm immediately went around my waist and I stiffened as he led me into a bar.

You will not touch a woman who is not your wife.

You will shun the appearance of evil.

This couldn't be right. He had to have another business meeting, I reasoned—perhaps on an upstairs floor. But inside, there was no staircase, no meeting area. He led me to a high-top table as Enzo took a seat at the bar itself.

Loud music played over the speakers. There were perhaps only four people total drinking and staring at a baseball game on the TV over the bar itself.

"This is a special place," Magnus said, leaning over the table toward me, his gaze falling to rest on my mouth.

I didn't see how that could be. It was dark and grimy, the guys at the bar slouched against it defeated by whatever had brought them here.

"How so?" I asked, trying to sound pleasant.

"When I was writing the third volume of my Testament, I used to come here to work," he said.

"Here?"

For a minute I wondered if there was an audience somewhere. If my response was being judged.

I'd spent countless days locked up in a white cell for listening to worldly music on Shae's phone. And now the man I'd come to know as a minor deity was telling me he'd written one of our holy Testaments in a *bar*?

Magnus Theisen was the Interpreter of God! God Himself had chosen Magnus to receive His new Testaments and record the precepts of salvation! Precepts Magnus had all but said needn't apply to us.

Which meant either everything I had been taught was a lie or that God had made a terrible mistake.

I could feel him waiting for some kind of answer. When I gave none, he turned his attention to a rut on the table, which he traced with his thumbnail as the waitress came over. But instead of asking for an order, she reached around Magnus and gave him a hug.

"I missed you!" she said, chewing out each word as though it were a piece of gum. He didn't look up. "Hey. Everything okay?"

"Sure," he said, and glanced at me. But his gaze was flat, his expression—so rapt before—was dead. "Order whatever you'd like," he said, sitting back, not looking at me.

"Juice. Whatever you have."

"Orange, cranberry, or tomato?"

"Tomato," I heard myself say.

"Magnus?" she asked, her brows drawn up in a concerned look.

"Just give me some water."

She gave me a look and turned to go to the bar, where Enzo was already drinking a beer from the bottle, apparently unafraid of the ramifications. Magnus, meanwhile, looked restless, ready to go. And though I didn't know what was happening in the air rapidly cooling between us, I knew I was somehow supposed to fix it. Because as much as I did not want this attention from him, spurning it, I somehow knew, would only turn out badly.

For me.

He sighed, refusing to look at me. "You know, maybe I shouldn't have brought you here."

In that instant I knew that as bad as life was before, it was about to get much worse. Because for me to commit my own sins was one thing. But for me to know and judge the sins of Magnus . . . would be unforgivable.

Not that anyone would believe me. And that was the worst part. There was no one I could go to with any of this. Including my sister, who had refused to hear it.

"No," I say quickly. "It actually makes me feel better."

"Better how?" he asked, impatient.

"I just like the thought of it. I like the thought of a lot of things I've never talked about," I said.

"Like what?"

Here, then, was the test.

"First, why don't you order what you really wanted to a minute ago?" I suggested.

He gave me a small smile and got up to go to the bar.

My mind was spinning, wondering what would happen if I got up, took off for the ladies' room, and ran out the back door. But I had nothing waiting for me on the other side and everything to lose.

Including my eternal salvation.

I glanced over at him leaning against the bar beside Enzo as the bartender made him a drink. He openly flirted with the waitress, the playful smile he had given me in the car toying about his lips.

I hated that smile, the smolder in his eyes. I wished I could unsee it, scrub it from my brain.

When he returned to the table, his posture was easy as he slid a drink in front of me and crossed his arms on the edge of the table.

"Tell me a secret," he said, gazing at me through his lashes and tracing the rim of his glass with a fingertip as he had the back of my hand the first day in the car.

I let out a slow breath. "My dad used to beat my mother. It's why we came to the Enclave."

"That's unfortunate," he said, his gaze falling past me. It wasn't what he wanted to hear. But if I could bore him, maybe he would forget about me.

"Yeah," I sighed. "Jaclyn probably doesn't talk about it much. It was pretty bad. He drank a lot. One time he gave our mom a black eye that lasted for weeks."

"Mm." He lifted his cocktail and took a long drink.

"We had to spend a couple weeks with her friend Julie. I kind of hoped we'd get to stay. I really hated living at home. Julie had cable, and she had a PlayStation. You ever play that? There was this game Jaclyn and I used to love, maybe she's told you about it—"

"So, Wynter," he said, sitting back. "Listen. I just wanted you to know that you should prepare to be married. It's time, and you've been upstanding—it's obvious you've done everything you should and . . . so." He drained the rest of his drink, clearly ready to leave.

No.

I grabbed his wrist.

It was too close to his hand, but my fingers dug into his cuff.

"You don't want to hear about my father, do you?" I said.

"No," he said, his expression blank.

"I don't want to talk about marriage," I said.

"Then tell me something interesting," he said brusquely.

In that instant, something switched off inside me. And something else switched on. Self-preservation. A search for any weapon I had.

"All my secrets are in my Penitence file. Haven't you read it?"

"No," he said. "Should I?"

"Probably not."

"Do tell."

"I used to talk about boys. A lot. And then I realized I wasn't supposed to think about that."

"It's natural," he said, his gaze more intense. "Of course you should think about it."

"The Admitter said I shouldn't."

"I don't want you to talk to the Admitter anymore. I want you to tell me instead. What did you think about? What did you want to do with those boys?"

"The usual."

"I want to hear you say it."

He studied me for a long moment, his breath catching. And I knew in that instant I'd made a mistake. He not only wanted to go down this road I had no way to navigate, but he *enjoyed* the fact that I was uncomfortable. Which meant nothing I said or agreed to would ever be enough. He would only demand more, no matter the cost to me.

"There's something else," I said. "It's—it's embarrassing. Wrong."

"Then tell me."

I looked away. "I can't. It's about you."

"Now you have to."

I glanced down. Did I imagine it, or did his breath halt for a fraction of an instant?

I pursed my lips and said, "You're the reason we joined the Enclave. I was obsessed with you the first time I met you. And now, just when I felt like I knew everything about you, I've suddenly learned *so* much more. About you. How complicated you are."

It wasn't the response he wanted. And I would not give him the kind of secrets I sensed he wanted from me. Had no arsenal to draw from, even if I'd wanted to.

But I'd seen the way he'd noticed me reading the article about him. The way no one spoke of the newspaper journalist calling, the magazines on the wall—openly displayed, never talked about. Needing to be admired.

"I mean, you're famous, aren't you?"

He gave a quiet chuckle.

"But you can't say it, can you? That the world knows your name. Because the others don't understand who you are in that world. What you give up to be with us. That you have to be two people."

He lifted his gaze to mine for a long moment.

"No," he said hoarsely. "They don't. They don't know what I go through for them. All that I've done. All that I do." His eyes fell to my mouth. "The way I pour myself out for them. Yes. I'm two people. I have to be. It's my great gift: faith. And it's my burden, calling home the Select, catering to their needs, unable to move forward in my own freedom. But I'm a man. With no one to share and unburden myself with. Which is why you're so important to me. Because you understand."

"Jaclyn would understand," I say quietly.

"I don't want to talk about Jaclyn. Come. It's time to go." He handed me a napkin. "Wipe that off your mouth."

In the car on the way back to the Enclave, I tried to rebraid my hair, elbows close to my sides.

"Let me," he said.

"Please," I whispered. "You're my sister's husband."

"For God's sake, it's just hair, Wynter."

I turned, reluctantly, in the back seat. Closed my eyes as his fingers brushed against my neck. He finished as we reached the heavy gate.

Pulling into the Enclave parking lot, Magnus straightened as the Prius came to a halt. This time he didn't gesture me out on his side but got swiftly out of the car and shut the door behind him. Unsure what had happened, I let myself out of the other side . . . just in time to see Jaclyn stop in the middle of the small parking lot in front of the counseling center van.

"My love," he said, walking to her side. He kissed her on the cheek, but her gaze fell on me.

"I've just finished hearing the story of your mother from my dear sister-in-law," he said, gesturing to me, before going on about how sad it had been to hear the circumstances that had brought us here.

I saw the way her gaze slid from me to him. Her thin smile in response as they moved toward their residence.

The minute I stepped foot inside the Factory, the air threatened to stifle me. It was too warm, the women too curiously deferential. Hurrying through the common area to the bathroom, I fell to my knees in a stall and puked up the contents of my stomach.

THE NEXT MORNING was rainy, uncommonly cool for summer. When Magnus got up to speak at service after the hymns, I could barely look at him, knowing he was seeking my gaze as he preached on the gift of children, who would be the true measure of God's blessing and bounty in the new Earth to come. By which God would repopulate the renewed world.

After so many sermons on the depravity of the world, a few women wept at the beauty of this vision. I did, too, for a different reason, grieving the thing I felt dying inside me.

I had never felt so alone in the company of the Select. Couldn't wait to leave even as Magnus revealed that he'd received a new revelation: as Adam was commanded to multiply and fill the Earth, so was New Adam commanded to do the same.

Which was why, as in the days of Jacob the Patriarch, David the friend of God, and Solomon the Wise, he, Magnus, had been commanded by God to take a second wife.

CHAPTER SEVENTEEN

Truly's . . . *father?*"

I hear the fear in my voice. Because I'm losing her, too fast.

"Don't look at me like that," she says. "I'm not crazy. Not yet."

"But—" The idea of Truly being fathered by anyone but Magnus was ludicrous. First, because Magnus would never allow himself to be so humiliated. Second, because Jackie would never do something like that.

Would she?

Jaclyn's talking to herself again, whispering in the darkness.

"Stop that," I say.

She does, and the silence is almost worse.

"Jackie . . . *how?*"

"How was I with Ashley?" she asks. She smiles. "I was handing out tracts outside the center. He walked by and I thought he was the most handsome man I'd ever met." She laughs softly. "We talked, and he came by again a few days later. After weeks like that, he asked me to meet him for coffee."

"And you *did*?"

"Yes. I told the other women I was going to hand out tracts closer to campus. And then I met him at a little shop and we talked—about everything. He was doing his veterinary infectious disease fellowship at the university. Something about diseases in livestock. He was—is—extremely smart."

I blink, trying to reconcile my sister having a relationship with a man of the world.

But I'm also thinking: *We could have left.* She could have gone and taken me with her.

I also know I wouldn't have—gone. Because I believed. The entire debacle with my engagement to Shae's dad hadn't happened yet. Magnus was still perfect, and I lived for the day we would see our mother again in the new Earth to come after the cataclysm.

"It was easy," Jackie says. "Forgetting who I was and that everything I wanted and felt and hoped for was wrong. Believing for a minute that it was all exactly right and as it should be. And it was exciting. Stealing moments alone. How do you think I recognized that look in Magnus's face? I *remember* that feeling."

"So . . . *what happened*?"

"He finished his fellowship at Iowa State. He got a job in Fort Collins at Colorado State University in an infectious disease center at the veterinary school. He asked me to go with him, live with him, marry him. I asked him to join the Enclave. But he wouldn't. He called New Earth a cult. I didn't know what to do—until he told me he had reported New Earth to several watchdog agencies. I felt betrayed. New Earth was all I knew. More than that, I was afraid. Three weeks later, my engagement was announced. I took it as a sign. He left. I married Magnus. I didn't know I was pregnant." She glances down. "I cried every night for weeks until I realized I was about to have a baby. Ashley's baby."

I exhale a stunned breath. It comes out like an unstable little laugh.

"Ashley will know what to do," she says quietly. She glances at my phone. "Please call him."

"Do you know his number?"

She shakes her head. "I haven't talked to him since before Truly was born. So that was . . . would be . . ." Her brow wrinkles.

I watch her struggle, my heart breaking at the sight of it. "Almost six years," I say gently. "Jackie—"

She smiles slightly. "I can't wait to talk to him."

My cell service is slow, stalls out twice, and finally loads on the third try with a page of information about his DVM from Kansas State, PhD in pathology, and research in emerging zoonotic and infectious diseases. Then, finally, a white page listing for an Ashley Neal on Juniper Lane. I've just dialed it when I stare at Jackie and say, "He doesn't know, does he?"

She shakes her head.

It takes a while for the first ring to sound. When it does, I put the phone on speaker and set it on the table between us.

It rings and rings.

Someone picks up, and Jackie comes closer, clutching the back of her chair.

"Hello?"

"Ash?"

Silence. And then: "Jackie?"

"It's me." Her voice wavers, she drags her coat sleeve across her eyes.

He sounds instantly awake. "Are you all right? Where are you?"

"I'm in Chicago, with Wynter . . ."

I've never heard her voice like that. Never heard Magnus speak to Jackie with the same tone, such concern.

I feel like an intruder. I gesture that I'll be back, pull on my boots, and grab my coat. Step outside onto the landing.

It's cold, crisp, and dark, the stars brittle overhead. I can hear Jackie's voice from inside, raised—in happiness? In dismay? I can't tell; she's crying.

But now so am I. And I wonder how this could happen. How Jackie and I could be reunited—here, on the outside, but without Truly, only to be separated again—seemingly by the catastrophe we'd been taught to expect all our lives.

And then I'm seething. Filled with an anger I have never felt before. What did Magnus plan to do with those samples? Trade them for a bacterial miracle meant to keep him healthy as the rest of the world dies around him, taking his detractors with it?

I tell myself I will find a way to end him. For what he did to Jackie, and Kestral before her. I will do whatever it takes.

And I will get Truly back.

Jackie's calling me and I step back inside. Find her sitting at the table, red-eyed, and the other end of the phone is so silent that I think the call is over until I glance down and see it's still connected.

"Hello?" I say into the silence.

"Wynter," Ashley says. He sounds shaken. I can hear him moving, pacing on what sounds like a wood floor.

"What do we have?"

"I don't know. I can't know until I see it. This whole thing is crazy—"

And I know he isn't just talking about the samples.

"Is it possible?" I ask.

"Sure, anything's possible, theoretically," he says. "I'm familiar with Magnus's projects. I read up on them when I met Jackie for reasons that you obviously know now. He's got money and knows a lot of people. Which means either it's nothing or it's—"

"He threatened to kill Jackie if this didn't get to whoever was supposed to come get it," I say. "It's not nothing."

He blows out a long breath. "That's what worries me. If it's any kind of link to the index case, it could be extremely helpful, which is why it's too bad your friend Ken isn't still there or in better shape. I don't want to scare you, but it could also be very bad in the wrong hands."

"What do we do?"

"Can you get to Fort Collins?"

I glance wildly around us. "Yes." Never mind that the farthest I've ever driven is the Walgreens less than a mile away. But I figure if Jackie can make it from Ames, the two of us should be able to get to Colorado.

"Okay, it's . . . nearly one a.m. here," Ashley says. "I'll head to campus this afternoon, expect you some time early evening."

He gives me an address and building.

"Wynter, do you mind if I talk to Jackie again?" he says. "Alone?"

"Of course not."

Outside, I key in the code to the side door of the garage. There's an entire storage unit filled full of the things we camped with at Indiana Dunes. I grab a couple sleeping bags, ski gloves, a stupid snowboard hat with a pom-pom on top, and the emergency kit. Pry open a plastic tote and find a cache of old gas station and AAA maps. Grab Colorado, Iowa, Nebraska, and Kansas as an afterthought before dumping out the tote and filling it with all the stuff. I carry the tote to the house garage and load it into the back of Julie's car, which I know for a fact has a full tank of gas.

Gas.

I search around the riding lawn mower for the red plastic gas can, find it half full, add it to the trunk.

Inside the house, I snatch up a spare set of batteries, the blanket from the couch, a couple masks and sets of gloves from Ken's office, a bag of things from the fridge and pantry, a case of water, one of the five canisters of Lysol wipes Julie picked up from her last trip to Costco, and the pepper spray she jogs with.

Pausing by the desk in the kitchen, I tear a piece of notepaper from the cube by the house phone.

> *Julie,*
> *I love you.*
> *W.*

I leave the note on the counter and quietly carry everything out, pile it all into the SUV.

Back up in the carriage house, I find Jackie staring off into the darkness.

"The car's loaded," I say. When she doesn't answer, I move toward her. "Jackie. Let's go."

"I'm not going with you."

"Don't be ridiculous."

She shakes her head. "I'd take these to Ashley myself, but I don't trust myself ten hours from now not to lose them or do something horrible. I've already seen her . . ."

"Seen who?" I say, not understanding.

"Mom."

A chill runs up my spine.

"You have to come with me," I say. "Especially if this is a cure—"

She shakes her head. "I asked him. There's no cure. Only the possibility of a vaccine. By the time there's any kind of treatment, I'll be long dead."

"You don't know that!"

"What I do know is that I can't risk getting you sick." She looks at me, something feverish in her eyes. "You have to get Truly."

"Please, Jackie—"

"Promise me!"

"I will. I promise!"

"Besides." She shakes her head. "I don't want him to see me, remember me, like this."

She gets to her feet, and I realize she's about to leave.

"What are you doing? There's food here—water in the fridge and more in the tub. If you won't come with me, you have to stay!"

"No. If they've followed me I need to be seen—going the opposite direction."

"*Where?*"

I move toward her, and she backs toward the door.

"I love you, Wynter," Jackie says.

The next instant, she's yanked open the door and is hurrying down the stairs. I run to the landing, lean out over the rail as she darts down the driveway.

"I love you," I whisper as her heels pound down the frozen street.

THE GOD OF my childhood was angry. A God to be obeyed and taken offerings of beer, who loved you if you parroted a joke you weren't old enough to understand—preferably with dirty language.

The God of my adolescence never cared about cuteness—only perfection. He was the fiery God of rolled-up sleeves concerned with the minutiae of sin with all-seeing eyes. The God you looked to, if only to make certain he still saw you, and whose punishments you accepted because negative attention is better than none. A God who could turn both the tables and the rules on you at a moment's notice. So that all you thought you had done to be right could be wrong. And all that was wrong was presumed right—no matter how wrong it still felt.

The day I was turned over to Satan for the destruction of my flesh, I knew Jackie had saved me in the only way she could. I knew, too, that I would save her in return. That there was a God waiting for me beyond those walls, ready to show me how.

But now, staring down at the empty street after Jaclyn disappeared, I wonder which God has taken her from me, here in the outside world. The God who requires childlike devotion or blood sacrifice for the sin of notice? Or the capricious God who cannot be followed for his equally changing ways?

Grief immobilizes. Stuns and turns you numb, like venom creeping toward your heart. It seized me up when Mom died and now threatens to paralyze me again. I don't know how to move, how to function in a world without Jackie.

It's the thought of Truly that makes me move, looking blindly around me in the gust of cold air from the open door. Grabbing the flashlight, I toss the contents of the fridge into the bag with the rest of the food. Pull the flash drive from my phone and drop both into my bag before slinging it over my shoulder and closing the carrier.

Back out in the house garage, I slide the carrier into the front seat of the Lexus, plug my phone into the charger, and get in, tossing the flashlight onto the floor.

Thirty seconds later, I'm accelerating toward the highway, glancing into my rearview mirror.

CHAPTER EIGHTEEN

Magnus showed up at the children's school while I was teaching, his sidelong smile for me alone. He appeared at the kitchen when I went to serve, his gaze loitering on me when backs were turned.

The only place he wouldn't deign to visit was the laundry.

But now, when I needed the work, no one would give it to me. Women who used to see through me rushed to relieve me, their attention cloying as syrup. The oblivion I had enjoyed for five years was gone; I was noticed everywhere, treated with a deference I did not want.

Yet, there was one person who made no effort to hide her displeasure at my sudden rise in favor.

Ara.

We had never been friendly except those first days when we were both seven, a thought that used to make me sad until she systematically turned all my friends against me—including Shae. Ara had mostly ignored me after that, and I had stayed out of her way. She had effectively replaced Kestral in her duties especially as they pertained to novices; Jaclyn had no real interest in dealing with the guests and, in all honesty, was probably not the most welcoming member of the Enclave. Whereas Ara had the same charm, when she chose to, that she had once shown me.

Now when I passed her, lasers shot from her eyes. She'd already given birth to one beautiful dark-haired little girl and was pregnant now with a second child. But somehow I'd always known she considered herself too good for any of the Elders.

Though Magnus's choice was a foregone conclusion to the Enclave, he hadn't announced our engagement. Which meant I still had time to bore him. I just didn't know how. I'd been careful to stay busy, make sure we were never alone—a thing he treated as a game that only fueled the fever in his eyes.

But now his patience was waning.

Five days after his revelation, he sent Magnolia out of the office on errands.

"Ask me to do something for you," he whispered, leaning over my desk. "Something secret that only you and I will know."

"What I'd really like you to do?"

He smiled slightly. "Yes?"

"Is ask Jaclyn that."

He pulled back, a dark look in his eyes. "No. I'm asking you."

"I'm sorry. I can't think of anything."

"I'm getting tired of this, Wynter."

When I didn't answer, he walked to the file cabinet that I now knew contained every sin of the Select. He pulled out the drawer marked M–Z. Traced a finger over the tops of the tabs and slowly pulled one of them out.

Mine.

"I read this, as you asked," he said quietly. "So many confessions. Such unbidden thoughts. I think you have many secrets." He lifted his gaze to me. "*I want to hear them. The ones you don't dare confess, even in your prayers. That you think about at night. The ones you try not to think about at all.*"

"All I have is there, and now you know them," I said evenly.

He considered the file, flipped through the pages. Seemed to weigh them in his hand.

"So . . . many . . . . troubling thoughts."

"Acts committed in thought are not the same as those in deed. You told me yourself."

"Why would I contradict the Testament?" he asked, tilting his head.

"That's what you said!"

"Did I?" But his expression said he was clearly concerned about the state of my mind. "Meanwhile, it would be worrisome if someone drew attention to the sheer volume of these. It reminds me a little of a girl named Lyssa. Remember her?"

I stared. What was he saying?

His face turned to flint. "I thought you were different from the others. I still think you are. But it's your choice. You have three days," he said, sliding the file back into the cabinet as Magnolia returned.

I FOUGHT FOR breath behind the Factory.

My choice? What choice did I have? I could survive Magnus as long as I was willing to debase myself, alienate my sister, and deceive the Enclave alongside him.

Or I could lose everything—along with Jaclyn and Truly—in three days' time.

I spent all day trying to sort through my too-few options. All night wondering what escape might mean for my soul. Knowing I would never leave Truly.

Which meant I had to convince Jaclyn to come with me.

CHAPTER NINETEEN

Just after 2 a.m., the streets are eerily dark, traffic lights like unseeing eyes in a city far too quiet. Twice on my way out of the neighborhood, I pass groups of people standing outside, staring at the heavens. A few cars drift along the street, silent as ghosts. No headlights behind me; they're all in the parking lot of Target, pointed at the shattered front doors, people coming and going with carts.

Three police cars whiz past, lights flashing. Silent. They don't stop.

At least the car's GPS still works. I follow the prompts to Highway 88. Nine hundred forty miles to go. Fourteen hours. Barring any delays, I will be there by early afternoon.

Assuming the world doesn't end.

The scratch in the back of my mind is back. Whispering that Julie and Ken and Dr. Reiker might be far more misguided than I. That in some twist of logic, someone as crooked as Magnus has heard a voice of God too faint for any other human ear.

In which case the samples beside me mean nothing and retrieving Truly will only push her to the front step of Hell.

Stop.

I tell myself God cannot be so petty, capricious, or cruel.

And then I think of Jackie.

I can't get my last image of her from my mind. Can't not hear her running down the street. Or stop wondering where she's gone.

She said Magnus threatened to kill her and thought she was being followed even as she admitted she was losing her grip on reality. It's possible the only thing following her was a pair of headlights headed in the same direction. But if they thought she was coming to warn me . . .

I dial Julie from the car's Bluetooth.

"Wynter." Her voice is soft but not yet groggy—the way people sound when they're trying to sleep and can't. "Everything okay?"

"Julie, listen to me," I say, craning to look back as I pass two vehicles in the ditch, headlights still on. "Don't wait till morning. Get up. Now. Go."

"What do you mean? You sound like you're in the car." I hear her sit up, instantly alert. "Wynter, where are you?"

"I'm sorry. I have to leave. It's an emergency." If I tell her where I'm going and why, I'll have to tell her about Ken. And I don't know what she'd do then.

"What? What are you talking about? Where are you going?" I can hear her, practically see her, getting out of bed. Flipping the duvet off of her, swinging her feet to the carpet before remembering the lights don't work and fumbling for the flashlight on her nightstand. I hear her click it on in the background.

"Julie, it isn't safe. You can't wait till morning to leave."

"We're not going without you!"

"I'm not coming."

"What are you talking about?"

"Jaclyn's sick. I promised to take care of Truly," I say, fighting to keep my voice stable.

"Wynter, listen to me. Truly's safer where she is right now, and you'll never make it there and back on a single tank of gas! Turn around. We'll wait for you."

"No. Don't. I'm not coming back."

"Wynter, there's nowhere to go! Especially with a child! You have no place to take her, protect her—what are you going to do for food, to stay warm, safe?"

"I'm . . ." I search for some lie. "I'm going back to the Enclave," I say. "I'm going to stay there with her."

"*What?* No! Wynter!"

Ambulance lights speed by, sirens off, as though the blackout has stolen all sound.

"Julie, please just trust me. You need to go. Now. Promise me."

"At least let us know that you made it there safe."

"I'll try. Julie?"

"Yeah?" she says, sounding shocked, hurt, and worried out of her mind.

"If things get worse, there's a place near Sidney, Nebraska. The Peterson farm."

"Okay, but what—"

"Say it back to me."

"The Peterson farm."

"Thank you, Julie. For everything." I choke out those last words. It hurts to say them. They're too much like good-bye.

I click off the phone but can't stand the sudden silence, the sound of Julie's confused hurt, Jackie's last words too loud in my head. I turn on the radio, the chatter of which does nothing but add to the undercurrent of anxiety twisting my stomach. Especially considering that my sick sister is somewhere doing everything they're saying not to:

Don't travel.

Don't go outside.

The radio broadcaster says the station is running on backup generators. Reads reports of emergency workers still trying to rescue people stranded in elevators, on the LA Metro, and in the Seattle Space Needle. Rumors of looting. Residents without heat in twenty-degree temperatures. Homes across the country without running water or soon to lose it.

I zoom out on the GPS with one hand, trying to figure how much highway I should cover before refueling somewhere in Iowa. Far enough to have burned some room in the gas tank but still several hours east of the initial blackout, where I assume there's already been a run on stations with backup generators to operate the pumps.

I count three cars in my rearview mirror. Wonder nervously how long they've been there as I pass a truck stop filled with the headlights of semis, the halogen beams of cars. I speed up.

The next radio station I stop on, the DJ has either finished or completely abandoned the standard alert script.

"Look," she says, and sighs. "It's been a long few weeks and months for all of us in the news. If you're tuning in tonight on your portable radio, I know you're scared. It's hard to make sense of what's going on. What's happening to our good men and women. Our schools. Our workplaces. Our churches. Right now I miss the shows where all I had was celebrity gossip or the latest viral video.

The problems that felt like big deals until all of this started happening.

"I don't know what's going to happen, but I believe God's with us. So I'm going to say a prayer for you and for me and for our great nation. And I'll be back with announcements and updates and the alerts, but for now, we're going to listen to some music."

She plays Bon Jovi's "Livin' on a Prayer," and then she's back with reports of explosions at two interconnection substations in what the White House is calling an act of terrorism in the prolonged attack on the US electrical grid.

"We don't know how long the blackout will last," the announcer says. "Stay warm. Stay indoors. Keep the doors locked. Emergency responders are working around the clock to keep order and help those who need it. I know you have questions. I know you may be afraid. Just remember that we're all going through this. And we'll get through it together. You are not alone."

I don't know that DJ. I don't know what religion she is—according to Magnus, God doesn't even hear the prayers of those outside the Enclave. And I know she's never heard my name and can't be speaking to me. But I imagine that the voice of God has found me here, in the outside world.

She plays some song about ridin' the storm out as I speed at eighty miles an hour through Sterling and then Prophetstown.

Which I salute with a single finger on account of its name.

As I pass north of Davenport, I'm surprised once again at the number of cars on the streets.

It's nearly 5 a.m. Cars line the off-ramp all the way to the giant truck stop and the overpass above. I slow as two forms dart across the highway ahead, ubiquitous red gas cans in both their hands. Just past town, I wonder if I should have stopped, topped off the tank.

Wonder how much worse things will get in the next hour and by morning.

DAWN THREATENS MY rearview mirror as I reach the outskirts of Des Moines. By the time I pass around the city, the sky is already casting a blue tint over a land without light.

I'd hoped to get gas here before the stations run dry; I'm down to a quarter tank with only a couple gallons at most in back. But the first truck stop in West Des Moines is deserted and the second is backed up along the entire right-hand lane leading to the exit. Police lights flash farther up the line; I can just make out an officer, patrol lights flashing, directing cross traffic at the turn.

It occurs to me that I'm only an hour south of the Enclave. From Truly. It's Friday; Rosella is already in the kitchen. The ovens still work, I'm sure; the Enclave has generators and a stockpile of fuel to last halfway to the afterlife if its members are frugal.

It takes everything in me not to turn north.

Truly's safe. For now. I chant it over and over in my head.

I click the button on the steering wheel. One hundred forty-five miles left in this tank. Enough to make it to Council Bluffs. I'm cutting it close, but once I get there, my next tank should see me all the way to Fort Collins.

Assuming I can find fuel.

I switch lanes, accelerate past the line of cars. Can see kids huddled in the back seats, pillows shoved against windows, phones glowing near their faces. Even watching an animated movie on the drop-down screen of a four-door pickup.

I scroll through radio stations recycling the same warnings to a heartland just waking up to cold houses, dead electronics, and unresponsive coffee machines. The president is calling the cyberattacks on the grid and the substations an act of war, urging Americans to keep the roads clear for emergency responders, stay indoors, and maintain law and order.

I can't find the radio show I was listening to earlier; maybe the DJ is done with her shift. I land on a station where the DJ is similarly tired of the same dire warnings and fuels breaks between the news with heavy metal. It's angry and defiant. And though the radio display says "Classic Metal," it's mostly new to me.

I'm delirious from the cocktail of adrenaline and grief, feeling untethered, alone, and a little unhinged.

I remind myself I have just one immediate, clear-cut goal. It keeps my foot near the accelerator, even though I'm back on cruise control—a thing I hate but have resorted to in the name of conserving fuel. For the moment, Truly's safe. I'll worry about how to get to her, what to do with her, later. For now, all that matters is the samples.

I think how crazy this is. How crazy it all is. I'd spent so long trying to be safe. Now here I am speeding across the Midwest with the disease turning the world crazy riding shotgun in the front seat. I wonder what Elder Decaro would say if he saw me now—plastic wrappers on the console beside me, "Highway to Hell" on the radio.

No doubt Magnus would think it delicious. Except for the fact that I have his carrier of pig tissue. Which makes me choke back an unhinged laugh. And I wonder if it's possible I'm crazy after all.

It occurs to me this is the closest I've ever come to acting on the intrusive thought of the hour—screaming during service, tossing an entire stack of plates onto the Enclave kitchen floor, grabbing the newest cute initiate in a lip lock if only for a taste of the world outside ("Welcome to New Earth!"). To breaking out of the obsessive need to check and recheck myself, caught up in the silent cyclone of personal desire and fear.

A black Jeep starts to pass me on the left. The driver is alone, like me, and I wonder where—or who—he's trying to get to. Unlike me, he's singing along to the radio. I know it's the radio, because he's bouncing his short-haired head to the beat of "Highway to Hell" blasting from my radio . . .

Until he looks over at me and stops, then quirks a grin.

I shove down the accelerator and speed past him.

A mile later I'm sobbing. Wishing I could talk to Jackie, that I could call her, tell her she can't be sick. That she has to live.

Because I don't know how I can do this.

An hour later, my back aches. My eyes hurt. I rub my forehead and squeeze my temples as I realize it's been nearly twenty-four hours since I last slept. I push my shoulders back, adjust the lumbar support on the seat as I pass an upturned vehicle in the ditch. Fumble in the bag of food for a can of green tea as a convoy of military trucks passes across the median, headed in the other direction.

I've dubbed most of the cars I've passed the last half hour in an effort to keep myself alert: Smoking Guy. The Nosepicker. The Lip Picker. The Clan Van with the four kids in back. Camper Man. I tagged the truck I passed a few miles back Redneck Survival Guy, if only for the coolers, white plastic chairs, grill, and entire mattress in the bed of the truck. He'd been ambling along, but now he's back in my rearview and closing in fast. I consider speeding ahead—according to the GPS screen, I curve left in half a mile—but the minute I see him swerve onto the shoulder, I rethink that. I've passed plenty of evidence of reckless driving since dawn: cars skidded to a halt in the meridian, others stuck after trying to detour off road. I even saw a car driving on the other side—in the wrong direction.

I didn't watch to see what happened.

Now, as Redneck Survival Guy comes up on me, I slow. But he's not changing lanes nearly fast enough. I speed up and angle right. My right tire hits the grading, the sound humming up through the SUV in a low whine. Just as I decide to speed ahead, he powers up alongside me, not completely in the left lane so that I have to drive on the shoulder just to avoid him. He's an older guy in a seed cap, lips tight around his teeth, gaze fixed right ahead as though he's chasing something. I lay on the horn, but he doesn't even seem to notice me.

By now he's practically in the center of the road and there's no way I'm spending the last few miles to Council Bluffs watching for him over my shoulder. I slow enough to let him pull ahead even as the GPS prompts me to stay left. He does, belatedly drifting into the left lane before abruptly swerving right—and onto the shoulder with a bump that sends the grill toppling out the back. It hits the pavement and bursts into pieces. A thud punches the front of the car, thumps along the undercarriage beneath me as the truck speeds ahead at the fork in the highway.

With shaking hands, I follow I-80 south. Whatever was trapped in the undercarriage seems to be gone, and I'm still moving. Which is good, since I'm surrounded by nothing but open prairie and farm-land.

Twenty-two miles to Council Bluffs and my best shot at a work-ing gas pump. I don't dare stop here to survey the damage—just my luck, I'd be the one to get mowed down by some granny in a Smart car.

Ten minutes ago I was unstoppable. Now I'm nervously watch-ing for each mile marker, listening for rattles in the undercarriage or any hint of a tire going flat.

What I notice instead is a syrupy smell inside the car. A few seconds later the thermometer symbol lights up on the dash.

Now I don't know what to do. I know how to refuel the car and—thanks to Ken—change a tire. My car emergency plan, however, has always and only consisted of asking whoever was driving with me what to do.

By the time white smoke starts wafting from the front of the hood, I know I've got problems. I'm trying not to freak out or entertain visions (too late) of the car erupting in flames and exploding—burning me and the samples in the front seat to high heaven.

I squint at the approaching sign for Underwood, Iowa, listing two gas stations, and a "truck stop"—which I find dubious but am in no position to refute.

By the time I turn from the off-ramp, I'm amazed to find the stop—a convenience store and Subway shop with four double pumps in front—swarming with activity, a large, handwritten *Cash only* sign at the turn where a man in a reflective vest is directing traffic from the cars lined up on either side of the street.

But right now gas is the least of my problems. I pull into the handicapped parking space in front of the convenience store (because who's going to fine me?), fumble in the back seat for my purse and a surgical mask. When I come around front of the SUV, I stop cold. The entire base of Redneck Guy's grill is protruding from the front of the Lexus by a metal leg.

When I tug on it, the thing won't even budge.

I walk to the front of the shop where handwritten gas prices are taped to the door—at least two dollars above the normal price per gallon. But when I go inside, the place is full; a line stretches the entire length of the shop's main aisle, one lone guy in a mask and latex gloves manning the register with an old-fashioned calculator.

The shelves are practically depleted, the dark coolers empty except for a few random bottles of Muscle Milk and cans of iced coffee. The radio's on, relaying the national power outage, as though we hadn't noticed.

I beeline toward the restroom, having had to pee for hours. I find it down a short hallway, an "Out of Service" sign taped to the door. I try the handle anyway.

Locked.

Back in the store, a man at the front of the line is arguing with the guy behind the counter, calling him names even as he forks over his money.

"You know this is price gouging!" he says.

"What I know is this is the only station between here and Council Bluffs with a generator. Which takes money to buy and gas to run," the man says, as though he's already repeated the same line twenty times today. He's thin and balding and doesn't seem the least bit ecstatic to be selling out of everything—even as more people come through the door. "You're welcome to buy your gas elsewhere if they have any left by the time you get there or wait for the next supply if and when it comes. Next, please!"

The man curses the guy out and throws the money in his face.

"Pump five," the man behind the counter says. "Next."

"Excuse me," I say to a woman in line. She's cradling a liter of pop and an entire box of salted nut rolls.

"The line's back there," she says.

"I just want to know if there's a repair shop here or anywhere nearby that's open?"

"There's one in the next building over," the man behind her says. "But I doubt anyone's working. This here and the church are the only places even open. Though that guy might be able to call a local mechanic for you if his phone's working. Probably charge you ten bucks, but—" He shrugs.

"Thanks," I say, and push out the doors to head to the truck repair shop. It isn't much more than a big garage, the bays closed. The human-sized door, when I try it, is locked.

It isn't the first time I haven't been allowed through a narrow gate.

I walk around the corner of the building and, with a quick glance over my shoulder, whip down my jeans and squat behind a dumpster.

Back at the SUV, which is still steaming, if not as badly as before, I unplug my phone, ready to throw myself at the mercy of the counter guy for a mechanic referral. My phone, at least, has a full battery, so he can't charge me for the call.

Straightening out of the driver's side, I don't register the shout at first. I'm preoccupied, worried about one thing: getting the SUV fixed so I can get back on the road. I'm also, like the Lexus, running on fumes. So it takes me a minute to notice the man at the pump twelve feet behind the Lexus—until he starts screaming.

All I can think is that the pump isn't working because he didn't see the cash sign. That he's the kind of person who shouts at inanimate objects—like the lady at the mall ATM a few weeks ago who yelled at it for a full two minutes when it wouldn't give her the option of taking out $30 even though the sticker said it dispensed only in increments of twenty.

Except he's not screaming at the pump, but about some chick named Jenny.

"You think you can hide what you really are?" he says to no one, waving the nozzle in front of him. "You think I don't know? That I haven't seen the *scales under your skin*?"

I go very still, afraid to slam the door and draw attention to myself.

Too late.

The man spins around, sees me. "You!"

He drops the nozzle and runs right for me. I dive into the driver's seat, slam the door. Fumble for the lock button. Hit the window one instead. It starts to go down. I punch it again—and the window stops.

"They're coming!" the man says, grabbing the edge of the window.

I hit the button again, and he grapples with the ledge, gets his fingers out just in time to keep them from getting caught. He pulls on the door, opening it. I grab the inside handle, but he's got more leverage than me. I let go, all at once. The door flies open and he stumbles back. I lean out, grab the door, and slam it shut. Punch the lock.

He springs back up. Slams a gun flat against the window so hard I'm surprised it doesn't break.

"Don't worry," he says, words muffled through the glass. "I won't let them get you. You saw them, too, right?"

But the sight of that gun has seized up my diaphragm.

"Say it!" he says, spittle flying from his lips. "I know you saw their scales. Don't deny it!"

I nod stiffly.

Crazy Man waves the gun around, ranting about illegal aliens. And somehow I don't think he means the Mexican kind.

I slide my fingers to the ignition button, wondering if I can start the engine and get it into gear before he shoots me in the head.

"Let me see it!" the man shouts, banging on the window with the butt of the gun. "Show me your skin!"

I have no idea what he means or what qualifies as skin on his planet. I hold up shaking hands.

"No! Your skin!" he screeches, then levels the gun against the glass.

That's when I see the figure crouched low in front of the hood of the car beside me. He lifts a latex-gloved finger to his lips over his surgical mask. I don't know what he plans to do, but I do know one thing: I cannot die. Not now. Not like this.

I rip off my mask. The crazy stares right at me. I hate, somehow, that he sees my face. "I'm immune!" I shout.

"What?" Crazy Man says.

"Look!" I unsnap the neck of my coat and turn my head slightly. Point to the birthmark I know is there. He cranes against the window hard enough to leave nostril prints. "Do you see it?"

"Yes! What is th—"

A rush of motion. A blur of red. Hard crack against the window.

The man drops, gun clattering to the ground.

I sit back, breathing hard as a second face peers at me through the window. Cropped hair. Good eyebrows.

"You okay?" he asks from behind his mask.

I swallow and nod.

"Hold on."

He bends down and I hear him set the gas can on the pavement. A few seconds later, he's dragged the man to the sidewalk. I put my mask back on, quickly get out, stepping over the gun.

"Careful!" I say. "He's sick."

"Kinda figured that," the guy says before retrieving the gun and emptying it. "By the way," he says, gesturing to the grill sticking out of the SUV. "I don't remember that being there when you passed me."

CHAPTER TWENTY

We couldn't go over the walls. At twelve feet high they weren't insurmountable and I knew where the ladders were stashed in the barn. But the electrified wires at the top meant to keep the unbelieving world from storming Heaven's gates at the start of the apocalypse posed a problem. A year before we arrived at the Enclave, some teenager had tried to escape over them and only ended up (not) meeting his Maker early.

It took two days for me to get her alone. Two days in which I'd run through dozens of scenarios in my head.

The game I'd play with Truly as we hid in the back of the van. The distraction Jackie would have to provide when we got to the counseling center in Ames. The story she'd tell about needing help with the lock or something inside. The way we'd tumble out the back and rush around the corner of the block—I imagined the center was in the middle of a block, but I didn't know. The way we'd wait for her to come get us.

We used to play hide-and-seek, Jackie and I. Used to know how to hide, especially, very well.

We had to.

We could do it again. We could survive together. The three of us.

I knew where Magnolia kept the petty cash. I was certain Jackie knew people in town after having been in charge of the center all these years. That there were people who helped women and children—I'd heard a neighbor talk to Mom about such a place. We could find one, I was sure, if we had to. Long enough to get away.

To be safe.

I finally caught up to her on her way to the storehouse just before lunch. Found her inside, an open bin of clothes from our last initiates on the ground beside her where she sat, fists curled in some garment of clothing or another, staring at nothing.

"Jackie," I said softly.

She jumped up at my arrival and started pulling things from the bin. "What do you want?" she said, not looking at me.

I glanced around and hurried toward her. "I want to leave," I whispered.

"What do you mean, 'leave'?" She glanced up as though I were out of my mind.

"The three of us, together. You, me, Truly." She laughed and shook her head. I grabbed her by the elbows. "Jackie, this isn't right anymore. None of it makes sense—"

"Then leave," she said simply.

"Not without you. Not without Truly."

"Truly is *my* daughter," she said, glaring at me. "She stays with me. And I'm not leaving. Not the Enclave, not my husband."

"Jackie, he isn't what he seems. To any of us, including you. Do you know he all but insinuated to me that you're not yourself? That you're somehow off?"

"You're lying."

"Why would I lie? I don't have to. And his so-called revelation?" I chuffed out a breath. "You *know* why he suddenly had that!"

She wheeled around. "You know what I think? You're jealous. You've always wanted what was mine. My daughter and now my husband. Ever since I had Truly!"

"*What?* I love Truly!" I wasn't jealous about her . . . was I?

It was no secret that I'd spent more time with her than Jaclyn herself, especially in the last year. Jaclyn worked at the center. She spent her evenings in the barrow she shared with Magnus and had a dozen other responsibilities across the Enclave as his wife.

I was the closest thing to a mother Truly had. The closest thing the Enclave would allow.

"Truly's your daughter," I said quietly. "But Magnus—"

"Is God's voice," she said shrilly. "And if he asks for you, who am I to gainsay him? And who are you?"

I blinked. "You can't possibly want that!"

She dropped the T-shirt and grabbed my hands. "No. I don't," she said, staring at me, fingers digging into my wrists. "But God never asked me what I wanted or what I liked. And He never asked you. This is all we have. All *I* have. The world is a terrifying place. I know that first-hand. I see it three days a week. Magnus is right. The end *is* coming."

"What if it's not?" I asked softly.

"How can you say that? *Why* would you say that?" she demanded.

I saw it then, in her eyes: fear.

I understood fear in all its forms.

Fear of being wrong. Fear of being right. Of the unknown. Of the future and of God.

Fear of oneself. Of one's own ability to do something so irrevocable that it could damn a soul for eternity. Fear powered the Enclave and every one of Magnus's impassioned sermons. But now I knew an equal fear: that everything we'd believed and based our entire lives on was a lie.

God, I believed, was real. Jackie, Truly, and my love for both of them were real.

That was all I knew anymore.

"Even if I wanted to, it would never work. Do you really think he'd ever let Truly go? Magnus is a powerful man." Her hands shook as she let me go. "He's watching you," she whispered before grabbing the tote and carrying it out.

She'd been right: despite his avoidance of me the last two days, I *knew* Magnus was watching, waiting for his answer.

Still, I clung to her last words. Terrified or not, she'd thought about it. I wondered, not for the first time, what her marriage these last five years had been like with an empathy I'd never felt for her before.

She'd come around. I could convince her.

But first I had to buy some time.

MAGNUS WAS SHUT up in his office on the phone with someone. He had barely looked at me the last two days, during which I'd breathed for the first time in weeks.

Now that was about to end.

When the sound of his voice faded, I got up, walked back, and rapped on his door.

It was against protocol. But so was everything.

"Come in," he murmured.

I did, quietly shutting the door behind me. I placed my palms together, level with my nose.

I took in the sitting area and three leather chairs. The low coffee table covered with several of New Earth's seed catalogs. The bookshelves packed with books, some of which I recognized. The Testament, in all its volumes, of course. Various copies of the Bible. Others with spines too worn to read. The credenza was stacked with folders and a ream's worth of printed paper held together by a rubber band. The heavy, carved desk sat facing the middle of the room, the throne of an important person set with the largest monitor I'd seen but dominated by the man himself.

He glanced up, annoyed. Gone the rapt fascination.

"Wynter."

I lowered my hands. "I've been thinking."

His brows lifted just perceptibly over the rims of his glasses. He was the Magnus of Sabbath service, of the coming end. The man I'd once thought looked like a baseball player, with shoulders broad enough beneath the taut cotton of his button-up to carry the burden so uniquely placed upon him. A figure to be revered, perhaps feared—at least a little. Whose even offhand remarks carried the tinge of inspiration.

The one I'd wanted him to be. The one he could never be again.

"I was just admiring the covers in the office . . ."

"Then admire them out there," he snapped.

"I have a secret I can't share with anyone," I blurted. "I can't talk about it because it's about you. Should I go to Penitence?"

He tilted his head. "It depends."

"On what?" I asked, studying him. This was dangerous. He was dangerous.

"On what it is."

"I was thinking . . ." I leaned back against the door. "About the time we kissed."

He blinked and gave a slight laugh. "What are you talking about? We've never kissed."

"Really?" I said, giving him a quizzical look as I moved toward his desk.

"I would have remembered that," he murmured. Now, in this light, I saw that other man and his need of admiration after reverence had gone dry. Who, with one glance, had killed the precepts I had spent years of my life memorizing chapters at a time.

I could never forgive him for that.

"But we have."

"Wynter, I don't know what game you're—"

"The Testament—your Testament—says time is not linear. That it does not exist for God. It happens all at once. All that will happen has happened already. Isn't it true?"

"Yes," he said slowly. "It is."

"So it's already done. That and much more."

He rose and moved from behind his desk, eyes fastened on me even after his phone began to buzz, lit up with a long series of digits. "This . . . kiss. Care to jog my memory?"

He reached back and grabbed the phone, started to turn it over, and then glanced at it. Hesitated.

"I came at a bad time," I said, moving to the door.

I expected him to say that we *would* finish this conversation. To demand that we meet somewhere later. Instead, to my surprise, he strode past me to the door, yanked it open, and stepped into the hallway.

"Everyone out."

My heart stuttered until I realized he was gesturing for me, too, to leave. "Magnolia, tell the Elders I need some privacy."

I moved past him to the front room where a startled Magnolia had just risen from her chair.

A second later he had locked himself in his office.

CHAPTER TWENTY-ONE

A few of the locals wrestle Lizard Man into a locked closet because no one knows how long it'll take the sheriff's department to get here.

"Dispatcher said it could be an hour before the sheriff can come take your statements," the guy at the counter says after locking the man's gun in the store safe and donning a fresh pair of gloves.

But that's exactly fifty-nine minutes longer than I want to stick around.

"I need a mechanic," I say.

He shakes his head. "Gone."

"Is there anyone nearby?" I say.

"Closest you'll find is Council Bluffs."

But that won't help me.

I shove out the door to find the hood of the Lexus propped open and Jeep Guy leaning out over the grill to peer down into the guts of the car. He's switched out the latex for a pair of work gloves that go far better with his thick brown jacket. I wonder if he works on a farm or something, though I've never seen a farmer drive a Jeep.

"Straight into the radiator," he says. "Surprised your engine didn't shut down."

"So . . . what does it need?"

He laughs. "A new radiator."

"Where do I get one?"

"Well, for this fancy soccer mom model—"

"It isn't mine," I say quickly.

"Stolen, huh?"

"No, it's not stolen!" I say, insulted.

It kind of is.

"No one here's going to have what you need. Or be able to order it anytime soon."

"What about Council Bluffs?"

He shakes his head. "You're not gonna make it that far before your engine shuts down. And nothing's going to be open anyway."

I turn away, fingers clasped over my head, as the last twenty-four hours catches up to me. Getting Jaclyn back only to lose her. Leaving Julie and Lauren. Ken. Truly. Having gone so long now without sleep that I can't think straight. What am I doing?

And I don't know what I'm in danger of most: crying or laughing in that way people do when they're on the verge of a breakdown.

I don't dare do either. Not in public, lest I end up in a truck stop broom closet. Desperation churns the pit of my stomach. I cannot stay here. I *have* to get to Colorado.

"Can I ride with you?" I blurt.

He gives me a wary, sidelong glance. "You don't even know where I'm headed."

"You've been going west for the last fifty miles. If you were headed south, you would've taken 35 from Des Moines."

"Maybe I'm going north."

"Are you going west or not?"

He lowers his head with a sigh.

"I have food," I say. "Water. A gas can I can fill up here. Money. I can pay you!"

He turns his head to look at me. "I could be a serial killer for all you know."

"Do serial killers usually point that out?"

He straightens up and drops the hood of the Lexus. Cocking a brow, he asks, "Are you trying to pick me up?"

"What—no!"

"I mean, we did have a moment back there."

"No, we didn't. We had no moment. But I still need that ride."

He blows out a sigh, scratches the back of his neck. "Okay, listen. I can take you as far as the panhandle. But it's gonna cost you that gas can. That *full* gas can."

"Done."

Ten minutes later, we've moved the Lexus to the side of the truck repair shop and shoved my stuff into a Jeep full of camping and fishing gear.

And then we're pulling out onto I-80 again.

Only then do I question my sanity for jumping into the car of a complete stranger as I start thinking of what a terrible position I've just put myself into. He could drive me anywhere. Rape me. Sneeze on me.

"So, um, I didn't ask how you were feeling," I say awkwardly. Neither one of us has taken off our masks, and I have yet to remove the latex gloves.

"Great, thanks," he says.

"No, I mean . . . you're not sick or seeing things?"

"No more than usual," he says, looking at me. "How 'bout you—relatively sane?"

"Define 'sane,'" I murmur.

He chuckles and holds out a work-gloved hand. "Chase Miller."

I glance at his hand without taking it. "Wynter. So where *are* you headed?"

He quirks a brow at his rebuffed gesture and gives a slight shrug. "Wyoming. Buddy of mine has a cabin there near some good ice fishing. Figure it's as good a place as any to ride out a few months."

We've already passed several overturned cars—especially across the median, coming from the west, Omaha and Council Bluffs. Makes me wonder what's happening in Chicago or even New York.

I glance in the side-view mirror, not having forgotten what Jackie said about being followed. By now there's dozens of cars behind us.

"What's in Colorado?" he asks.

"My mom," I lie. "She's disabled."

We ride in awkward silence for a mile before he turns on the radio. The president's back on. There's been some kind of attack on a transformer manufacturer.

"Someone's determined to keep the lights out in America for a looong time," Chase murmurs.

"Who do you think it is?"

"Probably Russia."

Reports of crashes, more crazies. Speculation about the crazy flu being bioterror. I think of the carrier in back. Did I imagine it, or did his gaze linger on it as I shoved it beneath a sleeping bag?

"You had enough news for now? How 'bout some music?"

"Anything's better than this."

He pulls off his glove and scrolls through the phone plugged into his dash as I rummage in back and offer him a bottle of water.

Classical music floods the Jeep.

"Vivaldi," he says.

I've been stealing glances at him all this time. He's got dark hair and olive skin, but his eyes are blue. He's younger than thirty but seems older than me. Then again, a lot of people do, if only because of how sheltered my existence has been until two months ago.

Sheltered. I actually hate that word. It implies safety.

"So who's going to get the unfortunate news about that SUV you were driving?" he asks.

"My aunt," I say. "It's hers. I live at her house. I'm a junior at North Central College outside of Chicago."

"Doesn't look like you'll get to finish out the semester."

"It closed a few weeks ago like everywhere else."

By now the initial alarm of Jaclyn's appearance and recent adrenaline of being confronted by a crazy man with a gun have all worn off. A few minutes later, classical music droning in my ear, I'm fighting to stay awake. I actually feel my head bob once as I jerk it upright.

"Sleep if you want," he says. "Looks like you could use it."

"I'm fine," I say, gazing at the side-view mirror again.

A few seconds later, I'm gone.

CHAPTER TWENTY-TWO

All that day I waited. For him to appear at the children's barrow or summon me to meet him at his car. Or his office itself. After all, it was abandoned. We'd be alone.

But no summons came. I went with Magnolia to the warehouse to check on the latest yields. When we returned, Magnus and his blue Prius were gone.

I must have looked out that office window fifty times throughout the afternoon—dreading its arrival even as I waited anxiously for the white van that would return my sister from Ames. I had to try to talk to her again.

But when it pulled in past the gate shortly after five, Jackie wasn't among those who got out.

I hurried out after one of the women—a girl named Mallory two years older than me.

"Where's Jaclyn?" I asked.

Her brows, so fair they barely existed, lifted in confusion. "Magnus picked her up in town."

Magnus?

"What for?" I asked.

"He didn't say," she said, clearly perplexed by my question. Of course she was; Magnus didn't need to explain himself to anyone, and no one would have asked.

Anxiety gnawed at my gut. Where had he taken her? Had my willingness to reengage him somehow tipped him off about my plan for her and . . .

Suddenly I was running for the children's ward and tearing up the steps of the barrow.

"Truly!" I shouted, barging through the front door into the open front room . . . where all the children were sitting in a circle reciting lines from the Testament with Arabella. I searched their faces, the floor tilting beneath me.

"Winnie!" Truly said, waving from across the room where she sat between two other girls.

"Are you going to marry Magnus?" a girl to Arabella's right asked. Another child tittered, covering her mouth with her hand.

"Well, you'll just have to wait and find out, won't you?" I said, before saying something about needing Truly to play with the daughter of a visiting family later this week, tugging on my earlobe, and leaving as she reached for her own.

Neither Magnus nor Jackie came to supper that night. And Enzo was nowhere to be seen.

I finally mustered the courage to seek out a Guardian.

"She's with Magnus," he said, barely looking at me. "Out of town."

And though I pressed, he either didn't know—or wouldn't say—more.

I'd never known Jaclyn to accompany Magnus anywhere before. Why now? Had he seen us talking and taken her as insurance against the possibility of my escape?

Would she tell him?

I thought back to that call, to his demand for privacy. Who'd been on the other end of that conversation?

That night as I lay in bed, I heard the gate grind open from my cot in the Factory through the window cracked open near my bed. Slipping out from beneath my quilt, I moved toward the window. I could see the twin beams of the Prius swing through the yard as the car rounded the drive toward the barrow Jaclyn and Magnus shared.

They were back. She was back.

Tomorrow I'd learn where they'd gone and what, if anything, she'd said. I could convince her. I thought back to her warning. Clung to the hesitation in her eyes.

My arms had just started twitching with sleep when something startled me: a whisper near my ear. I started, scared—until I saw the features of the woman standing over me. Jaclyn.

I hurried out of bed, instantly alert. "What is it?" I said, noting the gas lantern in her hands, the coat over her shoulders as I pulled my skirt over my nightgown and threw my shawl around my shoulders. Slipped into my shoes. But she said nothing as she took me by the hand and led me out, down the path toward the storehouse.

"Where've you been?" I said. "Where'd you go?"

"Quiet," she said. She sounded nervous as she pushed the door to the Quonset hut open, pulling me inside.

She set the lantern on a shelf near the entrance, illuminating the area where I'd found her two days ago, and pulled me toward her, her fingers cold in the late-night chill.

"You wanted to know where I was," she said.

"I was worried!" I said. "When the van came back without you—"

She cut me off with a sharp gesture, her face pale in the lantern light, ghastly shadows beneath her eyes. "I'm going to talk," she said. "And I want you to listen."

"Okay," I said slowly.

"I was with my husband in Des Moines, where he had meetings. What you don't realize is that he has to work very hard to find new seeds for our vault, a thing that requires a great deal of time, not to mention investors."

"But why take you?" I said, not understanding why we were even talking about this. We had plans to make.

"Because he wanted us to have some time together. To talk about you."

"About me." I gave a short, harsh laugh.

"And for me to have time away from my responsibilities to think. About the future. All of ours."

I narrowed my eyes. "You mean yours, mine, and—"

"Yours, mine, and the Enclave's," she says.

"Jackie! There isn't any—"

"Not another word!" she said, fingers digging into my arm. And then, more quietly: "There's far more at stake than your concerns for yourself. It's true that I've had questions. I've been proud . . . even jealous. But now I see that this is for the best."

"This . . . being . . . ?" There was a slow sinking in my gut.

"Your marriage to Magnus."

"How can you say that?"

"He needs sons to carry on his work in the coming age. To lead new nations. I haven't been able to give him another child since Truly was born."

"You're only twenty-seven!" But what I wanted to say was that Magnus could get them with someone else—after we were gone. It wouldn't be our problem anymore.

I took in the set of her jaw. The tight line of her mouth. And then I realized: he didn't take her with him just to give her time to think but to convince her he was right.

Because that's what Magnus did.

"Jackie," I said, taking her by the arms, something desperate in my voice.

"It's for the best," she said. "I wanted you to hear me say it before you talk to him."

I opened my mouth to say I didn't want to talk to him. I wouldn't. That I would do whatever it took to prove to her he wasn't what she believed.

Just then something moved in the shadows and I instinctively pushed Jackie back as a figure stepped into the light of the lantern.

Magnus.

I stared at him as Jackie moved past me to stand at his side. He laid a hand on her shoulder. "You see," he said. "Your fears about your sister are unfounded. In a few days, we'll all be family."

She gave me a last embrace before they returned to their barrow. And I felt her hand slip into my pocket.

Alone in a stall of the Factory bathroom ten minutes later, I withdrew the folded slip of paper. The message was only two words, penned in Jackie's hand:

Trust me.

My engagement was announced at next morning's service.

CHAPTER TWENTY-THREE

I dream of Jackie. Chased by an unmarked car. Getting run off the road. Careening from a bridge. Holing up in some shack and freezing to death only to be found days, weeks, or months from now, ravaged and twisted with decay and the telltale signs of her mad last hours.

I dream I die, but when I get to that Other Place, Jackie and Mom aren't there.

I sit up with a start, heart racing. Feel as though I'm suffocating in the mask.

Chase glances over at me, his own mask gone. "When you said you have water and food, you failed to mention that you snore," he says pointedly.

"What? I do not!"

He grins. He's got dimples. "I'm just teasing."

I look away.

The sky, stark blue this morning, has turned sullen gray. I search out the clock on the dash. One twenty-nine. Vivaldi's gone, the news back in its stead, turned low. Then I notice we're off the interstate on some two-lane county highway.

"Where are you going? Where are we?" I demand, pushing up straighter, glancing behind us.

"Relax," he says. "We're south of Omaha. Had to avoid the city. Sounds like it's a mess." He rubs his hand over his face with a faint scratch of whiskers. "I would *not* want to be an ambulance driver in any city right now, I can tell you that."

"Has that car been back there for a while?" I say, gesturing.

He frowns. "I think I turned in front of it. Why?"

"Paranoid, I guess."

"That isn't all bad. Do you trust her neighbors?"

"Whose?"

"Your mom's."

"Oh. They're nice. Though I guess you never really know what people are like. Why?"

"Anyone not already crazy from the disease is going to get mental really fast when they run out of food and water. Especially if they think you have some. And a lot of idiots are going to burn their own houses down trying to stay warm. Which means they'll be looking for a new place to stay."

"What are you, some kind of survival guy or something?"

"Or something."

"I forgot to ask where you're from."

"Cleveland, this time."

"'This time'?"

"I move around."

"What do you do?"

"Whatever I want," he says with a slight smile.

"Maybe you shouldn't say that to women riding with you."

"Sorry. I fought for a while after I left the service."

"Fought." Service.

"You know. Mixed martial arts?"

"Oh, yeah." No, I don't know.

"Traveled for a while," he says, sighing. "Switched to training for a while."

"Do you actually live anywhere?"

He looks over at me. "Do you?"

"Naperville. I told you. Where I'm in school at—"

"Where you loaded a single bag full of clothes into a two-year-old SUV your aunt loaned you not knowing when you'd be back. By the way, North Central's on a trimester system. Buddy of mine went there."

"What?"

"You're not missing out on the rest of the semester because they don't have semesters." He glances sidelong at me. "Just a tip for next time."

"It's really none of your business."

"At least that part's true," he says.

We ride past country homes and a small gas station. The lights are off, the place deserted. Meanwhile, the first snowflakes of winter have begun to fall, fat and sloppy against the windshield.

"THIS LOOKS LIKE it could get ugly," he says, glancing through the windshield up at the sky. The snow's been coming down progressively harder for the last half hour. And though I know what Chase means, there's nothing ugly about it. It looks like a starfield from the old Star Wars movies Jackie used to love. Which makes it both more beautiful and more devastating at once.

"Can you pull up any weather info?" he asks, unlocking his phone where it's plugged into the dash.

I take it from him and for a minute I wonder what kind of music and photos he has on it. The places he's been.

After a long pause, the weather app loads.

"Snow through the night," I say. I turn and dig around in the back, offer Chase a protein bar.

"Thanks," he says, but sets it on the console, opening the water instead.

"When did you leave Cleveland?" I ask.

"Couple hours before the electricity went out," he says, rubbing his eyes. "Figured it was coming."

"Want me to drive so you can sleep awhile?"

I say this having never driven in snow. But also because it's unnerving not being in control. I'm angry at myself for having fallen asleep earlier, his comment that he could be a serial killer still ringing in my head.

"I'm fine."

Chase pulls off the highway.

"What are we doing?" I say.

"Steering clear of Lincoln, crazy people, and idiots who can't drive in snow, hopefully," he says grimly.

All I know is we're losing time and could've been halfway across the state on a normal day by now.

But on a normal day, I'd have no reason to hightail it to Colorado, either. At least the car behind us is gone.

He turns onto a county road. Out here the farmland looks a lot—too much—like that near the Enclave. Silent. Remote. For a minute I entertain the idea that Chase is indeed a serial killer—or even just a one-off killer. And I remember Julie's pepper spray is buried in my bag.

Earlier today, blazing through Iowa, I had briefly entertained the idea that maybe God had meant for us to be at the Enclave. Not because Magnus was right or even for the sake of my soul but to get these samples to Ashley today.

In which case I wonder why God couldn't keep the electricity on. Or the weather warmer.

Or, barring that, a grill inside a pickup.

A few minutes later, I realize we've slowed, are coming to a stop. "What are you doing?" I say, heart thumping against my ribs. But Chase is squinting through the snow at something on the road.

"Hold on," he says, grabbing the protein bar and getting out.

I watch as he walks about twenty feet down the road and stops. A second later, he crouches down. Just as I'm eyeing the driver's seat, the key fob dangling from the ignition, caught between sliding over and throwing the Jeep into gear and getting out to see what's going on, he stands up and comes back carrying something beneath his jacket.

He gets back into the Jeep, snow on his hair and lashes. And there, peeking out from his jacket and shivering against him, is a little white-and-brown-splotched dog.

The puppy whines as Chase lifts him up in the warm air.

"He's a boy." He glances at me. "Hope you aren't allergic."

"To boys?"

He sets the puppy on the console, but it climbs back to Chase's lap on unsteady feet and peers out the window. "I think this one was waiting for someone who isn't coming back. Came right toward the car to see if he recognized us. See how he keeps looking?"

But at that moment I can't. I can't look. The mere thought threatens to break something thin and raw inside me.

"Probably going to be a lot of this in days to come, hate to say. Poor little hungry guy ate my lunch," he says, rubbing the dog's floppy ears. "Hey, buddy."

Chase buckles up and puts the car in gear, left arm curled around the dog that drops, in the space of a mile, into an exhausted sleep curled in his lap.

We go a few more miles before the snow is so thick we can barely see the section stretching in front of us. I glance at the speedometer: thirty-five miles an hour. Try to quell the panic rising up inside me. Every mile feels like torture; I'd hoped to be halfway across the state by now.

Thirty miles an hour. Twenty-five.

"You look on that side, I'll look on this one," Chase says.

"What are we looking for?"

"Somewhere to wait this out."

A few minutes later, he turns off into a field toward an open weathered wooden corncrib and drives in.

The second he turns the car off, I can hear the wind howling through the boards, feel it shudder in gusts against the Jeep.

He gets out, dog in one arm, and opens the back.

I get out, stretch stiff legs with each step as I move to the opening to gaze out at the landscape. Visibility's getting worse. The puppy runs out into the snow just far enough to do its thing and retreats back at a whistle from Chase. I didn't want to stop but if we have to, it's better that we're hidden.

I wonder where my sister is, where she went after she left Julie's house. If it's true that she was followed. If she's somewhere safe . . . or knows where she is at all.

Chase has the back of the Jeep open, is rummaging around in the front, the puppy lapping at a Thermos lid of water near his feet. I'm just coming back to get my sleeping bag when he steps back from the driver's side, a gun in his hand.

I go very still, breath frozen in my throat.

Before today, I'd seen exactly one gun in my life, and it was wielded by a man threatening to kill my mother.

The memories flash through my mind all at once: Dad, drunk. Mom, arms out, telling us to go to our room and lock the door. Mom, crying in the living room. Jackie and I hiding in the closet, our breath too loud. Magnus preached on family curses once. Is it ours—Mom's, Jackie's, mine—to fall victim to the men around us?

"Hey," Chase says. "Wynter, it's okay."

I back up a step and he lifts his hands.

"It's all right. This is for protection," he says, glancing up at it.

That's why Dad claimed he had a gun, too.

I spin toward the open end of the barn, stare wildly out at the storm. Back at the samples in the Jeep.

"Look, I'm putting it away." He reaches on top of the Jeep for a black case. Opens it and sets the gun inside. He latches the dark plastic box. "See?"

"It stays in back," I say, voice unsteady.

"It's not a lot of help back there . . ."

"We're in the middle of a snowstorm. Who's going to find us?"

"I'll make you a deal. It stays up front. On your side. Okay? Trouble comes, you hand it to me. Fast."

Magnus always taught that a gun sends two people to Hell—the one getting shot and the one doing the shooting.

Finally I nod.

I retrieve my sleeping bag and get back in front. Climb backward onto the seat to fumble through the emergency kit for a couple mylar blankets.

A few minutes later, I'm cocooned in my sleeping bag beneath a mylar sheet, my stupid hat on.

Chase turns the engine on long enough to warm up the inside as we eat pumpkin bread and string cheese from Julie's house, half of which he feeds to the dog curled in his lap before turning the engine off. Within seconds, I can feel the cold seeping in from the edges of the windshield, the window beside me. He pulls his sleeping bag over his shoulder and, a few minutes later, reaches back for the blanket from Julie's house, settling it over all three of us.

"Thanks," I murmur, pulling the edge of the blanket up over my nose, too conscious of the gun case at my feet.

I sit there awkwardly in the weird twilight of the storm as he closes his eyes. Unsure if I should say good night. Waiting for any indication of a snore. Wondering how I'm supposed to sleep this close to a man. A gun. A deadly disease.

"Just so you know," he says, not looking at me, "we're here because of the weather."

"Okay," I say, not sure what he's getting at.

"My mother raised me to be a gentleman. You're safe."

I don't know how to respond to that.

"You're not going to get in your sleeping bag?" I ask.

"Nah. Besides, I've got passenger number two curled up with me."

We lie in the semidarkness, wind blowing through the slats of the barn, and I start to think he might be asleep when he asks quietly, "Who's Jackie?"

I stiffen. Surprise—and then pain—stab through me at the sound of her name.

How would he even know to ask?

"You said her name earlier, when you were sleeping."

I look away.

If my lies are none of his business, the truth is even less so. But somehow, to refuse to acknowledge her seems tantamount to deny- ing her existence in this world. A form of murder and blasphemy at once.

"She's my sister." I whisper.

The last word comes out unevenly. I clamp my hand over my mouth beneath the blanket. My breath shudders out my nostrils and I squeeze my eyes shut against the tears. Against the sounds fighting to get out like so many demons even as I fight to hold them in.

Without a word, Chase shifts in his seat. Lifts the warm bundle of floppy ears and big feet curled against him over the console and, nudging aside the edge of the blanket, lays him against me.

I wrap my arms around the puppy and clutch him close, sobbing as he licks my cheek.

CHAPTER TWENTY-FOUR

rust me.

My first thought at Magnus's appearance had been that she'd betrayed me. But of course she had to have known he was there.

Trust me.

Or was it possible she meant my pending marriage? That she really believed it was for the best and all would be well?

No. She'd been too careful in our one-sided conversation, interrupting me before I could betray myself, my plan for us to leave. A plan she'd never committed to, I reminded myself.

I was desperate to talk to her, to find out what had happened in Des Moines. What she meant.

Trust me.

But there would be no opportunity for me to speak to Jackie alone with the frenzied preparations for my wedding under way.

That afternoon, I joined Rosella and her zealous minions in the pantry—a giant Quonset hut filled with wall-to-wall shelves of everything from canned carrots, pears, and peppers to whole cobs of corn—trying to feign interest in plans for my wedding banquet.

I tried on the white dress Jackie had worn for her wedding in the living room of the Factory. Stood like a mannequin as Iris and several others tucked and pinned it, all the while discussing whether it needed longer sleeves. Was told I was expected at a private session with the midwife after dinner for a private lecture on the marriage act—a thing I definitely did not want to think about and doubted I needed anyway, given all the stuff Shae had talked vividly and in great depth about before her initiation.

Trust me.

I had no chance to ask if Jackie's plan included saving me from my wedding night. Would she think it was petty for me to worry about a few nights when she had weathered nearly five years?

I showed up for work at the office, not having been told to do otherwise, and Magnus threw open his door.

"There she is. Isn't she a beautiful bride-to-be?" Magnus beamed so that even Elder Decaro, sorting through his mail, politely agreed.

"Wynter," he said, crooking his finger at me. "A word?"

I schooled my expression and followed him into his office, heart knocking against my ribs as he shut the door behind us.

"I feel like a boy," he said softly, lifting my fingers to his mouth. I forced a slight smile as he dragged my nails across his lower lip. "You have no idea how many times I've thought about what you said. About our kiss. About *everything* that's about to happen and has already."

"I thought you would," I managed. I glanced toward the door. "I don't think we're supposed to be alone . . ."

"What are they going to say? Besides. They're right out there. Did you meet with the midwife?"

"Not, um, yet."

"Good. Don't." His thumb traced my mouth, gently forcing it open. "We'll be like Adam and Eve in the garden. Two innocents exploring with no knowledge of good or evil. Get lots of sleep until then. Of course, you'll be in Penitence tomorrow night . . ."

"What?" I said, startled.

"You're marrying the Interpreter, Wynter," he said, frowning. "You can't expect to come to my bed without it."

As though I were the one who needed cleansing from my sins.

"Did . . . Jaclyn do the same?" I asked. Was she aware of this? I'd still been living in the girls' barrow when she'd married Magnus and I had no idea how she'd spent the night before her wedding.

"Of course." He smiled lazily and then leaned down to whisper against my ear. "I'll make sure they bring you an extra pillow."

My skin prickled all the way down my arm as I quickly calculated the hours until my fast would start tomorrow.

Whatever Jaclyn had planned, it would have to happen before then.

He was murmuring something, his arm winding around my waist. But the instant he started to nuzzle my neck, I jerked back, hand flat against his chest.

He stared at me, stunned, and I caught my breath in horror. But in that fleeting instant as I took in the shock on his face, I thought, *He sees this is a mistake. That I don't want him and never will.*

He grabbed me by the wrist. Yanked me hard against him.

"You. Don't get. To do that," he hissed before pressing his mouth against mine, forcing his tongue between my lips.

I struggled against him, fighting to breathe as he pulled me toward the desk and then shoved me down against it.

"Who knows," he said, breath hot in my ear, his weight smashing me against the cold mahogany. "Maybe I'll check on you myself."

I scrabbled as he grabbed my wrists, papers flying to the floor. "But we're not—we won't be married," I said raggedly, barely able to hear myself over the hammer of my heart.

"No one would ever know."

He shoved back and pulled me up to face him, fingers biting into my arm. And I thought, *This is what the face of Satan looks like*.

"Pull yourself together. Fix your hair before you leave," he said, turning away to snatch up a paper from the floor.

I straightened my blouse with shaking hands, unable to quiet the tremor quaking along my chin as I smoothed back my hair.

I barely nodded at Magnolia, who admonished me to enjoy my wedding plans. Outside, I hurried blindly through the yard past the barrows to the barn, where I curled up behind a hay bale as the walls closed in.

THE NEXT DAY, I pointed out my few personal possessions that were to be moved by Iris to the second bedroom in Magnus and Jackie's barrow. I said good-bye to each item in my mind, resolved that I would never see them again. I had no intention of sleeping a single night beneath that roof or on the new bed delivered from town that morning.

I had just over seventeen hours. Seventeen hours to save if not my life, then my dignity, my body, and whatever part of my soul was attached to it.

Where was Jackie?

With each hour, panic rose inside me until I was light-headed, my vision spotting until I barely recognized my own hands cutting the stuffed zucchini on my prenuptial plate that evening.

At 9 p.m., I entered Penitence between two Guardians.

A half hour later, I heard the slide of a desk chair as the Admitter prepared to leave for the night.

The minute his footsteps faded up the stairs, I struck the Testament from the altar and tore the picture of Magnus from the wall.

CHAPTER TWENTY-FIVE

jolt awake a short time later to headlights bouncing off the rear- and side-view mirrors, blinding me the instant I open my eyes.

The dog is in the driver's seat, front paws against the window. He growls and then gives a high-pitched bark.

Male voices outside. One of them irate, the other low and even.

I shove up, cheeks cold in the frigid air, twist around to squint at the two shadows standing in the twin beams filling the barn. Chase stands with his palms up in front of him. A second figure is holding a shotgun trained on Chase's chest.

I drop down behind the headrest, heart pounding as the puppy barks again and again. I grab and pull him against me, conscious of the gun at my feet.

I could never use it.

Could I?

I hear Chase talking. Glance at the side-view mirror. A truck idles mere feet from the entrance, blocking us in. If something happens to Chase, I can't even pull out of here—assuming I don't get shot through the window first.

I wiggle out of the sleeping bag, reach back for the carrier, fully prepared to make a run for that truck.

The voices come closer, around the other side of the car. An instant later, a man in a surgical mask and black cap peers into the driver's-side window. The dog goes crazy. Grabbing the carrier, I yank open the door, instantly on my feet in the chilly air.

"Wynter!" Chase says. "It's all right."

But now a whole new series of suspicions has crept into my mind in the space of the last second alone.

That Chase knows this place. That he's in league with the guy following me. They've been working together.

"This is Mr. Ingold," Chase says. "This is his property."

I move around the back of the Jeep, clutching the carrier against me as Chase scoops up the dog.

Mr. Ingold is a thin man with age spots on his face. He nods at me, shotgun lowered at his side.

"Hi," I say. The farmer nods.

"Snow's supposed to stop sometime tonight," he says, glancing from me back to Chase. "You should be on your way by morning."

"We will," Chase says. "We won't be any trouble. By the way, do you recognize this dog?"

"No," the farmer says, shaking his head. "Can't say I do. I wouldn't be picking up strays, myself, seeing as how things are about to get scarce, but suit yourself." He nods toward the entrance of the corn-crib. "There's a spigot on the west corner if you need fresh water."

"Thank you," Chase says.

Mr. Ingold starts to turn, then pauses. "Were you in Iraq?" he asks.

"Afghanistan," Chase says, then adds, "Welcome home, sir."

"Thank you," Mr. Ingold says. "Good night, now."

Mr. Ingold carries the shotgun to the truck. A few seconds later, he pulls away, his pickup cutting through half a foot of snow, leaving darkness in his wake.

"What did you mean, 'Welcome home'?" I ask.

"Did you see his hat? Guy's a Vietnam vet. They didn't get the kind of respect or homecoming the military do today."

I'm only vaguely aware of the Vietnam War and have no idea what kind of homecoming the military receive today.

"Isn't it . . . a little late?"

"Yeah," he says, looking at the carrier in my arms. "It is."

"Why'd he ask if you were in Iraq?" I ask as he leans in to start the Jeep.

"He saw the decal on my rear window," he says, setting the dog on the ground.

I back up, peer at the eagle, globe, and anchor in the corner of the window.

"What is it?"

"The emblem of the United States Marine Corps."

I also have only a vague idea what a Marine is, and only because of a TV series Ken watches.

Chase pats his knee and ruffs the puppy's short-haired head till it shakes with a flip-flap of ears. "C'mon, buddy," he says, play running to the entrance, looking over his shoulder as the dog bounds after him. "Need to go outside? I know I do."

I return the carrier to the back and watch them follow the truck's tire tracks out into the darkness. I walk out to the entrance as they disappear and I stop to stare up at the sky. No stars. Just the pale smear of moon through the clouds, the slanted flight of the snow falling silently to the ground. It reminds me of Iowa. Of the dark within the walls, from which we couldn't see even the nearest headlights passing at the end of the long Enclave drive. There were just the planes, flying into or out of Des Moines. I used to watch them ascend to the heavens at dawn on my way to the henhouse, wonder where all those people were going.

Chase comes jogging back, the puppy scampering on his heels. They chase each other on the dirt floor of the corncrib for a few minutes. I pick up an old corn cob, bend down, and show it to the dog. Toss it a little ways.

"Go get it," Chase says, pointing. The dog looks at him, bewildered. Then at me like I'm out of my mind.

"Was he upset?" I ask. "The farmer?"

Chase shrugs. "Startled is more like it. Can't say I blame him—I wouldn't be too keen to find someone else's vehicle in my barn."

"He held a gun on you."

"He didn't want to use it. Just needed to know we weren't out to steal from him or hurt anyone." He retrieves the cob, tries tossing it again. This time the dog runs after it then stops, as though forgetting what it was doing.

"Get it," Chase says, crouched on his heels. "Go get it, buddy!"

"Hungry?" I ask, and walk back to the Jeep. My legs feel thick and stupid, my neck stiff. I root around in one of the grocery bags, pull out a piece of white cheddar, an apple, a box of Julie's gluten-free crackers, and offer them to him. Chase gets back in and relegates the dog—who is far too curious about the impromptu picnic—to the back. He holds the box of crackers toward me. I shake my head.

"You originally from Colorado?" he asks.

"Yup."

I note the time. Nearly ten o'clock. I was supposed to be in Fort Collins by now. Yet here we are, barely west of the Iowa border. I pull out my phone, redial Ashley's number. I need to let him know I won't make it till tomorrow.

This time it doesn't even connect.

"Since we're both awake, can we leave?" I ask. Because we still have a lot of state to go.

"There's ice under that snow," he says, handing a piece of apple back to the dog. "Four-wheel drive isn't any help on ice—especially with idiots on a road we can barely see."

"How soon?" I ask.

"We'll see how warm it is in the morning. You always this jumpy?"

As though in response, I reach back for my bag, fish around for my medication, which I haven't taken in more than twenty-four hours. Opening the bottle, I pour out a tablet and then look inside.

Only five pills left. Five pills between me and my next crippling obsession about my eternal fate. Or possibly Truly's. Or whether I'll accidentally kill her with my own negligence, or if I'm sick and don't know it yet, or my tried-and-true favorite: what more I could have done to save Mom from dying.

"I don't suppose Walgreens is going to be open tomorrow," I murmur.

"Only to people willing to fight off looters and addicts. You might want to start tapering down."

I break the pill in half, and then one half in half again. Take three-quarters of a tablet and put the remaining quarter back.

"Anxiety?"

"Something like that."

"Any triggers I should know about?"

"Yeah. Vivaldi."

He chuckles, the sound warm. "I thought you looked a little twitchy back there."

I smile slightly.

He looks out the window for a second, then back at me. "You know if you get attacked, the best thing you can do is just get away. Or do everything you can to inflict enough damage . . . to get away."

"Okay," I say, not sure why he's telling me this.

"Which means you can't worry about stuff like that case back there."

It'd be good advice on any other day.

"What's in there, anyway?"

"Insulin," I say. "For my mom."

I CAN'T SLEEP. Can't get comfortable. Can't help listening for the sound of another car. Checking the rearview mirror.

Sometime after midnight I shimmy out of the sleeping bag as silently as I can, shove my feet into my cold shoes. Glance at Chase, who hasn't moved in the last hour. The puppy lifts his head. I stroke his ears.

"Go outside?" I whisper, gesturing over my shoulder. He doesn't move. I don't blame him.

I grab my gloves, let myself out of the Jeep. Close the door with a quiet click.

I pause at the entrance to the corncrib. Stare at the snow outside, the drift sloping to the earthen floor at my feet. If I stand still enough, I can hear it falling. The barely discernable *pat-pat-pat* of the flakes as they join the others on the ground like the dull glitter of burnt-out stars. A sound amplified by darkness, the open entrance of the corncrib, the canopy of clouds.

No cars. No city or farmhouse lights. Not even a barking dog.

On any other night I'd think the snow was beautiful. Tonight it feels like a shroud.

Squatting on the south side of the barn in the snow (I've been doing way too much of this outdoors lately), I debate whether to wake Chase. The wind has quit blowing. The Jeep has big tires. If we stick to gravel roads, shouldn't we be okay?

I finish, scoop up a handful of snow, brush my hands together, and then shove them in my pockets.

Now that I'm awake, all the restless energy of before comes back. The anxiety of not being on the road, of not moving anywhere at all. Stuck here, wondering where Jackie is and if she was followed or only imagined it. How far east she got on what remained of her gas.

And then there's the person—or persons—Jackie was supposed to meet. It couldn't have been Blaine; he's already dead.

I shudder in the freezing cold, wondering if Jackie would have been next. A simple mugging, a robbery at the center, a senseless murder—any one of those, and all traces of the samples could have disappeared and there'd have been no one to say anything about their existence.

I walk until my toes are frozen, my cheeks and ears numb. Until I'm light-headed from cold. And then I start back, following the shallow indentations of my tracks already filling with fresh snow. Wondering if I should wake Chase. Ready to plead my case about needing to get to my mom. To manufacture tears, if that's what it takes.

A glow emanates from the open entrance of the corncrib. Rounding the corner, I see that the dome light of the Jeep is on. It takes me a minute to register the fact that it's empty. Another to notice the form leaning against the driver's-side door.

Chase.

"You're awake," I say, surprised. "Does this mean we can go?"

He comes to meet me near the entrance, hands in his coat pockets. "That depends."

"On what?"

"Look. You seem like a really nice person. But there's something I need to know."

"What's that?" I ask warily. There's something strange about his posture. Something almost feline in that six-foot frame that sets me instantly on edge.

"What's in the carrier, Wynter?"

"I told you," I say warily.

"You also lied."

"It's also none of your business!"

"Normally I'd agree with you except this is my vehicle," he says, walking toward me. I force myself not to take a step back. "And I've just spent hours—with you—listening to radio reports about cyberattacks and possible bioterrorism, watching you check every fifteen minutes to see if we're being followed. So when I find a refrigerated carrier full of specimen samples and a USB drive with files about the Bellevue 13 and rapid early-onset dementia being carted around by a girl I *know* has been lying to me about why she's so desperate to get to Colorado . . . you can see why I'm ready for an explanation." He shrugs.

"I'm not a terrorist!" I exclaim, incredulous.

"You're going to have to do a lot better than that, honey," he says.

But I can't. I won't. Because Ashley voiced what I'd already suspected: that those samples in the wrong hands could be very bad. They'd been in the wrong hands once.

"No. Sorry," I say.

I don't know Chase. Not even a sliver as well as I knew my father or Magnus or Shae or any number of people I thought I knew—people for whom the chasm between who they pretended to be and who they really were was as wide as the one dividing Heaven from Hell.

I move toward the Jeep, ready to get the carrier, my things. Having no idea what I'll do next, but knowing it won't involve him.

He lifts the keys from his pocket, clicks the fob. The Jeep locks.

I stop, staring at the locked vehicle, my things trapped inside. I spin back.

"What are you going to do—*steal from me?*"

"I don't think that carrier belongs to you any more than that Lexus did."

"I told you, the SUV belonged to my aunt. I mean she's like an aunt. And those samples are for a grad school project," I say, remembering the empty fellowship form on the flash drive.

He takes a long look at me, turns on his heel, and walks to the Jeep.

I haul in a relieved breath as he unlocks it—until he gets in and slams the door shut. Relocks the door from the inside.

"No!" I run toward the Jeep as he starts the engine. Pound on the driver's-side window. "Stop!" I yell. "Please!"

He puts the Jeep into gear and I feel myself go hot in the chill air as he starts backing toward the entrance.

I scream, banging on the door, jogging alongside it, out into the snow. Clawing at the door handle.

He shoves the Jeep into gear and, before I can run around front and throw myself in front of the tires to stop him, plows through the snow toward the road.

I run after him, nightmare slow. Sink into a drift and lunge forward again. I'm light-headed, staggering through the snow, all the heat gone from my limbs, my head.

I feel like I'm going to vomit. A bright light shines in my face, but it isn't enough to keep the world from going dark.

CHAPTER TWENTY-SIX

A blinking eye stared from the corner above the toilet.

I hadn't minded the eye during my few days of self-imposed Penitence the last four years especially—probably because they had been fewer than before and mostly voluntary. But I probably should have thought twice before tearing down Magnus's picture. Luckily, the camera was at the wrong angle to capture the wall.

Tonight, that eye was my friend. By Magnus's own edict, the punishment for rape was expulsion and damnation, and the eye would know.

Not that anyone would ever see the evidence.

I counted the seconds—something I had done naturally entire portions of my life, even when I didn't need to. One minute. Five. Ten. Thirty.

At 10 p.m., lights out, my cell went dark. All except for the red dot of the eye.

Trust me.

But as the hours wore on, I started to panic.

I couldn't be here when they came to let me out for breakfast. To attend service. To be dressed by the women of the Factory for my wedding. Taken to the Banquet Table to celebrate over a meal, songs, congratulations. There'd be no chance to talk to Jackie—who would spend the night at the Factory to give us our privacy—before I was escorted to Magnus's barrow.

I got to my feet and began to pace blindly, hands over my eyes in the dark. And then I was feeling my way to the door, fingers going to the hinges, tugging on the pins, scratching at them like a caged animal.

I scrabbled in the dark for the worn copy of the Testament and, finding it, ripped the cover free. Fell down beside the door to pry at the hinge pins and then the screws of the lock. Finally I crawled toward the cot, feeling in the darkness for anything on the frame I could use. A strut, maybe—anything.

A sound outside the door. I stiffened at the sound of purposeful steps moving down the hall toward the Admitter's desk where monitors lined the wall and the log of Penitents—their check-in and check-out times with their room numbers—was kept.

No. No, no, no . . .

Rushing to the altar, I snatched up the cloth on it. Glanced at the blinking red light . . . just in time to watch it go out.

The footsteps neared and then stopped outside my door. I darted to the side of it and flattened myself against the wall, the cloth twisted between my hands.

A key slid into the lock. Turned, clicked.

The door opened the length of a blouse-clad arm as a figure eclipsed the hallway's lone fixture and slipped into the cell.

But it wasn't Magnus. It wasn't even a man.

And she was pregnant.

Ara.

I moved from the wall behind Ara, startling her.

"What are you doing here?" I blurted, blinking against the light.

Her gaze fell to the cloth. "What were you going to do—*strangle me?*"

"I—I didn't know it was you."

"I couldn't exactly announce it, could I?" she snapped.

My gaze flicked past her, already judging the distance between her swollen body and the hall. Between the hall and the stairs and the back door above. My legs tensed, ready to sprint past her, to shove her aside—until she pulled a slip of paper from her pocket.

"What's that?" I said, taking it.

Did I imagine it, or was it the same size as the one Jackie had given me just two nights ago? It contained only five digits: 4 0 7 1 5. Jackie's handwriting.

"Memorize it," she commanded.

I did, quickly. "What is it?"

"The Narrow Gate code," she said, putting it back into her pocket. "What time is it?"

"Just after four."

The Guardians changed shift at four thirty. The Narrow Gate would be unattended for a few minutes.

"Get Truly. Jackie's already out. She's waiting at the end of the road with a car."

My breath left me all at once. Clearly, I'd underestimated her.

I started past her and then stopped.

"Why?" I asked, turning back. "Why are you helping us?"

She lifted her chin. "Because with both of you gone, Magnus will need a wife."

"But you're already married," I said.

She gave a hard little laugh. "If he can have a revelation just to marry you, he can have another."

I caught her by the arm. "Ara. I know we haven't been friends for years. But thank you."

She fixed me with a level look. I used to think she was pretty, with eyes the color of sea glass. Now I realized just how brittle they'd become.

"Like I said. I'm not doing it for you. You've never been one of us."

I didn't know if she meant "us" the Enclave, or "us" the kind of person she imagined herself and Magnus to be.

It didn't matter.

"He likes secrets," I said as she turned to go.

She glanced over her shoulder at me, something glittering in her eyes. "I know."

She left then, striding swiftly down the hall despite her swollen belly. Before her steps had faded from the stairwell, I pulled the cell door shut with a soft click and hurried to the panel behind the Admitter's desk, where the panes on the screen had all gone dark, and switched the system on.

And then I was bolting down the hall and hurrying up the same stairs Ara had ascended seconds before.

I bypassed the metal side door at the top of the stairwell and turned down the corridor to emerge in the narthex of Percepta Hall. I could just make out Ara's form through the glass door, disappearing down the path.

I strode to the opposite door, skin prickling as I passed the sanctuary where I imagined shadows hulked behind the altar.

4 0 7 1 5.

I chanted the numbers in my head as I hurried past the Banquet Table, the Factory and storehouse, clinging to the shadows. I knew the way to the children's barrow so well, I could have found it blindfolded.

I slipped out of my shoes on the back porch. Let myself in through the door, which I left ajar as I crept through the children's sparse galley kitchen to the girls' dorm at the western end. Navigating past the faint glow of the bathroom night-light, I stopped midway down the row of small wooden-railed beds.

I didn't need to see her; I would have known the sound of her breath anywhere. The smell of her sweet, honeyed hair.

Sliding my arms beneath her, I picked her up, blanket and all. She stirred as I cradled her against me, her arms winding around my neck in sleep. She knew my sounds, my skin, as well.

I carried her out to the porch, toed back into my shoes. And then I was running through the shadow of the wall cast by the setting moon.

I crouched at the corner of the guesthouse, eyes fixed on the gate. It seemed somehow appropriate to me that I would wait here, at the edge of the cottage we had first stayed in fifteen years ago. That we had come in as three. That we would leave as three tonight.

Truly stirred and I pulled the blanket around her, my arms prickling in the chill September air.

"Hi!" I whispered.

"Winnie? Why are we—"

"We're playing a game," I murmured into her hair. "But if you want to win, if you want the prize . . . you can't talk. We have to be very quiet."

She held her finger to her lips. I scrunched my nose at her and nodded.

Movement in the darkness. The soft click of the guardhouse door. They were leaving, one Guardian from the front booth, the second from his post near the gate. My heart hammered against my ribs as I closed my eyes, resisting the urge to run this instant. Counting their steps to the garden path, listening for the crunch of their boots fading toward the Banquet Table where their reliefs were clattering empty mugs onto the pass-through counter as they got ready for their shifts.

A walkie-talkie crackled with a brief exchange from the Guardians at the southern end of the Enclave near the warehouse and its treasure: the seed bank. I was used to the walkie-talkies, the sounds of boot heels crunching on gravel—they were the sounds of security and safety I'd lain awake to so many sleepless nights. Sounds so mundane they belonged, in my mind, with those of the crickets and first birds of dawn.

I imagined the path up the drive, past the Factory, toward the Banquet Table kitchen, walking it in my mind until the sound of their muted conversation faded.

And then I was sprinting, all out, skirt swishing around my knees, Truly bouncing in my arms.

I threw my shoulder against the Narrow Gate door, shifted her to my right arm. Fumbled with the keypad in the darkness, finding the 1, 3, 7, and 9 at the corners.

4 . . . 0 . . . 7 . . . 1 . . . 5.

I waited for a click.

Nothing.

I tried the door handle. It didn't turn.

I exhaled a breath, willed my fingers to stop trembling.

"Winnie . . ." Truly whined.

4 . . . 0 . . . I carefully felt for each number. 7 . . . 1 . . . 5 . . .

I tried the handle. It wouldn't budge.

I pictured Jackie at the end of the long drive, waiting for us, engine running. Wondering where her daughter was. What was taking so long.

"Winnie—" Truly twisted in my arms.

"Hush!" I hissed.

Twice, in the last fifteen years, a Guardian had gotten the Narrow Gate code wrong enough times that the sirens on the four corners of the Enclave had sounded and the lights had come on, stadium bright, in the middle of the day. That must not happen now.

Truly started crying, wrenching this way and that. "Why are we leaving? I don't want to go!"

I said, more gently than before, "Mommy's waiting outside."

But it was the wrong thing to say. She didn't know Jackie as "Mommy" any more than I had known our mom as "Sylvia." There were no mommies here.

Voices in the distance.

My fingers hovered over the keypad, shaking worse than before. I counted the top row, found the 4.

Over, down, across the next row to the bottom.

0 . . .

I could hear boots against the gravel, coming down the path. Ten seconds. It was all we needed to slip through, to shut the door behind us. No one would see us running for the road on the other side.

7 . . .

A walkie-talkie crackled.

Top left corner.

1 . . .

Second row. Middle. I double-checked, counting the buttons, left to right and down.

5.

The Enclave lit up in stark relief like a picture thrown into negative as a siren blared to life above.

Truly screamed, hands over her ears. I threw myself against the door, keyed the code in again, and then again, in the light brighter than day. Praying to God, then begging, and finally screaming myself.

I snarled as they grabbed me, my arms locked around the little body inside them, Truly's hands like barnacles as she clung to my neck. Bit the Guardian who tried to pry Truly from me, backed against the gate like a rabid animal.

And that's when I saw her running toward me in her nightgown, a shawl tight around her shoulders.

Jackie.

What?

How was that possible? She was supposed to be waiting outside!

"Truly!" she cried, Magnus tight on her heels. "She's taking Truly!"

I swung my gaze around, uncomprehending. Ara had done this. She had always hated me. She had done this to us both. To us all.

Her pregnant figure stalked toward us from the shadows, finger pointed.

"She was stealing the child!" she shouted. "She was trying to leave with a child!"

It was a damning offense, trying to leave with another. Worse yet, trying to take a child. More damning, even, when that child belonged to Magnus.

They pried Truly screaming from my arms. Hauled me across the yard.

I stared at Jackie as they dragged me past her. At her wide eyes, her face so white in the darkness.

Did I imagine it, or did her lips move in a single, silent word? *Sorry.*

I was given one phone call to the number on my intake form filled out by our mother, I assumed, when we'd arrived. It had since been crossed out and replaced by another I didn't recognize with a 770 area code. I didn't know who had written it there or who it belonged to, but when the line rang, I knew the voice immediately.

"I'm coming" was all she said.

I cried after that.

On the morning of my wedding day, I did not eat the breakfast meant to honor me. I spent the service meant to celebrate my union with the Voice of God locked in a cell.

I was spared visitors. Just the red light blinking in the corner.

Until the Guardians came for me.

To send me into Hell.

CHAPTER TWENTY-SEVEN

Wynter, you with me?"

I try to talk around a thick tongue as my eyes pry open on a face far too close to mine.

Blue eyes. Good eyebrows.

Chase.

"Hey," he says, sounding relieved.

"What happened . . ."

"You passed out. How long has it been since you've eaten?"

I scrunch my eyes shut, feeling vaguely claustrophobic because there's a heavy band around me making it hard to move.

I open my eyes and then I realize: it's Chase, half on top of me, arm pinning me down.

My response is instant and animalistic. I flail beneath him as someone shouts for him to get off with a voice that sounds possessed. It's fury and offense and self-righteous wrath all balled up in one from a valve that, once tapped, spews twice as hard the second time.

He's up on his knees, hands in the air, and I'm swinging free of mylar sheets and sleeping bags to paste him across the jaw.

"Stop—geez—would you stop? I'm not doing anything! I haven't touched you!"

I'm in the back seat of the Jeep, which has been miraculously cleared of all the crap that was back here earlier. But I can't stop kicking at Chase, who finally backs out of the door at my feet.

It's a weird feeling, fury. A crazy, near-euphoric high.

I shove up, fumble around, looking for the carrier case. Find it lying in the front seat. We're back in the corncrib, though this time we're facing the entrance.

"It's there," Chase says. "It's fine. And despite what you might think, I wasn't going to leave you. Meanwhile, you're still not getting it back until I get some answers."

"I'm not a terrorist! I am trying . . . to save people," I say, feeling dangerously like I'm about to crack up and splinter. Or throw up. "To do the right thing. And to do that, I have to get that box"—I point to the carrier with shaking hands—"to someone in Colorado."

"To someone who isn't your mom."

"No. Not my mom. My mom is dead. My sister is sick." My hand goes to my head.

"I'm sorry," he says quietly.

I give a brittle laugh. "Now you believe me."

"I believed you before. Or wanted to. I don't know many terrorists who are petrified of guns, know nothing about cars, can't lie, and openly distrust men."

"I don't—"

"I get it. Most of us are pigs. But do you have any idea how this looks?" he says, gesturing at the carrier. "So I need some straight

answers now or I *will* dump you off at the first law enforcement station we see."

"Why don't you do that, Chase?" I say. "In fact, that'd be just fine."

"You sure? They're not going to give you a police escort to Colorado. You *stole a car*. They're going to take your cooler there and
lock you up. That's how it works, you know. Oh, wait. You *don't*
know, do you? Because you just came out of a cult."

I stare at him, feeling instantly more exposed than if I had come
to naked.

He lowers his gaze. "I'm sorry. I went through your phone. Tried
to call one of the numbers on your list—the Colorado one."

"Did you get through?"

"No," he says, looking surprised I even asked. "There's no service."

I wish he had. I'm worried Ashley will think something happened to me. Or that I changed my mind.

"But I did see your emails with that woman. Kestral."

I look away.

"And I saw your search history about New Earth and that guy,
Magnus," he adds, reluctantly.

"You're an ass," I say.

"I just want to know what I'm dealing with," he says, sounding
tired.

"I don't know," I say honestly. "And I won't until I get to Colorado."

"Is this . . . what I think it is?" he asks, pointing at the carrier.

"Depends on what you think it is," I say.

"Is this a *cure*?"

"There's no cure. But this could help with a vaccine." I weigh
whether to say more. Magnus was willing to go to great lengths for
the samples in that carrier.

"So the disease came from pigs? Where did you get this?"

"I don't know. My sister got it from Magnus. I don't know where Magnus got it. I just know he's a sociopath with a big corporate past and a lot of money. My sister, Jackie, is—was—his wife. She thinks he was trying to sell or trade it to the Russians. Someone came looking for it, he sent it out with her to hand off . . . But instead she drove to the Chicago area where the dad in the family I've been staying with is an epidemiologist. But he's out of town working on the disease. And now he's sick. And Jackie's sick." I feel my calm slipping. "And I'm trying to get it to the only other person we have access to who might know what to do with it!"

"Do the people she was supposed to give this to know where she went?" he says, eyes widening. "Do you even know who they were?"

"It doesn't matter—no one's there anymore. I made sure. And no, I don't know who they were! Just that Jackie thought it might be some Russians."

Now he's the one staring at me.

"Well, you can't exactly go to the CDC," he says flatly.

"No. I can't. Not like this. But the man I'm trying to get them to in Colorado can. He's a veterinarian who works on infectious diseases in animals."

Chase drops his head back to stare at the ceiling. Draws a long breath through his nose.

"So," I say more quietly. "Now that you know everything, I am begging you: just get me somewhere I can find a car. And then you can head off to your buddy's cabin to ice fish your heart out."

"I can't do that," he says at last, looking at me.

"What do you mean?" I demand, wondering if I've just made a terrible, terrible mistake, telling him all of this. For an instant, I can feel my remaining faith—in the world, in men, in humans in general—slipping away.

"Because I need to get you to Colorado," he says quietly.

"You sure?"

He gives me a quizzical look. "If that container can help people, how is there even a choice?"

"There's always a choice."

"Not if you want to do the right thing. Doesn't seem like you hesitated."

"No."

"All right, then," he says. "Colorado."

"Colorado," I say.

WE STARE UP at the sky, at the sliver of moon obscured by the snow falling in our hair and eyes. We agree to leave as soon as it lets up and we get some light.

Back in the Jeep, Chase turns toward me. "Good news is, no one's going to find us in this storm. Soon as the weather lets up, we get out of here. For now, I'd like to formally start over." He holds out his hand. It's not huge, but it's strong-looking. I wonder if he's ever killed anyone. "Just think. You and me, we're probably two of the few people willing to shake hands anymore," he says with a wry smile.

I hesitate. "I have OCD," I say, and take his hand.

"Chase Miller," he says. "I have hand sanitizer."

"Wynter Roth."

He gently squeezes my fingers. "It's nice to meet you, Wynter. I'm gonna make you a promise now, okay?"

"Okay," I say, not sure where he's going with this.

"I will do all within my power to get those—and you—to Colorado safely," he says. "And I'm going to ask for one thing in return."

I give a small smile . . . and then hesitate.

"Quit trying to punch me. At least until I show you how to make a proper fist."

He turns my hand over, folds my fingers in. Lays my thumb over my index and middle fingers. Rotates my fist and pushes two fingers against the top knuckles of the same fingers.

"Right here," he says softly.

I nod.

He lets go of my hand and searches for that second apple, insists that I eat. I do, for the first time since leaving Jackie.

"Did you have a special fight outfit?" I ask after a few minutes. "For your fights."

He chuckles. "What, like a red leotard? Jack Black in his 'stretchy pants'?"

I have no idea what he's talking about, but he's covering his mouth with his forearm, he's laughing so hard.

"*Nacho Libre?*" he says, eyes crinkling. I lift my brows. Finally he just says, "You ever even seen an MMA fight?"

"No," I say. "Cult Girl. Remember?"

"Ah, of course."

"So do you fight under your own name? If I googled you," I say, picking up my impotent phone, "what would I find?"

He exhales a long breath. "Hmm. Well, for one, you'd have to look up Cutter Buck."

"'Cutter Buck.'"

"Buck for Buckingham. My mom's maiden name."

"So if I googled 'Cutter Buck . . .'"

"You'd find my bio."

"Which would say?"

He lets out a long breath. "Twenty-six years old, six foot two, 190 pounds . . . maybe 185. Former Marine. National hero, friend to ladies everywhere, devastatingly handsome breaker of hearts." He grins.

"Show me how to make that fist again. I need to use it."

He laughs.

"So what are you?" I ask.

His brow furrows. "Is this a trick question?"

"Your ethnicity."

"Oh well, my dad's African American, Caucasian, and Native American. My mom's Middle Eastern and Caucasian."

"What else?"

"That isn't enough ingredients for you?"

"On my Google results."

"Oh." He thinks a minute. "You'd find a video of a fight you probably wouldn't want to watch. I mean, I don't want to watch it."

"Why's that?"

"I got my arm broken. Part of the reason I quit fighting."

"Eww."

"You'd find a statement I made about the nickname I used to have, which I didn't like. Something to the effect of 'I have two sisters, I respect women—I've had my ass handed to me too many times by them growing up not to. Being called "The Ripper" isn't something I want for them or myself. I love my fans, but please, if you love me, come up with something else.'"

"They called you 'The Ripper'? Why?"

"Sent a guy to the ER with thirteen stitches to his mouth and cheek."

"That's disgusting."

"Yeah, kind of was."

"Your sisters used to beat you up?"

"Oh, my God." He rolls his eyes. "All up and down the house. And the yard. And the street."

I laugh.

"What about you? If I googled Wynter Roth . . . ?"

I shrug. "I'm a nobody. My mom's mom was Hawaiian." I pause, wondering if that's why I long so much to see the ocean.

"Did you grow up in the uh . . . New Earth?"

"No. I was seven. Jackie was twelve. It was a safe place. It had walls."

"Safe from what?"

"My dad."

His jaw is working in the darkness.

"What?" I ask.

"Call me old-fashioned, but real men only fight a woman when she's part of an opposing army. I'm sorry. I'm sure you love your dad . . ."

"He's dead. I barely remember him."

"So this cult . . . why'd you leave?"

I'm quiet for a minute. And I realize I don't have the words to explain it. Or the desire to.

After a while he says, "I could show you some stuff if you ever need to defend yourself . . . if you want. If you're not going to sleep."

"I'm not. Show me."

I spend the next hours learning how to punch, kick, go for the throat, groin, eyes—all in order to get away.

"This is a rear naked choke, also called a sleeper hold," he says, pulling my arms around his neck, positioning them behind his head. "And when you're doing it, you hang on like a spider monkey. Here," he says, showing me where to put my legs.

"I don't know what a spider monkey is."

"Just get your hooks in," he says, planting my hand on my other arm.

Finally, around four in the morning, we're back in the Jeep. Chase dozes off, his breath a soft, even rumble. But I can't sleep. I'm staring at the snow outside and thinking of Jaclyn.

CHAPTER TWENTY-EIGHT

I stood, frozen between two worlds. The walls on either side of me. The wildflowers before me, parted by that perditious road. I took one last look back at Jaclyn where she stood, white-faced, in that crowd.

I'd relished leaving these walls before, entranced with the world beyond. But the same walls today were a gate to a foreign and dangerous place that might as well be a hellscape for Truly's and Jackie's absence within it.

Then I stepped out, wondering what would happen to me next as gravel crunched beneath my heels.

CHAPTER TWENTY-NINE

By dawn, the snow has let up to a thin flurry. We step outside as Mr. Ingold shows up a few minutes later with two shovels, warm sweet rolls, a Ziploc bag full of dog chow, and two Styrofoam cups full of coffee.

"Thought you might need a little digging out," he says.

I thank him and grab a shovel, start in on the nearest drift. I've shoveled a lot of snow in my life.

"She's showing you up," Mr. Ingold says, chuckling and pulling the second shovel from the truck.

"Thank you, sir. I got it," Chase says. "You hear any news?" he asks.

"Well, they're saying the cyberattack came from Russia," the farmer says, leaning against his pickup with a steaming Thermos cup of coffee. "Won't say how long the electricity's likely to be out. They're saying it could be weeks. Months, even."

"That long?" Chase says, his forehead wrinkling.

"Another substation exploded last night," the farmer says. "The president's declared a national state of emergency. You folks have enough gas to get where you're going? You're not going to find much at stations after today or tomorrow."

"We'll be okay," Chase says.

"They closed down a section of the interstate north of here due to accidents and the weather," Mr. Ingold says. "Ambulances in this area have been running all over the place. You're better off sticking to state highways anyway, assuming you stay out of the ditch." He takes his cap off and resets it.

"Will do," Chase says.

A half hour later, we've devoured the sweet rolls, fed Buddy, and made good on our promise to be on our way.

We pass houses with smoke rising from chimneys. I can smell the wood burning, even from inside the Jeep. We drive down the mostly quiet main streets of Hoag and Swanton and the equally small hamlet of Western (population 235). No gridlocks, no traffic here. The tiny downtown looks like something from a movie: a row of four buildings on each side—a couple with tall false fronts—and a grain silo right at the end of the street. There are even a few cars parked outside the corner church.

We've just turned onto Highway 74—a flat, straight stretch of narrow highway with shallow enough ditches that, were it not for a few fresh sets of tire tracks, it'd be hard to even know where they are.

Chase checks the rearview mirror every few minutes.

"So this Magnus guy . . ."

"They call him the Interpreter. Basically, he's our prophet. Their prophet."

"And no one knows he's a con artist?"

"No. They worship him," I say, for lack of a better word. "Thing is, I think he actually believes some of what he says. That his human whims are . . . I dunno. Divine edicts." I tell him how charismatic Magnus was—how perfect he and Kestral were together. How she was driven away and abandoned like an unwanted animal.

"Let me guess. Kestral was . . . what? Forty, when he got rid of her?"

"Around there. We didn't celebrate birthdays." Or Christmas or Thanksgiving or Valentine's Day or Fourth of July, for that matter.

"Dude's how old?" Chase says.

"In his fifties, I guess?"

We're just coming to the next town when we see something up ahead, across the road. A yellow school bus, blocking the main thoroughfare through several streets of businesses. Two men stand in front beside one of those portable signs, shotguns in their hands.

NO SERVICES. NO ENTRY.
TURN AROUND.

"That happened fast," Chase murmurs, pulling far enough right to make a three-point turn. We cut south a mile, go around. There's another school bus blocking the road to the town's residential area to our right at the intersection and two more men. One of them signals us to keep going straight. I glance at him as we pass. He stares after us. As I look into the side-view mirror, I see him lower his head to talk into a police-style radio.

"These are public roads, aren't they?" I say. "Can they do that?"

"I don't know, but they are."

We go a few more miles. The next town we come to is the size of Western. No school buses. No armed men on the road. Maybe the town's too small for any of that. What I do see are a few cars in front of the building every town has even in the absence of a post office: the local bar.

A large sign is posted in the front window:

OPEN FOR BUSINESS (COME IN!)
CASH ONLY. PROPRIETOR IS ARMED.

And then I smell it: the unmistakable smell of a grill in use.

Chase groans from the driver's seat. "God, I want a burger."

I'm hungry, too, for the first time since I left.

"C'mon," I say.

"We don't know who might be looking for us."

"Trust me, nobody knows who I am. I wasn't lying when I said I was a nobody. Come on. We'll get one to go."

Two seconds later, he's swinging around the corner to a side street, parking out back where a generator is running.

I grab the carrier as the dog leaps into Chase's empty seat. "I can't leave this," I say. Chase empties out half his duffle and sets it inside. Offers to carry it and puts the strap over my shoulder when I insist. We both loop on our masks. I can hear Chase's catching on his whiskers.

"Keep an eye on things, Buddy," he says, clicking the lock.

We walk around front where Chase gets the door. The first thing I notice as I step in past the ATM is the rumble of a generator from the direction of the dimly lit kitchen. The second is the TV over the bar.

The third is the onslaught of greasy-good smells.

There are maybe eight people in the place—including the bartender, who's pouring drinks in a surgical mask and pair of latex gloves.

We're the only other ones in masks.

"Welcome, strangers," he says, glancing up. A guy at the bar turns and, after sizing up Chase, nods.

"Thank you," Chase says, gesturing to an empty table near the door. He kicks out a chair for me without touching it.

I sit, staring at the TV, where the anchor is reporting an estimated ten thousand infected and a growing number of fatalities across the country under the headline "Nation in Crisis." News scrolls across the bottom of the screen: stores operating by candlelight, allowing only one or two customers in at a time. Looters of mom-and-pop stores being shot. Off-duty first responders reporting in by the hour. Footage of soldiers rolling into New York City as the president mobilizes the National Guard.

"What are you hungry for?"

"Anything without meat. Except grilled cheese."

He looks at me for a minute. "I'm pretty sure the vegetarian option out here is chicken, but I'll see what I can do."

He goes to the bar to order, at which the bartender informs him there's a five-dollar generator fee. Chase pulls out his wallet, and a few minutes later the bartender goes into the kitchen.

"You a military man?" one of the guys next to him asks. It's barely ten and he's already slurring.

The man goes on to regale him with some tale about some place he and his buddies were stationed. Chase nods and listens good-naturedly, and when the bartender comes back, the drunk guy says, "A shot for my friend here, on me." And then he's introducing himself and the guy hunched over his drink next to him and calling for the bartender.

"Jim, we got a Marine here—better pour us a couple more. And one for his lady."

"Essie, come say hi," he says.

Essie?

I get up awkwardly.

"This is Esmeralda," he says. I give a little wave as Chase hands me a plastic shot glass.

"Screw the Russians!" the drunk guy says. A few at the end of the bar lift their drinks. The rest ignore him.

Chase lowers his mask enough to drain the glass. I do likewise, take a sip, and sputter.

"That'll take care of more germs than that mask will," one of the guys says to me.

"Thank you," I say hoarsely.

"You guys had any cases around here?" Chase asks.

"Sure," the guy says. "Fella stole a neighbor's horse and went riding into town buck naked in twenty-degree weather. Local dentist. Used to take care of my kids' teeth when they was little. He's at the tri-city med center now. Guess he don't recognize his family anymore. Sad deal."

"When was this?" I ask.

"'Bout five days ago."

"There was another one in Ord," the guy next to him says.

"Oh, yup," the first guy says. "It ain't nearly as bad out here. Think I heard Lincoln had close to a hundred cases. That was a week ago."

We thank them for the shots. I carry the remainder of mine back to the table near the door.

"What is this?" I whisper, pretty sure I've burned out the lining of my esophagus.

"Fireball," he says.

"And who's Esmeralda?"

"The girl I promised to marry."

I straighten. "Oh."

"Until fourth grade started and she decided she liked my best friend better."

"Ouch."

The TV is replaying footage of an explosion, of the president condemning the attacks, telling Americans to be smart, be safe, and stay inside. That the Red Cross is establishing protocols for those needing water, food, assistance.

"You know who stands the most to gain from all this?" Drunk Guy at the bar says loudly. "North Korea! No one goes in, no one comes out. All they have to do is wait this whole thing out—or hurry it along with a little ballistic missile. Before you know it, that crazy Kim Jong-whatever'll be ruling the world."

"They're not going to need missiles," I murmur, looking at Chase.

"What do you mean?" he says, staring at me.

I can feel the alcohol spreading warmth through my stomach as I talk.

"The disease is spreading with the flu," I whisper.

"It's a *flu*?"

I shake my head. "Not the flu itself—something spread by the flu that started in Alaska with some pigs."

He sits back hard in his chair, his expression blank. "Do you know how many people get the flu each year? The season's just getting started!"

"Where's your family?" I ask.

"France," he says, distracted. "My parents and one of my sisters are. So they're safe."

"You said you had two sisters. Where's the other one?"

He shakes his head. "Lost her to breast cancer."

"I'm sorry."

"Took it three times to get her. She was a warrior. So . . . what you're saying is we're looking at tens or hundreds of thousands of cases—of *deaths*—by the time this thing runs its course?"

I say nothing. The silence does it for me.

He straightens as the bartender comes over with our food in Styrofoam containers—cheeseburger for him, veggie burger for me. Fries all over the place.

The aroma is more than I can take. I peer at the sandwich, then push my mask aside and take a bite right there and before I know it, we've wolfed down half our food and Chase is calling for two more shots.

"No. I can't," I say.

"If you can't drink at the end of the world, when can you?"

"Don't say that."

"Trigger time?"

"All Magnus talked about was the end of the world. Everything we did was to prepare for that. To survive—or not—to the new Earth to come as the rest of the world burned, died, drowned, or whatever, around us. So, yeah, you could say the end of the world triggers me. It makes me want to *walk* all the way to Fort Collins if I have to."

"You probably didn't know what to do with yourself once you got out," Chase says, considering his glass.

"No. I didn't," I say. "I daydreamed about it, lots. What it'd be like to do what I wanted when I wanted. Turns out I didn't know what I wanted. I hate to say this, but right now is the best I've felt in longer than I can remember. It feels *good* having a purpose in this life. In this moment, right now. I feel wrong, admitting that. With Jackie . . . all that's going on."

"Yes, it does feel good," he says quietly, lifting an intense blue gaze. "Thank you, Wynter Roth. You may not believe this, but we have more in common than you think."

I tilt my head, not sure how that could be.

He lifts a broad shoulder. "I didn't know what to do with myself after I decided not to re-up. I took a gig consulting on a movie set. Couldn't stand it. Got into fighting. Got out of fighting. I wasn't going to Cheyenne to just wait this thing out. The idea was to go figure things out. Figure myself out. Get a plan by the time the electricity came back on and the world started up again."

"Thank you, by the way," I say, studying him. He really is handsome. And I don't know whether it's the Fireball or the end of the world, but I don't mind letting my eyes tell him so.

"For what?" he says, his gaze drifting down to my mouth.

"Coming along when you did. And this."

He doesn't answer but reaches over to take my hand. The gesture sends an electric charge up my arm. A good one. So good, in fact, that I think I ought to pull away.

So good that I don't.

"You believe in God?" I hear myself ask.

"Pretty much have to," he says, though he doesn't explain why.

The bartender comes over with the shots. I'm actually disappointed when Chase lets go of my hand to pay him.

"What should we toast to?" he asks, after the bartender leaves.

"Saving the world," I say.

"To saving the world." We clink plastic cups and I shudder down another sip.

"Maybe when this is over . . ." He shrugs, turning his cup on the table. "You should try your hand at ice fishing."

"It could be a while," I say, drinking half the shot and sliding the rest toward him.

I don't say that I won't be around to ask. That I'll have a child to worry about.

"Should we get on with this world saving, then?" Chase says.

I grab the duffle and the food container with the last of my fries.

But I stop cold at the image on the TV.

It's a photo of Jaclyn.

CHAPTER THIRTY

"C hase," I whisper as I move unsteadily toward the bar. Dreading, bracing myself for what I'm about to hear. That she shot up a neonatal unit, rammed a bus full of people off a bridge, started a fire that burned down an entire building full of people—any act of madness so heinous as to warrant national coverage.

Anything other than what the anchor says next.

". . . what controversial religious leader and 'agricultural archaeologist' Magnus Theisen claimed was a promising lead in the ancient roots of the virus causing rapid early-onset dementia. The potentially life-saving research was stolen in a violent break-in at the New Earth lab in Ames that claimed the life of Theisen's wife, Jaclyn. Theisen was found dead yesterday morning in the office where she worked as an administrative . . ."

What?

I stagger back, Chase catching me by the arm as my knees threaten to buckle.

Jackie . . .

An off-site lab in Ames? Magnus claiming the research as his own?

Jackie dead.

No. She can't be. How could she have been found in Ames? She was going east.

I look at Chase, my eyes wild as he comes to stare at the TV.

". . . thought to have been murdered by twenty-two-year-old former organization member Wynter Roth . . ."

I swing my gaze back to the screen.

And find myself staring at a picture of myself.

"Federal authorities are asking that if you have seen this woman, please notify local law enforcement."

I turn away from the bar, checking my mask as Chase takes me by the elbow.

"They're lying," I whisper, unable to catch my breath.

"Go close up those takeout boxes," he murmurs, pulling me behind him.

I walk woodenly to the table and fumble with the boxes, fingers stupid on the Styrofoam tabs.

"Thanks, guys," Chase says, hand raised in a wave as he comes to collect the duffle bag.

"Need one for the road?" the bartender asks.

"Nope, we're all set, thanks."

"Hey," the man at the end of the bar says.

Chase pulls the keys from his pocket, puts them into my hand.

"'Scuse me," the guy says, sliding off his seat. He walks over. "What did you say your name was?"

"Crawford," Chase says, holding out his hand.

"Not you. Her," he says, pointing. Behind him, another man gets up from the bar.

Chase passes me the duffle.

"I wanna see her face!" the man says, pushing toward me.

"Whoa," Chase says, hand against his chest. "I think there's a misunderstanding here."

"Then let's clear it up. Let me see your face, miss."

"Essie," Chase says. "*Go.*"

I shove my way out the front door, skip the icy sidewalk and plow right through the snow, cutting the corner down the side of the building. A shadow skirts from the back door of the bar as I round the bumper, steps camouflaged by the generator's engine. One of the guys from the bar. He grabs me as I lunge for the door. I turn, lash out with a fist full of keys. Drive my shin up into his groin. Bring the hard part of the duffle down on his head. I don't stick around to see whether he gets up but click the fob and yank open the driver's-side door.

I climb in, shoving Buddy out of the way. Start the engine, throw the Jeep into reverse. Back out from behind the bar and shift into drive. Barrel toward the corner as Chase comes running out the front door. "Go!" he shouts, leaping up onto the running board, not even bothering to climb in.

I gun across the intersection and down the residential street. Stop two blocks down, just long enough for him to get in.

And then we're hightailing it out of town.

We drive in tense silence for several miles, Chase pointing me north and then east a mile. North again.

But all I can see is Jaclyn's picture pasted on that screen.

Found dead.

"Wynter."

"I didn't do it. Someone killed her." My vision blurs. "She said she thought someone was following her. Oh, God . . . *Jackie!*" The words spew from my mouth, foul as vomit as I cover my mouth with my arm.

Worse yet, there's no one to corroborate my story. The lights were out in Naperville. No electricity . . . no security cameras. Julie didn't see her; Jaclyn parked blocks away. I didn't even tell Julie why I was leaving. I told her I was going to the Enclave to get Truly—less than twenty minutes from Ames!

"I can't even prove that Jaclyn came to Illinois. And you—you didn't even see me on the interstate until we were west of Ames. You can't even say you saw me east of there, coming from Illinois!"

"I thought you and Jaclyn called Ken?" Chase says, glancing at me.

"Ken's sick. In a few days he won't remember his own name!" I clench the steering wheel, run back through that night again. The time the lights went off shortly after midnight. When Ken called after that. When I saw Julie in the RV—what time was that, 1 a.m.? When Jaclyn showed up maybe twenty minutes later. How long was she there? I fumble for my phone, for the time stamp when I finally called Julie to say I was leaving.

2:13 a.m.

"Wynter, pull over."

"I kept thinking if she had stayed in Ames to hand the samples over they might have killed her . . . Blaine, Magnus's former business partner, died less than two weeks after the handoff in September. They said it was an overdose, but was it? What if they're covering up the whole trail!"

"Wynter, let me drive."

I skid to a stop on the shoulder of a highway. I don't even know which one. Chase reaches over and puts the Jeep into park.

I get out. Walk around the back of the Jeep where Chase meets and takes me by the shoulders.

"I didn't kill my sister! She was sick!"

He pulls me against him, holds me tight.

"I've never even heard of an off-site New Earth lab," I say.

"Whatever's in those samples, somebody wants it really badly. Which means the sooner we get to Colorado and can hightail it back out of there, the better," he says. "Who did your sister think was following her—Magnus's men or the people she was supposed to deliver the samples to?"

"I—I don't know. I thought she was imagining it . . ." Because she was sick. Which means I was going to lose her.

But not like this.

Inside the Jeep, it takes me three tries to click in, Buddy clutched against me, as talons of grief and panic sink into my diaphragm, deeper than before.

Pull it together, Wynter.

Chase turns on the radio, scans the stations past the same tired public advisories to stay home, coverage of the president's address to the nation, the attack on the electric substation, new cities in the Pacific Northwest under formal quarantine . . .

He abruptly turns up the volume.

". . . Theisen found dead in an Ames, Iowa, lab where promising research on rapid early-onset dementia was allegedly stolen by a Wynter Roth . . ."

My heart drops. He scans through several more channels and lands on another station airing the same story, word for word.

I expect Chase to pull over, kick me out at any moment.

"Interesting that they failed to mention you're her sister," he says.

It's true; they haven't.

"So you believe me."

"I'm a pretty good judge of character. I also highly doubt anyone willing to kill for those samples would be desperate to get them to a college of *veterinary medicine* in Colorado. Wouldn't be my first choice, considering that the Russians no doubt pay better. The good news is they can't show your picture on the radio."

We pass by a small pond off the side of the road. All of a sudden, he hits the window button on his side of the car, grabs my phone, and chucks it out of the Jeep.

"What are you doing?" I shout, as I watch it break the icy surface.

"Making sure they can't track you any farther than they have. Who else knows about the Colorado connection?"

"No one." And then—oh, God. How am I supposed to tell Ashley what's happened to Jackie? Or has he already heard it somewhere on the news? What if he's called the police?

No. No. He talked to Jackie and me together. He knew she was with me in Naperville and that she was sick.

"How *did* you find this guy in Colorado?" he asks, glancing at me.

"He's . . . an old friend of Jackie's. What if I go to the police?"

"You'll be taken into custody for an attempted act of bioterrorism in addition to murder. With the grid down, the entire case could take . . . a long time. You could be locked up for years just waiting for a trial."

And then what would happen to Truly?

"No police," I say.

"No police. Right now nobody knows where the samples are—"

"Except a bunch of drunk guys back there."

"Who don't know where we're headed."

"I'm sorry I got you into this," I say quietly. "You need to get away from me. We need to find two new cars. You go to Wyoming, I'll take the—"

"No. Besides, the only gas you've got is now mine."

"Not if you don't get me to the panhandle. That was the deal."

"Are you going to turn me into a kidnapper?" he says, glancing at me.

"Those guys back there know what we're driving. And that farmer, Mr. Ingold, who fed us this morning? He not only knows what we're driving but what you used to do, what we look like—and our first names."

His jaw tightens. "There's no way I'm not seeing you to Fort Collins."

"You're aiding a fugitive!"

"As a Marine, I vowed to served this country, protect American people, and their way of life," he says.

"You're not a Marine anymore."

"Once a Marine, always a Marine. Besides. Remember what we said back there—about having a purpose in this mess?"

"Ruining your life isn't mine."

"Let me see that map," he says, nodding toward the folded mess on the dash.

I sigh, open it up, and, after a few seconds, point to where we are. He glances at it and then around us. The country is eerily quiet.

As much as I'm determined not to drag Chase into this any further than I have to, I'm actually grateful for his presence at this moment.

I'm also grief-stricken. Stunned.

Petrified.

I rub my eyes and then my temples. Try to banish the images of Jackie—bloodied, broken, and pale—from my mind. But I cannot *not* see her laying there, her eyes left open.

For the first time since leaving the Enclave, I miss those concrete walls.

We stop long enough to add some gas from one of the cans and then follow a single set of tire tracks down the two-lane highway till we see blue lights in the distance.

"Get down," he says, turning south. I unhook my seat belt, crouch onto the floor.

"Think that was for us?" I ask, sliding back into my seat a few minutes later.

"Didn't want to ask."

We relegate ourselves to county roads, moving slower than before.

I root around in my bag, take half a tablet from my prescription bottle and swallow it with a sip of water. Wonder vaguely how much of a basket case I'm going to be when the last quarter is gone—or whenever the half-life of this stuff wears off.

Chase turns on the radio. It's filled with reports of gridlocks on outbound highways from all major cities. National parks already experiencing the influx of those escaping the city as those in urban areas host impromptu block parties, grilling entire freezers full of defrosting meat.

And the search for Wynter Roth, last seen in south central Nebraska.

Outside, the landscape has started to change, the flat fields rolling into gentle hills. Shallow canyons rise up on either side of the road and cows wander sluggishly through the snow.

"What happened to the guy who ran out the back of the bar?" Chase asks suddenly.

I give him a blank look.

"The guy who followed you out of the bar?"

A brief flash of running for the Jeep. Slamming the duffle on someone's head.

"I dropped him."

Chase glances across the front seat at me in surprise. "Oorah," he says. His gaze falls to the Styrofoam container in my lap. "All while saving the leftovers."

I open the container that's been torturing Buddy this whole time and feed him the last of my fries.

The paranoid voice in the back of my brain says he could turn me in at any moment—that the one good thing I have going for me can't possibly be true. I go back again to the moment we met at the truck stop, searching, scrubbing my memory for any sign he isn't who he says he is. That he was working in tandem with Redneck Grill Guy. Following me. I go back again and then again, and then wonder if my medication is already wearing off.

A few minutes later, we see police lights again.

"Okay, new plan," he says, abruptly turning north. He drives faster, wheels chewing through snow.

"I didn't know we had an old one! What are you doing?"

He grimaces as though preparing for a blow that's going to hurt. "You're right. We need a different car."

We're just south of Hastings when I point ahead to an old red-and-white pickup abandoned on the side of the road, gas door open. Chase pulls in front of it, gets out, and goes to peer inside the truck.

He returns a few seconds later and opens the back of the Jeep. I put on my mask and get out in time to see him pulling out a length of cord and a screwdriver.

"Locked," he says.

We go back to the truck where he ties a slipknot in the cord. "Can you get your fingers in there?" he asks, nodding to the top of the door. I do, just enough to push the cord in around the seal until we can get it down far enough on either side for it to feel like we're flossing the door like some massive tooth.

"Just get that—yeah," he says, as I twist the cord just enough to get the slipknot over the knob.

We pull on both ends of the cord until the knot tightens on the knob, then yank it up.

Chase gets in, pulls the cover off the steering column. I grab the gas can off the back of the Jeep, fumble with the spout. The truck's ignition fires, or tries to. Chase seems satisfied.

"Okay," he says. And then I'm tipping the can up, standing there for what feels like forever as it trickles into the truck and Chase starts unloading the Jeep. He's murmuring under his breath—no. He's singing. I don't recognize the song, but he has a nice voice. For some reason that surprises me. I look down, pretend not to listen if only because I want to hear more.

How many roads must a man walk down
Before you call him a man?

I glance up at a distant sound: a truck coming down the road. I lower the can. "Chase."

"I see it." He comes around and takes the can. "Get in."

I climb in, pull my mask higher up over my nose just in time to hear Chase curse through the open front door.

"Get down!"

Something isn't right. I hear the erratic chug-and-go tread of tires in the snow.

The truck doesn't even slow—if anything it accelerates—as it approaches. I lift my head as it passes, just in time to watch it plow straight into an electrical pole with a deafening crash.

I get out, frozen. Stare as the pole buckles and then breaks like a matchstick where the front of the truck has wrapped around it, wires snapping.

Chase grabs my arm, yanks me back.

"Someone's still in there!" I say.

"I'll go."

I don't know if he's saying it to spare me or because he's worried they might be conscious enough to recognize me. I pause as he jogs ahead to skid into the ditch beside the cab. Watch as he dons his gloves and then tugs at the door, finally reaching through the broken window. A second later he walks around to look in the back of the truck, climbs up, and roots around in the rusty bed. That tells me all I need to know about the state of the driver. By the time he returns with an old gas can, I've already started loading our gear. But it's the thing in his other hand that has my attention.

A pistol.

He sets the gas can in back and digs in his pocket. "Here," he says, handing me a cell phone and several bills—two of which are hundreds.

"You *robbed* him?" I say.

"Trust me. He doesn't need it anymore," he says, checking the weapon.

As I finish loading the truck, which is running now in an effort to warm it up, Chase goes to work on the license plates of the Jeep, which he removes, along with the decal off the window. It seems wrong, somehow, for him to do that. And I feel guilty, as though I've somehow caused it. But he does it, wordlessly, and I say nothing.

Finally he stands back, hands on his hips, and just looks at the Jeep that he's stripped even of its spare tire. He exhales a long breath as I come to stand beside him. I wait for him to say that he really liked this Jeep. That it cost him his savings or that he worked for years to buy this particular tricked-out off-road model that, frankly, is far better suited to our purposes than the old truck behind us. But instead all he says is "Let's go."

I climb behind the wheel of the truck and follow the Jeep as Chase pulls away. We drive past the crash about a half mile to a copse of trees where Chase parks the Jeep out of sight. A minute later, he's jogging back up to the road. I slide over without a word, if only because I can't drive and duck out of view at the same time.

And then we turn north.

CHAPTER THIRTY-ONE

I crouch down in the front seat as we cross I-80.

"What do you see?" I ask.

"Cars in the ditch, few on the median—five total, more ahead. More traffic than I expected," he murmurs, driving across the overpass. "No cops, at least. Gas station at the exit is empty. Sign says no gas." He lays his hand on the edge of the seat between us, and I clasp his fingers. They curl around mine as we drive another mile.

"All clear," he says, pulling me up. I slide the pistol off the seat to the floor and refasten my seat belt as we emerge onto yet another county road in yet another stretch of Nebraska that's even flatter—if that's possible—than before.

"Listen," he says. "I don't know what your plans are once we get to Colorado and I'm not gonna tell you what to believe. But if anything happens to me and you need to protect yourself or someone else, you're gonna need to make friends with a gun."

It's the "someone else" that makes me look at him and say, "Show me."

He pulls over and I spend the next hour learning how to hold the pistol. Inserting and ejecting the empty magazine. Thumbing the safety. Chambering a round. All things I never thought I'd do until the moment I considered what it might mean to choose between someone else's life and Truly's.

At one point I catch him studying me sidelong.

"What?" I ask, wondering if I did it wrong.

"I was just thinking that fate's a funny thing."

"This isn't fate," I say bitterly.

"Really? I told myself I'd follow the road in front of me. I took a training job. My fighter got injured. I hung out in Columbus trying to figure out what to do until this started happening and I decided to bug out. Buddy of mine deployed overseas said I could go out to his place and wait out the Crazy for as long as I needed. So I packed my gear and headed that way. And then this girl catches me head banging on the interstate . . ."

"Anyone driving by would've seen you."

"Still, the minute I recognized you talking to that crazy down at the truck stop, I knew it had to be a sign."

"That's a coincidence, not a sign from God!"

"How do you know?"

"Because! A sign would look different. Be different." All of this would.

What does he know, anyway? How many nights has he spent in a white cell combing his soul for sin? How many times has he searched the eyes of the closest thing to God on Earth, looking for a sign, any indication of approval, assurance—only to find that God had vacated the premises and something else lived behind those eyes?

He squints in the sun. "You ever hear the story of the guy stranded on his roof during a flood praying for God to save him?"

"What?" I ask irritably.

"Guy's stranded on his roof and when a rowboat, a motorboat, and finally a helicopter come by telling him to get in, he tells them to go because God's going to save him. And then he drowns."

"That's a horrible story."

He holds up a finger. "When he gets to Heaven he asks God, 'Why didn't you save me?' And God says, 'I sent you two boats and a helicopter—what more did you want?' Well, *what more do you want, Wynter?*"

I give him a weird look. "So you're saying you're a *rowboat*?"

"I'm saying you keep thinking like that you're gonna drown."

When I don't answer, he shrugs. "Anyway, it's my sign. A private message from God to me. It's not supposed to make sense to you. It's code."

Such a thought would have been considered anathema in the Enclave. But I find myself wondering about what he's just said . . .

And feeling strangely envious.

"Meanwhile, it just occurred to me that if this disease started with pigs, there's a whole other application for what's in that carrier than saving people or making them sick."

I feel my eyes widen. It's an implication I wouldn't have thought of. "You mean farm animals. The meat industry."

He nods. "It wouldn't be hard to infect entire herds of commercial animals in one country just to drive up the value of meat in another. It's market sabotage. And not to be all conspiracy theorist-y, but I wouldn't put it beyond . . . well, a lot of countries. And while I know you won't understand this, I have an emotional relationship with bacon."

"Okay then," I say. "Save the bacon, save the world."

He nods. "Doing it for the bacon."

By the time we get back on the road there's a statewide search for my sister's killer.

For me.

Watching Chase squint at the gas gauge on the dash, I realize we may have a more immediate problem.

"How much of that tank did you put in here?" he asks.

"All of it." I lean over to peer at the gauge, wavering just above E. "That can't be right."

He pulls over and we get out. I crouch down as Chase crawls under the front of the truck. And then he's digging for his pocket-knife.

"Fuel line's rotten," he says and then curses.

"What now?"

He slides out and gets to his feet. "We either get a new hose or find a new vehicle."

"Okay. We do a gallon at a time till we find something else." I grab the other can.

We go as far as we can—which turns out to be about ten miles—before we have to stop and refuel again. Of course now, when we need a new car, there's nothing to be found on these back country roads.

We turn south, get back onto I-80. By now the traffic has picked back up, steady but cautious.

We finally spot an old Ford Bronco on the side of the highway and pull over behind it. Chase gets out to peer inside the window and then opens the door—it isn't even locked. A few minutes later, I'm following him to the next exit where we unload the truck and reload the Bronco. The inside smells like sweat and BO. There's a cup of some dark substance that definitely isn't coffee in the console that Buddy finds fascinating. Chase chucks it out the window as we turn northwest.

Meanwhile, we're down to our last four gallons.

"What we need," Chase says, craning his head as we pass an old, sagging barn, "is a farmer. One with a big enough operation to sell us some gas."

We peer down county roads at cross sections, scan the horizon for silos, grain trucks, farm signs. Just south of Tryon, we pass a sign for Foster Farms, spot a cluster of silos up a gravel road a hundred yards from three large Quonset buildings. I pull my mask up, tug down my stupid ski hat.

"Maybe I'd better wait by the windbreak," I say, pointing to a line of trees.

Chase shakes his head. "A couple is a lot less intimidating than a man my age traveling alone." He turns up the drive and parks a short distance from the main house. Hands me the pistol. "Anything goes wrong, you hightail it out of here."

Buddy whines from the back as Chase gets out, grabs the empty gas can, and heads toward the house where a figure is already moving behind the transom window.

A minute later, he and another man with a mask over his mouth head out from the house and off between a couple sheds. I slide behind the wheel and glance at the clock, laying the pistol on the seat beside me.

For the first time since I left the Enclave, I wonder what Magnus is doing right now, this very minute. Knowing, as he must, that the samples are in my possession. I imagine that smolder snuffed from his eyes as he paces his office, hand passing over the whiskers on his face.

I hope he's afraid. I want him to be—as afraid as anyone terrorized by fear. Of death, of retribution for some real or imagined sin.
Of being forsaken, or worse, forgotten by the God whose voice he
claimed to hear.

But I also know Magnus. Which is how I know he isn't afraid.
Not of God, or of losing the samples, or being tied to them.

And definitely not of me.

Not while he has Truly.

It occurs to me then that he knows. Not that someone else is
Truly's father—I fear for her life if that day ever comes—but that I
will come for her. And that he will continue to exercise power over
me, no matter where I may go, because he still has her.

And so that glint hardening his eyes as he paces in his office isn't
fear at all, but anticipation as he waits.

I've made two promises since the lights went out: one to Jaclyn
and one to myself.

I'm coming for you.

Chase comes jogging down the drive, gas can in hand. I turn on
the truck, put it in gear. Thirty seconds later, we're speeding down
the road.

THE EARTH HAS sprouted ridges and undulating hills that turn
into shallow canyons. We stop to buy gas from two more ranch-
ers. One of them sells us a couple gallons. The second just points
his shotgun at Chase, who lifts his hands and climbs back into
the car.

Chase is back in the driver's seat, and I've been glued to the
map for the last fifteen minutes. We've just skirted the sandy south
shore of Lake McConaughy, a place that looks more like an expanse

of wintry beach than something in horse and cattle land. It reminds
me of our trip to Indiana Dunes, which seems like a year ago.
Meanwhile, it's threatening twilight and we still haven't made it to
Colorado.

"We're thirty miles north of the border," I say. Never mind that
every highway and interstate in the area seems to converge just
south of us near Julesburg.

I measure the mile ruler with my finger. "Twenty more miles
west and we can drop straight south." I flip to the Colorado map. "If
we stay north of 76, we go into Fort Collins from there."

He shakes his head. "We need fuel."

I don't have to look to know. The light's been on for miles.

"How much do we have left?"

"Not much."

We travel five more miles through rolling wasteland until we
come to a drive with two posts on either side, an overhang across the
top: Sandhills Cattle Co.

Chase dons a seed cap from the back, palms the pistol, slides it
down near the front of his seat.

"Anything goes wrong, you know what to do," he says.

I nod.

We're met outside the main building by two men in surgical
masks carrying shotguns. They look like medical outlaws. A black
pickup is parked to the side, a series of pens beyond it. Cattle gather
at long troughs in the middle, seemingly impervious to the cold.
Buddy is frantic, alternating sniffing and barking in the direction of
the cows.

Chase pulls up his mask, rolls down his window.

"Howdy," the taller of the two says.

I smirk beneath my mask. *Howdy?*

"You folks lost?" one of the men asks, coming to peer inside the truck. Buddy swings around like a weathervane, barking straight at him.

"No, sir," Chase says, nudging Buddy back. "Just wondering if we could buy a few gallons of gas."

There's a muffled sound coming from an outbuilding adjacent to the main one. Chase cranes his head as a third man comes to stand outside the building. The first man steps in front of him, cutting off his line of sight.

"You got cash?"

"We do," he says. The sound grows louder. Someone's shouting. Chase cranes his head. "You boys having some trouble? Need any help?"

"One of the hands got sick, turned violent." He shakes his head. "Had to pen him in. Sad deal. Where you folks from?"

"Oklahoma," Chase says. "We were up visiting some relatives when the blackout hit. They were kind enough to loan us a vehicle."

"Surprised you didn't head back south," the man says. But his eyes are on me. Buddy won't stop barking. I pull him against my chest, his little body straining in my arms.

"Thought we'd head west. No point going back to the city."

"Well, you pry got that right. Though you'd best be careful."

"Why's that?"

"There's checkpoints all along 76 into Julesburg. Some fugitive they're after. Few dangerous crazies, too."

I fix my gaze on Buddy, heart thumping in my chest.

Everything inside me says we need to turn around, get out of here. But the Bronco's running on fumes.

"Thanks for the heads-up," Chase says. "We'll keep our eyes out."

"You do that."

"So about that gas," Chase says.

The man comes to lean on the driver's-side door, gaze roving over the interior of the truck. He glances in the back. "Sure. Why not. If you wanna come with me, we'll get you taken care of."

"Thank you," Chase says. "Appreciate it."

Chase pulls off to the side and parks, but leaves the engine running. After going around back for the gas can he stops by the open window. "Back in a minute, hon," he says. But he flicks his eyes toward the road, and I know he's telling me to go.

As the three of them move up the hill, the taller man whistles to the one stationed at the side building where the banging has gotten louder, shouts sounding like a series of barks. The man bangs on the steel siding, yelling a string of obscenities, and I lower Buddy to the floor. Climb across the console to the driver's seat as Buddy springs back up to the passenger seat. The bark issues again, muffled through corrugated steel. No, not a bark, but a word, repeated over and over: *Help.*

Movement from the corner of my eye. The man's crossed the drive and is closing the distance between us, shotgun over his shoulder. I drop my hand down, search for the pistol, unable to reach the grip.

"Sorry 'bout that," he says, coming to lean against the door. He's got a piece of jerky sticking out of his mouth. His eyes are yellow where they should be white, his skin furrowed and leathery. He reeks of booze and dried meat. "We had some trouble with a local. People see a big operation like ours and, well, they get greedy. Been waitin' on the sheriff but you know how it's been, with that manhunt—woman hunt, I guess you could call it—and all." He shrugs.

I glance toward the building, positive now I heard that shout right. Buddy, meanwhile, is going nuts, growling and barking at the man, who just grins and tosses the rest of the jerky onto the passenger-side floor. Buddy leaps down, on it like a bad rash.

"You with him?" He juts his chin in the direction Chase disappeared a minute ago.

"No," I murmur, searching for any sign of him. "He's with me."

He leans against my door, looks me up and down with a grin. "You're feisty."

"If you'll excuse me, I think I'll go see what's taking so long."

"Sorry," he says, shaking his head. "I need to ask you to stay here. Policy."

Just then a shot rings out beyond the line of trees. My head jerks in the direction of the sound and I grab the gearshift.

"Uh-uh," the man says, sliding the barrel of his shotgun casually over the sill. "Hands on the dash, Beautiful."

Something inside me breaks. I throw my forearm under the barrel, send it flying upward. A shot punches through the roof, deafening my ears as I dive for the pistol.

I come up shouting, pistol raised, unable to hear myself through the ringing in my head. He pumps the shotgun and then glances down at it. Lifts his gaze to me.

It's the look of a man who's just made a horrible realization.

I release my thumb from the safety. Reach for the gearshift instead.

The shotgun clatters to his feet as he charges the driver's-side door in a rage. I slam him across the forehead with the pistol grip, throw the car into gear, spit gravel up the drive.

Just beyond the trees I see them—Chase and one of the men, brawling in the dirt as the second man gimps toward the house. I lie on the horn, closing the distance between us. Floor the gas as Chase rolls away, the Bronco bucking over the second man with a jolt as I speed down the other side of the hill. Skidding to a halt before I crash into a pen, I wrench around, spot Chase running toward us, two shotguns in hand. Buddy's barking again, the sound dull, like a hammer through water, the ringing in my ears drowning out all else.

Chase is saying something but I can't make out the words. I gesture to my ear and shake my head. His head snaps up at something I cannot hear. In a single motion he grabs the pistol from my lap and aims it toward the trees. A moment later, he lowers it and then I see why: the black truck is speeding down the road.

When we return to the fuel tank, the guy I ran over is nowhere to be seen.

We start the generator. While the Bronco's fueling, Chase comes to examine my ear and neck.

He lets me go to study the pump, looking from the gauge to the generator. I see rather than hear him curse.

"What is it?"

I can't make out what he's saying, but I understand when he hangs up the pump and caps the Bronco's gas tank.

The ranch tank is empty.

"There's someone in the building shouting for help," I say, not sure how loud I'm talking. We drive back to the side building and Chase reaches for his shotgun.

He gestures with two fingers toward his eyes. I nod and follow him out.

The handles to the outbuilding have been zip tied together. Chase snicks them with his knife and yanks open one side, slips into the darkness as I watch the yard for movement.

He reemerges a few seconds later with an old rancher in a dirty coat with a felt cowboy hat on his head. I don't hear every word though I'm catching more of them than before, can tell that he's thanking us, saying something about his ranch hands and his wife being gone. He looks worried, worn, and surprisingly frail. Chase informs him that he's out of gas—that we took a few gallons, all that was left. The rancher, whose voice is fainter than Chase's, waves it off.

He asks us to come inside but Chase says that we can't stay. He makes us wait as he goes to another building and returns with a plastic bag with two frozen roasts.

"There was more," I think he says, "but those fellas took it."

"Sir, you don't need to—" Chase says.

But the rancher insists and walks us to the car where we thank him and take turns shaking his hand. When I do, I get close enough to see that he isn't just ruddy cheeked as I first thought.

He's feverish.

Those guys might have robbed the rancher, but they weren't lying about the sick part. And I wonder if we did the right thing setting him free.

WE PULL OUR gloves inside out, throw them into a plastic bag. I dig alcohol wipes from the emergency kit and we wipe off our hands, the door handles, steering wheel. I can't help thinking of that rancher, so gently confused. Even as we left, he turned and looked around as though he wasn't sure which building was the house.

"Wanna tell me how we got this hole in the roof?" Chase asks loudly. He's back behind the wheel and though my ears are still ringing, I can hear the air whistling overhead.

"Not really."

"What happened to 'If this goes sideways hightail it out of here'?" Chase says. He sounds angry. "Did you not see me tell you to go?"

"I tried. It didn't work."

"Wynter, there is no 'didn't work.' I tell you to bug out, you bug out."

"You're welcome."

"For what?"

"For coming back for you."

"I don't need you to rescue me! Your mission is to get to Fort Collins, whatever it takes."

"I don't take orders from you. And this was my 'mission' before it was yours."

Meanwhile, the needle on the gas gauge has barely lifted off the red.

"How far will that get us?"

He shakes his head. "Twenty miles if we're lucky. Probably closer to fifteen."

I grab the map, estimate the distance to Fort Collins. We've got at least two hundred miles to go, and that's if we drop down straight into Colorado on the highway. Which, with the roadblocks, is no longer an option.

I think about Kestral's email. The one I told Julie about in case she needed a safe place to go.

"Keep west," I say. "We need to get to Sidney."

CHAPTER THIRTY-TWO

It's twilight, the sky the color of faded denim, the snowy ground reflecting the anemic sunset.

I wonder if Ashley's given up on my arrival. If he's heard the news about Jackie.

If there's a cadre of police waiting on campus for me now.

I find my bottle of pills and take the half and quarter left over from last night.

Three left.

"You okay?" Chase says, glancing at me.

"Chase, what happened to the guy I ran over?"

"I'm pretty sure if he was dead, they would've left without him."

It used to be one of my fears when I first started driving: that I had run over someone and didn't know it. I'd even doubled back down streets just to be sure. It got better when I went on meds and Dr. Reiker said it was actually a common obsession for people with

OCD, but I still thought about it sometimes. And now here I'd done it on purpose.

I try not to remember the way the Bronco bumped over the man, throwing Buddy and the suitcase briefly up off the seat. But then I only remember it in more vivid detail.

"You're not a bad person," Chase says when I tell him about it. "You're trying to do something to help people and he was trying to stop you. Not that he knew that. In his mind . . . I don't even want to guess what he was thinking."

I don't either.

Headlights in the side-view mirror. I glance back at the black truck behind us and punch the dome light off.

"Is it them?" I ask.

Chase flicks a glance at the rearview mirror. "Think so. It's the same truck." He accelerates through snow that melted earlier in the day but is swiftly starting to crunch once more beneath our tires.

The truck's gaining, those twin beams coming closer. We speed faster, fishtail once, worn tires spinning through the snow. The sign ahead says the county road we're on is about to turn to gravel. Chase slows just enough to turn a sharp right north. I grab the overhead handle, sure we're going to end up pitched, headlong, into a canyon. When we don't, he accelerates—not fast enough. The truck taps our bumper.

Chase reaches for his shotgun. I grab the wheel as he rolls down his window. Unhooking his seat belt, he turns to fire. The head-lights swerve, drop back. We speed up, the old Bronco laboring on the snowy gravel road. Canyons slope away from the left shoulder, which is hemmed in by only a guardrail.

"There's supposed to be a highway coming up that heads straight north," I say, squinting in the darkness. "There—turn there!"

Chase grabs the wheel and floors it. Shouts, "Get down!" and then slows as much as he dares into the turn. I scream, hunched over the dog, sure the truck is going to bash right into us. Chase leans low and fires again. A second later our back left window shatters.

We barrel down the road, the truck creeping toward our back fender again, its front windshield a sinister spiderweb.

Chase slings his seat belt over his chest. I grab it and click it into place.

He taps the brake hard enough to let the truck surge ahead— and then turns our bumper into the truck's rear tire. I scream as the truck spins to the right directly in front of us and then rolls into the ditch with successive crashes even I can hear.

I swivel around, stare at the upturned truck through the back windshield.

"Anyone getting out?"

"Not that I can see."

Buddy trembles in my arms. Or maybe that's me.

We drive a mile in silence.

"How far off do you think we are?" Chase says, glancing at the gas gauge. The light's on again.

"Maybe ten miles."

At last we pull onto the highway, turn the Bronco north. We're the only car in sight.

We have to search longer for a radio station. When we finally find one, there's no more music; it's all news. Overcrowded hospitals, makeshift wards. American travelers quarantined in Hong Kong, Canada, Australia.

And in local news, a reward being offered for information leading to my arrest or that of the man with me.

Last seen traveling in a black Jeep.

We drive in tense silence, our gazes flicking between the gas light and the speedometer as the needle flutters downward. A few seconds later the engine shuts down and we coast toward the side of the road as the Bronco dies.

CHAPTER THIRTY-THREE

The stars are out, strewn against a black ice sky, and it feels as though the temperature has dropped twenty degrees since the sun set. I pull the hood of my coat down over my stupid pom-pom hat, the duffle bag bumping against my thigh with every step.

"You good?" Chase asks. He's carrying the food and as much gear as we could make fit into his backpack, including water and the six pounds of meat the rancher gave us—one of the best bargaining gifts we have. The rest we had no choice but to lock in the Bronco. Buddy, who walked the first half mile on a makeshift leash, peeks out from an equally makeshift sling fashioned out of Julie's sofa blanket around Chase's torso. It makes him look like some village woman carrying her baby and despite every horror of the last forty-eight hours—and who knows, maybe I'm finally losing it—every time I look at him, I can't help a small laugh.

"Go ahead, laugh," he says. "But there's a reason he likes me best."

We've been walking for nearly an hour and a half—an hour since he stopped at the first farmhouse we came to to ask for gas and then, when that was refused, for directions to the Peterson place while I hid in the trees. The farmer there directed him north, saying it was west of Gurly, about eight miles as the crow flies. Which I figure means we have maybe four more miles to go. We've already cut across two square-mile sections, eating protein bars as we go.

Adrenaline has left me; each step feels like my feet have frozen into blocks of ice.

"You sure about this?" he asks for the third time.

I had to convince him to take a chance on the mysterious Mr. Peterson—who has to have heard about me on the news by now, assuming he has a working radio. Which I assume everyone out here does.

"Yes," I say, as much for myself as for him. Because I'm banking on Kestral, that she'll vouch not just for me but for Magnus's sociopathic character and the lengths he'll go to get his way.

I stumble over cornstalk stubble, the rows the best indicator of our direction since the moon drifted behind a bank of clouds as we trudge staunchly northwest, scanning the horizon for any hint of light.

"You never said why you left," Chase says.

"Left what?"

"New Earth. From what I saw just briefly on your phone, it doesn't seem like many people leave."

"No. They don't."

"So why did you?"

"Because of Magnus."

He glances at me sidelong.

"He had a 'revelation' that he should take another wife."

"You."

"Yup."

"Ah, straight out of the David Koresh handbook."

I know who David Koresh is only from all the reading I've recently done on cults.

"Wait." He stops and looks at me strangely. "Are you . . . *married*? Not that it would be legal. I mean, if you are, you aren't. Unless he divorced your sister to legally marry you. Then . . ."

"No." I keep walking and he catches up in three strides.

"So what happened to the 'revelation'?"

I blow out a breath. "I got caught trying to escape. With my niece, Truly. The siren woke everyone up, they all saw it, and Magnus had no choice but to cast me out on our wedding day." I shrug.

"Wow," Chase says. And then: "Wow. So you planned all that?"

"No," I say quietly. "Jackie did. She set me up to get me out. Because she knew there was no way we'd be able to escape together. So she saved me instead."

"How old's your niece?"

"Five."

He's quiet a moment before he says, "You're going back for her, aren't you?"

I don't answer. He stops. I do, too.

I turn around. "She's all I've got left, Chase."

"You ever consider she's safer where she is?"

I shake my head. "Jackie isn't the only one who worked the center in Ames. Magnus himself leaves the compound regularly with his driver and God only knows how many places he goes. Chase, everyone in the Enclave lives in *community*. Sleeping fifteen, twenty to a barrow. Gathering every morning for service. Sitting at communal tables three times a day! One person. That's all it would take. One sick person. The disease would tear through there like fire!"

He studies me in the darkness and then nods, just perceptibly.

"I take it the locals know about the place."

"Of course." It's no secret that the Enclave has food, water, and room for more. "The Enclave has guards, but not enough to hold off a mob," I add, because I know what he's asking. And I've thought about that, too.

"How do you plan to get in?" he asks as we trudge forward again.

"I don't know."

It's something I've been thinking about in stolen moments and have yet to figure out.

Along with how and where we'll live.

The one thing I have going for me, assuming I do get Truly out, is the fact that the grid's down and might be for a long time. If that's true and the projections about the virus are right, by the time the lights come back on, tons of people will be unaccounted for.

Including Truly and me.

Not that I think it'll make living the life of a fugitive easier. I hadn't exactly planned on that part.

I hadn't planned any of this.

"Then I guess I'm going with you," Chase says.

I glance at him, surprised. "Truly isn't your problem."

"You know, the thing no one tells you about saving the world is that there's such a letdown afterward. I'm gonna need something to do."

"What happened to ice fishing?" I ask between labored breaths.

"Wynter. It's common knowledge that one should never ice fish after saving the world."

"See, no one tells me anything."

"Besides. The fish aren't going anywhere."

And as much as I want to tell Chase he's already done enough, when it comes to Truly, I'll never be too proud or stupid to turn away help.

I glance down at the feet I can't even feel anymore that somehow continue to step out in front of me.

"So you're saying you're a rowboat." I give him a small smile.

"I'm a helicopter, baby." He grins.

I give a soft laugh. "Just think, you could've been sitting in front of a fireplace in Wyoming right now."

"Bored out of my mind."

"Oh, you'd be helping some little old lady fix her roof or something."

"Nope, not me."

"Yeah, you would. Because you're good."

"I'm glad you think so," he murmurs. I cock my head at his tone.

The clouds drift overhead, the half-moon peeking out enough that I can pick my way through the rows without stabbing the soles of my shoes.

"Look," Chase says, pointing to something on the horizon.

A thin waft of smoke, as though from a fire.

Or a chimney.

We make our way to the northern edge of the section and west, to the intersection. I sag when I realize the smoke is still a way off. We stop just long enough to sip water that tastes about as cold as my fingers feel, despite the purported thermal lining of the ski gloves, and we trudge on—another mile, two.

We're just turning north when a set of headlights comes rolling down the road with a crunch of gravel. A pickup. But at least it's not black. Whoever it is, they're not in any hurry, have no particular destination despite the fact that fuel is scarce. It reminds me of something, that slow pace of someone surveying the area at night.

No. Patrolling.

We walk steadily as it comes toward us, squinting against the headlights. There's no point in running; we've already been spotted. Chase steps between me and the truck as it rolls to a stop alongside us.

By the glow of the dashboard I see the driver pull a mask up over his nose and mouth. The window drops down and a man in a cowboy hat I guess to be in his fifties leans out as a second man studies us from the passenger seat.

"You folks need help?"

"We're looking for a man named Peterson," Chase says.

"You got business with him?" the man asks, looking from Chase to me.

"Only if you know him," Chase says.

"We're part of the outfit," he says.

"I'm friends with Kestral," I say and realize I don't even know her last name now.

The man seems to frown. "Don't know a Kestral," he says.

I blink. "But she's the one who told me to come here!" Was it possible she'd only heard about the place but not stayed there personally? Or was she staying under a new, assumed name? I try to remember her alias in the article, but shock and exhaustion have done their job in effectively shutting down the nonessential functions of my brain.

"Were you driving a Bronco?"

"Yes, sir," Chase says. "We ran out of gas."

"You two wouldn't be responsible for a black truck in the ditch few miles southeast of here, would you?"

I flick a glance at Chase, can feel him weighing out his answer.

"I hope they weren't friends of yours," Chase says.

"They weren't anybody's friend. Came down from South Dakota and been causing trouble round here since the electricity went off. Either of you sick?"

"No, sir," Chase says.

"Armed?"

"Yes, sir," Chase says.

"If you'll surrender your weapons, we'll take you with us."

"Where?" I ask as Chase tenses beside me.

"To meet Mr. Peterson. But most of us call him Noah."

CHAPTER THIRTY-FOUR

The man who introduces himself as "Mel" pats Chase down, removes his pistol and pocketknife. "You'll get these back when you leave," he says, handing them to the second man.

When Mel pats me down, he asks if there are any more weapons.

"There's a second pistol in the duffle," I say, nodding to the bag on the ground. Chase looks away, unhappy. But I'm banking on this being the safe place Kestral claimed and need to prove I'm nothing like the person wanted on the radio.

Mel moves over, unzips the bag, and pulls the pistol out.

"Thank you for your honesty," he says. "Especially given that you two are all over the news."

My skin goes hot and then cold. And I wonder again what I've done in bringing us here.

They lock the guns in a box next to our bags in back. And I don't need to look at Chase to know that he's on razor's edge by now.

We drive less than a mile to an acreage ringed in with a metal fence maybe nine feet tall. It's lit at intervals by high, wan lights, which I assume to be solar. The gate opens as Mel presses a button on his visor flap. The man with him has already radioed ahead that they're bringing in visitors.

The sight of that fence has a strange effect on me. I note the barbed wire, the trees strategically planted around the perimeter to block both wind and prying eyes. The cluster of buildings hulking in the shadows, including what looks like a shed, a weathered barn, and the requisite Quonset building . . .

The headlights of a parked truck at the far corner of the section.

I know guards when I see them. And I wonder if the similarities drew Kestral to this place or were an aversion to overcome. If she'll be there to greet us . . . if she was ever here at all.

The plume of smoke we saw earlier rises from a ranch-style home. The windows looking out over the long front porch glow the color of an orange harvest moon.

As we roll up the drive, a figure emerges from the front door: dark-skinned, mug in his hand. He's wearing a high-collared sweater like I imagine a professor would. And though he isn't wearing a mask, he's donned a pair of blue latex gloves.

"Don't worry about your bags," Mel says. "I'll get 'em." We insist we're capable of carrying them, but the last thing we can afford is conflict or to appear overly concerned with the duffle as he waves us on.

"Welcome!" Noah says, as we make our way up the wooden steps to the porch. His short, gray hair curls against his scalp and I guess him to be in his sixties. His smile is warm. Something's cooking inside, the smell of it wafts through the half-open door. My stomach responds with a lurch and Buddy struggles to get free of his sling, sniffing at the air.

"Thank you," Chase says, offering his hand with his name.

"Chase, nice to meet you." Noah nods and turns to me. "And you must be . . . Wynter."

"Yes," I say. Because I'm a terrible liar.

"I wondered if we might expect you. It seems you're quite the person of interest these days."

Before I can form some kind of response—excuse or desperate plea—he turns to Buddy. "And who's this?" Noah asks, cupping the dog's head. Buddy responds by licking Noah's latex-clad palm. "Come, little friend. Bring your humans inside."

He leads us into an expansive living room with exposed wooden beams where he takes our coats and hangs them on a rack near the wide arch into the kitchen.

"Dinner isn't quite ready," Noah says. "But that will give us time to chat. I'm very curious about the turn of events that has led you to our doorstep." Turning to Chase, he says, "Go ahead and let the dog down. He wants to find the cat food in the mudroom."

A wood fire is crackling in the fireplace and the warmth burns my frozen cheeks, which are already heating from the panic of wondering if I've made a terrible mistake in throwing us at the mercy of a stranger.

Particularly one with patrols and a barbed-wire fence.

A door claps against its frame somewhere in the back. A few seconds later, a blond figure appears in the doorway.

"Wynter!"

She flies toward me, arms outstretched, and grabs me in a tight hug. I wrap my arms around her, flooded with relief and unexpected emotion.

"Oh, you have no idea how good it is to see you," she breathes. She smells like shampoo, rainwater, and the burning wood that emanates throughout the entire house. My fingers pin-tingle inside my gloves as I hold on to her for dear life, my cheek numb against her hair.

"They said they didn't know you," I say, bewildered.

"They don't know me by that name here. It's Celeste now. Oh, Wynter. We heard about Jackie. Is it true?"

"No!" I say, pulling away. "You *know* me. You know *him*! You have to know it's a lie!"

"Wynter. Of course I know," she says more gently, her eyes filled with a sadness I've never seen in them before. "What I meant was, is it true that Jackie's dead?"

I stare at her and she blurs before me. My cheek's wet and I don't remember when those tears fell.

"I don't know." And by saying it, I actually dare to hope that it's not. Until I remember that the story's everywhere. That there must be a body. And that even if it isn't hers, I do not expect I will see her alive again.

I swallow and turn away as Kestral—Celeste—introduces herself to Chase. I hear her say that she's known me since I was a girl "just this high" as I take in the overstuffed chairs and long leather sofa. The lantern on the coffee table that is the sole source of illumination other than the fireplace.

Nothing about this place is what I thought it would be even five minutes ago.

I expected wariness. Tension. An interrogation, even, to judge the extent to which we could be trusted. Whether they would help us at all.

I'd also expected others. Had assumed, when Kestral mentioned a "safe place," that it was some kind of halfway house or shelter. But from what I can tell, this is a simple farmhouse where Kestral and Noah live alone.

Which doesn't explain Mel and the other man, who have since disappeared with our bags, or the patrol at the end of the section.

"Beautiful place you have," Chase says as Noah returns with a tray of mugs.

"Thank you," he says, setting it down by the fireplace. "I acquired it twenty-five years ago from a man named Walt Peterson."

"Any relation?"

"None. My given name was Thurley. When I came back from Vietnam in 'sixty-nine, I didn't have much. Through a series of events I ended up stuck for a while here in Nebraska—only black man for miles around. Walt Peterson, who owned this place, hired me on to help with the harvest. Been here ever since, and after a while folks just started calling me 'Peterson,' too."

"Welcome home, sir," I say.

"Thank you," he says. "And tonight we have a reunion, it seems."

"I told Noah as soon as I heard from you," Kestral says. "I was so happy." She turns to Chase. "I don't know if you can understand, but we were like family."

"I might understand something like that," Chase says quietly.

"Wynter and Jackie were like my children. Wynter, I can't believe how much you look like your mother. Sylvia was a beauty. When she died . . ." Her voice catches as her eyes lift to me. "I felt responsible for so much after I left New Earth. The way I encouraged you to stay. The people I unknowingly defrauded of their belongings, their futures, their lives . . ."

I stare at her, my expression stark. Not prepared to hear this.

"You didn't know," I say, almost brusquely.

"No. But because of me, people gave up their livelihoods, signed everything they owned over to Magnus. Because of me, your mother . . ." Her lips tremble.

I look away.

"Your mother's cancer," she says, starting to cry. "If she had been allowed treatment—if she hadn't refused it because of what *we* told her was right—she might be alive today! Wynter, I am *so sorry!*"

I came here prepared to defend myself. Now all I want to defend myself from is the onslaught of emotions at the regret in her voice. At the memory of losing Mom all over again and the years of guilt that I failed to keep her alive. Especially now, in the wake of Jackie's death.

"I feel so responsible for everything that's happened to you and so many others. Forgive me. Forgive me," she says, weeping. I reach for her and in an instant, she's sobbing in my arms.

"There's nothing to forgive," I whisper. Because to point one finger would require another, pointed at my mother. And my father. And my selfish desire to replace him. And whatever need of Jackie's that made her want to stay.

I thought I blamed only one person: Magnus himself. But we were the ones who helped create him.

I look up to find Noah quietly pouring coffee from an old-fashioned metal pot retrieved from the fireplace coals, an oven mitt on his hand. Chase stands across the room gazing out at the back-yard, where solar path lights glow yellow wells in the snow.

I'm aware of the clock ticking on the mantel. That another day has passed since I expected to arrive in Fort Collins with the samples that could prove to be either shield or weapon.

"Where are our bags?" I ask, looking at Noah, arm still around a sniffling Kestral.

"In the guesthouse," he says, offering me a mug. I see Chase glance at me.

"But you know I'm wanted for murder and theft."

"I know enough of Magnus's character to doubt the veracity of his claim," Noah says quietly.

"Thank you," I say, taking the coffee. "But we have to get to Colorado. And while we appreciate the hospitality, what we really need is fuel."

"I doubt Colorado will be far enough to relieve your woes," Noah says, rising. "Or that you'll make it past the roadblocks."

"We're not trying to get away," I say. "We're trying to make something right."

Noah sits in one of the chairs and quietly sets his mug aside. "I have only two rules on my property. The first is safety, which means we'll retain your firearms and any weapons until you leave."

"And the second?" Chase says uneasily.

"Honesty. You're welcome to take refuge here. And you can leave anytime you like. But if you want my help, I need to know how you came to be here."

"What did he do to you, Wynter?" Kestral whispers.

I take the coffee and, with a glance at Chase, sit down on the edge of the sofa. "You might want to check on dinner first," I say. "To make sure it doesn't burn."

NOAH LISTENS IN silence as Chase paces near the window.

But it's Kestral I'm worried about. The shock of learning about Magnus's pursuit of serial wives. His willingness to flaunt his own vices. His increasingly shady deals and willingness to put Jaclyn in the danger that led to her death.

Kestral has her own stories to tell—about ancient seeds illegally acquired from archaeological dig sites, reengineered when they wouldn't germinate, and sold as genuine articles. That she knew he had ruined Blaine Owen's career, but that Blaine continued to broker deals for whatever Magnus would pay him, selling his dignity to fuel his drug habit.

At my request, Mel brings in the duffle. I show them the samples, the web pages and notes on the flash drive, hooked up to Chase's phone.

When I finally finish, Noah, silent all this time, stands at last. "How long have you two been on the road?" he asks, looking at me.

"Since the blackout," I say.

"I suggest we get some dinner in you, let you rest a little. We can talk about your fuel situation in the morning."

"Sir," Chase says. "We really need to get on the road. We can't possibly—"

"Son," Noah says, "You won't make it past those roadblocks without help. You might as well clean up for dinner." He picks up a walkie-talkie, and a minute later Mel shows up in the kitchen to escort us.

"Let the dog stay and chase the cat, if he can find her," Noah says. "Dinner will be ready when you are."

"You'll want your coats," Mel says to my surprise. I don't understand until we follow him—not to the end of the house, as I expected, or even to the basement, but out the back door past a set of cat dishes Buddy is obsessively licking clean.

"Noah's known for . . . certain eccentricities," Mel explains, leading us across the yard.

"Where are we going?" Chase says, moving in front of me. It's the same question I have because by all appearances the older man is leading us toward the shed.

Mel stops. "You're safe here. I know this may not look like

much, but . . . please come with me." He moves ahead and opens the shed door. Light spills out onto the dark earth the moment he does, from a set of overhead lights. The far wall is stocked with shelves of white plastic buckets, the adjacent one with tubs marked "dental hygiene," "soap," "linens," "towels," "unguents," and others.

I don't even know what an unguent is.

"All solar," Mel says, gesturing to the bank of lights as he goes to a door leading to a side room. When he opens it and flicks on another switch, however, I realize it doesn't go to a room at all but to a set of illuminated plywood stairs.

"Where—where does this go?" I ask, not understanding.

Chase looks nervously behind us.

"Follow me," Mel says, and heads down the stairs, the heels of his boots thumping with each step.

The end of the stairwell leads to a long hallway with motion-sensor lights, a sliding door on each side. I think I see another pair farther on. "You're the only guests at the moment," he says, gesturing to the first door. "Please."

With a glance at him, I move toward the first door and carefully pull it open. The motion must have set off a sensor, because the inside flickers to life. I catch my breath.

It's a rectangular room as long as a hallway, complete with a sitting area of mismatched chairs, a double bed with a thick comforter on it, and an antique-looking dresser. There's a small sink along the back wall—as well as a pocket door to what I assume is a closet or restroom. The floor has been laid with wood laminate flooring and a sprawling rug, the corrugated wall covered in mismatched art and a long set of bookshelves, but I know what this is . . .

"This is a shipping container," Chase says, with no small amount of wonder.

"Yes," Mel says.

And remarkably, it's warm.

Well, warmer than it is outside, at least.

"This heater runs off a lithium pack charged by solar panel," Mel says, showing us how to adjust it.

"How many are down here?"

"Six," Mel says. "Three on each side. The last two are double-wide, for larger families. So technically it's eight. Any more and we'd need a longer hall."

The shed above doesn't begin to cover the living space below it. It only disguises the stairwell.

"I never would have guessed this was down here," I say.

"That's the point," Mel says. "The two other doors upstairs are bathrooms. There's a shower as well. The pressure isn't great and you'll want to be fast, but it's better than nothing."

We thank him and he leaves, boots thumping up the stairs.

"Let's go look at the others," Chase says. We do, the hallway illuminating as we pass along it. Each room's different. One filled with kitschy knick-knacks and a retro dinette set. Another with an antique dining table and old traveling trunk filled with toys. The "double-wides" feel practically like homes with two beds and four bunks each.

Back in our room, I peel off the fleece jacket and carefully set the samples back into the carrier.

"This place is amazing," Chase says, looking around us. I sit down on the bed with an exhausted sigh.

"Did I do the right thing?" I ask, staring at the ceiling. "Telling them?"

He comes to sit down beside me and blows out a sigh. "My general rule is that you can't go wrong telling the truth. The hard part is finding the right person to tell it to. I admit, I felt uneasy coming in here. The fences, the patrol—"

"Me, too," I murmur. "You have no idea."

"But I like him. I really hope he's one of the good guys."

He shakes his head and gets up. The stubble on his cheeks has darkened and I think he must be handsome with a beard. "I don't know 'bout you, but I'm gonna shower."

"They think we're a couple."

He pauses, considers the duffle on the bed between us. "There's plenty of rooms down here, Wynter." He heads upstairs a moment later, fresh clothes in hand.

It's quiet. I wish there were a radio—something—as I grab some clothes and head up to the other bathroom.

It's spacious if cold, with towels and a loopy carpet. A sign taped to the wall has written instructions for using the composting toilet. Luckily for me, I already know all about it. Most important, it has running water. Doesn't matter that the sink tap is cold. That the shower spits more than it sprays. I close my eyes and thank God for plumbing and soap.

I dry off, tug my brush through my hair. Wish I had a hair dryer, but I'm not complaining. I spent fifteen years of my life without such modern marvels. I shove damp legs into black jeans, my arms into an embroidered blouse.

By the time I get downstairs, Chase is dressed in fresh jeans and a simple gray sweater.

The table's set by the time we return to the house. Just three places.

"Where's Kestral?" I ask.

"Tonight was difficult for her, as you might guess," Noah replies.

"She'll join us in the morning. Please," he says, bringing a cast-iron skillet to the table.

It's filled with buttery biscuits.

"Do you have a cooler someplace I can put these?" Chase says, holding up the bag of roasts. "I can pack them with snow . . ."

"The refrigerator is fine," Noah says, gesturing toward it.

Chase looks at him quizzically and then goes to open it. To my surprise, the light comes on.

"Mel and the other man aren't joining us?" I ask.

Noah leans toward us and whispers, "They don't like my cooking." He chuckles. "I suspect it's too basic for their tastes. But I like simple."

I try to remember if we passed Kestral, Mel, or the other man in the hallway beneath the shed. If I heard the sounds of anyone else. But I'm certain I didn't. Where have they gone?

We sit down to a dinner of green beans, baked potatoes, and even butter—as well as some kind of stew, which I politely refuse.

"Be advised that there's bacon in the beans . . . if you still want to eat it, knowing what you do," Noah says, sitting down. "Shall I say grace?"

It's the first time I've prayed with anyone in months. And it is a holier prayer than I've experienced in fifteen years, this one shared by unbelievers and apostates.

Glancing around the table as Noah asks for mercy, blessing, and the guidance to bless others, I feel gratitude for the first time in days. I think back to my conversations with Chase about signs and secret codes. And I think it's no coincidence that Julie's always loved us or that Jaclyn has always been more brave than she knew. No more coincidence than a grill tumbling from a truck or a doomsday prepper named Noah.

"Do you have family?" Chase asks as we eat. "I mean, there's so much space in your bunkhouse."

"Sure," Noah says, sucking on a tooth. "I just don't always know who they are until they show up. But I'm ready for them, whoever they are, when they do."

"During a disaster, you mean?"

He lets out a long sigh. "Hard times have been coming for a long time. Disasters. Cyberattacks . . . disease. I've always known something like this would arrive. No one believed me, but that didn't matter."

"You wanted to save them," I say.

"I wanted to save myself."

"You built all this . . . for yourself," I say.

"No. No building can save a person's soul." He crosses his arms across his belly. "When I was in Vietnam, I saw things I wish I hadn't. I did things in my life I regret. Probably much as you," he says, nodding at Chase. "Some were necessary. Others I questioned and struggled with. Mr. Peterson was a religious man. I never had been. In some ways, I'm still not. But after taking life, I felt dead. And so I understood what he meant when he said that to live, you have to give life to others. I feel very alive with you here. I felt very alive building this place."

"Where do the others stay?" I ask. "I didn't see them in the bunkhouse."

"Ah." His chuckle is low and mellow and melodic. I think he must have a nice singing voice. "I'll show you in the morning."

By the time we finish, we're sated and stupid, practically slumped in our chairs. The iron skillet is empty—as is every plate on the table.

"Thank you," I say.

"I should thank you," Noah says, rising. "For the bravery of what you're doing. Both of you, Wynter and Chase. Thank you for this service. Rest well tonight. Tomorrow, we'll get you to Colorado."

CHAPTER THIRTY-FIVE

It's late by the time we retreat to our makeshift bunk. We're silent as we descend the stairs. Buddy, the traitor, refused to leave the cat.

All the panic, the unease of before has deserted me with the last of my energy, leaving me strangely liberated, at the end of myself.

I sink down on the bed and Chase comes over to lay his arm around me, careful to broadcast his intention in a way he never has before. I saw the way he glanced at me as I told the story tonight. I didn't want to share the details of my time alone with Magnus—especially in front of him. It was Kestral who asked for them as outrage, anger, and strange injury played across her face. Now I regret sharing that much.

"Don't."

He hesitates and starts to let me go. I lay my hand along his thigh. He looks at it and then at me.

"Don't what?" he asks softly.

"Treat me like I'm fragile."

He leans toward me, brushes his lips against my neck. "Never," he whispers.

I close my eyes.

I could tilt my head and kiss him, he's so close.

When I make no move, he lets me go, rising to retrieve his back-pack from the end of the bed. Pausing at the door, he says, "There's a big difference between fragile and exquisite, Wynter."

He sets the lock and leaves, quietly shutting the door behind him. I hear the one across the hall close a few seconds later.

I lean over and flip off the light. Sit on the edge of the bed, gazing into the darkness. Reliving the warmth of his breath against my hair. Wondering what it would be like to turn my head and meet those lips, taste his mouth at last. Snared in a moment that will haunt me all night.

Ten seconds later, I'm striding out into the narrow hall to stand before his door.

I reach for the knob, not sure it will even turn. Not knowing what I'll say if he says something from inside.

But it isn't locked.

Chase rolls to an elbow in the shaft of dim light filtering in from the hallway.

"I—I don't . . ."

"It's all right," he says.

When I don't move, he pulls back the edge of the comforter. He's still dressed beneath it. Neither one of us speaks as I lock the door behind me and blindly cross the room. Just the quiet rustle of bedsheets as he gathers me in his arms.

SOMETIME LATER, A knock sounds at the sliding door. Mel's voice outside.

"Yeah?" Chase says, instantly alert, leaning up over me. I turn my face against his shoulder. He smells like warmth and musk and skin.

"Noah says be ready in half an hour."

THE HOUSE IS eerily quiet. Dark, except for the fireplace stoked to new life in the living room, and the kerosene lantern glowing on the table. Standing at the small kitchen window as Chase pours a cup of coffee, I can just make out a field of solar panels reflecting the pallid stars. It's barely 4 a.m. My eyes hurt, I'm so tired, but I'm very, very awake. Hyperaware of Chase, half my mind still back in the bunkhouse, tangled up in last night.

"Mel went to retrieve the rest of the things from your vehicle," Noah says, glancing up from the pan he's stirring on the old gas stove. "I'm sorry to report it's gone."

"That was fast," I murmur.

"Nor was there anyone in the truck you dispatched. I think it's safe to say that whatever possessions you left behind, they have now."

"Can you spare a vehicle?" Chase asks.

"We can. But first, breakfast," Noah says. A moment later he sets a bowl of scrambled eggs on the table. I stare at them quizzically.

"I didn't see a chicken house," I say. Granted, I've yet to see the place in sunlight, but upon arriving at those metal gates, took in everything I could.

"Ah," he says with a mysterious smile, gesturing us to help ourselves. "Just because you do not see them doesn't mean they are not here."

I feel as though there's far more to Noah than he's told us.

One thing I do know for sure: I'm going to miss hot meals.

"Thank you for your hospitality," Chase says as we finish eating. He's anxious to get moving, I know.

And despite the wonders of Noah's bunkhouse, so am I.

"You've trusted me with your lives," Noah says. "And in so doing, with the lives of countless others. Come, I want to show you something."

He pulls up his surgical mask and gestures for us to do the same as he leads us out toward the barn. It's built into the gentle rise of a hill, a closed door large enough to admit oversized farm equipment in the middle. We follow him in through a side entrance past a tractor, some kind of UTV, and an old work truck, past several empty horse stalls that still smell like hay to a wooden door framed into the back. When he opens it, there's another door beyond it . . . framed in concrete.

Chase cocks his head as Noah opens it and, as with Mel the night before, leads us down a set of stairs. Except this one descends four back-and-forth flights illuminated by fluorescent fixtures in the wells.

At the bottom of the last staircase we emerge into what seems like a dimly lit cavern until Noah flips a switch, bringing a spacious, round living room to life. Forget the kitschy antiques; the place is laid out with an L-shaped leather sofa, a pool table, and a television screen, all situated around a funnel-shaped chimney or exhaust system in the middle.

"What—" I look around, unsure what I'm trying to ask.

"Is this a missile silo?" Chase asks in obvious amazement.

"Decommissioned," Noah says, gesturing us to follow him across the room and into a large tunnel. The other end opens into a second round room lined with shelves and filled with books, a spiral staircase ascending and descending through the middle.

Stuffed chairs huddle in twos and threes between two large wooden tables with beautiful live edges. A man sits in one of the oversized chairs, reading to a boy perched on the cushioned arm. Both look up at our arrival, the man smiling pleasantly as the boy peers around him.

"Noah," he says, by way of greeting, pushing his glasses farther up his nose. I note he does not rise even as the boy comes over to wrap his arms around Noah's waist.

"This is Seth," Noah says, ruffling the boy's hair. "And his father Micah. He and his family have been with us for—how long has it been, Micah?"

"Long enough to have gotten our days and nights turned around." Micah grins and nods to us. "Welcome."

"Hi," I say, but my gaze is on the boy, his big brown eyes so much like Truly's.

"Are you going to live here?" Seth asks.

"These folks are just passing through for now," Noah says, patting the boy's shoulders before gesturing us toward the spiral staircase where we are met by Kestral.

She smiles as she puts her arm around me, but she's quiet as Noah leads us below.

The place is a multilevel underground of wonders: A dining hall filled with round tables. A kitchen one level below. A hydroponic garden complete with a wooden chicken coop and fenced-in run around the perimeter of the level. A gymnasium with workout equipment. An infirmary. Four entire levels of communal and private living quarters occupied by the thirty-two residents who live here and work to keep it running—several of whom come to greet us.

"There are three stories of supplies beneath us. The equipment room is above the library, the generator room above that. We run on three wells and as much solar energy as we can. But this is Nebraska." Noah chuckles.

"You built all this?" I say.

"Well, the silo was here. I simply repurposed it. My hope was to turn something built to house destruction into something life-giving and good."

"Who are these people?" Chase asks.

"Refugees."

"From . . . Syria?" I ask.

"From life," he says, glancing at Kestral, and then tilts his head as though acquiescing. "Rima is from Syria. She's a widow and our resident nurse."

"This is incredible," Chase says, looking around.

"Who's in charge of this place?" I ask. Because I have yet to see a framed picture of Noah or anyone else on these rounded walls. Even fast food restaurants have managers' pictures in the hallway to the bathroom.

"No one," Kestral says.

"They are," Noah says. "Though they've elected to keep me running things as long as our doors stay open."

"What do you mean, 'stay open'?" I glance at Kestral, but her eyes have clouded.

"Things have gotten worse in just the last day with the attacks," she says. "There'll be panic soon—over clean water, food, and basic supplies."

"This silo is self-sufficient," Noah says. "With a six-month time lock from the inside should things get ugly enough."

Back above ground, he regards us in the chilly barn. "So you see, we have traded secret for secret. And now that you know ours, you are welcome here. Both of you, if you should ever need it."

"Thank you," I say.

"Yes—thank you," Chase says, but is interrupted by the appearance of Mel, walkie-talkie in hand.

"National Guard is moving in. Someone called in a tip. Just came across the scanner."

"Thank you, Mel," Noah says, and turns to us. "We'd better get you on your way."

CHAPTER THIRTY-SIX

There was a radio song we used to sing with Mom back in Chicago. We had no clue what the song meant. We just liked to yell out the words.

Jackie later forgot the song, or so she claimed. I don't know how that's possible, given that Mom used to play it all the time and that the chorus only has four words, repeated over and over. I've always been prone to getting things stuck in my head. Someone called it an earworm once, which I thought sounded gross and not at all like what it's really like. More like a playlist with only one song stuck on repeat until it becomes the anthem of your life for hours or days at a time, whether you like it or not. I only recently learned, of course, that earworms are associated with OCD.

As I climb into the front seat of the truck in the darkness, that song comes back to me.

There's something wrong with the world today . . .

We leave Buddy behind. I didn't want to—Chase didn't, either. But we have no idea what we'll find once we enter Fort Collins. Buddy licks my face as I gather him up, remembering the feel of his little body in my arms that first night in the Jeep.

"He'll be here waiting," Noah assured us. "Healthy and bigger than before. Though I can't say what condition the cat will be in. Go in peace, my friends."

Mel takes us south, points silently to a set of blue lights up the interstate and another on the highway. I glance back at them in the distance as we turn west until the road splits into two trails, where we head southwest, winding first through scrubland and then earth scarred by tire tracks and cattle drives.

The trail ends at an old windmill standing lone sentry over a cluster of water tanks where the snow has been trampled by cattle into dark, frozen sludge. He turns off the headlights, cuts the engine. Getting out, I follow the two men around to the trailer in back where Mel has hopped up to unchain the UTV already loaded with our bags. The headlights glare against the back windshield of the truck as he backs it onto the ground.

It's eerily quiet, the snowscape barren beneath a moon sheathed in clouds.

"You're going to head southeast down that dry bed," Mel says, pointing. "See that line of red lights on the horizon? Those are wind turbines. They're a mile away on the Colorado side. Zach, who was with me last night, is waiting at the first one to the east."

Mel digs into his pocket and hands Chase his pocketknife. "Your pistol's in the glove compartment. I loaded the magazine. Watch the terrain. Point right toward that light—any farther west and you could end up in a ravine or driving off a bluff. Get there safe. Get the samples there safe."

Chase shakes his hand. "We will."

"Thank you," I say, giving Mel a hug. But the minute I do, he stiffens in my arms. It takes me a second to understand, to hear what he has over the rumble of the UTV: a tapping, a whir, swift as a flutter. The distant drone of an engine. Chase curses and my head swivels upward in the same direction as theirs—east, toward a glowing tail of a helicopter, a traveling beam of light.

"Go! Go!" Mel shouts. But we're already running for the UTV. Chase grabs the wheel as I slide in beside him. And then we're speeding down the dry bed as the helicopter roars closer, that cylinder of light sweeping the ground beneath. We hug the eastern edge of the wash, but our lights are a dead giveaway. The helicopter banks, coming right for us.

Chase veers down a steep tributary, hits a ridge that nearly sends me flying. Turns us west—the wrong way, the ground growing more treacherous beneath us.

"Cut the lights!" I shout.

"It won't be enough."

But it has to be. It cannot end like this. We've come too far with so much at stake.

That stupid song comes back to me.

There's something wrong with the world today . . .
Livin' on the edge

Come to think of it, I always hated that song.

The chopper roars toward us, so close I have to duck to see it from beneath the vehicle's low roof.

A voice issues from the loudspeaker: "Stop the vehicle. Repeat: Stop the vehicle or we will shoot." It's cold and practically mechanical. Detached as the voice of a distant god.

The headlights will get us killed. "Forget the UTV!" I shout. "Cut the lights—we have to run!"

I grip the strut as Chase makes an abrupt turn to speed along the earthen face of a low-lying bluff. The instant it blocks the chopper from sight, we skid to a stop. Chase tears open the glove compartment, shoves the pistol into my hand. I swing out of the UTV and grab the carrier, but when I turn back, Chase hasn't moved. The chopper roars toward us, practically overhead.

"Chase!"

"Count to five when I leave!" he yells. "And then run!"

"What? No! I'm not going without you!"

"You have to."

"No! I'm not leaving you!"

His eyes meet mine as he throws the UTV into gear. "You're the bravest person I know, Wynter."

"Chase!" I scream.

He takes off across the snowy wasteland toward the canyons beyond, the chopper trailing him like a kite.

I stare, breath frozen in my lungs.

Move.

I stagger a step, slip on the snow's frozen crust. Pick my way along the edge of the hill to the winding floor in the darkness.

A shot cracks across the landscape, echoes along the hills.

I spin back, stifling a scream. Search the darkness for any sign of the UTV beyond the ridge. The helicopter circles like a vulture as a second shot shatters the air.

I take off, legs churning. Grapple my way over the next ridge, tear across the dry river floor.

Sirens wail toward the east.

A third shot.

I drop to a crouch at the edge of the next rise, lose my footing and skid down the other side, carrier dragging across the ground. I can't hear the UTV anymore or even the chopper, the whir of the propeller drowned out by the heart hammering against my ribs.

I drag a sleeve over my eyes and blink hard at the horizon, searching for the red constellation, low and straight as an arrow. There. I shove to my feet and run, clutching the carrier against me. Cradling the disease that cost me my sister. That ruined Ken's brilliant mind. That brought me Chase and then took him away.

The landscape breaks abruptly into a corner field. I hurtle down the embankment, gasp as I tangle on a fence, barbs biting through my sleeves and gashing my cheek. Haul myself up over it, metal piercing my gloves as I scan the distance for lights, telltale flashing blue.

I cut across the field in a daze, pass through the fence on the far side, barbs snagging my hair, ripping through the nylon of my coat. The turbine rises like a giant with a single Cyclops eye. I sprint for it, tripping over shorn field stubble.

But when I get there, the road that dead-ends at the first turbine is empty. I bend over, hands on my knees, suck in a breath through my nose before starting off toward the second one as the helicopter veers away. Sirens converge in the distance.

I reach the second turbine, stagger on to the next. And the one after that.

I hear the silver Sierra before I see it; it's traveling with its headlights off. I wave my arms and then pull off my hood and rip open my coat to show the reflective collar of my zip-up beneath. The truck comes to a halt, Zach's face ghostly in the glow of the dash affixed with a fake in-transit sign, the Nebraska license plates removed.

He's barely put the truck into park before he's out. "I had to wait out the chopper to keep from drawing their attention. Was afraid you wouldn't make it."

"Chase didn't," I say dully.

"I'm sorry. I am. But once they realize they don't have you, they'll be all over the place. Hurry." He helps me into the driver's side of the idling truck. "Go hard west till you hit the mountains, all the way to Livermore. Go in from the northwest and you'll avoid the city. Take 287 down."

"What about you?" The plan had been for him to take the UTV back across to the water bins.

"I'll be fine. Go!" he says. And then he's running for the field.

CHAPTER THIRTY-SEVEN

The road blurs. I drive without seeing it or the landscape or the sunrise. Haunted by the sound of those shots. By Chase's last look at me.

This is the second time I've stared into the eyes of someone about to die.

I tell myself I barely knew him. That I'm a twenty-two-year-old two months out of a cult bonding with his dimples in a crisis. That any connection between us is just what happens at the end of the world.

And I tell myself I'm a liar.

The Rockies emerge from the last of the night, beautiful and foreboding. I've never seen mountains before. This isn't how I wanted it to happen.

It hurts.

Magnus was right: this world can't go on. Not with people like him preying on others. Not without more people like Chase.

I could throw the samples out the window. Let the world purge itself as, maybe, was always intended. Nothing could stop me and who would know? I imagine lowering the window, the icy blast of the air. One simple, irrevocable act like a step between Heaven and Hell.

How many more lives could crash to the pavement, shatter like a slide made of glass?

I reach for the carrier beside me. Test the latch. Still secured.

For now, Magnus's prediction might still come true—but it won't be because of me.

CHAPTER THIRTY-EIGHT

I turn south, wend along the foothills, barely registering the cars nosed into snowy ditches, backward on the median, abandoned on the shoulder; it's the same as everywhere else.

I pull up my mask, draw the hood of my coat over my head as 287 takes me directly into Fort Collins where it becomes College Avenue. The first intersection I come to is bottlenecked to a single, narrow pass through the wreckage of a collision where a semitruck lies on its side, trailer twisted at a wrong angle like a broken limb. The SUV crumpled against the curb has strewn wreckage across both lanes. A man in a hoodie stands in the middle, holding an invisible baton, arms weaving in the air. Conducting not traffic, but an orchestra only he can see.

Up ahead, the gas station is empty. The drug store is dark, the front window shattered, shelves empty. The hardware store is worse; the place looks gutted. Same for the Asian grill, though the thrift store appears unmolested.

An apartment building ahead is surrounded by portable chain-link fence and posted with a handwritten sign:

INFECTED

A police cruiser blocks the right-hand lane and I merge left, noting the spray-painted X on the front door.

Every other building after that is a bar.

The university has to be close.

More wreckage at the four-lane intersection of College and Laporte. More on Mountain Avenue, where I veer around three cars jigsaw-puzzled together and peer down the cross street, looking for the campus.

Blue lights flash ahead, silent against the indigo sky. I turn toward the mountains, skid to a stop as a truck hauling a camper runs the intersection in front of me without even slowing. I drive past an auditorium where a sign outside the door says WATER. A line nearly a hundred people long has already formed up outside, people in surgical and makeshift masks fixated on phones without service. A few turn to stare, their gazes dull. I wonder how many of them will live through the winter, the month, the week.

Six Porta Potties line the parking lot with a line of their own. It scatters as one of the booths begins quaking as though it contains a madman . . .

Which it very well might.

I cut through a residential area, worried that I've missed the university as the road empties into Laurel.

And then suddenly there it is, right in front of me.

Orange-and-white-striped barricades block the entrance. A campus security cruiser is parked behind it, the guard sitting inside the truck. I continue down the street without stopping, turn off into a residential area, and park. Locking the truck, I tug my hood low over my head, the carrier under my arm.

Crossing to the campus, I hurry through a parking lot, skirt the edge of a residential building. I glance up in time to see a curtain move in a third-floor window, but can't see who's watching from inside.

There's a path around back with another entrance. It's got a handmade DO NOT ENTER—INFECTED sign on the door. I wonder if the person I saw upstairs really is sick or simply using the only weapon at their disposal.

Once past the residential halls, I cut north of the stadium toward what looks like a more industrial set of stone and concrete buildings that I imagine hold classrooms, lecture halls. Maybe a lab. Unnerved by the open areas, but even more by the silence.

I don't trust it.

I try the door of the first building but of course it's locked. I round the corner—and stop short as a couple guys in jeans and hoodies come strolling my direction. They might be my age, though somehow I doubt they belong here any more than I do.

"Hey," the first one says, lifting his chin. He's got a shaved head and a single patch of hair shaped to a point beneath his lower lip, silver chains around black boots. "You got any food?"

"No. Can you tell me which way the veterinary college is?"

"Yeah. For some food," he says, his gaze going to the samples.

"I told you I don't have any."

"What's in the case?" he up-nods toward the carrier.

"Nothing you want to eat."

"We also accept cash."

I pull the pistol from my pocket and thumb off the safety. "Accept this."

They step back in unison, hands out before them.

"Whoa," he says. "No need to get twitchy."

They walk backward several steps, and the one spits before turning to saunter quickly the other way.

I glance up at the hall in front of me, follow the walk around back, looking for some kind of sign, pistol naked in my hand. I have no idea where the veterinary college is, let alone the microbiology building. Find myself walking aimlessly past a broad, arched entrance where I try the first door I come to. Locked.

But when I lift my eyes, there's a sign taped to the window:

WINTER →

I turn away and then stop. Ashley wouldn't know my name's spelled with a *y*. I follow the arrow to the next set of doors, where another sign points to the next building over. It's marked MICROBIOLOGY. I rush toward the entrance, which is cordoned off with yellow tape and a sign that says QUARANTINE: DO NOT ENTER. But fixed to the glass is another arrow pointing to a side entrance.

When I reach the black metal door I groan inwardly at the sight of the keypad. Beside it is a simple note: J.'S BIRTHDAY.

Jaclyn was born on July 3—every birthday of hers I can remember before Julie moved away involved sparklers instead of candles on a cake coated with ashes. It was the only cake I ever refused to eat, finding the prospect unappetizing even as a kid.

I enter the digits one at a time—0 . . . 7 . . . 0 . . . 3—flashing back as I enter the numbers to that night at the Narrow Gate, Truly in my arms. And I know that even if I can't see her, Jaclyn is with me now, as she was then.

Except that, as before, nothing happens. I glance around me in exasperation and enter the code again, prepared to back up and start shouting if I have to. Then, remembering the security system at Julie's house, I try the # button.

The door clicks open.

I find a second note inside next to the stairwell door: C321. A flashlight has been stuck to the wall beside it with a piece of adhesive Velcro. Pocketing the pistol, I grab the flashlight, turn it on, and take the stairs up two floors. Striding down a tiled hallway, I peer through the glass frames in dark office doors until I spy a denim-clad pair of legs resting on a couch in C321.

I rap, softly. The legs don't move. For a moment I assume the worst—that all of this has been for nothing. The thought is so terrible, so unthinkable, that I begin pounding on the door.

The legs jerk to life, feet swinging to the floor as the figure briefly disappears outside my line of vision. A few seconds later a lantern lights up the office interior and a man with long, tousled hair and a badge hanging from his neck strides into view.

"I'm looking for Dr. Neal," I say loudly, the words echoing down the hallway.

He searches my eyes through the window and I suck in a breath. I don't even need to read the name on his badge to know that it's him.

Truly has his mouth. She has his eyes.

"Wynter?"

I nod and yank down my mask. Because though I bear less of a resemblance to Jackie than my mom, the likeness is there.

He stares, and then swiftly loops his mask over his ears.

"Are you sick?" he asks, words muffled through mask and door.

"No," I say, and hope I'm still telling the truth.

He unlocks the door and lets me in, glancing out into the darkened hall before locking it behind me.

"You made it. I'd started to worry you wouldn't."

"Yeah," I say. "Me, too."

He doesn't look like how I imagined a professor or a veterinarian would, Def Leppard T-shirt haphazardly tucked into a pair of faded jeans that disappear into a set of shearling slippers. He's clearly disconcerted. Nervous, maybe. Which doesn't keep him from stealing glances at me.

"Sorry," he says, raking back his hair, a tendril snagging in his week-old beard. "You just look so much like—"

"It's okay," I say, not sure I can bear to hear him say her name.

He nods toward the carrier tucked beneath my arm. "Is that . . ."

"Yeah."

"I've got a generator hooked up in the lab. I can take a look at them right away."

But these are no longer just samples of some disease. They were purchased with lives to save many more. Lives precious to me. Which might be the reason it feels so hard to let them go.

When I don't move, he claps a hand to his head. "I have no manners—are you hungry? Can I get you some water? Coffee? I brewed some this morning. It's still hot." He moves to a credenza stacked with gallon jugs of water, a European-style kettle, and a corrugated box filled with processed food.

"Water would be great."

As he searches for a glass, I wander past the plaques jostling for wall space, the electric guitar on the stand in front of his desk. Study the framed photos on his shelves: Ashley, scuba diving underwater. Standing atop a mountain with three other men. Riding a bike down a red dirt path. I'm curious about the man Jackie so clearly loved, collecting details for the day Truly is ready.

I'm anxious, at the thought of her.

"Have you . . . heard from her?" he asks.

I turn, confused, to find him holding a mug, looking lost.

No, distraught.

"Heard from—" And then I realize whom he means.

"No," I say softly. Nor do I expect to.

"Then it's true, what they were saying on the news? Not that you killed her but that she's . . . Is it true?" he demands, his voice rising in pitch.

I swallow. I can't bring myself to say the words.

He takes a step back, hand going to his head, his expression that of a man sucker punched by grief.

By love.

"*He* did this, didn't he? You said that night on the phone Magnus threatened to kill her. I knew he was a fraud," he says, his voice ragged. But when he looks up, his eyes are dangerous. "I knew he was a narcissist. But what kind of monster does something like this?"

I set the carrier down on his desk.

"The kind you have to stop."

CHAPTER THIRTY-NINE

By the time Ashley returns from his lab, the office is dark. I push up in alarm, realizing I've slept the entire day.

"How'd it go—what happened?" I ask as he sets the LED lantern on the floor and sinks into a chair.

"It's a prion disease," he says, his face pale. He's wearing a lab coat, his hair pulled back in a ponytail. He rubs his face, the lantern accentuating the circles beneath his eyes, and says he's already been in contact with the CDC.

But all I can think is that Magnus *knew*. However he came by the samples, he knew what he had and that he had the resources to save hundreds—maybe thousands—of lives.

Like Ken's. And my sister's, for whom I hold him doubly responsible.

How many was he willing to let die? And for what? To hold the health of a nation hostage? To force the hand of God?

A monster, Ashley called him.

But he is something worse.

Ashley's still talking, though whether to himself or to me, I'm uncertain.

". . . an ancient virus causing prion proteins to misfold faster than *any* prion disease on record. And now it's become highly contagious by inserting its DNA into a strain of influenza."

I have no idea what he's just said. "Ashley, what does that mean?"

He looks up, his expression stark. "We're looking at a pandemic. And it's going to be bad."

IN THE LAB down the hall, Ashley opens his laptop and pulls up a group of files I recognize from the flash drive, starting with an obituary.

"The pigs belonged to this man," he says. An Alaskan farmer named John Coulter. Coulter raised Mangelitsas, an old Hungarian breed of hairy pigs that do well in climates like Siberia or Alaska because of their wool. They were nearly extinct by the 1990s, when an animal geneticist started a program encouraging farmers to protect the breed. The breed made a comeback and eventually arrived in the United States around 2007. Today, it's a gourmet specialty meat raised mostly by hobby farmers. Unlike commercial pigs, however, heritage breeds are generally free-ranging.

"The thing about pigs is they dig. And eat pretty much anything. In his account given to a grad student from UC Davis, John claimed that one of his boars dug up an old caribou carcass from the woods behind his farm, where the permafrost, frozen in Alaska for ten to— who knows—a hundred thousand years since the last ice age, has been melting. A few days later, all the pigs but one are dead. Discouraged, John decides to give up pig farming. He takes the surviving pig to slaughter but keeps the brains, which he scrambles with eggs for himself and a buddy from the slaughterhouse as a special treat."

"Gross."

"I agree. Especially when you see this," he says, opening a round image that looks like a close-up of a pink sponge. "This is a sample of one of the exhumed pig's brains. See these proteins here, all clumped together? That's what a prion disease does over the course of usually years, causing spongiform encephalopathy, a condition that affects the brain and nervous system with these holes. Mad cow disease, if you've heard of that, is a bovine form of spongiform encephalopathy. The human variant—usually acquired by eating meat tainted by infected brain or spinal matter—is called Creutzfeldt-Jakob disease. Or, in the case of cannibalism, kuru."

I make a face.

"It happens." He toggles to the Baconfest vendor list.

"In August, the farmer mysteriously dies. The pork from his Mangalitsa shows up at the Redmond, Washington, Baconfest in a tasting booth hosted by gourmet meat wholesaler North Woods Farms. Except the meat is tainted with nerve or spinal cord tissue. And now *everyone* who ate it is carrying the disease."

I think back to something Ken said that night on the phone. "But not everyone with the disease even eats meat."

Like Jackie.

"Right. So one of those prion-infected bacon eaters ends up in the hospital for an emergency appendectomy a few weeks later. Just one problem: you can't get rid of prions on surgical instruments with normal sterilization techniques."

"The Bellevue 13 . . ."

". . . all shared the same OR. So we have transmission from eating infected tissues and transmission through infected surgical instruments. So all of this is completely in line with what we know about prions. Except for one thing."

He switches to another slide. "This is a tissue sample from the caribou carcass. And you can see the misfolded prion proteins in the spinal tissue, which is what killed it. But there's something else: a virus. Meanwhile, back in Alaska"—he pulls up a second obituary—"the farmer's brain-eating buddy starts exhibiting erratic behavior. He dies in a grisly showdown between his head and a band saw."

He pauses and, with a curse, grabs a nearby notepad and pen to scribble "shut down Alaska slaughterhouse."

He pulls up a third obituary.

"A second slaughterhouse worker dies four days after that. But this second guy, according to his family, had recently switched to a vegetarian diet to lose weight for his upcoming wedding. He wasn't even eating meat. But he *was* diagnosed with influenza A three weeks before he died."

"Ken said something about the flu," I say. Was it only three days ago?

Ashley nods. "Right. So when that Mangalitsa boar dug up that caribou carcass, it didn't just infect itself by eating prion-tainted remains. Rooting around, snout in the carcass, it infected itself with the virus that caused the caribou's prion disease in the first place. Which means the slaughterhouse workers were also exposed to the virus when they handled the brains. When one of them caught influenza A, the two viruses in his cells did what smart viruses do: swapped and shared their DNA in a form of recombination that has created such viruses as the Spanish flu, which didn't exist before it killed more than three percent of the world's population."

But not all of it. I remind myself of that, refusing to give Magnus's voice volume. Meanwhile, I wish Ken could hear this—that he and his team were right. He deserves to know that. And I think he would have liked Ashley.

"So now our second slaughterhouse worker is infected with a new strain of influenza A that triggers prion proteins to rapidly misfold, causing the spongiform encephalopathy that looks like rapid early-onset dementia. And influenza A is much more contagious than the original caribou virus."

"Great," I murmur.

He pulls up the list of concert dates. "A week before he dies, this guy's friends take him on a bachelor party trip to Portland for a U2 concert. Within a month, new cases of rapid early-onset dementia show up throughout the Pacific Northwest. Except this time they start with the flu. The good news is that we can protect people against the flu. The bad news is that we don't know how to sterilize surgical instruments against prions. And with prion blood tests still in trials we have no way to monitor the safety of the blood supply."

Now I remember Ken saying the only way to test for the disease was by examining brain tissue after death.

"Meanwhile," Ashley says, "the soil those pigs were buried in: infected. No one—human or animal—can eat anything grown on that land for . . . I don't even know. The infected can't give blood, and people will continue to need surgery. You see why this is a problem."

"But now that you have these samples, you can find a cure," I say.

Ashley shakes his head. "That's the thing: by the time you're infected, it's already too late. No one's figured out a way to get antibodies past the blood-brain barrier, even by direct injection into the brain. Though a dose beforehand could offer some protection."

I stare at him. "Then what good are the samples? What was all this for?" For all I know, Chase is in custody, or a hospital with gunshot wounds, or lying in a canyon, dead. "Jackie gave her life for this!"

"Because now, at least, we can create a more accurate vaccine for the flu-borne version, which is the one that will kill the most people."

"That's it?"

Wynter, we'll probably never know how many lives you and Jackie saved."

"We had help," I say, feeling numb. "From a man—a Marine—named Chase. And another man named Noah." And Mel, and Ken, and Farmer Ingold . . . even the DJ on the radio. And I realize she was right: we were never alone.

Ashley closes the laptop and sits back with a sigh.

"The CDC field office across the street from the college's infectious disease laboratory closed down a few days ago, but I was able to reach Atlanta. The problem now will be manufacturing mass quantities of a new flu vaccine in the middle of a blackout." He pinches the bridge of his nose as though his head hurts. "Another month without power and lots of people will die of all kinds of complications. Those who survive will just be entering peak flu season. This thing is about to explode."

I tamp down the old panic. Fight to silence the voice saying that despite Magnus proving himself a fraud, it's still happening. That the cataclysm can't be stopped.

"Wynter," Ashley says quietly, desperation in his eyes. "I have no right to ask this . . ."

He doesn't need to.

"I will. I'm going to get her," I whisper. "But I need a favor."

CHAPTER FORTY

You wouldn't have a picture of her by chance, would you? Of Truly?" Ashley asks some time before morning.

I wish.

"Photos are anathema in the Enclave," I say, gazing out his office window. Dawn has tinged the horizon the color of denim. I wonder if Chase is out there. If he's even alive. I've lost track of the number of times I've stared down at the campus, tracking movement, listening for the shout of my name. The hope of his showing up is the one thing that has mitigated my impatience to get on the road these two days while Ashley works on the antibody doses for me and Truly.

"It's not perfect," he said yesterday. "But it'll at least offer you a level of protection, even if you do get the flu. You might get sick, but you won't go crazy and die."

"Her eyes look like yours," I say softly. "She's got curly hair, like you. Jackie's ears and nose."

He looks up, searches my reflection in the window, though I know it isn't for me. And I understand, having seen Jackie from the corner of my eye in it more than once tonight.

"She loves kittens and puzzles. She's so smart—already learning to read. And she gives the best hugs in the world." I trail off.

He looks away, swipes a forearm across his eyes. "So," he says at last. "Tell me about this silo."

I eat even though I'm not hungry. Let him inject me in one arm and then draw blood from the other. Trade off sharing the couch with Ashley, who sleeps only a few hours at a time, insisting I have to keep my immunity high.

"WYNTER, WAKE UP."

I startle upright, instantly alert, to find Ashley gathering several things into a tub—including a thick envelope from his desk.

"Is it ready?" I ask, looking for my shoes.

"Yes. It's here. But there's something you need to know. There's been an attack on the CDC."

I glance up. "*What?*"

It's the cataclysm. The coming Final Day.

Shut up.

He straightens and rakes back his hair. "I don't have details. I contacted them earlier to let them know the sequencing was almost complete. When I didn't hear back I managed to get hold of a colleague at the University of Georgia. He told me what happened."

"So what now?"

"I contacted the University of Nebraska Medical Center. It turns out your friend—Ken?—talked to someone there several days ago. Unfortunately, he either wasn't well enough to remember or couldn't reach you. They did confirm that the CDC's been compromised, if only because it's no longer safe for us or the samples here. They're arranging with the National Guard to send a helicopter. There's just one thing."

Isn't there always?

He comes to sit on the low table in front of me. Only then do I notice that the tub is filled with food and the rest of the water.

"You're still wanted for Jackie's murder. If you come with me, you'll be taken into custody. With everything shut down, you could be detained for months."

"That's not going to work," I say. Though it would have been cool to have taken that helicopter ride.

He leans forward to take my hands. "I will get this cleared up," he says, lifting his gaze to mine. "I swear to you, I won't stop till I do. But I can't get into the Enclave. So I'm begging you. Please go back for Truly and get her to that silo."

I squeeze his hands, eyes intent on his. "I promise you. Nothing is going to stop me."

He sits back and releases a long breath. "Thank you."

"I am going to need some things."

"Name it."

"A car and whatever gas you can find."

"Anything else?"

"Can you get me into the theater building?"

CHAPTER FORTY-ONE

Speeding from Fort Collins as the sun ducks behind the mountains, I pull the baseball cap lower over my cropped blond wig, my shoulder sore from the last injection Ashley gave me.

I check and then, unable to help it, pick at the beard glued to my jaw. Wink at the skinny guy staring back from the rearview mirror. Decide I wouldn't date me.

The world I left five days ago has changed once more in the space of hours. It's too quiet and strangely feral. Bright eyes of buildings gone dark. Entire towns closed off like feudal villages without walls.

There's nothing but static on the radio now, my name mercifully erased from the waves. Silence feels like its own form of insanity.

I thought traffic would decrease with the supply of fuel, but I was wrong; it's only lessened on the eastbound side of the interstate, which seems to be the same direction most of the military vehicles are traveling as well.

I'd planned to cut south to Kansas, keep to county roads. But the police cars so prevalent before have apparently retreated, gone off to calm cities on the verge of eruption. For as wary as I am about crazy people behind the wheel, I crane to catch sight of other drivers, wondering who they are, where they're going. The mission worth burning their last gallon of fuel.

Four hours into my drive and just past North Platte, Nebraska, a helicopter whirs overhead. I gaze up through the driver's side window. Wonder if Ashley can see me speeding in his black Camaro below. It's filled with my belongings and gas siphoned from Noah's truck, half a container from Ashley's garage, and another from a university maintenance shed. The tub of food, water, and cash sits in back, a square, soft-sided carrier bag in front.

It's dark by the time I rejoin the interstate after passing south of Omaha. Even from the outskirts I could see the police lights vying for order. I can only imagine what it must be like in Chicago.

I wonder if Julie and Lauren are all right. If they stayed at Julie's mother's. But Julie's strong, resourceful, and I have faith I'll see both of them again. One way or another.

I leave I-80 before reaching Des Moines, the lights of the city gone, replaced by an ambient glow, and then turn north at 169 on my last gallon of gas.

By the time the car dies a mile outside Story City, that song is back, playing at the forefront of my mind.

The car dies a mile outside Story City. As I get out, I can smell it. Smoke, traveling from the south . . .

Des Moines is burning.

CHAPTER FORTY-TWO

I unzip the carrier bag, carefully retrieve a cool vial and wrapped syringe. I slip them into my coat pocket, reach behind me for a bundle in the back.

Lastly, I pull the cap and wig from my head, peel the beard from my face.

But the woman who emerges is not the same one I knew before.

The gibbous moon is out tonight. The snow has mostly melted from a road that cuts like dark ribbon between hoary fields. I lock the car, slide the keys on top of the front tire, and start walking.

The gravel crunches beneath my boots, the sound crisp, brittle as the air. It feels good to walk after so many hours, though I have to cover my ears with one gloved hand and then the other to keep them from aching in the cold, switching the bundle from arm to arm.

Forty-five minutes later, I crouch near a copse of trees along the edge of an old creek bed and study the steeple of Percepta

Hall where it rises above the wall less than two hundred yards away.

I can just make out the Guardian parked in his black truck this side of the wall. But there's something else I didn't anticipate: a shadow moving near the corner. A second Guardian on foot.

They've doubled the guard.

But of course they have; the Enclave is loaded with food. Not just that but clothing, fresh well water, propane, generators, and enough living space for a thousand people in a pinch.

I circle back the way I came, drop the bundle into the ditch at the base of a skeletal tree. My cheeks, nose, and ears are frozen by now, and I'm shivering inside my coat as I start down the long drive I walked out by that day in late September.

For a place that barely evolved during the fifteen years I was there, a lot's changed in two-and-a-half months. Not only are there two Guardians in front, but one of them sits in a brand-new guardhouse outside the Narrow Gate. And there's a new tower looking out over the wall from inside that reminds me of a state penitentiary.

I'm maybe fifty yards away when the guard standing outside speaks swiftly into a walkie-talkie. He's wearing a ski mask, his mouth a fleshy hole in the darkness.

A second later a spotlight flicks to life on the tower overhead, its beam pointed directly at me.

"Stop! This is private property!" the guard on the ground outside shouts.

I keep walking.

The Guardian on the ground speaks into his walkie-talkie. "Yeah. We have another one." A few seconds later, he comes striding out. At the sight of me, he stops.

"Wynter?" he says, strangling on my name. And though I don't recognize him in his ski mask, he obviously knows me. "What are you doing here?"

"I have n-nowhere else to go," I say, my teeth chattering.

"You're cast out," the second guard says. "You need to leave!"

"That's against Testament," I grit out. "New Earth's g-gates are open to the penitent."

"They're closed to you."

I fall to my knees in the gravel, lift up my hands. "I repent!" I shout. "I r-renounce the fallen world!"

"Stop!" the second one says, and for a minute, I think he might backhand me or worse, grab the new Taser gleaming from his belt and drop me rigid.

"You really want to t-tell Magnus you turned me away?" I say. "He wanted to marry me once."

"You look like a whore," he spits, looking me up and down.

"I repent!" I repeat loudly. "I forsake my life before and renounce the fallen world!"

His fist flies at me, crashes into my cheek. I go sprawling, my head ringing. Gasping against the dirt.

Two thoughts occur to me at once. First: for once, New Earth isn't sheathing its policy toward women in polite language about protecting them. No more mincing words.

Second: I wonder if this happened to Kestral.

"What are you doing?" the first Guardian demands of the second, obviously horrified. "You heard what Magnus said!"

At that, a look like terror crosses the second Guardian's face.

I push up slowly as the first Guardian jerks his walkie-talkie from its holster and turns away. I hear my name, the crackle of static. A minute later, he's shouting up to the tower.

The lock clicks in the Narrow Gate in front of us.

"You're relieved of duty," the first Guardian informs the second. "Wynter, get up."

"Thank you," I murmur as he waits for me to walk ahead of him, too pious to touch me if he isn't forced to.

"Don't thank me. He's right. You look like a whore."

CHAPTER FORTY-THREE

The Guardian escorts me down the stairs beneath Percepta Hall. I stumble in the darkness and he's finally forced to grab my upper arm to steady me.

The Admitter on duty rises at the end of the hall. A kerosene lantern sits off to the side of his desk beside an open ledger. He looks confused and then concerned—probably at the reddening mark on my cheek—until recognition transforms his features and his eyes widen in surprise.

I lower my head, fasten my eyes on the floor.

"Did you call in a female for her reckoning?" he asks the Guardian. Clearly I'm pushing the limits of protocol. Even I have never seen an apostate returned.

"Please don't wake anyone," I say. "Here—" I open my coat and start to dig through my jeans pockets, producing a few dirty coins from one, a crimson lipstick from the other, both of which I drop onto the desk.

I lift my palms to show that they're empty.

All the while, the only thing I can think about is Truly. Of her asleep, this very minute, in the girls' barrow on the other side of the compound.

The Admitter glances up, questions naked in his eyes. What made me return. What happened to me in between. Questions he will, of course, have to ask in extraordinary detail. Until then, I swear I can *hear* him imagining what I had to do to survive, his explicit reconstruction of my sins.

I lower my head and unzip my coat. Lay it over the empty chair in front of the desk. Turn to face him, palms open at my sides.

He hesitates and then comes around the desk and begins to search me, too thoroughly, checking the pockets of my jeans, digging out a couple more coins and a chewing gum wrapper I didn't even know was there before feeling for anything concealed within my sweater. I toe out of my boots and he gives a cursory glance inside each one.

When he grabs the lantern and a ring of keys from the wall cell, I reach for my coat. He snatches it promptly from my hands.

"Please," I say. "I'm still really cold."

He opens the nearest cell and I move inside. But when I reach for the coat, he holds it out of reach.

"Please! 'Give mercy to the traveler,'" I say, quoting the Testament, volume three.

"You're not a traveler if you're back," he says and slams the door.

THE EYE STARES over the toilet in the corner, red and unblinking, kept alive by batteries. There might not be any power, but there are still priorities. And observing the shame of others will always be one of them.

The cell is cold, but there is, at least, one new concession: an extra blanket on the cot.

I wrap it around me where I sit on the floor, back against the wall.

He put me in my usual room where, I noted by the dim light of the hallway, the altar cloth is missing and the picture of Magnus has been replaced. It is familiar and alien to me at once, like the Enclave itself. Because although Ara, Magnolia, and countless others I lived with and saw every day are out there, sleeping in the same barrows, vying for the same things—Heaven, perfection, and, barring that, to be just a little more perfect than the person beside them—Jaclyn is missing.

But Truly is here. And if it's even remotely true, what Magnus said about all time existing at once, then she and I are already gone.

I think this even as I'm aware of the fact that I'm locked in a cell.

I drop my head against the concrete block behind me, stare up at the ceiling, and wait.

Almost an hour later I hear it: the purposeful step in the hall. It passes by my door. Stops near the desk.

A few seconds later a key turns in the lock.

I glance up.

The red light is off.

CHAPTER FORTY-FOUR

The lantern lights up my cell. I get to my feet and the blankets fall away as Magnus locks the door behind him, pocketing the keys.

I remember the day I first saw him in the yard. The way he impressed me. Not just because of the deference everyone showed him but for the fact that he didn't even notice. Unlike my father, whom I'd watched chase attention with dropped names, big ideas, and bad jokes, with his flattery, his money, and his eyes. Who had a knack for carrying conversations on too long with everyone but us.

I can still see in that silhouette, if I try, the Magnus I met as a child. Important because others said so, filled with divine whispers, cloaked in the glamour of God. He's wrong; he's not two people. He was never that man to begin with.

He sets the lantern on the altar and then, as though just noticing it, picks up the Testament beside it and studies the cover.

"I wrote this when I was twenty-eight," he says quietly. He turns it over in his hands, traces the letters of the title as though it were an alien thing. "I had just had an affair with a woman who felt, for the time we were together, like the answer to everything in my universe. She awakened my senses like a drug, crowding out all thoughts except for those about her. I was obsessed. I couldn't get enough. Until the day I realized that, like a drug, her effects had waned, leaving me bored.

"That same year I realized that everything I'd ever pursued— money, success, women, influence—had failed to fulfill me. I felt cheated. Unable to find pleasure. I left my home and rented a dingy apartment in Chicago hardly bigger than this cell—which became the basis of the Penitence you know now. For three months, I ate only as much as I needed to survive, drinking nothing but water, as I divested myself of every desire until the suffering I went through to find it became a high and its own form of addiction."

He pages through the volume, head tilted. "I wrote this entire Testament in an effort to capture a way of life so stringent and tightly controlled that I could spend myself trying to follow it the same way I had exhausted myself with the world." He closes it quietly. "And when I finally emerged, *everything* was fresh and beautiful to me again—for a while."

He tosses the book onto the altar. "I used to think that we're all just looking for something to feed us. For our next addiction. Something to call a greater purpose. But now I realize: deep down, we *want* to suffer."

He leans back against the wall, regarding me at last. "You may not realize it, Wynter, but you've given me a great gift. In wanting you, I knew I was pursuing something that couldn't last. Not you, but my desire for you. I knew it and craved you anyway. Then when you left"—he shakes his head—"I was angry. I felt betrayed. I pitied myself.

"You see, I had forgotten how to suffer. How much clarity it brings. I began to write again and a whole new Testament started to pour from me. I've worked tirelessly on it. I barely sleep. When it's finished in a few days, I plan to have all my previous volumes burned. All of them." He makes a sweeping movement with his arm. "Trash. But this new volume—my final Testament—will serve as the foundation of New Earth to come as we welcome thousands to our sacred ground."

I blink. Is he insane? "You can't bring thousands here! There's an epidemic going on and even if there wasn't, there isn't enough room!" I say, gesturing in the direction of the stairs outside.

He crosses his arms and tsks. "Wynter, you've missed out on so much. I don't mean here, but our new facility. We broke ground in October. We've designed an entire center to take in those in need, to quarantine them until they can be integrated or segregated for medical help, counseling . . ." He waves his hand, seeming bored already with the details.

I squint at him in the light of the lamp. A second Enclave. A growing congregation. A horde of new followers arriving out of desperation, hunger, sickness—to find meaning in a world gone insane.

But of course.

"New Earth will be a beacon of light. A new way. A city of hope in a world that has been waiting for just such a time as this. We'll create a new tier of Elders. Build a formal school."

Anyone outside, hearing these words, might shout "Amen!" I'd watched it happen for years—in service, in the yard. The Select straining to catch his words like crumbs. And I know a part of him is waiting for me to praise his new vision. To stand in astonishment, even now. To proclaim it the will of God.

"You framed me for Jackie's murder."

He regards me with a frown. "I framed no one. I simply reported that my wife was found dead and that our most promising property had gone missing. As I understand it, you're still at large. I could send a Guardian into town for the sheriff, and the entire country would be grateful—until they learned you no longer possessed our promising property. You think you're cast out here? The world is a cruel and unforgiving place. It will never take you in again. You will have no friend, no shelter, no safe haven." His lips pull back from his teeth.

He crosses the space between us and reaches out to cup my cheek, thumb brushing across my lips. "But that need not happen. So long as you're willing to provide me some much-needed new inspiration. To prove me wrong about how long desire can last. Though I'm afraid you'll have to remain in this cell. It wouldn't look right for you to return to us now. *It'll be our secret*," he whispers, straightening with a wink. But there's nothing playful in his expression.

"Let me see Truly," I say. "And I'll do anything you like."

He pulls something from his trouser pocket, lifts it to the light. "So you can give her this?"

The vial.

I lunge at him, and he holds it out over the concrete floor.

I freeze.

"Ah, ah. These little glass vials are so fragile. And so mysterious. You never can tell exactly what is inside. Should I guess? Let's see. *I* think you got this from someone you gave my samples to. That it is derived from something that was mine. But you didn't bring it back for me, did you?"

"Please!" I say, lifting my palms and then pressing them together before me the way I have so many times. "People are getting sick."

"Yes, I know," he says, giving the vial a little shake. "We had to release three to the world last week. Like animals, back to the wild."

I go still. Sick people—here. Already?

Am I too late?

He walks several steps away and pulls the syringe from his pocket. I rush after him, to fall at his feet, palms clasped high above my face. "Please! You have to save her. Truly's all I have left!"

"How do I do it?" he says, pulling the cap from the syringe with his teeth. "Like this? How much?"

"No! It's only one dose. It can't be split. Please, for the love of God—she's your daughter!"

"For the love . . . of God?" he says, expression darkening. "Have you not read the Testament? A daughter does me no good."

He plunges the syringe into the vial.

"Magnus, I'll do anything you want. I can give you a son!"

"You didn't hear?" he asks, filling the syringe, his gaze lazy. "Ara already did."

I blink—and then scream as he jabs himself in the forearm and pushes the plunger all the way down.

I don't move as the contents of that vial disappear into his veins, the serum Ashley labored over for hours gone within seconds.

"You'd endanger your own child," I whisper.

"Of course not," he says, withdrawing the needle and setting it, and the vial, firmly on the altar. "Truly and the baby have been moved to the guesthouse to keep them safe. Meanwhile, what would the world say if God's own Interpreter got sick?"

He straightens, fills his lungs with a long, slow breath, and exhales, as though a new man.

"Now then," he says.

In an instant, he's on me. Grabbing my arms, pushing me toward the cot—until my head snaps in the direction of the door.

Following my gaze, he pauses, extricates himself to check the lock.

And then I'm leaping up and onto his back, arm wrapped around his throat. Snaking a leg round his waist, I grab my opposite bicep and shove his head forward with the back of my hand until we're ear to ear.

He thrashes, takes us both onto the floor. But I hang on like a spider monkey as he goes limp in my arms.

CHAPTER FORTY-FIVE

I wonder what's happening in Nebraska. If tests might be running on Ashley's vaccine even now. If Ashley himself is crashed out on the sofa of an office or a chair in the UNMC doctors' lounge.

It occurs to me that none of us should have entered these walls. That we have never been "in but not of the world" here but in another world completely. That this was never faith, but seclusion in a place so safe that faith need never be tested even as we lived our lives of duality. Tempting new initiates with food that was forbidden, promising love but doling out judgment, giving away the clothes we deemed immoral at our ministry in the name of God.

A groggy groan issues five feet away on the floor.

Magnus grimaces, seems to be trying to focus his eyes. Works his jaw as though I punched him, which I might have accidentally done while he was out.

"What . . . did you do?" he mumbles. His face is flushed.

It's about 3:30 a.m. by my guess and my butt is sore from the cold concrete. I gather the blanket closer around me. The other one's thrown over Magnus's bare torso. I don't need to look to know that he is sweating. I can smell it.

"What I did is come back for my niece. What you did is inject yourself with an extremely virulent dose of the caribou flu. Mixed with a sedative. Though I'd like to take credit for the sleeper hold."

"Caribou flu?" he says, clearly confused.

"I don't know if that's what they'll call it," I say, plucking a ring of keys from the floor beside me. I roll off my tailbone with a groan and stiffly get to my feet to retrieve the kerosene lamp from the altar.

Magnus jerks and rolls onto his face, his hands tied behind him by the twisted sleeves of his shirt. It came off pretty easy with the sleeves rolled up like that.

"What are you saying? That I'm *infected*?" he cries as I move to the door. I can hear him trying to push up against the bed as I systematically try one key after the other until the doorknob turns.

Outside, I put the key into the lock, step back, and kick the head clean off. The ring drops to the floor with a clatter. I grab it up.

Hurrying to the Admitter's desk, I set the lamp down and sling on my coat, pocket the keys, and pull open a drawer. Finding a black marker, I stride back to the door of my cell where I can hear Magnus shouting from inside.

I scrawl a big X on the painted metal, write:

INFECTED!!
DO NOT ENTER
YOU WILL RISK THE LIVES OF EVERYONE INSIDE
THE ENCLAVE.
MAGNUS CHOSE TO MEET GOD IN PERSON.

I cap the marker, pause, and then toss it under the door. Just in case Magnus has any new revelations before he dies.

And then I'm bolting for the stairs, lantern in hand, taking them two at a time.

MY FIRST INSTINCT is to go straight for the guesthouse. Instead, I make my way through the shadows to the back door of the administrative building, trying each key in succession until I'm in and walking through Magnus's office door.

Inside, I turn up the lamp and shine it around until I spot his laptop. I grab and tuck it under my arm and am just on my way out when I notice a stack of papers on his credenza at least three inches thick. Moving toward it, I glance at the title page.

The Final Testament of Magnus Theisen.

He was a prophet after all.

I hurry out into the main office past the cabinets against the wall. The repository of every member's files, each one a litany of sins. Just beyond it is the mechanical room. Stepping inside, I study the pipes attached to the water tank, running to and from the air-conditioning unit and heater. Haul back and kick the yellow one—once, twice, until it tears away from the unit. Until I smell the odor of gas.

Back in the main office, I reconsider the laptop in my hands.

I leave it with the lantern on my old desk, not bothering to lock the door behind me.

CHAPTER FORTY-SIX

There's an eye in the corner but it's blind, the red light dark.

I let myself in the back door to the kitchen, fingers drifting along the counter. It was here that I envisioned a new future for us when we first arrived. And here I first saw the beach, blue and vivid on Shae's iPhone.

I move into the living room where Mom stood at the foot of the steps, pulling her short skirt lower on her hips as she prepared to meet with the Elders. Her eyes had been filled with such hope.

The stairs creak beneath my feet as I follow the bannister up to the bedroom where Jaclyn and I said farewell to our songs, ribbons, and stories and the outside world with them.

"Truly?" I whisper.

A figure rises from the corner in a white gown, an infant clutched to her breast.

"What are you doing here?" Ara asks, clearly startled. Even in the dark I imagine she looks older than her twenty-three years.

"I'm taking Truly," I say, and move to the first bed, the little form huddled beneath the quilt. It's the same one I slept beneath once.

Ara makes no move to stop me.

"Is the baby his?" I ask.

"I told him it was," she whispers. "But he was already tired of me."

I shake Truly's little shoulder. She barely stirs. I wrap her in her blanket and gather her, quilt and all, into my arms and turn to go.

"Winnie, where are we going?" she asks sleepily, as though she just saw me yesterday.

"Somewhere safe," I say, and clasp her against my shoulder.

"They hate me here," Ara blurts out as I reach the stairs. "Everyone."

I pause and slowly turn.

"You could come with us," I say. "You and the children."

She stares at me, her eyes white in the darkness, but makes no move to follow.

"Good-bye, Ara," I whisper, as I carry Truly downstairs.

THE GUARDIANS COME running within minutes of the explosion. Flares light the sky, signaling for help as charred papers rain to the ground.

I don't even have to key in the code; one of them leaves the Narrow Gate ajar as he rushes inside.

Conventional wisdom dictates that there's an insurmountable divide—an entire dimension of eternity and space—between Heaven and Hell.

But I can tell you it's closer to a foot and a half. The distance of a step.

Or a leap of faith.

I run for the Guardians' abandoned truck idling outside, climb in front, my terrified niece clinging to my neck.

"Where are we going?" she wails.

"Don't look back," I say, as we speed down the road.

Five minutes later I'm retrieving the bundle from the ditch, checking to make sure it's all there: the soft-sided carrier containing her antibodies, some breakfast bars, a letter from Ashley to Truly, and an envelope of money.

The Camaro has already been sought out and looted by the Guardians. I know this because the bin of clothing and food was sitting in the front seat of the truck when I got in.

I get Truly—calm but pensive, asking about the "big boom" as we left—buckled in back, noting the fuel gauge as I climb in. It hovers at a quarter tank. Not enough to get to Sidney.

I'll have to keep an eye out for a rowboat.

I'VE JUST PULLED out onto Highway 69 when a set of headlights crests the horizon. I squint at the truck as it begins to slow, my head swiveling to take in the two passengers . . .

The profile in the driver's seat.

I brake as firmly as I dare as the second truck skids to a stop in my rearview mirror. Opening the door, I leap from the truck and run down the asphalt in the glow of taillights. Chase swoops me up in his arms.

"I thought you were gone!" I say, incredulous.

"Turns out, four-wheeling in the Sandhills isn't a crime," Chase says, leaning in to kiss me.

I open my eyes to see Kestral moving toward me. Gone the otherworldly grace I once celebrated; her every stride is firmly of this world.

"He's in Penitence," I say as she wraps her arms around me in turn. "And sick. Only a matter of weeks. Maybe days."

After hugging Chase and kissing the top of Truly's head as we transfer vehicles, she shoulders her bag and starts off toward the Enclave.

"What are you doing?" Chase calls after her. "It's too cold to walk!"

She glances over her shoulder with a smile. "Siphon the gas. You're going to need it. Besides. I've walked this road before."

CHAPTER FORTY-SEVEN

When we reach the Peterson place late the next morning, guards are posted around the perimeter.

This time we're held in a cordoned off area where we wait after being administered rapid flu tests.

"Sorry," Mel says with a sympathetic look at Truly, who squirmed in my arms at the ordeal. "New protocol. I take it your journey was a success . . . ?" he says carefully, flicking a glance at the nurse working over a set of tubes on a rough table.

Neither Chase nor I would explain in her presence that two of the tests were unnecessary, that Truly and I both have antibodies to the disease. For the sake of Truly's safety no one else can know who her real father is or his role in the creation of a vaccine.

"Yes. Thank you," I say, trusting that he knows I mean for what he did to help get me to Colorado, and not just for asking. "How's Noah?"

"Looking forward to seeing you."

Chase, the one most at risk, paces until we're cleared. Blows out a breath in relief as we're released to follow Mel to the house.

Julie greets me on the porch with a tearful hug. She looks older in the week since I've seen her. Both stronger and more fragile at once.

"Where's Lauren?" I ask.

"Inside. She's asked about you every hour since we got here. You heard about Ken . . ." she says, unable to finish, her expression crumbling.

I ask about her mom and she shakes her head as Truly clings to my side.

"Noah says the ham radio operators are reporting a missile strike in Hawaii. Can that be true?" Her expression is frightened, lost. "Is it possible that crazy Magnus is right—that everything he said about the end of the world—"

"No," I say, confident in the answer. "It doesn't end this way."

I DIDN'T BELIEVE Julie at first when she said the silo was full, but she's right. More than thirty people have arrived in the last four days. Now, standing out in the yard with Noah, Chase and I take in the line of people coming down the road. Some in vehicles, most on foot, carrying pets and dragging suitcases.

"It's time," Noah says, and his eyes look worried. "The flood is coming."

"What happens to them?" I say. The bunkhouses across the yard are already full with those who arrived yesterday.

"Maybe there's something I can do to help," he says.

"How can you?" Chase says. "When we're all underground?"

Noah gives him a quiet smile. And then I understand.

"No!" I say, alarmed. "You built this. It's yours!" And then I realized I never told him I'd be coming back with Truly. That I can't ask him to give up his place. "I'll stay above ground. Take my niece in my place." But Noah shakes his head.

"It was never for me. Besides, someone has to set and hold the timer from both the inside and the outside in order to shut the door."

"No," Chase says, shaking his head. "I can't justify going inside for six months while you stay out here. What about you? Who protects you?"

"Fortunately, son," Noah says, clapping him on the shoulder, "the world still has need of folks like me. But it's gonna need people like you in days to come."

WE GATHER JUST before dusk on the upper level, silent, and nervous. At 4:59 p.m., the lights flash. A siren sounds once every ten seconds. Then every five. Every one of the last ten, more and more incessant until it's a flutter of sound. By then, anyone wanting to run out would never make it in time. Truly covers her ears. Julie looks ready to hyperventilate as a pale Lauren holds her hand.

On the final siren, the door thuds, echoing with the finality of a vault. Chase's arm tightens around me as the bolt slides into place. Do I imagine it, or does he flinch?

Silence. And then . . .

Somewhere below us, the power cycles with a soft whoosh of air.

Gasps escape all around me as the walls and ceiling glow to life, pixels undulating into sun, a meadow, grasses rippling in the breeze.

"Wynter!" Truly whispers. "Look!" She's pointing there—and there! At a field of flowers, and butterflies, the first, faint evening star.

And I realize she's never seen a meadow—or any other view— like this before, unimpeded by walls or delineating lines.

I kneel down beside her. "What do you see, Truly? What does it look like?" I ask, laying my arm around her.

Just then the image glitches—a stutter, nothing more.

Truly doesn't notice as she drops her head back, mouth gaping open in wonder.

"Beautiful," she whispers.

One day, I vow, I will show her the ocean.

But for now, I lift her into my arms as we watch the sun set beneath a twinkling sky.

EPILOGUE

I t's become ritual to climb the stairs to the atrium and watch the
sun emerge from the pixelated horizon each morning before I start
children's school, and to say goodnight beneath the electric stars.

We were fortunate those tense first days of medical observation,
when initial screenings could have proven false in any one of the
new arrivals.

None did.

We're not the only ones marking time; that first week the children made calendars to hang by their beds so they could color in
a square each night until Open Day—which is how I realized the
weather in the atrium is always attuned to the same sunny month:
June.

With an hour of leisure before dinner, I've convinced Chase
to sneak away from the maintenance level and sit with me in the
sun—a thing we haven't done in days. He's been pensive and quiet
since we arrived. We all have.

I wonder who we'll be when we emerge.

It's Christmas. And for the moment, we have the level to ourselves.

Chase rolls up onto his elbow and gives me a rare smile as a bee drifts by, so realistic I swear I can hear it. It seizes in mid-flight, flickers before droning on.

One hundred seventy days to go.

AUTHOR'S NOTE

In 2016, thawing permafrost in the Siberian Yamal Peninsula released spores of *Bacillus anthracis* from a formerly frozen reindeer carcass, sending twenty locals to the hospital, killing one boy and 2300 reindeer.

In May 2017, the BBC reported the likely revival of long-dormant bacteria and viruses as the temperature of the Arctic Circle continues to warm. ("There Are Diseases Hidden in the Ice and They Are Waking Up," BBC, May 4, 2017). A November 6, 2017, article in *The Atlantic* posits that "if there are microbes infectious to humans or human ancestors [in the melting permafrost], we are going to get them." It's a fascinating article on so-called "zombie microbes" you can read here: theatlantic.com/science/archive/2017/11/the-zombie-diseases-of-climate-change/544274/. And another by *Scientific American* here: scientificamerican.com/article/as-earth-warms-the-diseases-that-may-lie-within-permafrost-become-a-bigger-worry/.

The Russian scientist who injected himself with 3.5 million-year-old bacteria is taken straight from the news. (Life really is stranger than fiction.) In 2015, controversial scientist Anatoli Brouchkov, head of the Geocryology Department at Moscow State University, did just that, injecting himself with Bacillus F discovered in the Siberian permafrost after noticing that the local people who drink the water containing the bacteria tend to live longer. He claims he hasn't had the flu since.

As of the writing of this book there is no test for prion disease; as Ken said in the story, it happens by posthumously sampling brain tissue. There is no treatment at present, though there are organizations dedicated to studying prions across the globe—including the Prion Research Center at Colorado State University.

In 2014, the University of Nebraska Medical Center seized national headlines as the gold standard for treatment of Ebola and highly infectious diseases. In 2016, UNMC was awarded $19.8 million to develop a national training center for the fight against Ebola and other highly infectious diseases. To learn more about UNMC, check out the NET documentary *After Ebola* here: netnebraska.org/basic-page/news/after-ebola.

In his 2015 book, *Lights Out*, Ted Koppel asserts that a cyberattack on America's power grid is a possibility (that former secretary of homeland security Janet Napolitano estimated at 80–90% at the time) for which we are woefully unprepared. NatGeo's movie *American Blackout* is a research-driven drama that paints a picture of what those first days could look like. The US government has logged incursions into the operating systems of American power plants since 2013 and in March 2018 released a report on efforts to infiltrate America's "critical infrastructure," pointing the finger at Russia. The report can be found here: us-cert.gov/ncas/alerts/TA18-074A.

On a more positive note, seed hunters like Dr. Ken Street, the "Indiana Jones of agriculture," are real and scouring the earth for ancient varieties of vegetables lost to us today—a worthy pursuit in my opinion, given that 93% of our seed variety has been lost in the last eighty years. If you're interested in cultivating or enjoying heirloom and ancient vegetable varieties for yourself, consider checking out companies like Baker Creek Heirloom Seeds (you can even visit their farm in Mansfield, MO) and nonprofit seed conservation organization Native Seeds/SEARCH in Tucson, AZ, where you can order seeds or take workshops in person.

New Earth International is not based on any real group. For anyone thinking, "But they're diet-restricted/patriarchal/insular/apocalyptic people who live on a commune, and I know religions like that!" let me just remind us that cults, in the modern sense, are defined by behaviors that may include: mind control, pressure, isolation, intolerance of critical thinking or questions, secrecy, separation from friends and family, the supremacy of a leader with purported special powers (and therefore privileges) who may require constant admiration or humiliate others in public, exploitation (financial, physical, sexual), and dire consequences for leaving.

Meanwhile, this novel may seem like a quilt of dire and too-real news. But that's what makes it a fun survival story. As with any tragedy—I'm thinking of the rescue of twelve soccer team members and their coach from a cave system in Thailand that happened two days ago, as I write this—the real story is about the hearts of the heroes involved, those lights that shine brightest in darkness.

May we all be that light to someone.

As for a prion disease–inducing ancient virus recombining with the flu? Don't worry, it's fiction.

For now.

ACKNOWLEDGMENTS

Every book I write is crafted solely for the enjoyment of my readers. Thank you, you guys, for letting me take you away for a few hours at a time and distract you from whatever you should be doing.

Thank you to all the real-life heroes: Veterans, teachers, law enforcement, first responders, parents, and every other person who puts the well-being of another first.

Cindy Conger, I will never forget the time you sent me encouraging memes every hour my last night of deadline until I finished the next morning. Thank you for the way you invest your talents in unearthing the dreams of others.

Stephen Parolini, you went above and beyond with this one, bushwhacking and pointing north when I couldn't find my way out of the weeds. Thank you for being a steadfast friend with ready genius to share.

Thank you to my agent, Dan Raines, for listening to my crazy ideas and selling them for money. My kids, who require progressively bigger, cooler, and more expensive shoes, thank you for this alchemy. And I thank you for never telling me (to my face, at least) that I'm off my nut.

Thank you, Beth Adams, Becky Nesbitt, Kristen O'Neal, and the team at Simon & Schuster. Thank you, President and CEO Carolyn Reidy, for enjoying my books and for your thoughtful, handwritten notes with each one's success. Sorry about the sunburn with *The Progeny*.

Thank you to my sister, Dr. Amy Lee, for helping concoct new diseases to threaten the earth. I'm so glad you use your powers for good. Sorry about the Raggedy Ann thing when we were kids.

Thank you, Ben and Charis Erlichman (a.k.a. "The Cleaners") for stepping in at the eleventh hour when I needed all four of your eyeballs. Thank you, Meredith Efken, for reading the first chapters of that early draft. Ken Rittgarn, for answering my questions about the power grid.

My publicist, Mickey Mikkelson—you are a joy to work with. Thank you for being passionate about helping authors connect with readers.

My new/old siblings (haha, I can say that now that I'm a middle child) Jimmy and Julie: the last pieces of my world are in place now that you are in it.

Thank you, Mom, Amy, Joyce, Steph, Mary Ann, and Susan for reading every early version of this book (sorry there were more than usual). Thank you, Dad, for always being ready to encourage and give words of advice and cook ribs.

Wynter, Kayl, Kole, and Gage, thank you for being such good-hearted, kind, and hilarious kids. Sorry for telling you you'll get rickets if you don't eat your Brussels sprouts.

Bryan, ours is my favorite story. Thank you for being the face of love and grace in my life. Every woman should be so lucky to have a husband like you, every child so fortunate to have you as a father.

And to the Ultimate Author: thank you.

WYNTER'S STORY CONTINUES IN

A

SINGLE
LIGHT

TURN THE PAGE FOR A SNEAK PEAK

Day 14

I miss ice cream. The way it melts into a soupy mess if you draw out the enjoyment of eating it too long. That it has to be savored in a rush.

I miss the Internet, my cell phone, and Netflix. I was halfway through the first season of *Stranger Things* when the lights went out.

I miss the sky. The feel of wind—even when it carries the perfume of a neighboring pasture. The smell of coming rain.

But even fresh air is a small price to pay to be sane and alive. To be with the people you love.

The ones who are left, anyway. My five-year-old niece, Truly. My mom's former best friend, Julie, and her sixteen-year-old daughter, Lauren. And Chase—my (what? Boyfriend?)—who has made it his mission to keep me safe since we met three weeks ago.

We're five of the lucky sixty-three who have taken shelter from the flu-borne pandemic in an underground silo west of Gurly, Nebraska.

I used to hate that word—*lucky*. But there's no better way to describe the fortune of food and water. Amenities like heat, clothing, and a bed. Not to mention an infirmary, gymnasium, library, hydroponic garden, laying hens, and the company of uninfected others. All safe and living in relative comfort due to the foresight of a "doomsday prepper" named Noah, who thought of everything—including the pixelated walls and ceiling of the upper lounge aglow with a virtual meadowscape of billowing grasses and lazy bees beneath an artificial sky.

We spent the first four days confined to two of the silo's dorm levels with the rest of the last-minute arrivals, waiting to confirm the rapid tests administered upon our arrival. Mourning the loss of Julie's husband and Lauren's father, Ken, and my sister, Jaclyn— Truly's mother. Stiffening at any hint of a cough across the communal bunkroom, fully aware that there is no fleeing whatever we may have brought with us; the silo door is on a time lock, sealed for six months.

By which time the grid will be back up and the disease causing fatal madness in its patients should have died out with the flu season . . .

Along with most of its victims.

Luckily (there's that word again), the tests held true and we emerged from quarantine to find our places in this new community.

That was nine days ago. Nine days of meeting and learning about the others here, of feeding chickens on the garden level, starting a formal children's school, and assuming new responsibilities on the kitchen, laundry, and cleaning crews.

Of speculating about what's happening in the world above as we watch the electric sunset after dinner.

That first week I helped the children make calendars to hang by their beds so they could color in a square each night until Open Day—which is how I realized the scene in the atrium lounge is always attuned to the same sunny month: June.

If we had come here in June, would we be looking out on a snowscape more closely resembling the December weather above?

Yesterday was Christmas—the first one I've observed in fifteen years. I caught Julie crying and knew she was thinking of Ken, and wished, for the thousandth time, that Jaclyn was with us as Truly and I decorated a construction paper Christmas tree.

She asks questions at night. About why I took her away from the compound we grew up in. Why her daddy couldn't come. Questions I answer with lies.

I take a seat on the floor near the end of the L-shaped sofa in the atrium, one of the last to arrive. It's become regular practice for the community to gather on the upper level beneath the pixelated stars after the children are asleep. To sing songs everyone but me knows the words to as Preston, who used to run a bait and tackle shop, plays the guitar.

But mostly to share what we know about the disease. To mine hearsay for information in the absence of any real news, which is a scarce commodity.

Especially down here.

The chatter is lively tonight. I gaze up at the constellations I had no names for (I'd been taught it was a sin to see anything in the heavens but God) until the night Chase and I brought a sky map up from the library below and spent an hour lying on the floor, tracing their shapes in the air.

I rarely speak at these gatherings. My story of growing up in a religious commune, while apparently fascinating, has little to offer these discussions.

Julie, however, is the widow of the former field epidemiologist who caught the disease traveling with the CDC team that linked its spread to the flu. As such, she's routinely peppered with questions.

"Do they have any idea of the virus's origin?" Rima, our resident nurse and one of the first people here, asks. Her adult son, Karam, told me yesterday she used to be a doctor when they lived in Syria. "Is it a bird flu, or swine?"

"Forget the origin," Nelise, a retired rancher who oversees the hydroponic garden with an obsessive fixation that could give even my OCD a run for its money, says. "What about a cure?"

She's asked the same question every night since we were cleared to leave quarantine.

"Too long for anyone sick," Julie says. She's changed in the three weeks since I left her in Naperville. The woman who suffered no idiots is gone. She's thinner, her complexion ashen as the lusterless gray taking over her once-blond roots.

But I know there is no cure. That the best anyone can hope for is a vaccine. That the fatal disease eroding the sanity of North America emerged with a caribou carcass from the melting Alaskan permafrost to infect a herd of pigs and mutated when an infected slaughterhouse worker also became ill with the flu.

I know this, because I carried the index case samples myself to the man who is, at this moment, involved in the creation of a vaccine.

Truly's father.

"Winnie?" Piper, our resident fitness instructor, says, startling me. It's what Truly calls me, the name I gave on our arrival—the closest I dare get to my real name, which I will never speak again.

Piper is the thirty-something wife of Jax Lacey (also known as Jax Daniels for the cases of whiskey he brought with him), who preps meat in the kitchen—including a few hundred pounds of frozen game he shot himself. It's apparently delicious, not that I would know; meat wasn't allowed in the compound I grew up in.

And these days I'm glad to be vegetarian.

I glance at Piper and then follow her gaze across the room, where Chase has just emerged from the tunnel connecting the subterranean atrium to the silo itself. The short crop of his hair has grown an inch in the three weeks since we met and he hasn't shaved for days. I like the rogue scruff even if it does obscure his dimples, but the tight line of his mouth worries me.

"How did you two meet?" Piper asks as I slide over to make room for Chase on the floor.

She thinks we're married. That my last name isn't Roth, but Miller.

"Oh, it's a long story."

I can't say that it was while fleeing with the stolen index case samples.

Or that I'm wanted for murder.

I wouldn't have even revealed my history with the cult I grew up in except I couldn't risk Truly, whom I took from there just fifteen days ago, contradicting my story. At least the only people who've seen my picture on the news were those who had generators—and then only as long as stations managed to stay on air.

For now, I'm banking on the hope that by the time the lock opens and we emerge from the earth like fat cicadas, the hunt for me will be forgotten as the fugitive Wynter Roth becomes just one of thousands—possibly tens of thousands—missing in the aftermath of the disease. We have time to plan the rest.

169 days, to be exact.

In the meantime, I like to tease Chase that he's stuck with me, which is more fact than joke. But at least he seems okay with that.

"What'd I miss?" Chase says.

"Piper wants to know how we met," I say. I note the way she's looking at him, taking in his fighter's physique and olive skin. The mixture of ethnicities and striking blue eyes that would snag anyone's gaze for a second, appreciative glance.

Chase chuckles. "The short version is Winnie's car broke down while she was learning to drive—"

"After getting kicked out of that cult, right?" she says.

"After she had gone to live with Julie's family, yes," Chase says, stretching his legs out before him. "So there she was, stranded on the highway without a valid driver's license. In Julie's stolen Lexus."

I roll my eyes. "It wasn't stolen."

It kind of was.

He leaves out the fact that it happened the morning after the grid went down as panic dawned with the day. That I barreled my way into his car—and his life—out of desperation to get the samples to Truly's father at Colorado State.

"Ooh, so you're an outlaw," Piper purrs, glancing at me.

More than she knows.

I'm relieved when Nelise starts back in about the time she caught a cattle thief on his way to the auction house with two of her cows.

It always goes like this at night: speculation about the disease, and then stories from before. Some meant to impress. Some to reminisce. Others to entertain.

All of them pointless.

We will never be those people again. Julie, the Naperville socialite, whose money can't buy her a single meal or gallon of fuel. Chase Miller, the former MMA fighter and Marine, unable to combat the killer running rampant within our borders. Lauren, the popular high school junior who may never see her friends alive again.

Me, just starting over in the outside world, only to retreat from it more radically than before.

Today a hospice center janitor is our chief engineer. An insurance broker heads up laundry. Julie runs a cleaning crew. Reverend Richel preaches on Sundays and is the only one Nelise trusts near the tomatoes. Chase works maintenance and teaches jujitsu. Delaney, who ran a food bank in South Dakota, plans our menus; and Braden, who flipped burgers at Wendy's, oversees the cooking.

I teach, as I did the last five years of my life inside the Enclave, and rotate between kitchen and cleaning shifts. I look after Truly. I am her caretaker now.

Micah, the computer programmer whose son has become Truly's new best friend, glances at his watch. At the simple gesture, conversations fade to expectant silence.

At eleven thirty-five exactly, the scene on the curved wall before us breaks, a shooting star frozen in mid-flight. And then the night sky vanishes, replaced by lines of static before the screen goes dark. A moment later it glows back to life, pixels reconfiguring into the form of a face.

It's larger than life, the top of his head extending onto the curved ceiling. I've grown fond of the gray whiskers on his dark-skinned cheeks, the gaps between his front teeth. Even the rogue white hairs in his otherwise black brows that I wanted to pluck the first time I met him.

They are as endearing to me now as the man himself.

Noah.

He's a man resolved to save his own soul by saving the lives of others and the only other person here who knows my real name. This is his ark.

But he is not with us. The time lock meant to keep intruders, chemical weapons, or nuclear fallout at bay requires someone from both the inside and outside to set it.

Noah sits in an office chair, plaid shirt peeking through the neck of a tan fleece jacket. The clock in the round wooden frame on the wall behind him shows just past five thirty. The usual time he records these briefings.

"Greetings, Denizens," he says, with the calm assurance that is as much a part of him as the creases around his aging eyes.

"Hello, Noah!" Jax calls as similar greetings echo throughout the room.

"If you can hear this, knock twice," Noah says with a grin. Chuckles issue around me. Last night it was "if you can see me, blink twice." It's a running joke; the atrium is three stories belowground and video communication is strictly one-way. Our messages to the top have consisted of nothing more than a digital "all is well" and "thank you" once a week since Day 1.

"What news we have is sobering," Noah says. "Our ham radio operator reports dire circumstances in cities. Shortages of water, sanitary conditions, medicines, food, and fuel have led to more riots, fires, and the kinds of acts good men resort to when desperate. The death toll of those dependent on life-support machines will climb steeply in days and weeks to come as those devices shut down, I'm sorry to say."

Preston, sitting across from me, rubs his brows as though his head hurts, and Julie sits with a fist to her mouth. I know she's thinking about her grown sons in New Mexico and Ohio. About her mother, already sick by the time she and Lauren fled the city for her house. Who turned them away without opening her door.

I think of Kestral, who first told me about this place. Whose return to the religious compound I grew up in must have induced a few coronaries given that our spiritual leader told everyone she was dead in order to marry my sister. I hope Kestral's safe. That even Ara, my friend and enemy, is, too.

"The greatest shortage after food, water, and fuel, of course, is reliable information," Noah continues. "We are in the Middle Ages once more, operating on hearsay and what radio operators report. What I can tell you is that the attack on the substation in California three weeks ago appears to be the act of terrorists working in conjunction with the cyberassault on the grid in order to prolong the blackout. The consensus is Russia, though there are those celebrating in pockets of the Middle East and Pakistan and groups claiming unlikely credit."

"What about the attack on the CDC?" Nelise says.

"It's got to be them," Preston says.

"How is it possible we've harbored Russian terrorists in our country and not even—"

"Shh!" several others hiss as Noah continues.

"The president has not been heard from since his last radio address last week. Foreign borders remain closed to Americans, and our neighbors to the north and south have sworn to vigorously defend their borders in an effort to stem the tide of Americans attempting to enter Canada and Mexico illegally. They don't want us there, folks." He hesitates a moment, and then says, as though against his better judgment: "There are reports that an Alaskan cruise ship full of Americans was deliberately sunk when it wandered into Russian waters."

Piper glances from person to person with a wide-eyed stare. Chase sits unmoving on my other side, jaw tight. There was news of a missile strike in Hawaii hours before we entered the silo. But that turned out to be only a rumor.

"There's talk of aid from our neighbors and allies in the form of food, fuel, generators, relief workers, and engineers. How much and how quickly remain to be seen. I imagine sharing information toward the creation of a vaccine in exchange for help manufacturing it will be a part of that discussion. Our knowledge of the disease will be the best bargaining chip we have," he says, gazing meaningfully at the camera with a slight nod.

"What knowledge?" Nelise says, too loudly. She's unaware that not only does Noah know about the samples being used in the production of a vaccine but that two of his crew helped us get them over state lines in the middle of a manhunt. And I realize his pause is a silent acknowledgment of Chase and me.

"Meanwhile, we hear it may be March before the first power grids come back online. By which time we hope to have not only vaccinations but your favorite television shows waiting when you all reemerge. I will, of course, keep you apprised as we learn more. Hey, Mel—" he calls, leaning out in his chair. "Remind me to get a television, will you?"

Quiet laughter around me.

Noah looks back into the camera and smiles.

"We are well up here. You may be interested to know we've acquired our first acupuncturist, as well as a zookeeper specializing in reptiles. We number fifty-three. As you might guess, the bunkhouse is full, as is the main house. Packed to the gills. There's a long line for the showers—those of us who grew up in houses with only one bathroom never knew we had it so good."

He chuckles, and then says, more somberly, "I'm sorry to report that we have had to close our gates. I hope the day does not come that we have to defend them. And so our number stands at one hundred and sixteen souls above- and belowground. Too few, at the risk of being too many."

He pauses, and I hate the disappointment etched into his features. That causes his lip to tremble as he looks away.

Gazes drop to hands and laps around me. Julie swipes at her eyes.

A few seconds later, Noah continues: "Five of our number have assembled a country band. Which leads me to say that I hope you're making good use of the keyboard and guitar in the library. Perhaps this summer we'll enjoy an old-fashioned summer jam—" His attention goes to something below the edge of the screen. "We have someone who wants to say hello." He turns away in his chair and reaches down.

When he straightens, there's a dog in his arms—a brown and white mix of churning feet and floppy ears panting happily at the screen.

"Buddy!" I shout happily at sight of the puppy Chase rescued during our journey west. A round of "aww" circles the chamber. I wish Truly was awake to see him. It'd been difficult to leave him topside, but in the end, practicality won out over the comfort of his presence.

Chase laughs and glances at me. "Can you believe how big he is?"

"You won't believe how big this fella has gotten," Noah says, and Chase points at the screen as Noah steals his words. "Artemis the cat, on the other hand, has become strangely thin despite the fact that I fill her bowl repeatedly throughout the day." Chuckles issue around me as Noah lifts one of Buddy's paws and waves.

"We're signing off for now. I wish you a good night's rest, a happy Boxing Day, as it were. A holiday I'm fond of for its—"

The screen freezes, Noah's face separated into two disjointed planes by a line of static.

We wait, collective breath held, for the video to buffer and finish.

The screen goes blank instead.

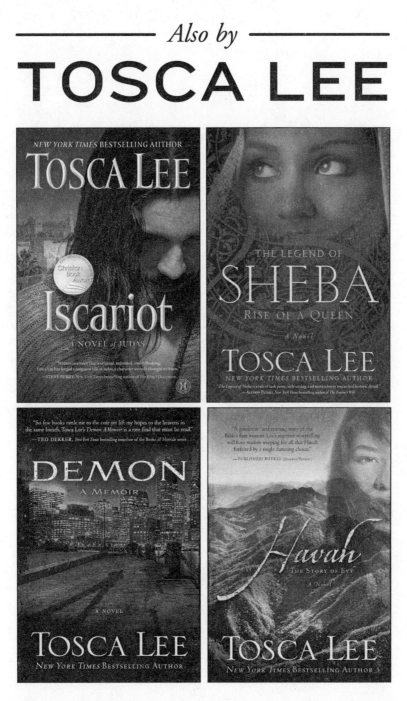

THE HOUSE
OF BATHORY
series

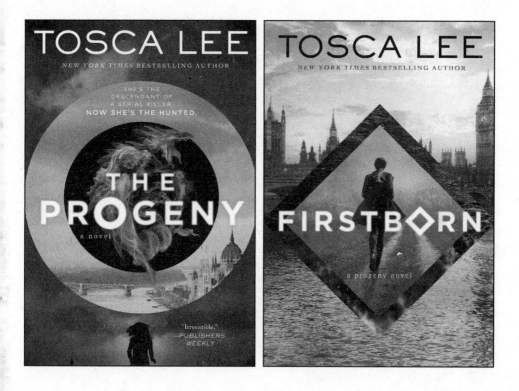